AF437596

THE ODDITY

BOOK ONE OF THE COVENS

CICI MYERS

ASIN: B0B69QFS92
ISBN-13: 979-8-218-08893-4

Cover design by: Benjamin Richard
Typography by: Kristy Lynae Moore
Font created by: Struvictory.art
Interior designs use and permission by Canva Pro

Printed in the United States of America.

This book contains references to death, bloody and gruesome scenes, sexual assult, drugs and addiction, and sex scenes with multiple people.

For anyone who has felt the utter loss of a loved one
and found the strength to heal your grief.
They are gone but never forgotten.

Prologue

Love can be all-consuming, bloody, raw, and enraging. Grief can be large and take over your entire being or be a small moment in time that passes through you, always creeping back in during your darkest moments. What they don't say is how empty it is. Even though it crushes your heart in a moment, it can be almost freeing.

What they also don't tell you is that sorrow can sneak into your heart and live there forever if you let it.

Chapter One

I sat on a wooden stool with my grimoire open, reading the sleeping spell in front of me. Wrinkling my forehead, I focused on cutting the echinacea root before me into tiny, thin, transparent strips. As I snipped the last of the root, I felt a trickle of sweat fall down my temple. I looked up at the light from the afternoon sun glistening through the stained-glass windows. Its rays hit the side of my face, and the heat washed over my cheeks down to my neck.

The pretty pink petals lay gathered to the side so I could muddle them down and place them in a small boiling black cauldron later. A light pink smoke drifted into the air from the cauldron, filling the space with the scent of lavender.

"STOP! You're doing it wrong!" yelled a gruff voice from behind my ear.

I jumped in surprise, slicing my thumb on the blade of my knife. Daniels, my mentor, was a tall older gentleman with bright blue eyes, snow-white hair, and a handlebar mustache to match. He was in his early 50s, but his face didn't show his age as much as his hair did. It was completely white for as long as I could remember, even when I was a kid.

A sting of pain in my thumb caught my attention. "Seriously, Daniels," I growled, narrowing my eyes at him. He glanced at the thin line of blood forming across my finger and raised a brow. The old man always kept a mischievous twinkle in his eye.

Daniels was trying to teach me the basics of potions and healing magic that belonged to our coven. The Silver Pearl Coven was one of three covens in Providence Village; we were mostly water fae with sirens, a few distinct centaurs, griffins, gorgons, succubi, and echidnae. Not many were mixed like me. "Mixing" used to be looked down upon by the elders, as they wanted to keep the lines "pure." I thought it was B.S. Like, if we mixed, it would weaken us somehow.

Our coven tended to be the more relaxed of the three; we wanted to keep the peace and keep the elements equal. It's not like we didn't mix with humans or other fae all the time. How do you think the legends of the ancient gods and goddesses came to be? Humans knew about us—we worked together a lot—but they got it all wrong. They thought of us like Hollywood stars, something you can see but never touch.

Sighing, I got up and walked to the first-aid kit on the long old wooden table in the middle of the conservatory, its green glass shining like the glowing portals I grew up seeing in the depths of the forest. Ignoring the pain, I started to clean the wound and placed a bandage on the top of my thumb.

The conservatory was my father's idea back when I was younger, but it was my mother who cared for the plants and made the life that grew here. I gazed out over the space, trying to remember the way she looked. You'd think after their death I would remember everything, but the truth is, that isn't how grief works. I tended to forget things, like the way she smiled or how my father used to smell like the forest after a rain. I think that is why I spent most of my free time here.

Looking up at the glass dome that rose above us, I smiled as a stream of sunlight danced over the hundreds of plants and flowers that we kept here. A small pond in the corner had a trickling waterfall that led to a stream which flowed down the entirety of the conservatory. Small fish and frogs called it home, and a few small café tables sat to one side, where we enjoyed tea or lunch. A spiral staircase led to the second level where more poisonous and dangerous plants lived. An apothecary table sat in the middle of the second floor, filled with all kinds of tonics, medicine, and potions. I wasn't allowed up there until I could master the basics of alchemy, but there were plants from all parts of the world, some that could kill you in a heartbeat, and flowers that could cure anything from a zit on your chin to death itself.

Death. That was one thing I was keenly aware of. When

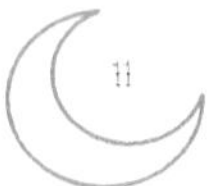

I found my parents dead at sixteen, it completely changed my view on life. I became wary of people, kept them at a distance; the wall I built around myself was solid and no one could penetrate it, not even those closest to me, those who loved me. This is why the conservatory felt like home—not the giant estate that sat isolated in the distance.

The conservatory was far enough away from the main house where my Aunt Coco and her boyfriend Jason lived now. I sure as hell would never sleep in that house again— the hallways always seemed too dark, and it was too quiet. My dad's laughter, which once filled the house, was gone, and my mom's singing, which once made us all comfortable, was missing. The conservatory gave me a bit of peace from the chaos of the main house. Our coven regularly visited the house for monthly meetings or social outings, but I spent most of my time here, escaping to read, study, or simply help Daniels take care of the plants and flowers. It was the one place where I could clear my head when it was full of darkness and when the nightmares seeped into my mind once the sun went down.

The conservatory was also my father and mother's favorite place, so I always felt closer to them when I was here. My father always said, "If you ever feel lost or alone, coming here and getting your hands dirty can always help you find your way back."

The memories flooded their way in: the way my father would hold my mother's hand while she planted the tiny pots around the conservatory, or the way my mother's eyes twinkled when she planned a surprise for my father. Tears threatened to spill as I tried not to think about the night

my parents died.

I remember going to the funeral and hearing the whispers circling like smoke in the air. "Did you know the girl found them? I heard that her crazy aunt will take care of her. She's just a kid, an orphan now, with no one to love her." Which wasn't true. I had Coco and Jason who I loved as much as my own parents. They have been together for years. Best friends since they were young until one day, they finally realized they loved each other just a bit more than any other friendship they had. They were true soulmates whose lives weaved through each other.

I closed my eyes, trying to wash the memories of that night away, but no matter what I did, I knew I would be standing there in that room again.

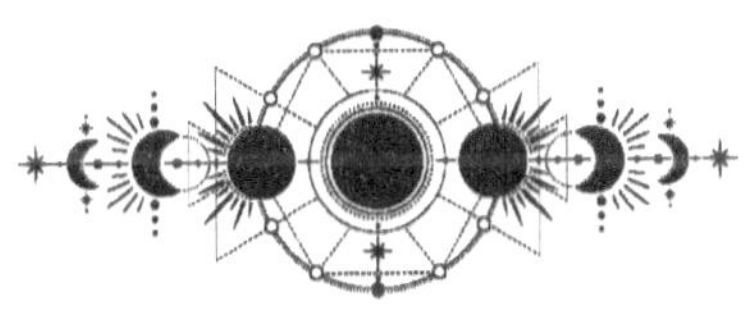

I was staying at my childhood friend Ella's house that night, but I had other reasons for wanting to sleep over. Ella's older brother, Sebastian, was back from a fancy private school he attended two towns over and, well, we had a bit of a crush on each other. Or maybe it was just me with the crush.

Sebastian, or "Bash" as everyone called him, was there with his two friends that night, Aden and Tristian. My heart gave a small tug at the thought I would see Aden. We were friends since we were little. He was this small, nerdy kid,

but once he got older and transitioned into a full-grown vampire, he was different—colder and more aggressive. It was like a switch flipped in him. Then once he became a member of The Blood Moon Coven, he was determined to be at the top with Bash. I wasn't clear on how they became friends, but I knew Bash, Aden, and Tristian were starting to make a name for themselves within the covens. People called them The Devils; they were the enforcers for The Blood Coven, the men who were called when the evil that lived among us needed to be "put down." They were the most terrifying men to walk Providence Village, treated like gods but feared by all, just as their namesake indicated.

That night started out amazing: Ella and I danced in her room to our favorite music, ate all the junk food, and binged our favorite movies. She recently started dating Aden's older brother, Ethan, so she kept checking her phone and smiling when he would send a message. It was sickening yet cute, and I was happy she found someone.

We were in the middle of a movie when the storm knocked out the power in the main house and plunged us into complete darkness.

Ella yawned. "I'm gonna go to bed. You wanna come?"

We walked to her room, which was dressed in soft grey and blue colors, her walls covered with pictures of her favorite bands and a photo collage of us. We climbed into her bed, and Ella fell asleep almost immediately, but I, being the night owl that I was, wandered around the house hoping to run into Bash and the other two so we could hang out and not have to deal with the blackout.

The house was too still. Thunder boomed in the distance,

and I jumped in surprise and bumped into a table, nearly breaking a vase. I caught it and steadied it back on the table, catching my breath. Outside the window, I saw the pool house lit up and shadows moving around inside. That must be where the guys went. I made my way down the winding staircase to the back doors that led out to the massive pool, which looked more like a lagoon. I thought my parents had money, but Ella's... Well, she was on another level.

The rain came down in sheets and plastered my shirt to my skin. I approached the door and heard a burst of deep laughter. Before I could knock, the door wrenched open, and I came face to face with my former best friend.

"Well, well, well... Hey, Lex, you come to play with the big boys?" He was drunk, swaying and slurring his words at me. Aden Charmante had grown into quite a man standing six foot four with dark hair and steel grey eyes that looked at me with interest that made me uncomfortable. I shuffled my feet slightly, took a deep breath, and played it cool with him.

I shrugged. "The power in the house is completely out, and Ella is sleeping. I wanted to see if you guys could fix it or if I could just hang out."

Aden tilted his head as if he was trying to figure out what he wanted to do. I crossed my arms and rolled my eyes. "Aden. Come on, don't be a dick."

He was about to give a snappy comeback when a deep voice said, "Let her in."

Sebastian Ryder. I'd know him anywhere.

I peered around Aden and there he was—every girl's fantasy with a tall frame, classically handsome features, and deep green eyes that made you feel like you were being hypnotized. I shivered, and not because I was cold. Bash simply had that effect on me. His voice made me feel hot and cold for him all at once.

Aden moved so I could pass him as I stepped into the pool house. The place was huge, with two bedrooms, a massive kitchen with a formal dining room, a bar area, and a living room that had a fireplace and an eighty inch TV on the wall.

"Thanks." I gave a small smile to Bash, who sat on the couch in dark jeans and a grey Henley that showed off his wide shoulders, larger than I'd seen last time.

He was still lean, but the skinny kid I had known all those years had turned into a man who looked dangerous. His cocky smirk played across his mouth. That same smirk he gave me so many times when we were alone, but this time it was different. He didn't look at me the way he normally did. It made me want to smack it off his face.

"So, the lights are out in the main house," I pointed out nervously.

Bash smiled and bit his bottom lip. "You said that already, Princess." He arched that perfectly gorgeous eyebrow and stood to meet me.

Princess. Ugh, that damn nickname drove me nuts! He started calling me that when we were little because I was the heir to The Silver Pearl Coven. My parents were the current leaders, just as my father's parents were before him. It was stupid because Bash's own father was the leader of The Blood Moon Coven. If I was considered a princess of Silver Pearl, then Bash would be the prince.

I looked down at my shirt, which was drenched from the

rain. "Do you have any extra clothes?"

Bash smiled. "A bit wet outside?" he teased.

"Obviously," I murmured. I glanced around the house nervously and saw Tristian walk from the bathroom.

"Okay, douche canoes, I am going to kick your ass in— hello, Lil' Star." He eyed me as if I was a mouse and he was the cat. If Bash and Aden were the darker ones of the group, Tristian was all light with blond hair and copper eyes, his movements like that of a tiger. "Pray tell, what brings you all the way out here to us?" His eyes sparkled at the idea that I came out here on my own just to see him.

Tristian Cassium, a legend of his own, was flirty and friendly with anyone. The "Lil' Star" name, which he recently gave me, was annoying. I wasn't sure why he called me "Lil' Star" other than to be an annoying eighteen-year-old boy. I crossed my arms and glared at him as I opened my mouth to tell him to fuck off.

"House is blacked out," Aden said as he put his arm around me, smiling. "So, Lex came to play with us." I shrugged his arm off, moving closer to the door; I didn't trust them as far as I could throw them.

"Can I get those clothes now, please?" I looked up at Bash, feeling the raindrops fall between my chest. Bash's eyes followed those raindrops and when he met my eyes again, I saw—for a brief second— lust. Then he turned and entered a back room.

"Aww but..." Tristian whined before Bash shot him a glare that made him seal his mouth shut.

I felt my nipples peak through the cold, wet shirt. Ahh, fuck. I cleared my throat. "On second thought, maybe I will

just head back." I turned to leave, but I ran straight into Aden's hard chest. The days of him being the skinny kid were definitely long gone. He wasn't as big as Tristian or Bash, but he was getting there.

"Bash will be right back, Lex; just chill." The way he said "Lex" was like it was a curse on his tongue.

I frowned at him and was about to tell him off when Bash walked back in with sweats and a shirt for me. He handed them to me, and our fingers brushed, causing a shock of electricity to run along with them, and our eyes met. I could see the fire behind them, and I knew in an instant that Bash saw my own eyes dancing with the flames back at him.

"Bathroom is that way, Princess."

I quickly walked back to the bathroom. It was huge, with a clawfoot tub and a massive open shower with a rainfall showerhead and white marble throughout the entire room. It screamed "luxury!" Not that I was expecting anything less from the Ryder family.

With a sigh, I removed my wet clothes. I tied the sweatpants tight, so they wouldn't fall off of me, and pulled the shirt on over my head. I gathered my clothes together in a small bundle and stepped out into the living room to see the Three Devils playing a video game about a guy on a quest for gold. I heard the soft whispers over the low music of the game, and one voice especially caught my attention.

"Wait, so you've hooked up... with her," I heard Aden whisper harshly to Bash as he concentrated on the game in front of him.

Tristian pulled out a large blunt, lit it, and inhaled. He

coughed for a second before looking over at Bash and asking dreamily "Dude that's...WOW...you faked the whole thing?"

"I had to. He wanted me to get closer to her. She's not like any girl I'd ever go for. I mean, look at her! But I am getting closer to knowing more about The Silver Pearl Coven and soon we will get what we are owed. Then my father will let us lead." His grip tightened on the controller as I let the words he was saying sink in. "Hey, and her cunt isn't bad, she tastes amazing, and the way she gives..." He raised his fist to his mouth, imitating a blow job.

I decided I had heard enough, and the anger I felt inside radiated off of me. I looked around and found a bowl of pinecones and picked one up, throwing it with all my might as I screamed, "Fuck you, Sebastian Ryder!" It hit him across the head, and he flinched. I folded my arms and glared at him.

Bash stiffened in surprise as his head whipped around, the realization that I heard everything he just said setting into his eyes. As his eyes widened in surprise, he raised his hand toward me. Aden and Tristian's gazes snapped to me. Aden looked pissed as hell, and Tristian seemed intrigued, trying not to laugh. Bash was in front of me in an instant, his face shifted to an utterly calm state. He lifted his hand to caress my cheek, then ran his knuckle up and down it. His eyes softened and he gave me a smile that felt like it was just for me.

"Ahh, Princess, you didn't think this,"—he gestured between us—"was real? Did you? Do you think I would do this willingly? No, Lexi, not without payment. You just bought my boys and me a clear, straight path to the top of the chain." He nodded towards Aden and Tristian before turning back to me with a cruel smile playing on his lips. "Though you will be glad to know that your pussy is just as sweet as I thought it would be."

That was the final nail in the coffin.

I felt the tears pool in my eyes. I couldn't believe he would do this. I searched his eyes for an answer, some hint of a joke, but I saw nothing but hate in them. That's when I looked back and Tristian had his phone out with a smirk, but his eyes screamed something else. Pity, maybe? Aden had a camera connected to the computer, his eyes full of rage.

Before I could even ask, Aden spoke in a low, dark voice, "It's live, Lex. Don't worry, we wouldn't want the whole Blood Moon Coven to miss this. Pearl Silver Coven's princess got her cherry popped by The Blood Coven's prince." He snarled the last words at me.

Laughter came through the other side of the laptop. I balked when I saw a ton of small squares full of Blood Moon members laughing and whispering. Cassandra, who was the biggest "snob girl" in our class, always talking about Bash, was smirking back with half of Pearl Silver's teenagers—our entire class.

I felt my magic move through my body, and I looked back at Bash with all the vengeance I could muster. "You are nothing, Sebastian Ryder, but a lonely, desperate parasite. I hope one day you know the pain you've caused, but lucky for you, I have enough hate to last a lifetime, and I won't be around to witness it. You are beneath me." I poked my finger into his chest. "You aren't worth a single tear." I gathered up all of the pent-up rage within me and slapped him across his face hard enough to make him lurch to the side. "I hope you rot in the depths of Hell, asshat!" I stormed outside, realized I was still in his clothes, and suddenly needed to get out of them as soon as possible. I ran quickly back into the main house so I could change, then get the hell out of there.

I thought at first maybe I could wake up Ella, but I shook that thought away immediately. I knew how much she adored her older brother, and I could never bring that hurt to her. Bash might be the biggest douchebag, but he would burn the world down for his baby sister. I knew I needed to keep this between us. It was coven drama, not best friend drama.

I heard the door open and froze as Ella's father, Morgan, walked in with a tiny blonde on his arm and his assistant following closely behind. She was this tall leggy thing who always trailed after him. Then, surprisingly, a kid about my age came in and closed the door, looking more than annoyed to be there.

"You stay here," ordered Legs.

The kid huffed. "Fine. I'll be in the library. Enjoy the fuck, Step-Mommy," he spat out before he stomped off.

She huffed and rolled her eyes. "Should have sent his ass to boarding school," she muttered. They started to make their way up the stairs that headed to another wing of the house.

Thinking I might be able to get past them without any-one noticing me, I made my way to the door. But just as I was about to grab the handle, I ran right into a metal statue and sent it crashing to the floor.

"Shit!" I yelped as it clattered.

Everyone turned to me. Morgan sped over to me with a concerned look on his face "Lexi, what are you doing up?" He spoke to me in a stern but quiet voice.

I bit my lip, deciding that we would go with half-truths. "All the lights went out in the main house, and I went to ask Bash if he could help find a fuse box, but my clothes got wet, so he gave me dry ones." I shrugged, trying to look nonchalant.

Morgan nodded. "Bash, he was... kind enough to help you out?" He questioned me as if he knew I was lying to him, and after what I had just heard from Bash, my mouth went dry instantly. Oh my gosh, Ella's dad knows!

I whispered in a shaky voice, "I just need to go home." I felt the tears spring back as the embarrassment settled into me. I could feel Morgan stiffen his posture.

"Sure, Lexi, I can drive you."

I shook my head. "I'll call a taxi."

Morgan nodded as if that idea was his own. "Great, well then, umm... I'll tell Ella your parents needed you home early, so I took you." He hesitated, then said in a low and careful tone, "I'll keep your secret if you keep mine." He checked his watch as if I was boring him.

"Deal." I didn't need to say anything more. I turned and walked back out into the rain. I wasn't going to wait for a taxi—I needed to get away now. I walked the five blocks to my home; my home that was comfortable; my home that had my mom who would hold me as I cried over a boy who never really loved me, to a father who would protect me from the world at all costs.

The rain pounded down on me in the cold night air, but I couldn't feel it anymore. I let myself cry, my tears mixed with the storm, and I found myself listening to the squish of my shoes. I somehow stopped crying; the storm washed away the pain, and I felt clean, numb. Then the anger settled in. I felt disgusted with Tristian and his dirty little smirk. Aden was dead to me. I would never feel sorrow for him again.

I breathed in the hatred I felt for Sebastian Ryder and knew I would one day destroy him. Yes, I would get my revenge one day, but I had to be patient, needed to bide my time, and then, only then, it would be mine.

He would regret messing with Lexi Rose.

I would have my vengeance.

I was lost in thought when I saw the dim light on my home's front porch.

We lived in a nice area of town. Large houses lined the street, and gas lamps illuminated red brick roads giving off an old-world vibe with a modern twist. Our house, or "The Estate" as most people called it, was at the end of a cul-de-sac. It was a two-story house with two huge, white columns climbing their way up to the roof. A driveway made a lazy half-circle where a white fountain with women lifting a vase up to the sky stood, water flowing down into a pool filled with stone sirens lounging upon the sides as I approached the driveway, a streak of sorrow embedded in my memory of each event that happened that night. I would never forget how Bash used me for his own advantage, how the strike to my heart shattered it. Then he drove the knife in more by exposing me to his whole coven. I just wanted my bed, a shower, and to never see Sebastian Ryder's face ever again.

Dad built this house for my mother when I was born. We had small nods to The Silver Pearl Coven surrounding our home. It was our way of remembering who we were and where we came from. We were the children of the witches they couldn't burn. Witches and sirens went back centuries; we helped the sirens trap men who tried to burn them, and the witches gave us protection. We shared a bond with the power of the elements, and it made us stronger together. Many of the witches fell in love or found their bonded mates through the sirens. My parents, grandparents, and many more follow the line of sirens and witches, although there were rarely any like me who controlled the magic of both species.

The soft glow from the moon gave just enough light for me to get my keys out. I assumed the door was locked since it was late. I turned the knob and slowly opened the door. It was eerily quiet. No music, no TV, no snoring, nothing but the sound of my shoes squishing through the hallway, making muddy prints behind me; I'd clean it up in the morning. I assumed my parents were in bed.

I crept up the stairs as quietly as I could, but I saw a small beam of light peeking through the bottom of my parents' door. My heart felt heavy and started to drum rapidly against my chest.

It was almost three in the morning.... Why is their light on? Maybe they were reading. I knocked softly on the door, but when no one answered, I knew something was wrong. I tried to open the door, but it wouldn't budge. It was as if something had been pushed up against it. I leaned into it with my shoulder, and it flew open, banging against the wall with a thud. I fell onto my hands and knees.

That was when I saw the deep red blood pooling its way to the door. My mom was on her side, eyes wide open and her mouth distorted in a silent scream. Dad was face-down on the floor.

Both of their throats were slit.

The pool of blood slowly reached my hands and feet, and I could only stare as it seeped around my hands. The dark red color was sticky to the touch. I thought blood shouldn't be this color. Blood was life. It should be bright red, not this dark and sticky.

I knew I needed to move. I needed to call someone. But all I could think was, Why them? Why take them? I lifted my head to look back at my mother, her blue eyes staring right back at me with no life in them. I would never see them sparkle when my father kissed her or light up when I gave her a hug and told her I loved her. It now felt cruel that I had her eyes. I lifted my cell phone and dialed.

"Hello, 9-1-1. What is your emergency...?"

I tried to catch my breath to speak, but nothing but tears ran down my face.

Chapter Two

The memory of that night ten years ago has always been clear to me. I could still feel tears that had fallen, and my heart broke for that girl. She was so lost, and possibly still is. But I shook myself; I did not want to relive the nightmare again.

I now noticed the steady drip of blood trailing down my thumb through my band-aid to the ground, forming a heart-shaped splatter on the conservatory floor. I tilted my head to examine the shape it created. Hmmm... interesting. I quickly snapped myself back to cleaning my cut and placed a gauze and fresh bandage around it. As tears threatened to invade my eyes again, I murmured, "Don't cry, don't do it."

Daniels moved closer to me, a gentle smile pulled at his mouth, but it didn't quite reach his eyes. "Tears shed for another person are not a sign of weakness. They are a sign of a pure heart."

I shook my head from my thoughts. "Wise words, Obi-wan." I smirked and nudged him, teasing him.

He gently placed a hand on my shoulder. "Now, get back to work." He pointed to the grimoire on the long wooden table. "If you are going to take over for me, you have to master every skill the coven will need you to complete." I was going to take over the coven once Daniels retired, but being part siren and part witch meant that I needed to prove myself even more. Most of our coven didn't care if you were mixed; still, some of our elder members did, and they held a lot of influence over the group. It was a bunch of political crap.

Daniels told me the other day, "You need to reach your full potential to run the coven and control its powers during the rituals we perform." It's not that I didn't want to run the coven. I just didn't feel like I was ready. Daniels did a fine job on his own since he took over after my parents' deaths, but many of the other covens were in talks about the true leaders needing to take their place.

I guess that made me "the true leader," but honestly, I just wanted to become an expert at alchemy.

I knew that Daniels was ready to hand over the coven to me. I could see how exhausted he was from the rituals we performed, and his eyes showed signs of his age. His powers drained more every time he met with the covens.

It was common knowledge that I was stronger than him, but we needed to wait until I could hone my power and build my skills so I could perform the rituals as "the one true leader." This Spring, our ritual was to pay tribute to the equinox, Ostara, which was to bring a time of balance and equilibrium to the covens. We would create an altar and place all different colors of flowers, black or white candles, honey, citrine, quartz, and honeymilk for the pixies. The High Priestess always adorned the altar with chalices of wine.

I pulled a notebook to my side and opened the grimoire to the page that outlined the history of our covens in Providence Village. Each page detailed every different form of fae that walked among us. I kept thinking how funny it was the way mortals tended to see the fae. Vampires weren't immortal, and they didn't glitter. Some were dangerous warriors whose bite could be addicting; with a lesser fae, it could enslave them and they would only want to serve that vampire, even if it meant their own death, and a vampire's compulsion was just as strong as a siren's. We sirens weren't cannibals either; we didn't drag sailors down to their doom. I mean, a siren could, but that would just be mean. Besides, witches were not fae, and we didn't have magical schools or wands.

The fae were everywhere, from trolls to dragons and pixies.

Providence Village had three covens that maintained order among us. The first page of the grimoire was dedicated to my coven, the symbol of a crescent moon with infinity crosses connected to each other forming a circle, which protected our coven's magic. Our coven had a huge mix of all different types of fae besides vampire, werewolves, and trolls. They liked to stay together with their own kind or kinds like their own; of course, some covens were more elitist like The Blood Moon Coven. We were the less aggressive coven, mainly focusing on family, friends, and community. We wanted to celebrate each other. We had our fair share of troublemakers, but as a coven in general we were more family-focused and heavily into water and earth magic. We helped the crops grow, performed rituals dedicated to the seasons, and had huge celebrations during the Winter and Summer Solstices as well as the Spring and Autumn Equinoxes.

I flipped to the next page to see another ancient symbol, one of darkness, blood, and death. I sucked in a sharp breath, recognizing the symbol for The Blood Moon Coven. Ella belonged to them, but she wasn't like most of her coven. Now her brother was the prince of the Blood Moon Coven and acted that way.

Just thinking about the asshat made my blood boil. Sebastian Ryder was the bane of my existence. No, I hadn't seen him much in the last ten years, but every time we saw each other, we got into a screaming match. It was wise for us to stay apart as much as possible.

The Blood Moon Coven was the wildest of us all; they were the gatekeepers, judges, jury, and executioners. They kept us safe but also were the cruelest out of us. They were the ones we called last when there was no other hope, and Bash and his Devils were the ones to take care of "problems." The kind of creatures they had were obviously vampires,

but also most of the fire witches and warlocks, phoenixes, basilisks, sphinxes, imps, and hellhounds—all dangerous in one way or another.

To be fair, most fae were deadly; we all could kill a human pretty easily. It was what made people write stories about us even though they were more or less completely wrong.

The Trinity Coven was more of a mystery. They were our neutral coven; they made the final decisions when Pearl or Blood couldn't come to an agreement. No one really knew much about Trinity. They kept out of the way and lived near the mountains. Their leader, Grayson, won his spot by killing his uncle who, from what I heard from Daniels, was a bastard of a man. Trinity Coven had the earth witches versus the water witches from the Silver Pearl, and then Blood Moon had the fire and air witches and warlocks. The werewolves, gnomes, unicorns, and even pixies.

Not a lot was known about each coven. They lived in secrecy for a long time. Only in the last few hundred years have we shared information about ourselves with each other. Treaties were formed between covens so we would benefit from each other and have a strong allied stance for whatever may come.

I scanned through each page to see if I missed anything, feeling dread tug at my insides. I closed my eyes rubbing my temple when a hand took mine. "Hey! What the hell, Daniels?"

He grunted and re-bandaged my thumb. "So, Ella and Ethan's engagement is tonight, huh?" He began to add an extra bandage. When he was finished, he walked over to a monkshood plant, picked up his gloves, and put them on as he started to examine its leaves with a slight frown on his face.

"Yeah, the engagement of the year, according to Ella's mother," I said, rolling my eyes. I love Ella and I would do anything for her, but the rest of her family gave me a headache.

Daniels smirked at me as he trimmed the leaves of a very poisonous plant, checked the soil levels, and added a mixture of soil and plant food to the little purple flower. "I guess the all-mighty Lord Morgan Ryder and his crew will be there. Keep an eye out for anyone or anything that might ruin Ella's day" Looking up, he narrowed his eyes at me "And you promise you'll be safe, won't you?" He acted as if he wanted to say more, but there was hesitation in his eyes. Daniels never wanted to make it seem like he was parenting me but, truthfully, he was the closest thing I had to a parent. I held up a hand "I will be safe, so as long as I stay out of Bash's and his crew's way," I mumbled.

The Blood Moon Coven generally ran most of Providence Village, and its leader was no other than Morgan Ryder. Of course, he made his son an authority of the coven. Morgan Ryder wasn't just a vampire; he was powerful, rich, and ruthless to his core. He would take down anyone by any means. He ran the biggest tech company, most of the local stores, and several restaurants. Sebastian was the only male heir to the fortune, and he was a thousand times worse than his father. Sebastian owned three different businesses under the Ryder name. One restaurant, Mi Belle Rose, one nightclub, Over the Rainbow, and one new-and-upcoming whiskey bar that he co-owned with

Tristian, The Gold Rush.

The whole town was enthralled with him; half the women wanted to land the coven's heir and the other half wanted to see him dead. Bash and the Devils acted more like a gang than a coven, though. At least The Silver Pearl was all about helping our community and supporting local charities. Bash's Coven was more into raising havoc and chaos.

PING

PING

Daniels's eyebrow arched up at the sound of my phone going off. I reached for it and saw the messages were from Ella. "Ella is officially freaking out over her shoes being the wrong color of cream... Is that even possible?" Daniels gave a soft chuckle, shrugging his shoulders. "I don't know fashion, kid," he said nonchalantly.

I folded up my notebook and placed the grimoire back on the small bookshelf that held it by our supply table. "Well, I guess I better head out. Can I come by tomorrow? Maybe help out and practice more on my potions? I still need to get the angle right when I cut the echinacea; it's not working as it should."

Daniels gave a full-on laugh and a wide grin. "Yeah, sure, that's the reason it's not working."

I threw a pair of gardening gloves at him. "Hey, old man! Listen, you might be right, but come on, I'm trying." I stuck my tongue out at him and laughed.

I knew the truth about why I needed practice. I refused for a long time, not wanting to learn anything about our coven or magic in general after my parents' deaths. While other witches in our coven could cause weather and storms to appear, I couldn't even do a simple casting spell. It was my fault, but I still felt like I needed to catch up as much as I could.

I gathered my purse and keys from the long table where my potion sat. "I'll stop by tomorrow and maybe, if you are nice, I'll bring you a coffee and blueberry danish from Coco's Bakery."

Daniels perked up and smiled at me. "Ahh, kid, your bribes are the best." He pulled me into a hug and whispered into my hair, "Love ya, kid." I smiled and hugged him back, feeling a bit sad leaving him here on his own. He looked down at me. "I swear to be on my best behavior here, if you swear to be on your worst with Bash tonight. Give him hell, kid."

I let out a laugh. Daniels knew everything that happened that night and saw the whole thing since Bash streamed it to all the covens. I took a deep breath, knowing that one day I would get my revenge on that asshat and his goons, but today was not that day. Today was all about Ella. "I swear. I will bring you Coco's best batch tomorrow." I kissed his cheek and walked to the door.

PING

PING

"Dammit, Ella. I know, I know," I grumbled. What I wouldn't give to have one of my aunt's famous iced coffees or pastries right now. Coco ran the best damn coffee shop and bakery in town. Her food could literally cure any common cold; it was that delicious.

I walked out to where I had my little red SUV parked. It

wasn't anything fancy, but it was new-ish. I started to text Ella as fast as I possibly could and as I was about to hit "send", my phone began to ring.

An unknown number popped up on the screen. I hesitated to answer, but I knew it was Ella calling from the hotel. "Ella, I swear I am not late. I am on my way, and I swear to sparkly unicorns and fire goblins—"

I was cut off by a deep, masculine chuckle. "Well, well, well. If it isn't the princess herself..." Sebastian's rich voice filled my ears, and my anger swelled up.

"Bash. What the fuck do you want?" I growled.

Bash sounded amused. "Listen here, Princess. Tonight is my baby sister's engagement. You love her, I love her, so I am playing her errand boy today. Ella says you have the perfect pair of shoes to go with her dress. Now, normally I would just break into your little excuse of a house and get them for myself, but since you probably have a hex on your lock, I figured I would save myself the headache and have you bring the shoes to her. Think you manage that, Lexi Rose?"

I huffed as I yanked open my door. I looked at my reflection in the window and saw my eyes changing from their bright blue to a deep purple. It felt as if someone was putting a blindfold made of fire over my eyes. I pushed past the pain as they burned and watered. "Fine. I'll be at the hotel in about thirty minutes with the shoes for Ella," I ground out.

"Great. Nice talking to you, Princess. I'll see you tonight." He paused for a second. I thought he hung up, but then I heard a small growl. "I bet you'll look delicious. I mean, we do get to share a dance together tonight, as it is a family tradition. Just promise not to get too worked up when my hands are on you."

Chapter Three

Oh, hell no! He did not say that! "Go fuck yourself, Bash! You are not coming within ten feet of me tonight. I will be friendly to you and your goons, but don't forget I would rather drown myself than be near you." I hung up, slumped into the seat of my car, threw my phone onto the passenger seat, and screamed into the steering wheel.

I didn't live on my parents' estate. It was too big, too sad, too painful, and too lonely. The nightmares were the worst when I slept there. Instead, I had a small house by the ocean to help strengthen my powers when I needed them. Coco and Jason took care of the estate, along with Daniels. The place was so big that it took all three of them to care for it properly. Coco didn't want staff if she could help it. I would stay the night sometimes, but that was mostly due to too much wine.

My small house was on the north side of town; the sunsets with orange, pink, and purple skies over the water were one of my favorite things. The waves that came in every day brought peace to my mind when at times I just felt fury. To be able to walk along the ocean helped my siren stay calm when I felt like the world was just too much to handle.

The water seemed to help me more than anything. I was always more relaxed in the depths of the coves, swimming around with the fish, finding hidden treasures from boats, or even visiting an old shipwreck that lay near the coast.

I drove through the mountains, the winding road putting my mind at ease. I began to sing softly to Billie Elish's "Happier than Ever" as her dream-like voice filled the car. Soon, I was pulling up to the gated community where I lived. After inputting my code to our neighborhood, I drove to the end of the street where my house sat. I was surrounded by McMansions, but a few of the original beach cottages still stood the test of time. Mine was one of them, built in the 1920's. It was cozy with modern upgrades.

Daniels and Jason both insisted that if I lived away from the estate then I had to have the best security. I fought them on it for weeks until Coco sat me down and explained it was more for them and their nerves versus wanting to keep me locked away. When I saw it from Coco's point of view, I couldn't disagree. If someone could kill my parents so easily, then why wouldn't they try to kill me?

This was the question we all wanted to ask and never had the courage to try to answer: Why didn't they kill me, too?

My quaint cream-colored house was set back away from the main road with a large wrap-around porch behind big, beautiful weeping willows. Supposedly, it was once owned by a famous Hollywood actress when she was starting out in the industry. Even though it was small, I felt like it was perfect for me. I didn't need fancy; I just needed my own space.

My only neighbor close to me was Mrs. Wilson. She was from London and had moved out here after her husband died twenty years ago. I never saw her without a caftan and a martini glass in her hand. You can tell she was beautiful when she was younger, and even now, she was just as pretty. Her grey hair was long and flowed down her back wild and free. Her amazing hazel eyes always seemed like they were looking for trouble, but she was a real sweetheart. She looked out for me and always asked if I was drinking enough water. She was just a kind woman who needed a friend to talk to.

I climbed out of my car and walked towards my door. I had an uneasy feeling someone might be watching me; I glanced around but didn't notice anything or anyone out of the ordinary. As I unlocked the door, I was smacked in the face with cool air. As hot as the day was, it felt good.

When I stepped into the entryway, I heard a "MEEEEEEOOOOOOOWWWW!"

I snickered as my Persian cat slinked out of her hiding spot, her big blue eyes staring right back into mine. "Okay, okay, Dyna, I hear you." She wove through my legs with short little mews. It didn't take a translation spell to know that she meant, Feed me now! I picked her up and I snuggled her to my chest. "Ma'am, keep it down! You're gonna wake up the whole neighborhood!"

A long island sat in the middle of my kitchen with ocean-blue cabinets shining under the soft light. Full floor-to-ceiling windows overlooked the afternoon sun, and I could hear the waves lapping against the rocky shore. I grabbed the closest can of cat food I could find and walked over to Dyna's dish, where I poured the food out into her bowl and refilled her water as well. "There, Your Highness. You are fed and watered now. I gotta go, but I'll be back tonight. You're in charge while I'm gone. Don't go inviting the local tomcats in for any crazy parties." I put her down in the front of her food, and her tail whapped at my leg. I sighed heavily.

I made my way into the master bedroom right off the kitchen and started to strip out of my clothes. The only thing I let Coco take control over was my closet because, as much as I tried not to, I loved shoes and purses. My walk-in closet was a true masterpiece. A black chandelier glistened above me with tiny crystals dropping down like it was raining black diamonds from the sky. One side was full of clothes, from a few designer dresses to my second-hand thrift finds collected over the years and drawers all neatly organized with my everyday clothes. The whole other side, however, was dedicated to rows and rows of shoes and a wall of purses in cubbies, all dramatically lit. Dozens of Louboutins lined the wall, along with an exclusive collection of Blahniks and the sexist pair of thigh-high Chanel boots.

My purses were neatly organized in their cubbies, from small clutches shaped like pineapples to fancy travel bags. I have a problem. To be fair, I did love them all. I wore the shoes and used the bags on a regular basis. I picked up the most gorgeous pair of Manolo Blahnik's; they were cream-colored shoes, with an ankle strap bow and crystals cascading down the heel. I knew these were what Ella wanted. She'd had her eyes on them for a while.

I pulled on a pair of comfy tights and my favorite Mermaid Hair Don't Care sweatshirt. Then I hopped over to my hanging clothes and pulled out a clear garment bag protecting a long satin emerald-green dress with a sweetheart neckline and off-the-shoulder straps. It was sexy, but elegant. I threw my overnight bag over my shoulder and pulled my favorite lace Louboutins out of their cubby.

But I paused as I looked in the mirror taking in my state. My long chocolate-brown hair was pulled up in a messy bun, my skin was the color of porcelain and clear of makeup with just a few smudges of dirt left over from helping Daniels in the conservatory. My bright blue eyes stared back at me. They were my mother's eyes, a cruel reminder for this orphaned girl. I missed my mom. I wish I could talk to her one more time. Ask her for advice about love and life in general.

I looked like my mother with her eyes and hair, but my face resembled my father with his sleek nose and the heart-shaped lips; I was the perfect mix of them. I definitely didn't look like most sirens who were thin and had long, luscious blonde hair. I sighed, dreading having to mix and mingle with the different covens this evening.

I glanced at the clock and noticed the time. "Shit, I need to go." Luckily, Ella had hair and makeup waiting for us so I could go this way, and no one would care if I showed up looking like a drowned rat.

It took about fifteen minutes to get to the luxury hotel

where Ella was having her nearly 300-person engagement party. The Grand Dore was a massive resort made out of white marble, twenty-four-carat gold doors, and a labyrinth maze in the back for dark deeds and biddings.

They once lost an entire group of high schoolers in the maze; it took three days to find them. I pulled my small red SUV up to the valet, where a young man stood looking bored.

"Ummm, no parking lot?" I asked.

He perked up and shook his head. "No, ma'am, not at The Grand Dore."

Shrugging, I handed the keys to him and headed inside. The lobby was palatial, with large gold columns and a huge, mirrored front desk, along with a small alcove with a few sofas set to the side.

I headed straight to the glass elevators as they opened up and pushed the button for the penthouse suite. The Ryders were always flashy, so of course, it was the penthouse suite for the bridal party. Ella didn't actually care about the glam, but I knew she wanted to please her family, so she went along with it. I walked down the tiny hallway and knocked on the double doors to the suite. It swung open with a jolt, revealing the person I hated almost as much as Sebastian Ryder.

Standing at six foot three was my former friend, Aden Charmante. He stared down at me, his steel eyes gazing into my blue ones, and a look of surprise passed his face. Aden was the one person I'd trusted with my whole heart back then. He knew things that even Ella didn't, but he crushed my heart the night he chose Bash instead of me.

I know why he did it: to get power. But that's the thing with power; it can change you. I knew this was the way of The Blood Moon Coven, but it still didn't take the sting away any less. I knew for years everyone wanted to know why I shut myself away after the night my parents died. They would ask why I hid behind books, alchemy, and magic.

That night, I couldn't face anyone, and for a long time I blamed these three Devils. Maybe I always would. My heart was stone-cold to them now, and hatred reared its ugly head once again.

I looked into Aden's eyes and noticed something I had never seen before. Jealousy. Something dawned on me. All the nights of us just playfully flirting, the times where he just wanted it to be me and him. Was he jealous of Bash, because he took what he couldn't have? I liked Aden as a friend once upon a time, and maybe it could have been more if time allowed, but now? I didn't think my heart could forgive him for what he did. The pain of that night lived in me more than anyone knew. A cruel smile formed on my lips as I knew that Aden Charmante took a beating that night too. He lost the one thing he wanted—me. It was a crack in his shield, and I caused that. It gave me more joy than I could express.

I guess I wasn't the only one who had scars on our hearts from that night.

Aden was insanely smart but had a rebel streak. His dark brown hair seemed sloppy on purpose, and those steel grey eyes looked like they were undressing me. A cupid's bow lip adorned his mouth. The biggest difference was the massive number of tattoos he had. His white tux shirt hung open, revealing a demon tattoo with its tongue snaking out across his fit stomach. Aden was completely covered in tattoos, from the top of his neck to the sharp V that reached his lower stomach. His slacks were unbuttoned, and his black boxers peeked out from behind them.

I hadn't seen him since then, so I had to quickly hide my shock at how much he'd grown. Holy shit! Where was the lanky, sweet-looking, nerdy kid I knew? Aden was now dark and dangerously gorgeous.

And yet, regardless of how he looked, I just kept thinking, They broke me.

I quickly looked away and started to move past him, trying to make my way to Ella.

Aden grabbed my wrist as he purred, "Well, that's rude. Hello, Lex." He used an old name he and Ella called me once when we were little. I just stared up at him, glaring as he continued to look smug. "Good to see you, too. You have grown up a bit, haven't you?"

It sounded like he just whispered dirty things into my ear. I blinked at him, slowly, and bit my lip because I could play this game. I was a siren, for goodness' sake. In my most seductive voice, I breathed, "Aden, I see you have grown a lot, too, but tell me... are you still a good little bitch for Bash?" I gave him a flirty smile and batted my lashes. "I am so glad it's working out for you. I didn't know you babysat these days; what do you charge, twenty dollars an hour?"

Aden's gaze suddenly turned cold, and he pulled me closer, snarling through his teeth, "Welcome home, Lexi. You're in for a hell of an awakening. We've been waiting for you." I stiffened for a second because Aden never raised his voice to me, let alone threatened me, but I gathered my strength and pulled my hand from his grasp. I casually flipped him the bird as I walked down the hall to where I heard a steady hum of "Toxic" by Brittany Spears playing through the loudspeaker.

Chapter Four

I laughed out loud as I entered the suite where Ella was sitting. "Ella! It's an engagement party, not a girl's night out!"

Champagne bottles were scattered everywhere. A few of Ella's friends were lounging about, giggling and staring at Aden as he followed me in. They stood and began to circle him, smiling and pulling him to dance with them. Aden played it up as he danced and laughed. He even kissed one girl's neck. I felt the hint of jealousy, not in a way of wanting him, but more that I missed his smile and his laugh.

It cut deeper to know he never mourned our friendship.

Ella sat in a high black chair getting her nails, hair, and makeup done at the same time. She smiled widely at me, and I couldn't help but smile back. Ella looked like a model with long, sleek blonde hair and big, cobalt blue doe eyes. She was known widely as a graceful beauty. If Ella reminded me of the sun, then Bash was the moon. They were complete opposites in every way possible.

That's why I loved her.

She didn't have her brother's snobbish behavior or attitude. Ella always said it was because she was raised in Paris and not in the states. She had nannies, aunties, and staff rather than her horrid mother to raise her. Ella and Bash's mother left their father years ago and, from what I knew, remarried some duke. Ella's stepsisters were awful to her. One day, her stepsisters were so cruel that they cut off her hair as a joke. To top it off, they ripped her favorite toy bear apart.

Ella called her dad in tears and told him everything that had been happening. He was furious. By then Morgan had remarried. Wife number two was very kind and wanted kids. Morgan, being the king he was, had Ella relocated and told his ex-wife to never contact either kid again.

Ella's family and mine went back even farther in our covens. My father and Morgan not only grew up together, but they even went to the same school, were on the same sports team, and they were always in competition with each other. Eventually, they ran multiple companies as partners, all while managing the covens themselves, too. They brought in more of the fae and more businesses, turning Providence Village into a growing city that was now more popular for local tourists and other companies.

"LEXI!" screamed Ella, jumping up and hugging me.

Somehow, she didn't mess up her makeup as she planted a kiss on my cheek.

Ella had everything an heiress needed to rule: brains, beauty, kindness, and she was more cunning than others gave her credit for. She paid attention to the room and was trusted by many fae, always the first to know of something going on but never telling a soul; she kept secrets close to her chest.

I hugged her back and then sat down next to her as the makeup artist glanced at my dirt-covered face. "No!" She pointed to me. "You shower now," she said in her French accent. I was about to argue and lay into her when Ella said, "Yeah, Lex, I love you, but you smell like manure." She waved her hand in front of my face.

I laughed and scrunched my nose and pursed my lips. Yeah, she was right. I did smell a bit like Daniels's special manure, and no one wanted that. I reached into my bag and pulled out the heels. "Here are the shoes you wanted." I placed them in Ella's lap as she squeaked, grinning wildly at them.

"You know you could have texted me about them and not have Satan himself call me."

Ella blushed. She knew that Bash and I didn't get along. She thought it was about the coven's rivalry, but I never had the heart to tell her what Bash did that night. "Sorry, amie, I was a bit upset after my cream shoes came back... Well, they came back yellow, and I kind of freaked. Ethan came in, and, well, he had to calm me down."

She turned even redder. I knew what Ethan did to calm her down.

Ella cleared her throat. "So, I asked Bash to call you for a pair that would work. Then I kind of was... well... you know... with Ethan, so I forgot to forewarn you."

"Well, as long as you aren't freaking out anymore, we're good. I'll be out in a few minutes" I kissed her cheeks as I headed back to the bathroom at the end of the hallway.

I stepped inside, dreamily looking at the deep tub that I would kill to soak in, but time was of the essence, so I decided on the steam shower with multiple showerheads. "A girl could really get relaxed in here," I murmured as I switched the shower on, making steam billow through the room. I stepped out of the spraying water and into a fluffy white towel.

The door suddenly burst open, and I was face-first with Mr. Casually Cruel himself.

I was knocked straight into that hard chest, making me stumble back a few steps as I held my nose. "Fuck! Damn it!" My towel loosened and fell to the ground. "Oh shit!" I scrambled to pull the towel up, but I was now twisted around trying to cover myself at the same time.

My ass landed right on Bash's crotch.

I felt his slight arousal as he held onto my hips to steady me. "Shit, shit, shit," I whispered, "Please be a dream, please don't be real..." I closed my eyes and took a deep breath, then turned my head to look up into the face of the Devil himself.

Menacing eyes stared right back at me as if I was an irritation, which was how I felt around Bash anyways. We didn't see each other often, but every now and then we had to endure time together. It was dismal, and we usually

ended up screaming at each other.

He reached down to pick up the towel like he hadn't seen me the whole time and dangled it on one finger. "Missing something, Princess?"

I narrowed my eyes, snatched the towel out of his hand, and quickly wrapped it around me. "You could try knocking next time." My face flushed with embarrassment. I grabbed the robe and quickly wrapped it around me as I struggled not to tie the sash too tight. I glared at him the entire time. "What the hell do you want?"

He raised an eyebrow at me. I tried to move around him, but he was so big that he filled the entire door.

I huffed, "I am in a hurry to get my hair and makeup done so we can be there for Ella and Ethan."

As soon as I said Ella, his glare softened. He lifted his arm above my head, so I had the space I needed to move through the doorway. Of course, it only left me a sliver of space to pass. The moment our bodies brushed each other, it was like an electrical current sweeping through us. I gasped and Bash turned towards me, eyes widening in surprise. His fingers ran down my arm, sending small tingles through his touch. I shivered, and he looked like he wanted to say more.

A shrieking cry filled the hallway, and we both turned our heads to see a familiar tall woman walking toward us. "Bashy Babe! Did you find it?"

I sighed. Cassandra went to high school with Ella and me. She was known to only date higher fae. She looked nothing like she did in high school. Her tighter-than-skin nude dress was completely inappropriate for the party, and it came just below her lady parts, exposing her gorgeous long legs. Her red hair flew about, landing in long curls on her back as she came stomping up to us looking like she was about to spit venom at me.

I raised my brow and smirked at the new nickname. "Bashy?"

"Don't say a fucking word, Lexi," Bash muttered.

"Of course, I would never." I smiled sweetly. I glanced down at my wrist as if I had a watch on it and looked at Cassandra. "Look at the time! I gotta run. Bye, Bashy!" Just to cause a ruckus and to piss him off more, I rose on my tiptoes and planted a chaste kiss on his cheek close to his lips.

"Enjoy the party, Sebastian," I teased. I turned quickly and went to join Ella.

The last thing I heard was, "Bashy, you don't want that reject, do you?" Cassandra's whiny voice snapped. Oh, hell no, she didn't! But I remembered it was Ella's party and I needed to be here for her. So, I kept walking and thought of many ways to accidentally spill wine onto Cassandra later in the evening.

I slid into the makeup chair next to Ella as she was animatedly talking to her hairstylist, who was curling her hair in long, soft waves. I smiled thinking how much Ella had come out of her shell in these last ten years. I remember the day we met.

One day, I was riding my bike and saw a small little blonde girl who looked about my age sitting under a tree. She was knitting a pink and purple hat. I asked her what she was doing, and she said, "Making my new best friend a hat." As she finished the last loop, she jumped up and ran

over to hand it to me. We've been best friends ever since. From our dance party nights to dealing with my parents' death and deciding which colleges we wanted to go to, Ella had been there through it all. Her friendship meant so much to me. So, I swallowed my pride and hate towards Bash, and I stood next to her to celebrate the fact that she found her person.

"Ahhh. I see! I told you! Much better, mon amie." The makeup artist broke me out of my memory.

After what seemed like hours of hair and makeup, Ella and I were both ready to party. I adamantly ignored Bash and Aden while they hung out on the sofa. Bash left about halfway through me getting my makeup done, muttering something about showing the photographer where to set up. Aden stayed the whole time, sitting right across from Ella and talking to her every now and then but completely ignoring me besides throwing the occasional glare my way, which I was perfectly fine with.

I eventually pulled out my phone, scrolled through my socials, and then opened up the most recent novel I was reading. I was deeply immersed in my book when I heard Ella shout, "Lexi!"

I snapped up from my book. "What?"

She smiled and rolled her eyes. "I swear you are always off in your own world. What do you think?"

Ella was a vision in a creamy dress with delicate lace running up the bodice. Her hair fell over one shoulder, and she wore simple diamonds in her ears with a small chain necklace that belonged to her mother. Her engagement ring shone as it sat on her hand. She looked like a model from a bridal magazine.

"You look beautiful, El." I smiled. "I can't believe you're getting married!"

She blushed. "I know. I love him so much, Lexi. I hope one day you find that, too."

I didn't let the pain show in my eyes because the truth was, after what all three of them did to me, I would never trust a man again. Daniels and Jason were the only two I truly trusted, but they were family. I had a few boyfriends, and I tended to have a few guy friends I hooked up with when I needed to, but I didn't want to give up my heart like that ever again.

I glanced over at Aden, who was staring at me with a dare in his smile as if I would tell her. "I should be almost done. Why don't you find Ethan? I will come and find you tonight." I grinned at her.

"Sure, see you two later. Don't do anything I wouldn't do." She smirked.

Aden stood with her. "I will walk you out, Ella." He led her out the door towards the entryway.

"Please finish," I begged the makeup artist.

She flicked her gaze between me and Aden's back. "No worries, mon amie, I will get you out of here. That boy is nothing but trouble."

I sighed. "You don't know half of it."

Once I was all glammed up, I made my way to the second bedroom in the suite where my dress and overnight bag were laid out on the bed. Ella would be staying with Ethan tonight, so I had her entire suite to myself; perks of being the B.F.F. I took my dress out of the bag and began to undo

my robe. I heard a small noise and turned around to see Aden leaning against the doorway, staring intensely at me.

"You could at least turn around; I am not giving out a free show here," I snapped.

He smirked and turned pointedly around, crossing his arms. "Happy?"

I just glared at him and slipped my legs into the dress. The silky fabric fell down my legs as I smoothed the dress out, and I was getting the bodice in place when I realized... "Shit," I whispered. I couldn't reach my zipper and hold the top of the dress up against my chest. "Damn it."

Aden looked over his shoulder. "What's wrong, Lex?"

I fiddled with the back trying to work the zipper up. "It's the dress. Can you get Ella? I need help with the zipper and... Ugh, damn! My shoes, too."

I tried not to blush, but I felt the heat in my cheeks. I refused to show him how embarrassed I was, so I held my head high. I heard him move to go get Ella and released a sigh.

Warm breath fanned on my neck, and immediately I knew it was Aden. I swallowed hard as his hands rested on my lower back, slowly zipping the dress up with one hand while the other guided the material. Goosebumps raised on my arms, and I shivered slightly at his cool touch.

Biting my lip, I realized how attracted I was to Aden. It wasn't just physical. Yes, Aden was hot in a tattooed beat-your-ex bad boy way, but I missed our friendship. I missed how we used to laugh, and knowing that I missed him just made it worse. To know that he left me empty and betrayed. Knowing we would never get that back again made my heart ache.

"Don't be afraid of me, Lexi," he whispered.

I turned to face him. "I'm not afraid of you Aden, I..." Sighing, I finally just said what I felt. "I don't know how to act around you. We don't like each other, remember?" I looked up at his face, trying to remember the boy he used to be. "But I do know this, I will always remember the good times, before your betrayal, before my heart broke into a million pieces."

His grey eyes gazed into mine as if he was trying to figure out a puzzle. Suddenly, he fell down onto one knee. I bit my tongue to stifle my gasp. He pulled my dress up enough to grasp my ankle, and I let out a flirty laugh as his warm hands moved up my leg to make me lift my foot and slide the black shoe on. He looked up at me with a mischievous grin.

"I wouldn't say I don't like you, Lexi." With the height difference of the heel, I grasped his shoulder as he got the other ready. "I would say I do like you, but it's not up to me, and you made your decision ten years ago." He glanced up at me knowingly. I shook my head, but he continued on. "I grew up and moved on; you should do the same." He lifted my foot into the shoe, his touch so light and gentle. "And if you didn't notice, the person who is helping you isn't Bash. I would like to think one day we could be friends again, but Lex, it's not up to me. It's up to you and him to get past your shit."

His hand moved up my leg leaving a tingle behind. "If you need anything else tonight, let me know," he whispered, standing and turning to walk out the door.

I bit my lip and found the courage. "Aden..."

He tilted his head to me.

"Th... thank you."

He nodded once and left the room, leaving me thinking, WHAT THE FUCK JUST HAPPENED? I did not have time to deal with old crushes and the fucking Devils of The Blood Moon Coven.

Chapter Five

Ethan and Ella had returned to the suite and were in each other's arms kissing when I came out. I smirked at the cuteness, giving them a few more seconds before I yelled, "Ella! You ready?" They jumped apart from each other, laughing.

"Yep, Now let's go find my family and get this thing done with. If it was up to me, we would have just had this at the Charmante's Estate with only family and friends," she huffed out.

She wasn't in love with a big wedding, but she knew for her family and Ethan's it was something they had to do. Ethan Charmante stood next to her in his boy-next-door manner. With his bright blond hair and blue eyes, he looked like a typical surfer, but Ethan was kind of amazing. He was kind, caring, and, for a vamp, he was the poster child for how all fae should act.

I laughed, "Ella you would still have like 200 people to get through. Let's just consider this practice for the big day." I walked up to her, giving her a hug. "You look gorg, Ella. Now, let's party it up" I hooked my arm through hers and we headed out of the suite to the elevator to meet Aden and Bash.

Except Bash and Aden were nowhere in sight. Cassandra was waiting in the hall heading towards the elevator, now in a different tiny black dress that was so tight I wasn't sure how she breathed. "Does she not own anything else?" I muttered, and Ella giggled.

"She is... Well, she is Cassandra."

I rolled my eyes as we approached her. She was staring down at her phone and lifted her head as we walked over, a smile plastered to her face. "Ells! O-M-G, aren't you just so excited it's your engagement?" She did a little dance, grabbing Ella's hand and looking at the massive ring—a huge three-carat cushion-cut diamond sat on Ella's finger with small diamonds circling the band.

I felt a hint of jealousy in Cassandra's gaze over the ring. It truly was beautiful, but Ella deserved it all. She was the best person I knew, and Ethan made her insanely happy.

Ella reddened slightly. "Yes, I am absolutely thrilled. Thank you, Cassandra. Did I introduce you to Lexi? Cassandra, Lexi. Lexi, Cassandra. Cassandra went to school with us, Lexi."

Cassandra turned towards me still smiling, but her eyes

held a threatening glare behind them. "Yes, I ran into her as she had her hands on Bashy, but she had just slipped, so it's totally fine." She scrunched her nose and gave me a toothy smile. She reminded me of a Regina George—nice to your face but would destroy you in a heartbeat.

I raised both of my eyebrows and laughed in her face. "Oh, you can have Bashy all you want, sweetheart. The farther I am away from him, the better. I never want to be that close to Sebastian Ryder ever again. In fact, if you want the job to distract him tonight, then by all means you should do that." I walked past her to the elevator, pushing the button and silently urging it to hurry.

Just as the doors opened, I saw the infamous Three Devils standing like GQ models. Bash wore a crisp, inky-black suit. His white shirt curved over his broad chest with black buttons descending to his perfectly tailored, matching pants. A black bowtie adored his throat. I was at a loss for words. Bash looked like a classic Hollywood Star. His amazing green eyes twinkled as he stared at me, taking in my dress and stopping for a moment at my chest. When he reached my eyes, I froze in place.

What I saw was pure lust, just for a moment, and then they turned dark and into something more sinister. I felt like I was a deer looking into the wolf's eyes. "The better to eat you with, my dear," popped into my head. Yep, he was definitely all predator at this moment. This couldn't be right because Sebastian Ryder hated me.

Aden looked the exact opposite of Bash. He wore a navy velvet blazer with a stark white shirt and navy tie to match, which was loosened at the neck. A few of his top buttons

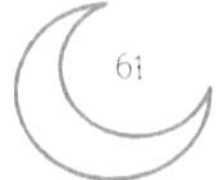

were undone so you got a peek at his tattoos. He smirked at me, biting his lip, which made a blush form across my cheeks. A tingle radiated throughout my body. The heat of his eyes hit down below, and I shifted from one foot to another as my blush deepened.

Finally, the last of the three (who was the only mildly tolerable one of the group) was Bash's best friend Tristian Cassium. Tristian was known as the "fun" one, always playful and super flirty. Some people thought he was just an airhead, but I knew it was all an act. Not only was Tristian insanely smart, but he was cunning, too.

He had his own set of businesses in Providence Village: a few gyms and a local pub. He also ran an insane Instagram account which was mostly him without a shirt drinking coffee while reading a book. It was called @evenblondesread. He had over two million followers. He was Providence Village's mini-celebrity; a true entrepreneur.

Plus, he wasn't too bad to look at. Besides the blond hair, he had copper eyes like a tiger; he was handsome, intelligent, and ruthless to say the least. Tristian was looking at his phone typing something out when he walked into Aden's back. His phone tumbled to the ground, sliding its way to my feet. He reached down in a sweeping motion, grabbing it quickly. When he raised his head to meet my face, his eyes widened. He hid his shock, quickly turning it into a sexy smirk.

I followed his movements, his eyes boring into mine as he stood up inches from my face. "Ms. Rose, you look utterly delectable tonight." He turned to Ella, who was glaring at him.

"Ella, you look lovely." He grabbed her hand, kissed it, and then twirled her in his arms.

Ella burst out laughing. "Geez, Tristian! I swear you wouldn't last a day without flirting. Now all of you, get out of my way! I have an engagement party to get to and hopefully sneak away early from." Turning to me, she said, "Lex, have I ever told you what Ethan can do with his tongue and a cherry?"

I rolled my eyes. "Ella, I do not wanna hear how big Ethan's dick is. Please, spare us all the gritty details."

Ella looked around the group, giving me an evil smile. "Uh, excuse me for being made to orgasm multiple times by a man who knows where the g-spot is."

Tristian looked shocked and shook his head. "No, no, Ella. Don't. Just don't." He looked terrified.

I put my head into my hands "No. I do not need, nor want, to know that."

A deep rumble came from Bash. "That makes two of us! Or did you forget your very dangerous older brother is standing right here? It would be such a shame if I had to kill your fiancé before the wedding day."

I looked over at Ethan, and he seemed genuinely scared of Bash. I sighed, rolling my eyes. "Fucking barbarian," I whispered to Ella.

Ella looked up at Bash with her big blue eyes, pouting. "Bash, you're no fun."

Bash arched an eyebrow and looked around at us. "Ella, Ethan, and Cassandra, you guys go downstairs to Father and the Charmantes; they are waiting on you." It wasn't a request but more of a command and, to my surprise, they all went.

Ella headed inside the elevator and turned to look at me, tilting her head. "Lexi, you coming?" But before I could move, Bash was guiding Cassandra in and hitting the fifth-floor button where the party was being held. The doors closed with a swish.

I turned to look at the three of them and crossed my arms. "That was extremely rude, Asshat". I gathered all the courage I could muster and huffed out, "So... is this like a meeting or are you just wanting to ogle me some more?" I examined my nails and glanced up at Bash. Before I could even move, Bash was in my face faster than I had ever seen someone move. I sometimes forgot how powerful Sebastian was.

"Hello, Princess, you look... edible." He smirked.

I bit my lip from the anger that formed at the center of my chest. I concentrated on the black buttons on his shirt. I gathered my strength, pushing my influence into him as I looked back at those deep green eyes "What do you want, Bash? Don't bullshit me. What the fuck do you want from me?" I snapped.

Bash seemed surprised but recovered quickly and stepped more into my space. His eyes blazed a fiery green as I felt his own compulsion sweep over me. I moved back instantly and found myself hitting something warm and hard. I turned to glance and noticed it was Aden. He immediately wrapped his strong arms around me, and I gasped, swallowing my scream. I tried to push away from his grasp, but Tristian stepped in, not once looking up from his phone as he typed out a text.

I was cornered by three lions, and I was on the menu tonight. Aden dropped his head near my ear and his hands

roamed down my arm lightly. "Shh, Lexi, we won't hurt you. Bash here just wants to make sure you are going to be a good little siren tonight," he whispered into my neck, and he gently kissed the spot right under my ear. "You'll be good, right?" He teased my earlobe. I felt my influence flow through me and pushed the emotion of fear into Aden. His grip loosened, and I wiggled from his hold.

I didn't dare look at anyone but Bash because I knew this was a test, a test to see if I would do anything against him tonight. It was always political with him. I sighed and pulled my influence from them. "No. Tonight is about Ella, and, as I have told you a million times before, I do not want anything to do with you, your businesses, or your little gang." I was shaking so much with anger that I felt my power growing inside of me. It wanted to come out to play. The problem with that was I didn't have enough control of my power yet, and I could cause more harm than good.

Bash knew that, too. He saw it in my eyes. His fangs peeked out from his teeth. "I would suggest you control yourself, Ms. Rose. You know it would lead to a deadly result."

Grinding my teeth, I took a deep breath and closed my eyes.

"Little Star, I don't think I've ever been more entertained by you," laughed Tristian, finally looking up from his phone. "Look, I would love as much as the next person to see a power struggle between the two most powerful covens, but we need to get downstairs." He went back to his phone as he turned and walked to the elevator, pushing the button.

"Couldn't have said it better myself, Tristian." I turned on my heel and walked over to the elevator doors. I stood next to him with my arms crossed and stared at the golden elevator doors, willing the damn thing to get here faster before any tears fell from anger.

Aden and Bash huddled together behind us, talking in whispers to each other. Tristian touched my arm and gazed down at me "You okay, Lil' Star?"

I shook my head. "Just drop it. Okay, Tristian?"

His lips thinned as if he wanted to say more, but he nodded. "You got it, Lil' Star."

I sighed, glancing his way. "You ever gonna tell me why you call me that?" I whispered.

He smirked. "Maybe one day, sweetheart, but today is not that day. Plus, he'd kill me. He is weird about you. Are you sure you're okay?"

Was I okay? No. Aden had my feelings twisted inside, and Bash, fucking Bash. I never knew if he hated me or not. He always walked a thin line between both. He was hot, then cold, and he needed to make up his damn mind. Either I was his enemy, or I was his friend.

When I found my voice, it wasn't loud, it wasn't cruel. It was powerful because I made up my mind about the Three Devils standing before me.

I turned to Tristian. "No, Tristian, I am not okay." I walked back over to Bash and slapped him across the face with all my might. "Ten years ago, you humiliated me. Then you manipulated me into having feelings for you. Why? Because of what your father wanted you to do for what, your coven?" The tears pooled in my eyes, threatening to spill, but I had to get this out. "You were my first kiss, my first everything, and then like a fucking fool I fell in love

with you. You kept me a secret, but I kept you like an oath because I thought it was more."

Sebastian wasn't the only one to blame for that night. All three of them had to answer for what they did.

I whipped towards Aden and pointed at him "And you!" He crossed his arms over his chest and smirked at me "You! One of the best friends I had. You knew more about me than ELLA! You betrayed not only my trust, but you broke our friendship, and I will never forgive you for what you did, Aden Charmante." Aden's shoulders drop in shame.

Tristian chuckled, and I turned and walked over to him and looked at him in his copper-colored eyes "I wouldn't laugh, Tristian. You are no better. You let them do this. You didn't have the courage to stand up to both of them. That's just as bad."

I hissed the last out because I knew the tears were coming, I turned to Sebastian and let him see my eyes filled with tears and the hate I wore on my face.

"Does that clear up why I might hate you three as much as I do? I am hurt, I am angry, and you should be worried because I am going to destroy you, asshole. You will be on your knees soon because I swear, Sebastian, you made a mistake that night. You underestimated me...you just turned this princess into a villain."

The elevator doors opened, and I turned and walked in, Tristian following me, Aden close behind. They stood on opposite sides, not looking at either of us, and Bash glared at me with fire in his eyes. He sped in just as the doors closed and we descended down to the fifth floor.

Bash stood so close that I felt his hardness pushing up

into my stomach. I gasped at the literal balls he had as I pushed him back, but he didn't move. He took my chin in his fingers, looked at my lips and then to my eyes. "I love a little competition, Princess." He pulled me closer, his lips brushing over my cheek to my ear as he breathed, "That slap is going to cost you dearly, darling."

Chapter Six

The doors opened, and a live band was playing a soft jazz number as Bash sped out of the elevator to join the party. Cassandra sprinted after him, pulling him off in one direction to a small group of his father's friends who were always at every party. They all smiled while clapping his back and shaking his hand. He gave polite nods before he grabbed a waiter to fetch him a drink. He looked at me and smirked, as if he knew our discussion was not over. Rolling my eyes, I headed in the opposite direction, directly to the bar which was situated in the back of the ballroom. I needed something strong to drink, and I needed it now.

The ballroom was decorated similarly to the hotel it-self, all in gold from the mirrored doors to the chandeliers dripping diamonds and glitter. The huge fireplace roared as people and fae danced passed me. There were fairies, goblins, minotaurs, and all kinds of witches celebrating the newly engaged couple. A few harpies and hippogriffs were taking shots while a tiny pixie girl was fast asleep on a table already. One thing the Ryders did know was how to throw a party. The first time Ella and I ever drank was at their annual Winter Solstice Party. I don't think I've ever had more fun than that night, dancing with strangers and laughing the night away with Ella. We paid the price the next day.

I scanned the room to find Ella and saw her smiling and laughing with a few of our older friends from school. She looked like she was in good hands. I soon reached the bar situated on the back patio. It was near the large labyrinth garden and was so clear it looked like it was made entirely out of glass. I laid my hands on it and jumped at how cold it was.

"It's ice, Lexi," a cool voice said behind me. I turned around and saw a girl with long black hair that looked almost blue when the light shone on it. Her skin was so pale it was ethereal.

She had a bored look on her face which I had seen many times in school. I smiled at her. "Hey, Nyx. I didn't know you'd be here."

She smirked as she walked by me. "The witches of the coven did it." She nodded to the bar. "Yeah, Ella and I are working on the same event for the Trinity Coven next month. She invited me last minute. So, the elusive Silver

Pearl daughter has come out of hiding?"

I shook my head. "I don't hide."

She signaled the bartender. "Yeah, you do, but I guess that's expected since, you know, the murders."

I raised my eyebrows. Normally people avoided talking about my parents' deaths, but Nyx was never one to go with what other people did, which was a reason I liked her so much. She was brutally honest.

"You know people could say you're too blunt, right?"

She laughed. "You love it, don't you?"

I grinned. "Sure do. So, how's life?"

We watched as a young bartender who looked barely twenty-one served multiple drinks, tossing cocktail shakers in the air and flipping around martini glasses before pouring colorful drinks into them. His ears were pointed— definitely an elf— and his eyes had a yellow hue that told me he was part of the local fairy clan, too.

"Life is okay. My sister and I just moved in with a few friends, but... I don't know, four girls in a tiny apartment is a bit..."

I smirked. "Overwhelming?" I finished for her.

She glanced at me. "That's saying it nicely. One girl is just a lot."

"I'm sure! Well, if you ever need a break, you know where to find me."

She raised one perfectly arched eyebrow. "Do I?"

I nodded. "Sure! Ask Ella, and here, I will give you my number." She handed over her phone so I could type it in.

The bartender nodded to me as he headed over to us. I knew the drinks would not only be strong, but they would

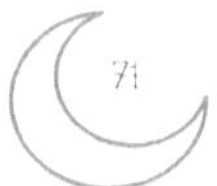

be potentially deadly. "Ms. Rose, good evening." I bowed my head in respect as it was tradition in the elven culture. He produced a shaker and two champagne flutes in front of me as he began to mix a drink for Nyx and me, pouring a sparkling silver liquid into mine. "Here. I can sense your rage. Drink this; it will help." His eyes sparkled a bit when I held the glass to my lips for a sip.

"It's good."

He shrugged. "I know," he said in a bored tone.

"Cheers," I told Nyx. "To the happy couple."

She shook her head "Cheers, Lexi. Hey, I gotta go get my sister, but I might take you up on the offer to escape."

I smiled. "That would be great! See ya later, Nyx."

I downed the drink, and the elf poured me another round without a word. I would have thanked him, but I knew you never thanked an elf. This would imply a favor would be owed and could end badly if you didn't want to pay the price of their kindness. I did leave him a hefty tip, though. I took the champagne and walked to the edge of the paved patio that overlooked the labyrinth. I felt some-one come up behind me, and I turned to see a younger guy with pale blond hair, a straight nose, and pointed features; he appeared almost skeletal.

His voice was soft as he spoke to me. "Did you know that the labyrinth was here before the hotel? A group of mino-taurs designed it over a hundred years ago. The point of the maze was to keep people out, but people ran through the maze as if it were their own personal playground, sneaking off to the dark corners to hide from the party. I even heard that at the center sat a fairy ring to take you to another dimension."

I tilted my head as he spoke and took a sip, savoring the way the silvery liquid hit my tongue. "Why not let them have fun? They don't mean any harm. Besides, if the minotaurs had a problem with them, wouldn't they shut the labyrinth down?"

He squinted his eyes and shook his head in disgust. "Don't you see? They are the problem, the frivolous fae and their whimsical ways. I swear humans have it so much easier."

I examined him a bit closer, wondering why he was so open and how he looked so familiar to me. "I don't know. Maybe they do, but I love being a siren and a witch. Humans have their own set of problems; though, I don't think any one life is perfect." I looked down, watching the fireflies dance to the music in a hypnotic way.

"Pretty night," he said, closer to me than before.

"Hmmm, yes. I'm Lexi—"

He raised his brow. "I know. Mr. Ryder asked me to get you."

I sighed. "Tell Mr. Ryder to fuck off and I will find him in a few minutes."

The man looked shocked as I waved him off. I turned away from him and walked to the steps of the garden, ready to go run into the labyrinth. I finished the last of my drink and set my glass on the banister, and my anger subsided.

I was still mad, but at least I could focus on what mattered. "Ella," I said sadly to myself. I turned around and scanned the room for her. I found her at the center of attention standing next to Ethan, who looked immaculate next to her. They were happy, laughing and talking to a group of people. A few girls were ogling Ella's ring, and Ethan looked down at her with pride in his eyes. He was so kind and caring and truly looked at Ella like she was the sun. She deserved all the happiness in the world.

I felt someone come to my side and I took in a deep breath because I knew it was one of the Three Devils. "You know, people don't believe we are brothers half the time." I turned to Aden, who held a tumbler of dark liquid in his hand. He took a sip and stared at Ethan. "He is so different from me that I sometimes don't believe it myself. I hear what my father says to my mother about me. He thinks I am nothing… and the way he talks about Ethan? You would think he was a god." He looked down at his drink, then slid a glance at me.

"Everyone is different, Aden. Just because Ethan looks nothing like you and has none of the same personality traits doesn't mean he doesn't share the same values as you or that he doesn't know your heart just as much as you know his. Your mother knows your heart and soul, and she loves you so much. So what if your father doesn't? Not all parents are perfect, and not all parents should have been parents." I placed my hand on his shoulder. I missed my old friend, but I was glad he was still inside there.

Aden turned and leaned over the rail. There was a frown on his face, and it looked like he wanted to say more to me. "You meant it, didn't you, what you said to Bash?" He shook his head. "You would destroy him if given the chance."

I moved to lean next to him, looking out at the night. "It's a chess game, Aden. If Bash tries to destroy me, he needs to know I will fight back. My queen never fails." I stood back up, seeing a familiar face in the crowd looking over his

drink at me. His green eyes held mine as he motioned for me to come over. I glared at him, letting my anger return "Also, I do not need a fucking babysitter. Did you really come to take me over to him, Aden?" I turned on my heel, flipped him off, and walked away with a sway to my hips on my way over to Ella. As soon as I crossed the floor, the effect of the silver drinks hit me full force. Damn, I should have asked what he put in it. Damned elves always causing mischief.

I felt light as a feather—like I could dance all night. I smiled at Ethan, hooking his arm in mine. "Congrats, Ethan, on getting the best girl I know!" I smiled. "Can I steal her for a few moments? I really need to dance and be away from the Devils."

Ethan slightly frowned. "Oh Lexi, I wish we could, but that's why Bash was looking for you. We need to do the formal dances now. Ella and I will start then you and..." He looked around and waved a hand. "BASH! Come over here and get your dance partner, frere." I groaned as Bash made his way over to us. "You and Bash will follow; it's tradition, and my family is pretty adamant about it happening, but after, I promise you can have her for the rest of the night until we get back to my room." He nuzzled her neck. Ella giggled and hit his arm playfully.

Bash joined the group and I looked anywhere but at him. A waiter with champagne flutes passed. I grabbed two and handed one to Ella, who gave me a snarky look.

"What?"

"Nothing!" She laughed as she sipped her champagne.

I tipped mine back and drank mine in one go. "Fine" I plastered on a fake smile. "Let's do this, then."

The music changed to a soft, romantic song as Ethan made a grand gesture to Ella and swept her into his arms. They began to dance, and the entire room quietly watched them. I saw their love fill the space, and my heart ached a bit, wanting to feel that way one day. I knew Ethan was perfect for her because he only saw her in the room. It made everyone stop and watch in awe. I sensed Bash behind me as he closed in. I glanced back to find he was staring at me. His green eyes were so intense and his jaw so sharp, any girl would die to have him hold them and dance the night away. I was that girl ten years ago. I would have gone to the ends of the world for him. As I thought of what would have been, my heart cracked, and I could feel my face shift from adoration for Ella to loathing for her brother.

He reached out his hand for me to take, and I yanked mine back, but Bash was fast and grasped it tightly as he walked us out. In one smooth motion, he pulled me around until I was facing him. I placed my hand on his shoulder and he pulled me closer at the waist. We began to move to the music, sweeping across the room as I scanned his eyes for any answers he might give. I saw nothing on his face to give away what he was feeling.

He bent his head to my ear and whispered, "Smile, Princess. Our covens are both watching us like hawks. Any weakness they see will give them a reason to move against us."

I stiffened slightly, then realized I needed to play the game of a leader for once. I bit the inside of my cheek and hissed, "Fine, but I don't like it, asshole." I slowly let a sweet smile show and softened my eyes as if I was infatuated with Bash,

trying not to think of five different ways I could punch him.

I moved to the music, and Bash twirled me out pulling me back right into his arms. I gasped in surprise and felt the words move through me as he dipped me so low to the ground that my hair brushed the floor. I glanced over at the crowd that had formed and Aden and Tristian were staring at me with something other than anger in their eyes. "Keep your eyes on me, Lexi," Bash said as he moved us through the floor.

I snapped my head back toward his as more dancers joined us on the floor. "Why? Jealous that someone else might want to steal me away?" I teased.

He huffed. "As if anyone would try to. Do you know who I am, Princess?"

I rolled my eyes. "Everyone knows who you are, Bash, but I would pay money to see someone stand up to you for once."

He chuckled. "You really dislike me that much, don't you?"

I shook my head. "Dislike? I despise you, Bash. You and your band of Devils think they can run this town, but you don't own the town, and you don't own me." I was about to pull away when Bash lifted me into the air and his hands moved right below my breasts, sliding back down to my waist. His fingers left a feeling of hot scorch marks down my side, and I was blushing bright red. Was it the music, the dancing, or was it just us? I didn't think we would ever know.

As the music stopped, an explosion of applause erupted throughout the room. I looked around to see everyone looking at us. Ella looked concerned, but Ethan had a smile on his face. Bash dropped his head to my ear and whispered, "It wasn't all fake, Lexi."

I whipped my head to ask him what he meant by that, but Bash was already gone, his back disappearing in the crowd. I stood, watching him leave, wondering what the hell I was going to do with that bit of information.

Chapter Seven

Ella came up to me with a wild smile. "Don't hate me, but Ethan and I are sneaking off into the maze, then to our room. Can we talk tomorrow?"

I laughed. "Yes go, go have fun and don't do anything I wouldn't do." I winked at her and Ethan.

Ella laughed with me. "Oh, I plan on doing a whole lot worse." She was pulled away by Ethan, who just gave me a tiny mocking wave.

I looked around and realized I didn't know anyone here besides Ella and Nyx. I suddenly wanted to leave. As I passed a goblin and a fire witch, I overheard their hushed gossiping.

"Did you see her dancing with Sebastian Ryder?"

"I know! Maybe we will see a coven wedding; those two are meant to be together."

I stopped to stare at them, and they froze up as I raised a brow. The fire witch tried to cover herself. "Ms. Rose… um, I—"

I cut her off and smiled. "Don't worry about it. As much as I… admire the compliment, Sebastian Ryder and I are just mutuals." I blew out a breath and walked away.

I wanted to scream and shout, but I knew this was part of the game, to smile and nod. I turned to go back to the bar when I noticed a small parlor room off to the side.

Quiet. That was what I needed—to sneak away until I could make one more round and head back to the room. I spotted Bash looking at me. If I could avoid the asshat Devils, even better. I headed into the dark parlor to a large window that overlooked the labyrinth. I sat on the window seat, lifted my knees to my chest, and laid my head on them. Today was exhausting; so many emotions ran through my mind. I knew I needed to get each of them under control in this quiet place away from the noise. It was a perfect spot for me.

Being a siren had many great aspects, but sensing the emotions of each person could be draining. We felt everyone's emotions more intensely. If you were angry, it burned our skin, sadness sat like a pit in our stomach, and when someone was truly happy, it was the biggest high you ever felt. If someone was close enough to touch, their emotions could overflow into you and become even more intense. It could be overwhelming if you didn't have a strong enough shield to keep that feeling out. With a large group like tonight, I had to make sure my shield was up at all times.

I rubbed my temple. I needed to expel these emotions soon or they would drive me into a deep depression. I heard the door creak open behind me. I turned my head to see a tall shadow walk in. "Go away, Sebastian. I need to be alone, and I do not want to fight anymore." My frustration came right back.

"It's not Bash," Aden replied in a low hum.

I froze. I remembered the hungry look in his eyes when Bash held me close while we were dancing. "What do you want?" I whispered.

"Look, I know you are mad, Lexi. I am not here to fight, but maybe we can, I don't know, come to a compromise?" He held his hands out to me.

I couldn't deal with this back-and-forth emotional rollercoaster anymore. "No, Aden, if Bash wants a compromise, he needs to be here. He needs to talk to me like an adult and not badger me at his little sister's engagement party. He doesn't get to send one of his Devils after me." I pushed from the spot by the window and walked over to Aden, arms crossed, slightly wavering as the effects of the booze finally hit me. Aden's eyes narrowed and he tugged at his tie, loosening it from his neck.

"He doesn't know I am here, baby... I am just... fuck!" He threw his jacket down in frustration and sat down on a couch, rolling up his sleeves and revealing more of his tattoos. "Lexi, I know what I did ten years ago was fucked up, I know that... I beat the shit out of myself for it daily, and I still care about you. I don't want to see you destroyed by the Ryders. Look, I love Bash like a brother, but he will take you down without any mercy. I do not want you to lose to them."

I was so tired of fighting tonight. I sat down next to him, my dress pooling out as I pulled his arm into my lap. "Tell me about your tattoos." I traced my fingers over his arm. "Like this one, why would you get this one?" It was a glass shoe wrapped in a rose. I knew what it meant, but I needed to hear it from him. "It is for Ella... and you. But you know that, Lexi, you two drew it for me sixteen years ago."

I smiled sadly into the night. "I know, but we were only ten when we did it. It's nice to know you had a real artist make our drawing come alive. It suits your whole anti-Prince Charming attitude."

Aden chuckled lightly, looking up at me. "The truth is, Lexi, I am always alive when I am near you. That's why I ruined us so many years ago."

My eyes widened as Aden cupped my cheek and pulled me to him. I let my eyes flutter closed as his lips brushed mine in a sweet, light kiss. He pulled back and looked at me, his face half hidden in shadows and the other half lit by the moon. He was so handsome. I saw, for an instant, that my friend who I loved since I was ten years old was here with me. I knew we could be something more this time, something unstoppable. I traced his jaw up to his cheek and smiled at him. I leaned forward, and he deepened our kiss.

I moaned into his mouth, and his hands brushed over my throat as he fought within himself to fend off the craving. I reached up to wrap my arms around his neck, kissing him as much I had wanted to since seeing him this afternoon. I felt his emotions rush over me; he was jealous, angry, and lustful, but underneath all that, I found love. The comfort

I had with Aden returned. He didn't care who I was or how powerful I was; he just wanted me to be me, which was one of Aden's best qualities but also his downfall. Because sometimes you disappoint that person who holds you on a pedestal.

He lifted me, pulling me onto his lap while moving my dress out of the way so I could straddle him.

"Aden, we should stop." I continued to kiss him breathlessly.

He nodded. "Yeah... stop..." He met each of my kisses with his own.

I laughed. "No, seriously, we need to stop." I pushed away from him and slid off of his lap.

He smirked at me and held his hands up in defeat. "Okay, but you can't tell me that wasn't hot, baby." He walked up to me, cupping my cheek. "That was like my world exploded, and it was just a kiss, Lexi."

I sighed into his hand, reining in the lust that passed through me. "It was hot, Aden, but it won't happen again." I backed up and went to the window.

"You can't hang on to the anger forever, Lexi," Aden whispered to the night.

A loud BANG, BANG, BANG came from the other side of the door. My head snapped up, and I looked at Aden. "Who knows we're in here?" Aden started to move towards the door when I heard from the other side, "Aden, get the fuck out here." Tristian's voice came out in an irritated rage. "I know you are in there with Lexi, and I can smell the lust."

I don't think I've ever heard Tristian sound this angry. I turned and motioned for Aden to open the door. "Let him in; let's see what the third Devil wants."

Tristian stood there with a grim look on his face. As he walked in, he looked between me and Aden and frowned at us. "About fucking time, you two. I have been hunting for you for twenty minutes. Do either of you not keep your phone on you?"

I shrugged, patting my dress. "No pockets; my phone is upstairs."

Aden leaned against the couch with his arms crossed. "Phone was on silent, frere." He pulled it from his pocket and looked down. The shock was written all over his face.

I went on high alert and walked towards the two of them. "What's going on?" But before he could say anything, an FBI Agent I knew all too well walked in. Bash was in handcuffs, looking like he wanted to murder someone.

I glanced between the two of them and suddenly felt scared for Sebastian, which was weird since I despised him. "What the hell is going on? Agent Rengard, what are you doing here? Why is Sebastian Ryder in cuffs?" The shock must have resonated in my voice. Rengard was assigned to my parents' murder case. "Is Coco okay?" I looked over to Tristian, but he stared down at the ground, avoiding my eyes. Aden's expression was grim, his lips thinned, crossing his arms and standing beside Tristian.

Agent Rengard looked over at me with a small smile, holding up a hand to stop me. "Ms. Rose, Coco is fine, but... do you know Steven Daniels?" he asked in a rough voice.

My world began to narrow as black spots threatened my vision, and my heart began pounding a mile a minute. I couldn't breathe. I felt an overwhelming heat burn through

me, and I sat on something before my legs gave out. On the floor or a chair? I wasn't sure; all I felt in the moment was how my whole world exploded again. I searched the room and found myself looking into green eyes as my mouth dropped open.

"No... not again."

CHAPTER EIGHT

"Ms. Rose, do you know a Steven Daniels?" Agent Rengard repeated.

I didn't move my gaze from Sebastian's as my brain tried to compute what Agent Rengard just said. "Why does Bash have handcuffs on?" I asked Agent Rengard again. Bash's eyes bore into mine as if he was saying, Don't believe them. My chest felt tight because I knew... I knew what was going on. An FBI Agent didn't just show up in the middle of a party if everything was okay. Tears pooled in my eyes, and I looked over at Rengard.

"Just answer the question, Lexi." He softened his voice as he reached out to touch my arm.

The look in his eyes told me all I needed to know. "You

know I know him. Daniels is dead, isn't he?" I let the pain sink into me. I just saw him this morning; how could he be gone? I have to get him coffee tomorrow... We have to finish our lesson... He has to be there for me, for our coven. I felt like my heart was cracking open.

From behind me, I heard Aden take in a shaky breath and move with Tristian towards Sebastian. They formed a protective circle around Bash, but I was completely alone. It wasn't until I lifted my gaze to Bash, whose eyes never left me; I saw all of his emotions, anger, rage, and sadness sit below the stoic mask.

"I am so sorry, Lexi. We found Daniels this evening," Agent Rengard said, his voice hesitant, as if he wanted to say more but couldn't.

I just lost the one person who believed in me and didn't pity me like the others did. I wasn't just a sad tragedy to Daniels; he saw my strength. Daniels was more than a friend; he was like another father to me. I nodded at Agent Rengard. "Thank you." My voice was soft.

"Tristian, please keep Ella and Ethan away from us. She... she doesn't need to hear about Daniels, see Lexi like this, or her brother in cuffs," Bash demanded loudly.

Tristian looked up at me then nodded to Bash. He quickly turned and headed to the security standing at the door, whispering instructions in their ears.

Bash's gaze was still fixed on me as if I would break right before his eyes.

"Why can't Ella know? Doesn't she have the right?"

Bash just shook his head. "Lexi, you are not in the right state of mind to make that call."

I felt the anger surge. "Not... the... right... state?" I poked a finger in his chest. "You have no right! We aren't your puppets! She has every right now to know what happens to you... to me!" I let my anger hit him like a punch. "You stand there high and mighty playing us like GOD, Sebastian. But you're not!" I walked away, wrapping my arms around myself and staring down at the floor.

"Lexi..." Aden moved in front of me, his face full of sorrow. I glanced over to Tristian, who watched me with pity in his eyes, and Bash stood stoic as could be. "Lexi, look at me." I turned to Aden and glared into his grey eyes. "Bash wasn't saying that at all. He was saying that he didn't want Ella to find out tonight, that he would tell her himself. It's her engagement party. If she finds out now, then it's all she'll remember."

I nodded, but the anger still whirled inside me, the pain too raw for me to see that I was being unreasonable. I whispered, "I hate him."

Aden put a hand on my shoulder. "I know." He pulled me into his arms, and I let the tears that I held go. They fell down my cheeks as I held onto Aden, the one bright light I could see right now in a sea of dark.

I wasn't sure how long I stayed in Aden's arms, but I felt Agent Rengard shuffle at the uncomfortable air in the room. I wiped my tears and stepped away from Aden. Glancing over at Bash, I saw for the first time his eyes shining in pain. I looked at Agent Rengard.

"Bash was here at the hotel. Tristian was with him most of the night. If you want an alibi, I think all three of us can vouch for him. You can remove the cuffs now," I said impassively. I moved like a robot, turning around and walking to the group of chairs gathered around a small coffee table.

"I am sorry, Ms. Rose, but unfortunately we cannot remove the cuffs yet."

I let my eyes roam over the room, seeing the thrown pillows on the floor from Aden and myself. I absently touched my fingers to my lips, knowing they were swollen from his kisses. Bash suddenly sat next to me and breathed, "Don't say a word. We will get the lawyers."

I nodded numbly as the tears continued to fall, wiping them away before I continued. Of course, I knew that was what we should do, but Bash was acting like he'd already given up. I wouldn't let Bash go to jail for a crime I knew he didn't commit.

I may hate him, but this was not the revenge I wanted.

Agent Rengard sat across from us, pulling out a small pad and a pen. Glaring at Sebastian but giving me a small smile, he placed his hand on my knee. "Ready?"

I looked at his hand and then up at him. "Yes, but please do not touch me. I can't control my power right now, and all I get is your anger for Bash, and Agent Rengard, I have enough anger right now to destroy a nation." He removed his hand as if I burned him, his eyes flashing in fury for a moment before softening. "Excuse me, Ms. Rose. I was just trying to be reassuring. A bit unprofessional, I admit. Forgive me." He bowed his head to me and sat up straighter in the chair.

Aden and Tristian stood behind Bash and me, forming a united front. "Daniels was found this evening in his home.

All doors were locked, no forced entry, no prints, no evidence, except his throat was slit and a note was addressed to you, Ms. Rose."

My head shot straight up. "A note?" I rasped out.

"Yes, a note. I can't read it, as it's been spelled; you are the only one who can open it." He reached into his jacket pocket and retrieved a black envelope with a red wax seal, the Blood Moon Coven's symbol etched into it in gold foiling.

I took the envelope with trembling hands and stared at it like I was hoping it would give me some type of answer. "Bash..." My voice came out hoarse, so I tried again and cleared my throat. "Sebastian, how do I open this?" I didn't dare to look at him because I knew I would break if I did. I would allow myself to break down later when I was home alone with no one to watch.

I felt Bash move before I felt him take my hand and raise it to his mouth. He bit down on one finger with the tip of his fang. The sting made me hiss. I should have known—blood was a life source, and it would be the perfect way to accuse Bash of the crime. So, of course it would need blood to open. I pulled my finger back and held it over the wax symbol until a drop of blood fell onto the dark envelope. A stream of smoke escaped the seal, and the envelope felt heavier. The flap unfolded to reveal black stationery with the Blood Moon Symbol embossed on the top scrolled with elegant handwriting in white ink. I read the letter aloud.

My Little Rose,

Did you miss me? Our night was cut so short ten years ago, but I never left. I kept my distance but have always watched you. I watched you grow into a strong, beautiful, powerful siren.

I know you better than you know yourself. You hide your powers, your abilities, but I see you for who you are, my little siren, my special girl.

Don't worry, Little Rose. I know your every thought, your every wish, and I am here to grant them. You needed Daniels out of the way so you could show your true power.

I set you free many years ago, free of the bonds that chained you to your life. And I have set you free again.

I will be watching. I will see how else I can help you, who else I can remove so you are free to become who you need to be.

Then your greatest wish will be fulfilled—we can finally be together.

With undying love,
Wishmaker

I looked up from the letter with a frown. "I have no clue what this is. It's utter nonsense. You can't make sense of it. It is a madman's work." I handed the letter back to Agent Rengard.

He pulled on gloves and placed the letter in a plastic bag. His eyes narrowed as if he was trying to work something out, reading the letter again to himself. "Doesn't help much," he whispered. "Do you know anyone who would want to hurt Daniels?"

I shook my head. "No, our coven, everyone pretty much loved him. We had a few bad apples but none who would resort to killing him."

Agent Rengard nodded in agreement, making notes in his small notebook. He looked up and turned to Bash. "This is your coven's stationery; is this your seal?"

Bash looked annoyed. "It is our stationery, it is our seal, but I did not write that letter. I have hundreds of coven members. Any one of them could have done this. It doesn't mean it was a vampire, Agent Rengard. A witch, a basilisk, or—hell, even the pixies have access to all of our spells."

Rengard glared at Bash. "I'm sorry, Mr. Ryder, but a powerful fae from the Pearl Coven was killed tonight and we have evidence that points to you, since the only person who could have bespelled the letter had to be someone in your coven and have access to your personal letterhead. Now tell me, Mr. Ryder, how that doesn't make you look like the main suspect?"

Bash raised an eyebrow, keeping his face neutral. "I was here the entire day and night. I have multiple witnesses; how could I have snuck out and killed someone who I had no ill will towards?" He almost sounded bored. "Plus, I have an alibi, as Lexi said earlier. We were together when the murder happened."

The agent narrowed his eyes. "Are you saying that there is no way you arranged anything? You do not have to be the one who did the actual killing to still organize the murder, Mr. Ryder." He glared over at Aden and Tristian. "You have people who work for you, do you not?"

Bash laughed, standing to walk over to the fireplace. "Please tell me why I would want to take over the Silver Pearl, why I would want to kill Daniels? Hell, the old man was more tolerable than my own! Look, I have no desire to babysit a bunch of useless fae. No, I did not kill Daniels."

It was one thing to talk about me, but to talk about my coven and to disrespect the craft we wielded made me grind my teeth, pissed as hell. I felt the pressure bubble up into my chest as my power slipped in. The anger from earlier returned, and the pride I had for my coven raised its hackles. I raised my hand and summoned a ball of fire in my palm, fully intending to launch it at that damned cocky-ass vampire. Bash moved faster and stumbled into the bookcase, gasping at me in surprise.

"Talk about my coven like that again. I will make sure your ass is fried, Sebastian Ryder."

Tristian moved to help Bash up and Aden placed a hand on my shoulder, holding me down. Fucking traitors.

"MISS ROSE!" Agent Rengard yelled. "Get yourself together! I understand you are grieving, but if you attack Mr. Ryder, you will be arrested for assault and thrown in the Witches Tower for a few days."

I barely heard Rengard but as I looked at Bash his eyes flashed with surprise. Then a smirk formed at the edge of his lips as if he was itching for a fight. I glared at him, sending him a final warning, "Don't you dare speak about the Silver Pearl that way again, Sebastian. You may think we are useless, but I promise you, we hold more power than you can imagine." It took all my strength to rein in my power. My teeth were aching to sharpen, my gums were sore, and my eyes were cloudy with the haze of the siren challenging me to start the transformation.

I walked up to Bash, looking over at him to see if I could find any truth in his words. "Swear it, Sebastian, swear it to me." He looked at me with such intensity that his green eyes almost seemed like they had a fire beneath them.

"I swear on the Blood Moon, I do not know who killed Daniels, Lexi, but I will help you find out who did as long as I breathe. We will bring down The Wishmaker together." I saw it in his eyes. He was telling the truth. Sebastian Ryder might have hated me, but I knew he would never hurt me, not this way. This was a blow to not just me but to both of our covens.

"I believe him, Agent Rengard, Bash is a bastard on his best day, but he respected Daniels. He wouldn't have done this. This was done by the same person who killed my parents. You have the confession here." I pointed to the envelope in his hands.

I glanced at Bash and saw him swallowing hard, his Adam's apple bobbing up and down. He murmured just low enough for me, "I would never, Princess."

My eyes had new tears threatening to spill, and I turned

to Agent Rengard. "We are done here, then. Please contact me with any more questions, but I am exhausted and just want to get home." I clenched my hands at my side, my nails digging into my palm trying to hold the pain in. I knew if I held on tight enough, I wouldn't spill it out.

Agent Rengard's eyes softened as I saw his own pain. "Of course, Ms. Rose. I'll be in touch. Daniels was a good friend of mine. Rest knowing that I will do all I can to find who did this to him."

I realized then that Rengard was grieving as much as I was. He stood up, smoothing out his jacket. Then he raised his hands over Bash's magical bound cuffs. After a whirlwind of movements, they broke with a golden sizzle.

Bash shook out his hands. "Thanks."

Rengard nodded as he handed both of us a card. "In case you 'remember' anything else."

I took his card and shook his hand. "Thank you. I promise that if I find anything, I will be in touch."

He hesitated like he wanted to say more. "I am so sorry for your loss, Ms. Rose." He nodded to Bash and the others, walking to the door and leaving us behind—leaving us all wondering what the future held for the covens of Providence Village.

Chapter Nine

Tristian followed Agent Rengard and closed the door behind him. We all stood in silence. All I wanted was to get out of these clothes and shoes. I ran my fingers through my hair, needing something for them to do. As I gazed at the fire, I spoke in a low voice, "Look, I know you three are waiting for me to break, but let me just get through this. I want to go home, shower, drink a huge glass of whiskey, cuddle my cat, and sleep for twelve hours."

Bash frowned at me. "I can help with one of those now." He walked to the bar and opened a crystal decanter. Then he poured the dark golden liquid into four small glasses and placed them on the small table in front of us. He handed me one of them. "Here, Princess."

My hand curled around the drink as I took it from him. I closed my eyes and took a deep swig, relishing the whiskey's spicy flavor running down my throat. I let out a low moan and took another drink before I opened my eyes. All three vampires looked at me with interest.

Tristian's eyebrows raised to the ceiling, and a smile played on his lips like I was there for his entertainment.

Aden was standing next to him, smirking and running his tongue across his bottom lip, making me remember earlier.

Bash looked at me like he was hungry. His fangs were fully out, and his eyes locked onto me with a carnal need. A small gasp left my lips, and Bash moved forward as if he was going in for a kiss.

He lifted my chin so I was looking into his eyes, and he bent down just enough to hover over my lips. I could feel his lust, his want, but I felt his sorrow too.

I let him breathe in, his nose running along my chin to my neck. My breaths came out heavy as my eyes fluttered closed.

"Sebastian..." I warned. His breath hitched, and his fangs scraped over my neck. I knew he wouldn't bite me.

He kissed behind my ear, and I shivered. "Lexi, I love the way you say my name."

I whispered, "With hate?"

He smirked as he kissed my neck. "Not hate, Princess; as if it's a promise. But one thing I promise you—we will find out who did this because if they want one coven, they will want all of us." He switched sides, moving to my throat and

placing a kiss on my neck.

Before I could even breathe out a snarky comment, I heard a growl from beside us. I looked up to see Aden seething, his fangs fully on display.

Bash looked at him in surprise but rose to the occasion in his domineering way, hissing at Aden. "You better back down, frere."

Aden bit back. "She just lost someone she loves; she doesn't need your bullshit right now."

My eyes widened, and I looked at Aden. "Don't, Aden." I could see the pain in his eyes. Daniels was a big part of his life, too. Daniels always let Aden run around when he was younger and the older he got, Daniels taught him that making a mistake was a learning experience, unlike his picture-perfect family who always looked as if nothing was out of place.

Aden glanced between Bash and me. "Why the hell not, Lex? He can't just piss on you like a dog. He has been doing this crap for years; he doesn't own you." I was confused, and I looked over to Bash with a questioning gaze.

"Charmante, you best not say any more, or I will shut your mouth for you."

Aden smirked. "My mouth can say one thing, Ryder. Yes, Lexi does taste like candy." He sucked his bottom lip.

I pointed to both of them. "No, we aren't doing this right now. I am not doing this right now."

I turned and saw Tristian, who had a childish grin stamped across his face.

"Don't even start, Cassium." I pointed to him, and he mimed zipping his mouth.

I slipped out of my shoes and walked out of the parlor through the middle of Aden and Bash, making them move to the side. I made a beeline for the elevator and pushed the button repeatedly. The doors opened, and Morgan Ryder stood there with his phone to his ear.

I froze. "Yes, it is very unfortunate. You have all of my condolences, Coco, but rest assured that Lexi is fine. She is standing right in front of me."

He raised an eyebrow at something my aunt said.

"Yes, I am sure she would, I will have her call her as soon as I have her returned to her home with security... No, I planned on sending the boys with her... Yes, Bash will keep her safe... No, this isn't for you; it's for her own good. We wouldn't want any of that blood spilled. She is head of the coven now, and we must protect each other. We will all rise together against this monster.

"Yes, yes I will have her call you; I must go and speak to Lexi and Sebastian." He hung up the phone and, as I was about to bolt, I heard three sets of footsteps rushing towards us.

"Lexi, don't you dare leave," Morgan said sternly as if he knew I was running from them.

He walked to Bash and placed a hand on his shoulder.

"Sebastian, you will take Lexi home. We do not know if the hotel is safe for her. Franklin has her things at the front desk. Tristian will place wards at her home and Aden... I want the best security team in place with access to all the cameras so we can monitor them. We have to make sure she is safe; she is not to leave your side until we find the killer, so pack a bag, boys. You are her new head of security." He

said all of this as he typed something into his phone.

I groaned, "Look, Mr. Ryder, as much as I appreciate it, I really don't want them in my home."

Morgan glanced up at me, tilting his head as if I told him that I wanted to live under a bridge with a troll. "Lexi, it is about your coven's safety and yours. You will be in good hands. We have to take your safety seriously since you have now had multiple people die for you."

He said this so bluntly. It stung, but I tried to stand my ground. "Sir, no. I don't want them—"

He cut me off. "Coco agrees with me, Lexi. Just do it for her."

I sighed. Coco was worried. He didn't need to spell it out for me. I ground my teeth, hating that I was making this decision. "Fine."

Bash's voice came from behind me "Of course, Father, but is it necessary for us to stay with her? I can have a team watch Lexi's house. It's beneath our skillset. We should be investigating the murder instead."

Morgan looked up from his phone for a moment as if he would consider the idea. Then he gripped Bash's shoulder. Bash flinched but stayed still.

"Sebastian, I do not need to explain to you that Lexi is now head of her coven. She is the actual rightful heir to the Silver Moon, and her blood holds the power yours would if I died. So, no, I don't think asking you to take care of the girl is out of your skillset." He moved closer to Bash's face and hissed, "If I want you to babysit a fucking group of baby pegasus and change diapers filled with rainbow shit, you will because I am the head of your precious Blood Moon Coven!"

Tristian and Aden moved closer to Bash. He nodded stiffly as he walked over and took my arm in his. He led me toward the lobby through a set of revolving doors. My feet hit the cold marble as we walked to the valet stand. I didn't say a word. I was in shock. I had never seen Morgan Ryder raise his voice to anyone. He always seemed cool, calm, collected, and bored by everyone and everything.

He was the most powerful vampire I knew. He ran his company Anderson & Ryder dealing with everything tech from the biggest social media platform called "Interfaes" to medical companies "ABV Positive", which helped fund research for deadly fae diseases.

On top of all of this, he was the Blood Moon leader. Yes, he let Bash run most of the coven and take care of anything that didn't deem worth his time. He was always more of an observer and never lost his temper.

I didn't say a word as Bash led me to the elevator, hearing the steps following behind us. I knew it was Aden and Tristian showing Morgan that they were a united front and would follow the orders he demanded. Aden had my bag in his hand, and Tristian's eyes were sweeping around to check for anything suspicious.

That's when I noticed Tristian was armed. It was very subtle, but I could see the outline of his holster shift underneath his jacket.

Bash whipped out a card from his wallet and handed it to the valet, a poor zit-face teen who jumped up. "Mr. Ryder, you're like, that famous vampire, aren't you? Bro, dude, do you like, sparkle and shit?"

Bash rolled his eyes, gave the poor kid an evil stare, and

nodded, throwing his ticket at him. "Get her car, too."

The valet looked at me. "I don't have my ticket," I said in a panic.

Tristian stepped up. "Let me save the day, Lil' Star." He handed over my ticket to the kid, who grabbed it and ran away to get each of our cars.

Aden and Tristian surrounded the valet stand with us in a stiff posture, scanning the outside like they were waiting for someone to attack us. Everyone was tense, and the silence between us was deafening. That is when I noticed Bash also had a gun on his hip.

I looked at Aden and whispered, "Are you armed, too?" Aden raised an eyebrow and pulled his jacket back, revealing two small pistols in a gun holster over his shoulders.

"How the fuck did I miss that?" I whispered to myself, thinking of how I had been straddling him. How the hell did I not notice two guns? Okay, maybe I should be more aware of my surroundings.

"Actually... I took it off before I sat down. You just didn't notice at the time because you were distracted." He spoke gently to me but looked at Bash with an evil grin and said, "But me kissing you could have been another reason you didn't notice."

Bash slammed his hand on the valet stand, sending a ton of keys flying to the ground.

He spun around, grabbing Aden by the collar and pulling him close to his face. "Treading on ice with me, Aden."

Aden snarled back at Bash, "You don't like it, then let's go, Pretty Boy."

I rubbed my temples. Good god, the fucking toxic mas-

culinity that ran between the three of them was infuriating. Tristian's arms were casually crossed as he leaned against the stand. His teasing smile said he was enjoying the pissing contest between the two of them. I rolled my eyes at him and glared at the other two. It looked like soon they would start throwing punches at each other.

Tristian laughed. "Jeez, where is the popcorn? Tell me, Lil' Star, do you really taste that good?" He licked his lips, and his eyes bore into mine with a gleam of lightning behind them.

I frowned at him and crossed my arms. "Stop encouraging them, Trist." I turned to the other two Devils before me. Bash had Aden in a vice grip around his neck, and Aden was throwing a punch to his side. "For fuck's sake, you two," I huffed as I moved between them and pushed Bash back by the chest.

He didn't budge. Jeez, how heavy was this asshat? He looked at my hand with a raised eyebrow.

"Just stop fighting for tonight, please, you two. I am exhausted, and I just need to... survive." My voice broke, and Bash snapped from a stony, cold vampire to the normal Bash, the semi-cold vampire we all knew.

He bent down to me, cupping his hands around my face. "No, don't... hold it in, Princess. I promise tonight you can fall apart, but for now, hold it in. Then once we are alone, you can let it out." He brushed the single tear that left my eye, and I took a deep breath, bringing my grief back inside once more.

"Yeah, baby, I promise we will be good for the rest of the night. We will find out who did this," Aden murmured softly.

He touched the small of my back, running circles along it.

Tristian even moved closer to me and gave me a wicked grin. "Then, Lil' Star, we will get revenge for you."

Revenge. Now, that sounded good. Nodding, I said, "I'm good," with as much confidence as I could muster.

"That's my girl," Aden whispered.

Bash was right. I couldn't show anyone my pain because my coven needed me now. Our covens needed us to be strong. We had to show a united front, that even with this loss we would survive. We had to.

Just like that, the Three Devils were back in my life.

Chapter Ten

The door flew open, and Ella, Ethan, and Cassandra walked toward us in a group. Ethan was comforting Ella. I could see her tears from here. As soon as she looked up and saw me, she ran from Ethan straight into my open arms.

"I thought she wasn't going to find out tonight," I whispered right before I caught her weight and pulled her into a tight hug. She hit me with all of her strength. I knew it was coming, so I was prepared.

The weight of our bodies pushed me back into Bash, but he was able to hold onto both of us, his hand supporting me.

Ella looked up at me with new tears pooling in her eyes and rolling down her cheeks. "Lexi, Father just told me.

I can't believe it. I am so sorry. What do you need?"

I loved her for asking, but the problem with grief was that it couldn't be fixed. It can't be stopped. Grief was like the tide: it rose and fell every day. It always came back. It was hard, it was ugly, and it ripped through your soul, leaving a little mark behind each time.

I cupped her face, fixing her hair and giving her a sad smile. "Ella, thank you, but I will be okay. I just want to go home and then I will deal with all of this in some peaceful way... It's too intense and busy here," I said with a wave of my hand.

Ethan walked up to us, chatting in a low voice with Aden and Tristian, but Cassandra hung back, texting on her phone a small smirk playing at her mouth. I wanted to punch her.

Ethan hugged all of the guys in that bro, I got you way, and then he pulled me into a group hug with Ella. "Just let me know if you need anything tomorrow. Go home and sleep, Lex." He looked over the group and with a sigh and a frown. "We all should get some rest."

Ella silently nodded and kissed my cheek. Bash and I started to walk with Ella and Ethan to the door, but Ethan just gave a small nod. "I've got it."

We stopped, watching them head into the hotel. The grief that they felt was thick around them. Then Ella called out. "Text me when you get home, 'kay? Father told me he was sending the boys with you tonight. I feel so much better knowing they will be there just in case anything happens."

I sighed. Okay, first Coco, and now Ella. I nodded. "Yeah, it might be nice to have a security team," I lied, still hating

the idea of them invading my own personal space.

Her eyes flew to Bash. "You better be on your best behavior! If I hear that you are being an asshole in any way tonight, I swear I will kick you so hard in the balls you will wish I would have cut them off." She scowled at him.

Bash stepped back from his little sister and moved his hands over his balls protectively. "Geez, Ells, calm down! I am just going to be on guard duty tonight. I promise no fuckery will be happening." He looked a little scared of his tiny five foot three blonde-hair-with-big-brown-eyes sister. I chuckled quietly, smiling at Ella.

"Sebastian promises no funny business. Thanks, Ella, I promise I will talk soon, okay?"

Ella hugged me again. "Yeah. I am bringing coffee and pastries tomorrow; screw it, I will bring wine, too. It's never too early to start drinking." She kissed my cheek as Ethan pulled her towards the doors.

I gave a small wave and turned to Bash with a smirk. "Big Bad Vampy scared of the little wolf?" I teased him.

"You heard Ella, we have to behave, so shall we get going?" Bash added with a mumble, "You've never been kicked in the balls by Ella; the little firecracker has a mean kick."

I laughed, biting my bottom lip as Bash gave me the tiniest smile. His eyes softened, and he moved closer to me. I panicked—but thank God because Cassandra took that moment to strut over to us with a flip of her hair like the night was just an inconvenience. She walked to Bash, wrapped her arms around him, and pouted.

"Bashy, take me home. My feet hurt, and I have been waiting for you for over an hour."

Jealousy poured out of me. I wanted to slap her face and rip her hair out and pull her away from Bash; maybe break a few of her ribs, too, while I was at it. Grinding my teeth I thought, great, now you are that crazy girl who is jealous of a man you never had—yep, this was a great way to deal with the anger and pain. My brain and body had a different idea. I glowered at Cassandra and started to walk up to her to give her a piece of my mind when I felt hands grab at me, then arms wrapping around my waist.

I yelped in fright, not knowing who had just grabbed me. I squirmed at the arms that held me in a tight grip. I looked down and saw "open book" tattoos on hands and knuckles, which told me exactly who was holding me. "What the actual fuck, Trist?!"

He chuckled. "Shh, let Bash handle her, because I tell you, it's gonna be amazing," Tristian whispered into my hair. I relaxed and he set me down, still holding me close. "Watch, he is going to destroy her."

Aden joined us with a smile on his face as he crossed his arms over his chest. "She is gonna get Bashed, isn't she?"

I glanced between both of them. "Okay dorks, what is 'bashed'?"

Tristian and Aden busted out laughing. "Bash is brutal when he breaks up with someone—as the girls in our coven say, you either get Bashed by Bash or you get Bashed by Bash."

I rolled my eyes at them. I turned my head to see Bash's Bashing, curious to watch the drama unfold, but Bash's eyes were on me and not on the girl who was wildly yelling at him. His eyes flicked to Tristian's arms where they held

me, and they narrowed. I could have sworn I saw his fangs slide out.

Cassandra looked at me with disgust, her brows pinched and her nose wrinkled up with a frown on her lips. She glared between me, Aden, and Tristian. "Are you fucking both of them? God, no wonder everyone calls you a scaly whore."

An inhuman hiss escaped my lips, and I dug my fingers into my hands. The pain laced through me. She had the audacity to look shocked. Before I could come up with a witty comeback, Aden smoothed his fingers over my stomach and Tristian's arm. "Hmmm, now that's something I could onboard for. Would you like to feel both of us inside you, baby?" he asked in a husky voice, biting his lip.

I wanted nothing to do with this. I didn't need to be rescued from her. I guess I was Cassandra's weak point, or she wanted all three of them, but that thought made my blood boil. She wouldn't touch them. The Devils might see me as a helpless princess, and I might be hurt, but I could handle girls like Cassandra.

I removed Tristian's arm from around me and brushed away Aden's hands. "I got this," I whispered low enough for them.

I flicked my gaze to Bash, arching a brow to silently ask if he was going to play my game. He gave the slightest nod, and I let his arms circle me, turning me to face Cassandra as I leaned back into his strong chest. I gave her an icy smile. "No, I am not fucking Aden or Tristian... but Bash...."

I smiled at him, then tilted my head to the side. He bent to meet me, his fangs fully extended, his breath tickling my neck as he skimmed them over my pulse, sending a delicious shiver down my spine. I looked at Cassandra. "I've ridden him like he was my own personal pony. Now excuse me, but Sebastian is taking me home, and maybe this time I'll let him take me how he likes me. What are you in the mood for, baby?"

I turned in his arms and rubbed my hands over his chest. Bash pulled me close, gazing at me with a sparkle of promise in his eyes.

"I am going to bend you over and make you hold on tight, Princess, because you are going to scream my name to the stars tonight when I am done with you."

Her lips popped open in surprise, and she didn't say a word. A smile tugged at my lips as I pulled away, and I started to walk with a sway in my hips towards the valet as our cars were pulling up. I looked back at Bash and smiled at him. "Coming, handsome?"

Cassandra's eyes widened and she screeched like the banshee we all knew she was. "Bashy! If you go with her, we are done!"

Bash straightened his cuffs and grinned. "Cassandra, there was never an 'us'; you were just a convenient fuck. Tits are Grade A, baby, but your pussy... mediocre. But that,"—he pointed to me—"is pure perfection." He strolled away from Cassandra without a backward glance and stood next to me. "Good job, Princess, we might just make you a coven leader yet."

I smirked up at him. "You're welcome. Any other girls I need to break up for you this evening?" Yep, it felt amazing to do the "Bashing" for once.

Bash's fancy Aston Martin pulled forward right behind

my run-down red SUV. I stood with my arms crossed as the wind picked up and wound its way around my body. I shivered as the valet started to hand me my keys, but Tristian swooped in and snatched it out of his hand. "Tristian, I can drive myself." I tried to grab them.

"No can do, Lil' Star." He held them over his head. "Aden and I will take your car. Go with Bash so he can keep you safe."

I planted my hands on my hips. "No one is going to get me when you three are following me."

"No, but they could run you off the road, plant a bomb, or hide in your trunk and kidnap you. The first rule of security is to think like a criminal, baby."

I knew they wouldn't drop it. "Fine." It was easier to give them the keys than fight with him for ten minutes in the cold night air. I pursed my lips. "You know, this is exactly what I did not want to happen, to be treated like I can't take care of myself. It shows weakness, Tristian, and I am not weak."

He frowned slightly. "I know you are not weak, Lil' Star, but just let us do this." I nodded to him, and relief washed over his face that he wasn't going to have to fight with me. "Thanks, Lil' Star. I will see you at home." He gave me his 100-watt smile and quickly kissed my cheek.

I couldn't help but give a small smile back and shake my head. That was the thing with Tristian—he could make anyone smile on their worst days, like a literal walking sunbeam. "Don't hurt her! She is a good car!" I shouted as he headed back to the others.

"Scout's honor, I will be the perfect driver." He gave me a salute and wrapped his arm around Aden's shoulder.

Bash took the keys from the valet and handed a fifty-dol-

lar bill over to the young kid, who looked stunned by the amount. He shook in fear to see the actual Three Devils of Providence Village in person. I headed to the passenger side of the Aston Martin to open my door, but Aden was faster.

He threw his arm out in a sweeping bow. "My Lady, your carriage awaits."

I knew he was trying to make sure I didn't get a chance to stop and think about the night's events, and it was working. I knew once I was alone that I would be hit with all the emotions I buried down.

Sliding into the creamy leather seats, I stuck my head out and looked up at Aden. "Tell Bash to hurry or I might turn into a pumpkin."

Aden grinned. "Don't worry, Cinderella. We will get you back in one piece, with all of your shoes and everything." He gently shut the door as I waited for Bash. The car smelled like leather with a hint of Bash's cologne, a blend of rich woods and spices.

Bash was whispering words with Tristian and Aden in what seemed to be an intense conversation. The worried look in Aden's eyes said a lot; Tristian's smile was gone, his fist curled up ready to fight, his jaw clenched so hard I thought he would break his teeth. I saw the fire in all three of their eyes which made me realize something: Not only were they the scariest assholes I ever met, but they were also mad as hell about what happened tonight.

I finally saw what everyone in this town was afraid of.

I closed my eyes as the events of the night played out, from running into Bash early on to the dance, then Daniels's death, to Sebastian getting arrested and almost taken to jail,

to the letter of a madman. I felt the weight of the fear on me, but as I looked at all three of them, I thought, Yeeeaaah, now I know why everyone calls them the Three Devils.

I hated these men down to my bones, but the one thing I knew, regardless of how I felt, was that they would protect me at all costs.

Chapter Eleven

Bash slid into the driver's seat and reached over to my side to pull the seat belt around me and click it into place. I arched an eyebrow at him. He smirked. "No snarky comment?"

I scrunched up my nose. "No, not yet."

The car started with a purr that went straight down to my center. Jesus, is this why girls love guys with these cars? He zipped out of the driveway of the hotel onto the busy streets of Providence Village. Bash drove fast, but he was being safe. I assumed he didn't want to give the FBI or local police any more reason to arrest us.

We sat in silence for about ten minutes until I couldn't stand it anymore. "Soooo... you and Cassandra? How long have you been, you know...."

Bash raised a brow and glanced over at me, clearing his throat. "One, that is a set-up from my father; it's an arrangement. Two, I am not dating her. She was a convenient lay."

Why did that give me the warm fuzzies? Lexi, get it together! You are not supposed to like Sebastian Ryder! So I went with irritation instead. "Got it, how convenient for you. So how long will you guys be staying with me?" (I also opted to change the subject.)

"You heard my father, until the killer is caught."

My eyes widened. "No. I do not have space for you three stooges, I have a life and a cat who needs me, and... and I have two guest rooms so I guess you three can draw straws or something." I was grasping at anything to prevent them from staying with me long-term.

"Princess, we do not want to stay with you any more than you want us there, so let's just find whoever killed Daniels quickly and we can all move on with our lives."

I felt a tug at my gut with grief. He was right, I needed to find out who killed Daniels. I stared out the window as light rain started to sprinkle down on it and just as the rain came down, so did my tears. I quickly wiped them away.

My life was just flipped upside down and the one person who I wanted to run to for comfort, support, and a hug... was dead. I couldn't hold it in anymore, and I just let the tears flow. Bash yanked the car over to the side and turned it off. He took my hand in his, and his thumb made lazy circles on my skin. It was soothing and comforting. I never thought I would see this side of him again.

"Let it out, Lexi, no one will know."

So I did. I released all the sadness, the grief, the anger, and the fear. I screamed, I sobbed, I let everything out.

I wasn't sure how long we were there on the side of the road, but I briefly felt Bash unclip my belt and pull me into his lap. I buried my head into his chest, sobbing. Bash kissed my hair. "I promise, I will make whoever did this pay. You are safe with us, Princess," he whispered. I knew he would make good on all of his promises.

My tears finally stopped and when I looked up, we were driving again. I panicked, trying to move back to my seat, but Bash held onto me. "Don't," he said, and he gripped me tighter to him. "Just stay until we get to the gate."

"Okay," I whispered hoarsely. I looked out the windshield and over the rolling hills that led down to the ocean.

I knew my body was begging for the water. I could feel myself desperate for the cold ocean spray to hit my skin. I needed to see the iridescent scales line my body, my eyes to shift to the protective layer that allowed me to see. I needed the slits to form upon my neck so I could stay for hours to recharge my power, and I needed to race into the depths of the ocean to give myself the outlet it desired.

I would change into my form tomorrow. I knew I needed to let these emotions out somehow. I let my anger sink back into me and transform... into a deep need for vengeance against whoever murdered Daniels.

As I turned my head to Bash, a loose strand of my hair brushed his face, and he pushed it behind my ear. His eyes searched mine. A smirk played at his lips as he saw my resolve and he breathed.

"Show them what you're made of, Princess. I can't wait

to see you paint the room red with their blood." His fangs slid out. I gazed up into his beautiful green eyes and traced his jaw with my fingertips. He flinched slightly, but his eyes never wavered from the road.

"Thank you for letting me... thank you."

He nodded. "Lexi, we are not perfect. When you love someone... I want you to get your revenge, Princess, and I promise the anger will fade once you do."

I laid my head on his shoulder and murmured, "That is the thing Sebastian, when your heart has been ripped out and beaten for years, you are always angry. I am not angry, Bash, I am enraged, and I will find them and unleash my wrath upon them."

He furrowed his brows, and I could tell he wanted to say more, but the car stopped at the gate to my home. I didn't want his pity or for him to feel sad for me. I looked into his forest-green eyes. "Welcome home, Sunshine," I said sarcastically, giving him the smartass smile I always gave him. "I say let's find this bastard and when I do, I will rip him into pieces. I promise to let you help."

Bash chuckled. "I like it when you get violent."

He pushed his hips up to me just to show me how much he liked me being a little psychopath. He was rock hard as he ground into my ass. "Let's send the other two to bed and I will show you how much I like it," he growled into my ear.

I bit my lip and slid off his lap, moving to the passenger seat as the gate opened. Aden and Tristian were waiting for us on the porch. "I don't want to be the fool again, Bash. It will be a cold day in hell before I touch you like that again." I opened the door and got out of the warm car into the cold night air. I walked up to the porch and into the arms of the other two Devils.

Both of them had already grabbed my bags and placed them by the door. "Bash looks pissed! What did ya do, Lil' Star?" Tristian asked with a huge-ass grin plastered across his face. Aden hid his own amusement with a hand over his mouth and chin.

A blush spread across my cheeks. "Nothing. He is just in need of a cold shower," I said quickly as I went to unlock the door.

"Yeah, an ice-cold shower," chuckled Aden.

Bash finally came up the steps. "What needs to be done, Aden?" He was typing out a text on his phone and looked up. "I already have a guard coming for the gates and a few to walk the surroundings. I want you both to check the inside for what we need. Aden, just order whatever you think we should get. Money isn't an issue when it comes to her safety." I rolled my eyes and walked in as the guys followed.

I knew Aden was big into computers and tech, but I never knew he would be their go-to security guy. "Cameras; she has none. Biometric lock on the front door, sensors on all windows, glass break sensors, door braces, secure all sliding doors and reinforce door jambs—she doesn't even have a deadbolt—keypad entry wireless, cameras inside main areas. Could we get a safe box in here, you think?" Aden rattled it off quickly, and my eyebrows shot to my forehead.

"Aden, how the fuck...?"

He grinned. "How did I know all of that? Well, Lex, you haven't seen me in a while. I grew up a bit, and I specialize

in cyber ops."

Tristian swung his arm around Aden's neck and grinned. "Yeah, Aden is kind of the best of the best, Lil' Star. He could literally kill a man with his pinkie." He wiggled his pinky in my face to demonstrate.

Aden cocked a brow and shook his head, pushing Tristian off of him. I smiled and shook my head, then headed to the kitchen and pulled out four bottles of beer. I didn't drink beer often, but Ethan had been over with Ella last weekend, and these were left over. "Okay, I am going to change while Bash finishes up. I'll be right back." I headed towards my master and a whistle stopped me as I turned around with my hands on my hips.

"Yesssss?" I hissed. Who the fuck whistles at someone?

Aden stood there with a smug look on his face, beckoning me with his finger. "You need help with that zipper... right, Lex?"

Damn it, he was right. I glared at him and walked over to him turning around so he could unzip me.

"Or was that bullshit?" he whispered into my neck.

I turned bright red, having completely forgotten about it. Tristian and Bash stood in front of me, arms crossed to see how I would react. Well, screw them. I turned around so my back was to Aden. If he wanted to unzip me in front of Tristian and Bash, fine, but I was determined to show them that it didn't bother me one bit. Aden slowly lowered the zipper down. Once it was low enough, I stepped forward and let the dress fall from my shoulders, pooling around my feet.

Tristian grinned. "Nice... Well, nice everything, Lil' Star."

I rolled my eyes and looked at Bash. His eyes were ablaze, but he kept them on my face, never drifting lower. "Well… thanks, asshats."

I stepped out of the dress and as I bent forward to gather it up, my ass brushed Aden's pants, and I heard him groan. I smiled evilly, knowing they were getting a show, but I sure as hell wasn't going to give them anything. I walked forward, throwing my middle finger in the air at all three of them.

I walked into my room and kicked the door shut. I hung up my dress and pulled on my softest leggings and a bright pink lace bralette that looked more like a crop top. I slipped on a long white tank with arm holes that were so big you saw my tan stomach and most of the bralette. Heading back into the kitchen, I grabbed the beer on the counter, opened the bottle with a pop, and drank deeply from it.

Bash looked up from his phone. "Thirsty?"

I opened another one and took a sip as I handed him a beer. I passed the other two out to Aden and Tristian. "Do you guys want a tour?" Bash gestured with a sweep of his arm for me to show them around. Taking another drink, I waved my hand over my head around the open-concept room. "Obviously this is the kitchen, living room, and small dining room. Two guest rooms are down that hall." I pointed out to the hallway by the patio doors. "My bedroom is back there, off the living room, and no, I am not sharing my bed. You guys figure out who sleeps where."

I batted my eyelashes at Bash. Fuck all three of them if they think that I would just welcome them into my bed.

I walked to the huge sliding glass doors that overlooked the backyard. "Come on, boys." I turned to look at them over my shoulder. Aden shrugged and followed me out, with the other two close behind. We made our way to the fire pit and sat around in large loungers as Bash started the fire. Tristan sat next to me. A smile adorned his lips, but it didn't quite reach his eyes. Aden and Bash sat opposite us.

I gazed out over the ocean, listening to the waves hit the rocks below, and I felt a calm come over me, remembering how Daniels and I would sit out here talking until all hours of the night. He always knew what to say when I was unsure of something. I wondered what he would tell me now. The ache in my heart grew, and I felt all these little holes and cracks that wouldn't stay closed filling with darkness. I shook myself out of my own thoughts; I knew if I kept thinking about them, I would sink lower into a darkness that was impossible to recover from.

Bash broke the silence and in his deep voice said, "I set up a meeting with Grayson tomorrow for us all to discuss what we need. For tonight, you need to get some sleep, but I don't trust you to be alone without a guard. You are now in charge of your entire coven, Lexi; you have to protect yourself and them at any cost." He gave me a somber look

that told me he was deadly serious about me having one of them with me all the time.

I glared at him over my beer bottle. "I told you no one is staying with me." I took a swig of my beer, settling my eyes back on Bash, who looked like he was about to explode at me. Suddenly, a big fluffy white cat leaped up onto Bash's lap.

I looked down in surprise at the white furball. "Traitor," I mumbled as my cat Dyna twirled around his lap, laying her head down with a deep purr. Bash automatically started to pet her. Dyna nuzzled down even more into his lap. The cat liked him more than me. "You know who feeds you, right?" I glared at her.

"Lexi, can you please just let us protect you?" Aden's soft voice came from beside me. He reached out and took my hand, flipping it over to trace the lines of my palm. It shouldn't have felt so intimate, but I felt something break for Aden. I missed his friendship so much over the years, and after losing someone else who was my family, I realized I don't have many people in my life who knew me that way.

I took a deep breath, removing my hand from his. I walked to the edge of my yard where it met the small hill that led down to the beach. Crossing my arms to bring some kind of warmth to them, I looked out to the ocean, seeing the waves come and go. At night, the ocean looked like ink—so dark, intense, and deadly, like the three of them.

I knew Bash was right. I needed to be careful, but I let myself be selfish for a moment. I didn't notice the tears falling down my face at first, but I quickly wiped them away before anyone could see.

"Fine. One of you can stay with me on the floor, but I swear

if there is any snoring, I'm done." All three smirked and nodded in agreement. "Great, but I am getting drunk first before we start playing house." Walking to my outside bar, I found the lightning whiskey made by a storm dragon. It was the strongest thing I had. I poured four glasses and handed them to the boys. "To Daniels," I said.

"To Daniels."

We cheered, and I took the whiskey in one full gulp. It was strong and sent electric tingles down my throat to my stomach. Aden coughed, and Bash's face was passive. As Tristian took his shot, his face skewered up, and I smirked. "Fucking hell, that was hot!" He said, his mouth hanging open.

"It's got a bit of a kick."

Tristian returned my smile, his eyes filled with mischief. "My dick is so hard right now for you, Lil' Star."

Aden laughed, and Bash grumbled, "Put your cock away, dude. She wants nothing to do with you."

I couldn't help but laugh.

"Tristian, know your audience," Aden scolded, throwing one of the decorative pillows at his head. I poured another and sipped this one slowly, taking my time to let the warmth of the whiskey settle into me. Curling up on the large lounger, I listened to the boys strategize and talk about what to discuss with Grayson tomorrow.

My eyes felt heavier as I listened to Bash's voice, Aden's comforting humming, and Tristian's laugh in the background. My eyes fluttered closed and soon I found a dreamless sleep. I didn't know if it was twenty minutes or three hours later, but I felt a nudge on my shoulder and slowly opened my eyes. It was Bash, his green eyes staring into my blue ones.

"Princess, let's get you in a real bed," he said softly.

I sat up. Tristian was passed out on the outdoor sofa with Dyna curled up on his chest, and Aden had a gentle smile on his face with a book in his hand.

"Is that a dick drawn on his face?" I looked closer at Tristian's face. Yep, they drew a dick. It was very detailed, too, with hair and veins. "Real mature, guys." I stretched my body up letting my shit ride up.

They both chuckled. "Yeah, well, he'd do the same to us," said Aden in a bored voice. He dropped the book and held his hand out to me. "Come on let's get some rest, Lex."

I looked at Bash. "Okay, Goodnight."

He nodded at me, lifting his drink. "I will see you in the morning. We are going to rotate the sleeping patterns. Aden is staying with you tonight," he stated in a matter-of-fact tone, making me think he wasn't happy about it at all.

Aden gave my hand a slight tug as we went inside. Blinking at the bright lights, I walked over to dim them down. "Better?" Aden asked.

"Too bright." I scrunched up my nose as I walked to my bedroom. I walked into the dark, throwing off my top and pants and walking into my closet to grab a pair of soft grey shorts and a matching pajama top.

Not sexy at all, but the long-sleeved top with white trim was the comfiest I had to sleep in. I washed my face, brushed my teeth, and by the time I walked out to my room, I grabbed a few pillows and a blanket and threw them on the floor at Aden's feet. Aden was shirtless, standing in only his pants with his hand on the back of his neck, looking frustrated but cute as hell.

I raised an eyebrow. "What?"

He looked up and his cheeks were flushed. "I, umm... just don't have anything on underneath these pants. I will just leave them on, I guess." He was too tired to figure out sleeping logistics.

"It's fine, Aden, just take them off, but no funny business. I mean it. I am far too tired."

He smiled. "Cross my heart and hope to die." He made a cross over his chest.

I crawled into bed, snuggling into my pillows and turning my back to Aden. I felt the bed dip as Aden leaned toward me. "Good night, Lex."

I turned to him. "Goodnight, Aden."

He smirked and kissed my cheek. "Get some rest, baby."

I closed my eyes, trying not to think about Daniels, but deep grief seeped into my chest—the same grief that I felt all those years ago. Aden slipped off the bed and laid on his back with his hand behind his head. His eyes closed, and his chest slowly raised.

I lay on my side listening to Aden's deep breathing and willing sleep to come. Aden opened his eyes. "You okay?"

I shook my head. "No," I choked out, and he sat up.

"Move over." I immediately shook my head. He smirked. "Relax, Lexi, I'm just trying to get you to relax. Close your eyes and think of the ocean." He crawled into the bed, wrapping me in his strong arms. "Let me be here for you as a friend, nothing more."

I brushed my tears and nodded. "Okay," I said in a small voice. The warmth of his chest and arms surrounding me made me feel safe and comforted, which was what I needed.

I needed to know it was okay not to be okay. Being able to give myself over to someone who would take care of me for once was what my aching heart wanted.

Once sleep finally hit me, I dreamed of blood and gore and Daniels's eyes fading into the light. I woke up in fright to an empty bed. I felt the tears stain my cheeks. Aden wasn't there. I looked around. I pulled my knees up to my chest and buried my head, letting the tears take control. I heard the door creak open and looked up, hoping it was Aden, but Bash walked in.

"I heard... I heard... are you crying?"

I tried to speak, but my voice was caught in my throat. He rushed over and pulled me into his arms. "I got you. I have you. I'm here, it's okay. Let it go, Lexi, let it out." He held me as I let the tears take hold of me. He kept whispering soothing words, but at that moment, I never felt more alone in this world. I was letting a man who I swore to hate for the rest of my life hold me tight and comfort me.

I could pretend that we hated each other and that he was protecting me for other reasons, but at that moment, I didn't care what his reason was. I let myself hold onto him as he rubbed my back in slow circles. I let Bash see the vulnerability that only a few have seen in me throughout the years. We stayed this way for a while until the last of the tears left my eyes.

One thought kept running through my head—maybe, just maybe, I didn't truly hate Sebastian Ryder. Maybe I never truly did.

I lifted my head and looked into those green eyes. "Thank you," I breathed.

He smirked. "I will always protect you, Princess; I just wish I could take the pain away."

I nodded into his chest and closed my eyes as I felt exhaustion creep back in. I laid in this man's arms, this man who had hurt me so much. He was here for me now, so what did it mean to me, to us? It was a dangerous line we were toeing.

Chapter Thirteen

The sunlight streamed through the window, casting a soft yellow light onto the bed. I stirred and arched into a stretch. A hard body was against me, an arm flung over my stomach, pulling me closer. I snuggled closer to the warm body, my ass pushing back into something very hard and ready. I moaned, and his fingers trailed down my side, leaving a line of heat behind them. He kissed right behind my ear.

"Good morning, Princess." His stubble tickled my neck.

"Bash?" I whispered. "What are you doing here?" He let a rumble out, pulling me closer to his chest.

"Aden went to the gym. I didn't want you to be alone, and I'm not sleeping on the floor."

I nodded sleepily, snuggling back into him. "You're warm. Did you just feed?" I sighed. I felt him smile against my shoulder.

"I am, and I did." He pushed more into me.

I bit my lip. "Bash... we can't."

He kissed my lips softly. "Can you be quiet?"

I turned and wrapped my arms around his neck.

"You know I can." I brought him down to me, kissing him softly, our tongues teasing each other. Finally giving in to what we both have wanted for so long.

I closed my eyes as he made his way down my neck, his hands trailing over me, sending shockwaves throughout my body. "You feel so good. Why do you have to feel this good?"

Bash's kisses turned cold, and his fingers clawed at my skin, leaving red lines down my arms. I pushed at him, but when he sat back, his face was hidden by a hooded cloak. I screamed, looking around.

I was in a different room; I was chained up on a black platform. I pulled at the shackles trying to free myself. "It won't help you now, Ms. Rose," an inhuman voice said. I cranked my neck to see the face of my captor, but all I could see was a person in a dark cloak with a hood standing at my feet, their face completely hidden. "I warned you, the next one would be even worse."

I wasn't sure what they were saying, and they raised their arm up to show me a severed head. I knew those green eyes, and I felt my fears become reality. Bash's mouth was open in a scream.

"My Rose, all I needed was you, and you had to ruin it with them. So now I will ruin you."

I screamed with all of the air in my lungs. "No... no... What do you want!?!" I struggled to try to break free, but my wrists started to drip blood down my arms. First my parents, then Daniels, and now Bash.

My screams echoed through the room as I saw cages and small bodies curled within them. He was a monster, a demon of nightmares. I fought with all my strength to get free, but the more I fought against the restraints, the more they tightened.

A whisper echoed through my mind. Someone was calling my name, and it was a small ray of light, filling me with hope. "Lexi, wake up. Lexi, baby, please. Lil' Star, open your eyes."

I blinked my eyes open and felt the sweat drip down my spine as a set of arms wrapped around me.

"Shh, Lexi, it's okay, it's okay—it's a dream."

The tears fell down my face and, as I came to, I saw the afternoon light shining through my windows. Tristian was next to me with concern etched in his face, not Sebastian. I sat up, looking frantically around the room.

"Where is Sebastian? Tell me he's okay! Tristian, where is he?!"

Tristan grabbed my face and made me look into his eyes. "Lexi, Sebastian had an earlier meeting with Morgan. He is fine. He woke me up so you wouldn't be alone. Aden is at the gym. You are safe. No one will take you or hurt you."

I nodded, hugging myself, not answering. I needed to get myself to calm down.

"Come on, Lil' Star. Let me get you coffee and you'll feel more like yourself." He hugged me closer, his hard-on digging into my back.

"Tristian!" I gasped.

"Hmmm," he said as he kissed my shoulder. "Sorry, Lil' Star, but I can't help it." His fingers moved to my shoulders; the lightest touch had me shivering.

"Tell me something real, Tristian."

He thought about that, his eyes searching my face. "Okay, but only if you tell me something real, too." He leaned back, pulling me to lay on his chest. "I hate what we do. I hate that people are afraid of us. I think if the covens knew the dark deeds we did for them kept everyone safe, then people wouldn't view us as some type of monster, though we are."

I looked up at him, running my fingers down his cheek. "Why do you guys hide it all? If you told people, wouldn't they see you differently?"

He shook his head. "Nah, they need someone to hate, so we are them. You don't see it, do you?"

I sat up, tracing his tattoos with my fingers. "I don't think everything is black and white. Everything is grey. You do what you need to, to protect the coven, and for that, I am grateful for you three."

He twirled a strand of my long brown hair into his hand. "You see how we protect our covens, yet you can't forgive us for something that three stupid teenagers did?" There wasn't any anger behind his words, it was just fact.

I smirked. "If I said I forgave you all, would it go away? Would it make everything better?" I tilted my head in curiosity.

He sat up. "I think forgiveness is something that needs to be earned, Lil' Star. If you need me to pass your test, I will, but Lexi, I will earn it one day. Take the time you need to

figure out what you want, but know this: One day, we will belong to each other." He reached out, running his fingers down the side of my face, leaning down to kiss my cheek, whispering, "You stole my heart, so I want yours in return."

I gasped as he leaned in and kissed my lips softly. He was so gentle. He cradled my head, our kisses soft and sweet. He tasted like sunshine and the beach. I moaned into his mouth as he pulled me on top of him. His hands roamed down my sides as he hooked my leg over his hips, and he dug himself into me. I arched my back, racking my nails down his back.

He pulled back and smirked. "You didn't have a clue, did you?"

I blushed and shook my head "You were Bash's best friend. I never thought... I mean, Trist, it's you, you are like..."

He stopped me and kissed me harder, his tongue tangling with mine as if he was starving. I wanted fewer clothes between us and started to unbutton my top when I heard the door open.

"Damn me for going to the gym." I turned to Aden's voice from the doorway. He was shirtless and only in gym shorts. Sweat gleamed on his chest, his tattoos on display, and he had a look in his eyes that was either lust or pure rage.

I licked bit my lip. "Good morning, Aden." A blush crept up into my cheeks.

Tristian popped out of the bed, pulling on a tank top.

"Well, I am getting coffee," he said cheerfully as he headed out of the room to the kitchen. Aden growled at him as he passed, and Tristian slapped Aden's cheek. "Don't be too sad, buddy. I can't help it if she wants me, too." I buttoned up my top and walked past Aden.

"Hey..." He looked down and pulled me close to him, bringing me in for a soft kiss. "Hey Lex." Then he frowned at me. "I can smell him on you." He pushed away from me and stomped down the hall into the guest bathroom.

I frowned and walked into the kitchen, where Tristian was pouring two cups of coffee for us. I sat down at the island, taking the cup as he handed it over to me. "He will be okay, Lil' Star," he said, kissing the top of my head. "I think deep down we all have known how long we have wanted you and for a long time, Bash claimed you for himself. If anyone looked your way, he made sure they knew not to touch you."

I pulled away to stare at him. "You have got to be kidding me, right? He just put a claim on me like that?"

Tristian threw his hands up in defense. "Hey, Lil' Star, I am just telling you the truth. You asked for it. I'm telling you what I know," he said with a shrug.

"That explains a lot, actually." How most guys just wanted to be friends and hook up. The few guys I did date never lasted long. They always blew me off after a few weeks. I sipped my coffee, being even more irritated by the fact that Sebastian had been pussy blocking me for the last ten years. Damn possessive vampires.

Tristian came up behind me, kissing the side of my head. "Ask Bash if you need more answers. He doesn't share that truth with us, Lil' Star."

Speak of the Devil and he shall appear. Bash walked into the kitchen in a pair of dark slacks, a white button-up shirt,

and rolled sleeves showing off his tan skin. He was texting on his phone while drinking an espresso and talking to Aden, who had a protein shake in his hand.

Bash looked at my coffee, glaring at the cup. He nodded to the espresso machine. "Tristian makes shit coffee. I made you one of mine; it's still hot."

I pursed my lips as he handed me the small cup of espresso. "I like all coffee, asshat; no such thing as a bad cup." I took the last gulp of my coffee before I turned to the cup Bash handed me and took a sip.

It was pure perfection. Holy shit, this man knew how to make espresso. I moaned as the tangy-sweet flavor rolled over my tongue. All three guys were looking at me with interest.

"Good coffee," Aden purred as he approached me.

I nodded. "It's delicious. Are you still mad at me?" I set my cup down and hopped up on the counter.

Aden walked to me, bending his head to my ear. "A bit, but maybe I'll punish you later." He gave me a quick kiss, and I looked over to Bash. His arms were folded, and he was glaring at Aden.

I sighed. "No more lies or half-truths, Sebastian. If we want the covens to work together, if we want us to work together, then you have to be honest with us. So, you wanna explain to me why none of the men in Providence Village ever wanted to commit to me? Or how you three made a dumb claim to me years ago?"

I glared at him playfully. Bash stood and walked over to me. "So, what is this, a negotiation? To accomplish what? Dating all three of us or just fucking all three of us? Tell me, Princess, is that what you think would happen?" He stood in his spot, arms crossed as if he was trying to intimidate me.

I played coy, taking a sip of my coffee and looking up from under my eyelashes at him. "Sounds like you have been fantasizing about that a lot more than me, Bash." I bit my lip just thinking about what it would be like to have all three of them at once. I dug a little more at him. "Tristian sure knew how to wake me up this morning, though."

Bash twisted around as Tristian stalked over to him. "Did you fuck her?" He pointed back to me. Tristian's grin dropped, and his face morphed into something I'd never seen in him before; rage sat behind his eyes. Calmly, Tristian looked to me, then back to Bash.

"You don't own her, frere. You don't get to dictate our lives. You think you have some sick right to her because of something that happened years ago. That doesn't mean you own her. If she wants me, then I want her."

Slamming his coffee cup down, he shoved past Bash and walked over to me, grabbing my neck and pulling me into a brutal kiss. I gasped as his lips collided with mine, his tongue stroked me, and I grew wet just having him kiss me. Damn, he was good. He pulled away just as quickly and headed to the guest room, slamming the door. In shock, I touched my lips and looked over to Bash, who was seething in anger. I couldn't get a breath out before Bash rushed up to me. I put my hands out in front of me to stop him, but he halted about an inch from me, reaching around to grab the whiskey bottle we left out last night.

His eyes never left mine as he took the lid off and took a long drink. "Stay in the house, Lexi, or take one of us with you if you need to leave. We have a meeting with the

covens tonight. We got another letter this morning from your number one fan."

I straighten up in alarm. "Where?"

Bash sighed. "Pinned to the gates. Here." He pulled the letter from his back pocket and dropped it to the coffee table. "Read it or not, but be ready at dark. It's the covens, so anything could happen. Make sure you are ready both physically and mentally."

I looked at the black envelope; what the hell did he want?

"Oh, and Princess." I glanced back at him as he gave me a cocky grin. "I am next on the list, and just so you know—when it's just us, you'll forget about everything else."

He ran his fingers through my hair, tilting my head back to look into my eyes.

"You forget I've had you before and I know what you like." He let me go, his fingers trailing their way down the column of my throat, leaving me breathless. He turned away and walked out onto the backyard, continuing to head down to the beach as his silhouette sank into the glaring sun.

I glared after him, and I yelled to no one, "Just because you deflowered me doesn't mean I like the same thing, asshat!"

Dyna perked her head up and walked over to me, jumping on the counter as she rubbed her head against my hand. "Men," I sighed. "They are complicated. Stay away from that one, Dyna." She meowed as if she agreed and jumped down to go to her bowl to have her breakfast.

I took my espresso and moved to the couch, picking up the letter in my hands. The black envelope had the Blood Moon symbol stamped into it just like the other one. Slightly trembling, I opened the letter, prepping myself for what it said:

My Darling Rose,

Gifts are my specialty. Do you like what I gave you?

You've given me a torn heart. I saw the way you shine in the night sky with those demons who do nothing but lie, cheat, and steal. They are stealing from me, and they must be stopped.

The blame is not all theirs. You are a siren, pure and true, luring anyone who crosses your path to their demise. Let me help you, sweet siren. Let me dash those devils against the rocks, starting with him. I'll hang his tattoos on my wall as a tapestry of warning: Never touch what is mine.

Never fear me, my beloved. You are my queen, and I your king. We'll rule them all together. We'll teach them all what real fear is.

I will see you again tonight. Do not worry; I am the shadows that move in the dark.

Always yours,
The Wishmaker

I felt sick to my stomach. I wanted to crumple the note up, light it on fire, and burn it to nothing. I closed my eyes and ground my teeth.

"I need to get to water," I announced to the empty room.

The beach was the usual place I'd go to think, but since Bash was sulking there, I chose my backyard. Thank heavens I had a pool. Don't get me wrong, I would choose the ocean over the pool most days, but every now and then I wanted to dip in and out without having to deal with a grumpy vampire. I walked to my room and picked my favorite suit—a black bikini. It was simple, but covered everything and didn't ride up my butt like the others.

I threw it on and went to get a towel from the linen closet. When I stepped back into the living room, Aden was standing there with his hands in his pockets, looking down at the letter with a frown drawn on his face. He looked up as I walked in.

I gestured to the letter. "Did Bash... read this?"

He looked over at me, noticing the bikini and towel. "No, but I need..." He tilted his head knowingly. "Yeah... Let's go, Lex. I will sit while you swim."

I gave him a small smile. "You could join me?"

He shook his head with a smirk. "No way, babe, I need to make sure it's safe, and I can't do that if I am distracted."

I gave him a flirty smile as I trailed my fingers along with the countertop. "God forbid I distract you." I turned with a swish as I walked to the door and took a left to the rectangle pool sitting to the side of the house with a raised, built-in hot tub. A small waterfall poured into the saltwater pool, loungers sat around so I could lay out, and a small table with an umbrella sat near the end of a built-in BBQ. It was a great house for entertaining, which I rarely did, and now I would probably never get to. Sighing, I dropped the towel onto a lounger.

"Do you want me to apologize on behalf of them, Lex?" I turned to Aden. His eyes were furrowed, his lips curved down sadly.

"I don't know what I want, Aden. This is all very fast, and I am still hurt from the three of you."

Aden wrapped his arms around me, pulling me close to him. "I'm sorry for everything." He kissed the top of my head and held me tightly against him.

"I just want our friendship again, Aden, so let's start with that. Maybe one day soon forgiveness will come." I pulled away from him, setting my towel down.

"I can try friendship, baby, but it's hard when you look like you do and make my heart feel again."

I laughed. "Are you saying if I were ugly, you wouldn't want me then?"

He smiled wickedly, popping on a pair of black aviator sunglasses. "Nah, even if you had warts on your nose, I'd still want you." I shook my head as I laid out on the lounger feeling the sun's rays warm me. "We will figure this out. Give us time to deal with it. Bash is protective of you, he always has been, and Trist, well, he knows what buttons to push, but he's also looked at you with a fierceness I have never seen before with anyone else."

I ran my fingers along his tattooed arm, tracing the images. "And you, Aden?" I looked up into his eyes as he stared back into mine.

"Me? I'm easy. I have been in love with you since I was eight, baby. I tried to get over it, but I don't think you've ever really left me. I have always watched over you whether you knew it or not."

I raised my eyebrow. "Like a stalker?"

He laughed. "No, more like I always checked in with Ella, Coco, Jason, and Daniels every week. I went out of my way to get coffee at Coco's so maybe I would see you every now and then."

I bit my lip. "We never saw each other that often, sometimes you were by yourself, but other times Bash or Tristian were with you. I assumed you were obsessed with the bakery like everyone else in Providence."

He laughed harder. "Well, I am! Her devil food chocolate cake is the best, that is true. Oh, and her croissants are out of this world. As much as I love Coco's pastries, we were there for you. We've been protecting you long before now, Lexi." He shrugged and walked me closer to the edge of the pool with an evil grin. I knew what he was going to do; I was no dummy.

"Oh no, you don't." I gripped his shirt and pulled him close. "I will take you down with me, asshat."

He smirked and lifted me; I wrapped my legs around his waist as he pulled me close. To distract him, I kissed his neck and ground into him. Aden's hands moved to my ass to hold me as he moaned. I giggled and tried to get out of his hold. Before I could do anything, he launched us into the water. A girly scream escaped as the cool water swept over me. I let go of him, swimming away, feeling the tension leave my body. Letting my siren take over, I felt myself shift.

The pain radiated through my body as I felt my hands elongate into sharp claws, and my skin formed scales on my arms and legs. My back arched as my whole body changed, and my eyes hazed over so I could see underwater clearly. My neck split open so the gills could come through as I breathed in deep. My eyes shifted as the film formed over them. I could see through the water as if it was glass.

Sirens could stay under for at least two hours before feeling any need for air. I was not sure how long I stayed under, but after a while, I pulled myself to the surface, seeing Aden's shirt and pants off as he lazily lay in the sun to dry off. He had a book in his hand and looked up at me. "Better?"

I smiled. "Not even close, but I will get there."

He looked relaxed, but I could tell he was on full alert, looking for anything out of the ordinary. I started to do laps, feeling the water move over me and work with me, my muscles getting stronger, my body feeling the pull of the magic within me. An hour later, I saw a shadow above the surface when I reached the edge. I pulled myself out, changing back. Aden walked up with a towel in his hands, wrapping it around me to keep me warm. I looked up at him as water sat on my eyelashes. "Truly beautiful" he whispered, tracing the water droplets slowly cascading down my cheeks. Goosebumps appeared on my arm, but it wasn't from the cold.

"We should go in," I whispered back.

"Hmm." He leaned closer to lightly kiss my cheek, then my other side. He inched closer to my mouth. "Yeah, we should, but I'm a Devil, baby, so let me enjoy this small moment." His mouth was so close to mine that it would

only take a small movement to claim a kiss.

"Yo, Aden, you gotta see this!" Tristian yelled from the patio with Dyna in his arms. He was full belly up, getting all of the attention.

"She is such a snuggle slut with you guys," I grumbled. I could swear that cat had all three of them wrapped around her tiny murder paws.

Shaking my head, I walked to Tristian, stopping to look down at Dyna. Her fluffy white head raised to me, then went right back down, purring louder into Tristian's strong arms.

"Traitor," I muttered as I went inside.

CHAPTER FOURTEEN

The smell of garlic, onion, and basil hit me as I walked into the living room, making my mouth water. The biggest surprise wasn't the smell of food cooking. It was Bash wearing my pink floral apron with lace on the edges.

I burst out laughing. "Why, Sebastian Ryder, I have never seen a more delicious man than you right now," I teased in a southern accent.

Bash looked up from the pasta sauce he was stirring and smirked. "I rock this apron, and wait until I give you a taste."

My voice dried up in my throat, so instead of saying a snarky comment, I walked over to see what he was cooking. The chicken was simmering in a pesto sauce and tomatoes.

I saw a pot on the side, steam billowing out of the lid. I opened it and found fresh penne pasta.

Bash pulled out focaccia bread that looked like heaven.

"Sebastian, did you make focaccia bread?"

He placed the bread on the trivet as he shrugged. "It's no big deal, Princess."

I moved to the bar stools on the other side. "Bash, this looks amazing!" He poured me a chilled glass of rose—my favorite kind, which I knew I didn't have in the house because Ella and I finished the bottle last week. "How did you know my favorite wine, Sebastian?"

He smirked, leaning closer to me. "One of my many talents is being observant. Like how I know that your favorite flower is from the small city of Providence. You love the smell of lilacs, but not fake scents from a candle or spray. You love the lilac that blows in over a warm spring day. You love warm blankets and hot chocolate on rainy days. You don't care about clothes that much but you like shoes and purses. I know that you make sure everyone else is okay first before you assess your own feelings. You are scared to train because once you do that, you will officially take over the coven, but that also means your parents' deaths are final, and lastly, I know you don't want to feel those feelings about us. You know it's not in your nature to want only one of us. I know that once you accept those feelings, you'll forgive us, and you don't want that because the anger is what you are holding onto after all these years. I know you, Lexi, because I've been paying attention for years." He pointed a wooden spoon at me.

As the truth hit me in the face, I crossed my arms. I bit

the inside of my cheek, tasting the tangy taste of blood filling my mouth. "Fuck you, Sebastian." I glared at him.

He was right, but he didn't deserve to psychoanalyze me. He didn't earn that right yet. I couldn't stand that he paid that close attention to me after all these years, which made Aden's words from earlier true. He cared and I couldn't have him care. Tears filled my eyes, but it wasn't sadness; this was filled with hurt, grief, and anger. I stood and walked away into my bedroom. It was childish, but I wasn't ready to see myself like that yet. I wasn't ready to face what I knew: Sebastian Ryder knew me better than I knew myself.

I heard the tiny pitter-patter of feet behind me as Dyna caught up to me, head in the air and her fluffy white tail swishing as she walked like it was a middle finger to Sebastian. I smirked and threw mine in the air, too. Solidarity, sister! I let Dyna enter first, then turned to see all three boys looking at me. I dropped my towel and slammed my door on them.

After I showered and got dressed in a simple t-shirt dress and sandals, I dried my hair and did my makeup, knowing it was time for negotiation between the Three Devils.

I strolled out with my head held high and sat on the barstool to look Bash square in the face. He had his arms crossed and glared at me. I picked up my wine glass and took a deep drink.

Tristian was next to him fixing a plate of food. He smiled widely at me, handing me a plate. "Hey, Lil' Star, here ya go!"

"Thank you, Trist." I took the plate from him and picked up the focaccia bread. I stared at Bash with a grin and took a bite. Bash growled at me, but I just kept smiling. "Now, now,

Sebastian, don't get your panties twisted. I come in peace." I took another sip of my wine.

He huffed. "I thought you would just stroll away again like the damn brat you are."

Aden walked in, freshly showered and dressed in dark jeans and a white tee. He kissed the top of my head. "Babe, it looks good." He smiled crookedly at Bash, who was still glaring at me. I hold up my fork for Aden to take a bite of the pasta. He slowly pulled the fork to his mouth, taking a bite. "Mmmmm. Damn, Bash, I think I just might marry you."

I leaned over to Tristian and smirked as I loudly whispered, "Is he always this grumpy?" Bash glared at us and then, as he was about to snap at me, Aden's phone buzzed. He pulled his phone out of his pocket to read whatever text just came through.

Bash snapped out of his piss-poor attitude and looked to Aden. "News?"

Aden finished his bite of food, swallowing. "Yeah, it looks like Grayson has some news for us tonight. Also, he is sending over two guys to help our guards out."

Bash glanced over at me with a stern look on his face as I took another deep drink from my wine and took a bite of chicken. Holy crap, was it delicious.

My eyes rolled up. "OH MY GOD, Bash, Aden is right. You might be the biggest ass I know, but damn you can cook."

Bash leaned on his elbows, gazing at me. "If you like that, then you should see how I fuck, Princess."

A blush creeped up, and I cleared my throat. "So... about, umm, all of this. I think we should have a few rules."

That got all of their attention as they all turned their faces towards me. Tristian's hoarse voice came beside me. "You care to explain that a bit more, Lil' Star?"

I bit my lip and looked at each of them. "Yeah, so we should have a set of rules... so we don't have the fights we've been having."

Aden broke into a huge smile. "Deal, baby, deal. What are you thinking?"

I grabbed the bottle of wine and poured a hefty amount into my glass.

I held up my fingers, rambling off the rules I came up with while getting ready. "One. Equal time with each other. We rotate days where one of you is with me. We spend time together, whatever that may be. Two. I need to train not only in magic, but in fighting. Bash was right: I can't be seen as weak. Tristian can train me in magic, Bash and Aden in fighting. Bash is the best with weapons and Aden in hand-to-hand combat. Three. I'm included in the planning of anything we do for the covens. Four. Bash cooks for us one night a week and we sit and have dinner as a group, no excuse." I picked up the focaccia bread and dipped it into the pesto sauce, taking a bite.

Tristian typed out the rules in a document on his phone and he smiled up at me. "Done, but I want to add Number Five. We each get to sleep in your bed on the day we have you."

I rolled my eyes. "Done," I conceded, taking another sip of wine.

Aden ran his fingers up my spine. "Six. We get to take you on a date of our choice once a month," he whispered into my ear.

"I didn't think you were a flower and date kind of guy, Aden."

Bash took his wine and leaned closer to me, stealing my attention away from Aden. "Seven. I want to choose what you wear to bed when it's our day." He grinned with a gleam of lust in his eyes.

I glared, shaking my head. "FINE, done. Eight. We kill The Wishmaker together and save our covens. We get our vengeance."

A smile danced across all of their faces, and I realized how scary they were.

"Princess, you have yourself a deal." Bash held his hand out to me, and I shook it. I wasn't sure what I just got myself into, but if it ensured that my Coven was safe, that my friends and family were safe, then I would walk through hell with the Three Devils next to me.

I spent the afternoon sunbathing on the patio, listening to a singer talk about her former lovers. Aden stayed out by me doing laps in the pool and hanging out next to me in the loungers. Tristian took calls about his new speakeasy, Belladonna, that was going to open up in the next few months. Sebastian stayed inside cleaning up lunch and typing on his laptop, something about business for his dad.

As the sun set over the ocean, Aden pulled himself out of the pool. My eyes lingered on his tattoos, seeing how intricate they were, curving over his shoulders, down his arms, then meeting at his stomach down the sharp V cut

that led to the top of his trunks. I looked up to his face, his cut jaw with a sharp five o'clock shadow, and his eyes so deeply grey they sent you into a trance. He had water droplets running down his face onto his hard chest over his pierced nipples... Wait, he had his nipples pierced? Holy shit! What else does he have pierced?

I raised my sunglasses and smiled. "Aden, why do you have your nipples pierced?"

He sat down next to me, his cool skin hitting my warm thigh. "Well, Lex, I think that question is a bit personal? The question is, why don't you have anything pierced?" He gave me a teasing smile as he laid across my lap.

"Seriously, why all the tattoos and the piercings? I like them... a lot, but I knew you to be this quiet, sweet, and, well, kind of a geeky kid when we were younger. What changed?" I ran my fingers back through his dark hair to get the loose strands out of his face. He purred, snuggling closer to my lap.

"Honestly?"

I smiled down at him. "Yes, honestly."

"After what I... we did to you and then the initiation into the coven... I felt I needed to do this, sort of like having armor. It also allowed me to finally express myself. You know what my family is like..." He struggled to find the words.

"Picture perfect?" I suggested.

He laughed. "That's one way of saying it, yeah, picture perfect. I was never perfect. I was never like Ethan. I always had this devil in me, so I decided I would put the devil out for everyone to see."

I ran my finger down his face over his lips. "I see you,

Aden, and I am glad you could finally come to light."

I kissed his cheeks slowly. Then, as light as a feather, I kissed his lips.

"Princess!" Bash called from the patio. "Stop kissing my third and get your ass dressed or you're gonna miss your first coven meeting!"

I rolled my eyes. "We are coming! So you can kindly FUCK RIGHT OFF!" Aden laughed into my lap and the feeling of his breath so close to me made me squirm. "Okay, not-so-Prince Charming, get off of me so I can get ready."

Aden looked tempted to say more, but he sat up, and I wrapped a towel around myself, gathered my sunglasses and phone, and headed inside.

I looked at Bash. "So, what is the attire for tonight? I assume it isn't black tie?"

Sebastian laughed. "Nope, definitely not black tie, but dress..."

Tristian looked up from his phone. "Sexy? Hot? Not that it is hard for you to do, Lil' Star, but add a bit of badassery to it." He winked at me.

I turned back to Bash. "Badassery?"

With an eyebrow raised, he chuckled in his deep voice "He's not wrong, Princess. Look to kill, literally."

Thinking about it, I nodded. "Okay, I think I get it." I headed back to my bedroom to find an appropriate outfit. I settled on black leather pants, a sweetheart black velvet corset, and a cropped leather jacket with thigh-high combat boots. The perfect combination of sexy and dangerous. I was finishing painting my lips red when Bash walked in wearing dark jeans and a gray button-up showing off his

wide chest. He was playing with a watch when he looked up and stared at me in the mirror. His eyes widened.

I put the lipstick down and stood up, worried that I got the wrong idea of what the meeting was about. "What? Is it not right? I can choose something less..."

He blinked as if he fought his way out of a trance.

"No, it's perfect, Lexi." He walked to me and pushed my hair behind my shoulders. "You look stunning, but you might want to wear this." He produced a royal blue velvet box in front of me.

"It was your coven's. Your mother used to wear it, so it only seems fitting you should have it." He held the box open for me. Inside was a beautiful ruby teardrop necklace with diamonds that were small and delicate surrounding the ruby.

"Bash, this is gorgeous. I can't."

He moved my hair to the side and carefully took the necklace out. "Well, technically, it's yours. Daniels had me place it in a safety deposit box for him when he took over the coven. The necklace represents the coven, but as Daniels wasn't into the lavish lifestyle, he put it away in a safe spot." He placed the necklace on me and gave me a half smile. "I would say that it is now back with its rightful owner."

I touched the ruby, just trying to feel a part of my mother; it felt warm and soothing against my skin. "Thank you, Bash." I turned and reached for him, kissing his cheek. "But you are still a dick," I jokingly added.

He chuckled. "And you are a pain in my ass. Let's go." He lightly pushed me to the door. We walked out to the living room where Aden and Tristian stood. Aden was wearing all black—black motorcycle boots, black jeans with a black Henley, and a black leather motorcycle jacket. His dark hair was swooped back. He looked like a demon ready to lay claim to a throne. He was deadly, and Tristian appeared the opposite in tight grey jeans, a white shirt, and a long silver chain with a tiger's eye inserted.

He had a black leather holster over him with two silver-handled guns gleaming inside. Both of them looked like they stepped off of the runway of Hitman GQ. I wondered what danger was ahead of us tonight and hoped I could be equally intimidating and confident. It didn't happen often, but now and then another coven member could take the place of the leader if need be, and I had a feeling I might be challenged more than once tonight.

I turned to Bash. "Ready?" He was checking his gun and put the safety on and holstered it.

Aden and Tristian walked over to me. "Yep, but this is for you, Lil' Star." Tristian handed me a small, thin case; I opened the case to a slightly curved deadly black blade; its handle was a matte black with a sprinkle of dark grey diamonds encasing the hilt.

"Is that an onyx blade?" I swallowed nervously. An onyx blade was one of the deadliest blades around for any fae. It could cause death in seconds if used correctly, but a slice not only would leave a nasty scar, but it would also taint the mind and make you go crazy.

"It is, and I am hoping you won't have to use it tonight, but you never know what will happen at these meetings. Strap it to your thigh. Just wearing it alone will tell people not to mess with you." I looked at the hilt, carefully examined

it, then returned it to its holster and attempted to attach it.

"Motherfucker! How the fuck do you attach this thing?" I mumbled, hearing a chuckle from behind me. I looked up, seeing Tristian leaning against the wall, seeming amused as hell at my attempt. "Like you can do any better?" I glared.

Tristian threw his hands up into the air. "Nooo, Lil' Star, you keep it up." He crossed his arms with a smug look on his face.

After five minutes and Bash yelling twice at me to hurry up, I threw my hands up. "Tristian, just help me. I cannot be a badass bitch if I can't get the deadliest knife I know on my damn thigh."

He raised an eyebrow "Okay, Xena: Warrior Princess, but ask nicely."

I could hear the smirk in his voice. "Tristian..." I growled. "Please." I grit my teeth and smiled at him, trying to hide my frustration.

"See? It wasn't that hard, Lil' Star." He pushed away from the wall and strutted—yes, strutted—to me and kneeled gracefully down onto one knee, starting to attach the holster to my leg while humming a tune I couldn't quite place.

"Tristian, are you singing Taylor Swift?" I laughed.

"Hey, don't hate T-Swizzle; the girl can write a hell of a song."

I pretended to zip my lips. "My lips are sealed."

His fingers fixed the last strap and lingered on my thigh a second longer, circling his finger on the inside of my leg, causing me to bite down on my lip.

"We should go, or else Bash is going to have a fit."

Tristian looked up at me with heat in his eyes. "Can't

have Mr. Grouchy Pants upset now, can we? I just can't stop remembering the kiss from this morning." He leaned in, placing a light kiss on my inner thigh. "I plan on exploring these leather pants more tonight, Lexi." He ran his hands up the back of my thighs to my ass and pulled me closer so his nose was right on me. "God, you are so warm. You know vampires run on the colder side when we haven't fed, so anything warm makes us want to snuggle, and I could snuggle you here all day long."

His gruff voice sent vibrations up into my stomach. I wove my hand into his hair. "Tristian, you aren't playing fair," I moaned. God, I wanted to just say screw all of this, then just screw him until I couldn't feel anything anymore.

He laughed. "All's fair in love and war, Lil' Star; now, we've got bigger fish to fry." He pulled back and stood up in one motion, walking to the door. I almost fell back but caught myself, glaring at him as he looked back with a cocky smirk. "Coming, Lexi?" I bit my lip and stalked towards him, putting an extra swing in my hips and stomping down to the car where Aden and Bash stood.

They looked up at me with interest. I said nothing as I pushed myself into the passenger seat of Aden's big, black Escalade, slamming the door and folding my arms in a pout. Tristian came out of the house, locking the door with the biometric lock. He walked with a swagger. Bash and Aden said something to him I couldn't hear, and Tristian laughed out loud. Bash looked pissed, and Tristian looked pleased with the little joke he pulled.

Aden jogged around and hopped into the driver's side, as Bash and Tristian slid into the back. "Hey, I got a surprise

stop before we head to the cabin." I looked over at him, waiting for him to tell me. "We are going to see our favorite pastry chef."

I grinned, thinking of my aunt. "Really?"

Aden nodded.

"Then what are you waiting for, Charming? Show me how fast this hunk of metal can go."

Chapter Fifteen

We pulled up to the gate that surrounded my family's home. Two huge guys were standing outside it. "Those have to be trolls, right?" The sheer size of these guys was intense. They each were at least six foot six and as wide as a linebacker.

Tristian laughed. "Oh yeah, baby, that's Deke, the one with the blue mohawk. Sonny is the one who looks like he could eat you."

The larger one, Sonny, came up to Aden's driver's side window. Aden rolled the window down about three inches, and I noticed that he had discreetly pulled out his gun on his lap, placing his hand on it just in case he needed to take action. "Aden," a low, gravelly voice said as he nodded to

Bash and Tristian. "This the one everyone is all up in arms about?"

Aden smiled. "Yep. Lexi Rose, meet Sonny Accardo."

I gave a small smile and a little wave. "Hello, how do you do?" Sonny gave a full belly laugh.

"Well, I'll be damned, aren't you the sweetest thing? What the fuck are you doing around the Three Devils?"

I smirked. "What makes them so devilish? Maybe they are just puppies with fangs?"

He smiled, showing off his insanely white teeth. "Aww, smart and beautiful! You got your hands full with that one, Aden. Is the boss man in there with you?" Tristian rolled his window down, and Bash saluted Sonny. "How's the family, Sonny?"

He smirked. "Good. Dela just got into Princeton, and Dani just got varsity for lacrosse."

Bash nodded. "Good! Dani the size of you yet?"

Sonny smiled a toothy grin. "Not yet, but soon. Anyway, Coco said you were on your way—head on in. Jason will escort you the rest of the way." The other guard, Deke, stood back, glaring at the window as we drove by.

"He seems friendly," I said sarcastically.

Aden smirked. "Yeah, that's Deke's normal face, but he is one hell of a fighter. He can have a shit attitude sometimes, but he will put someone down if it comes to it."

I saw Jason standing on the porch as we approached. His normally smiling face was gone, and lines of worry were etched in a frown. I didn't think what the news of Daniels would do to Jason. They were like father and son.

Daniels pretty much raised me, but only because Jason

and Coco were young when my parents died. Daniels stepped up and was like a father to all of us. It made my heart crack. I hoped Daniels knew how much he meant to us all. I wanted to scream at the heavens again.

The pain that The Wishmaker caused by taking the one truly good person from my family was crushing me all over again. I felt tears fill my eyes as Coco came to the door, wrapping her hand around Jason's arm. I leaped out of the car before it fully stopped and did a full-out run into Coco and Jason's arms.

"FUCK, ADEN! Park this fucking car now!" I heard Bash shout. He jumped out of the backseat and ran up to me. "Lexi, you can't..." He stopped suddenly, letting my family and I have this moment. I hadn't realized it, but the tears came down so hard I was a mess all over again.

"Coco, I am so sorry! Oh god, what are we going to do?" I was finally realizing how much I needed my family. They kept me grounded in this crazy, fucked up world.

"Shh, Lexi, shh. I know, sweet girl, I know. We all loved Daniels so much." Her voice cracked at the end, but she took me into her arms, holding onto me as tightly as I was holding her.

I nodded. "I'm okay, I just... I didn't realize how much I missed you two. The last twenty-four hours have been a bit crazy. God, this is stupid. I saw you yesterday." I looked at Coco. Her hazel eyes brimmed with tears, and she wiped mine away from my cheek.

"We missed you, too, honey, but I am glad these three troublemakers are keeping you safe."

Coco was what you would call a classic beauty, with

fiery red hair, big hazel eyes, and a sharp chin. She was the "cool" aunt. She traveled the world hanging out with rock stars and once was offered a modeling gig in Paris in the 90s where she lived for most of my life until my parents died. She flew out the next day and never left my side, saying "family stays together."

I felt Jason's hand on my shoulder, and I gave him a small smile. Jason was boy-next-door handsome with rich sepia skin and kind eyes. I knew he loved Coco even before they figured it out. He grew up next door and was always over to help Coco out with whatever she needed—tire change, picking ingredients from the garden; the man was hopeless for her.

I smiled at him and pulled him into a massive bear hug. "Jason, I missed you. I think we are long overdue for one of our famous baking nights with Coco."

Jason chuckled. "You should do one soon. Coco's got me making croissants and macarons. I don't think I'll keep my figure much longer if she makes me taste one more cookie."

I felt a small laugh come out. "Okay, soon, I swear."

He pointed his finger at me. "Pinky promise?" He flipped up his pinkie.

"Pinkie promise." I wrapped mine around his.

I looked back seeing all three of my Devils standing at the bottom of the porch with their hands in their pockets, letting us have a moment.

I cleared my throat. "Coco, you know Sebastian Ryder, Tristian Cassium, and Aden Charmante. Morgan Ryder assigned these three to me as bodyguards until the killer is caught."

Coco knew them, of course, and she disliked them as much as I did. She heard about the tapes, and she saw how I was that night. She quickly put two and two together that I was upset about more than just my parents' deaths.

Except, the more time I spent with the three of them, the more I seemed to forget what they did to me. The real question that I was afraid to ask myself was… would I forgive them one day and move on?

Coco's voice broke through my thoughts. "Actually, we have someone here who wanted to meet with you four before you headed to the covens meeting."

I stared at her questionably. "Who?"

She smiled. "Kane Anderson. He was a good friend of Daniels, and—"

Bash interrupted her as he and the other two Devils met us on the porch, "And he's my father's business partner."

Coco nodded to Bash. "He's in the conservatory."

"Okay, I'll see you soon. I am serious about a girls' night."

She smiled and hugged me once more. "Deal."

I unwrapped myself from her, reluctantly heading towards the side of the house where the conservatory sat. Green radiated in the night sky as the moon shone onto the verdant glass. A showdown of a man stood at a bench as we entered, and the steady sound of water filled the room. I glanced over all of the plants. It all was so familiar, but also foreign, that it held more sadness within its walls now.

"Lexi, Sebastian, thank you for seeing me," said a deep voice. Kane Anderson was a tall man with a rugged look to him. Standing with his hands clasped behind his back, he wore dark navy pants and a grey turtleneck sweater. He had an air of confidence about him, and I felt comfortable in his presence. I knew we could trust him but used my compulsion just to make sure he was being honest and true with us. I let the magic slowly slink out of me as a shiver ran down my spine.

"Mr. Anderson, not to be blunt, but we have a long evening ahead of us, so forgive me, but what do you want?"

I felt Bash stiffen, but as we approached Kane, he was chuckling. "I see why Daniels liked you, Lexi. He always talked so highly of you." He played with a small plant on the table. "Daniels was a friend. Damn he was closer to a brother to me than my own or anyone else." He looked at Bash's eyes as something passed between them like a silent understanding. "I want to help you figure out why the hell he was murdered. He was helping me buy back my company's stock. To say that his death is an inconvenience is an understatement," he sighed, turning his focus back to me. "And I feel like I might be responsible for his death. I think someone found out what we were doing and wanted to ruin us in the worst possible way." He slammed his fist down on the table, shaking the plant and tools.

Something wasn't adding up. "Wait, are you saying that Daniels was helping you, what, out of goodness of his heart? Because you were friends?" I pushed my compulsion into Kane, and his eyes unfocused as my lure encompassed him.

He looked over at me in disbelief. "No, I was helping him with the pixie dust problem, trying to find out who was the manufacturer behind it all."

My lips popped open. Pixie dust wasn't actually made by pixies, and it was becoming a problem around the city.

Daniel had spoken to Coco, Jason, and myself about the problem for the past year.

Pixie dust came in small glass vials. It was sparkly and alluring, and its effects were the same on each person or fae who consumed it. From what I'd heard, it made you feel as if you were riding high on life; happiness filled your entire body, but the downfall was the worst depression you had ever felt that stayed with you until you received your next hit.

I shook my head. Something just wasn't right. Why would Daniels be involved with pixie dust?

"Bash... do you think...?"

He nodded his head in disbelief. "Yeah, Princess, it all comes back to the dust," he growled out.

"Fuck!" Aden and Tristian grumbled in unison. I dropped my lure. Kane's fist unclenched and brushed the dirt off of his pants.

Kane's eyes became clear, and he shook his head. "You believe me?"

I turned to look at him and nodded stiffly. "Yeah, Mr. Anderson, we do."

"Start at his home, Lexi. Do you have a key?"

I shook my head. "No, Daniels was pretty private. He usually came to the estate."

Anderson nodded in agreement. "Yes, Daniel's was very private, but one thing Daniels gave me a few weeks ago was a key to his home. Here, take this and use it to start your search for anything that might help, and here..." He handed me a business card. "Call me if you find something or need any more help. Let's find this bastard and fucking burn him."

My smile didn't quite reach my eyes as I looked at him.

"I couldn't agree more, Mr. Anderson."

He left an old ornate gold key in Bash's hand because, of course, Daniels would have an ancient gold key to his home. The old man loved the antiquity of it all. He didn't say another word but headed to the door of the conservatory, stopping and turning back to me. "Lexi, I am so sorry about Daniels. He was truly an amazing person, and he did love you as his own." He gave me a small smile, which I returned.

"Thank you, Mr. Anderson."

He held up a hand. "Kane, please. Mr. Anderson makes me feel old."

I nodded. "Kane, we will find his killer." He nodded once and exited the door.

"Well, shit just got real," Tristian said as he held his head in his hands.

Bash was watching Kane leave. "It really did." He turned to Tristian and Aden.

"But can we trust him?" Aden said as he looked at me.

"I don't think we can trust anyone but us four," I spoke to them.

Bash turned to me and brushed the hair from my face. "Do you truly trust us, Princess?"

I looked up into his green eyes. "I don't think I have a choice in the matter, Bash, but yes—in this, I know I can trust you Devils."

Bash examined the skeleton key. "Let's go check out Daniels's home first. We have time. Then we can head to the Trinity Coven. We need to talk to the other leaders of the coven. Grayson might know more than he is letting on."

I headed toward the exit. "Well, let's go throw ourselves

to the wolves, then. But first, I am stopping and getting pastries. If Coco is stress baking, then it's gonna be heaven."

Aden ran past me. "Only if you beat me there!"

Tristian was on his heels. "DUDE! Do you think she has those coconut crisp cookies she makes?"

Bash walked up to me, wrapping his fingers around mine as we walked to the house. "Think she has her famous chocolate éclair?"

I smiled up at him. "Sebastian Ryder, I never knew you to be a man who would lust after an éclair."

His eyes were sultry. "Oh, I lust after a certain siren witch, but the chocolate éclair is second to her."

I grinned up at him. "Well, maybe if you weren't a giant ass and paid more attention to me than the éclairs, then you could have had me instead," I teased.

Bash pulled me close, peering down at me, his lips so close to mine. I closed my eyes in a sigh, leaning into the kiss he seemed to want to give. "Princess... I would never give up those éclairs!" He pulled away, laughing and taking off to the estate. I rolled my eyes, chuckling as I ran after him.

Chapter Sixteen

After Coco gave us three whole boxes full of delicious pastries, we all gathered back into the car. This time, I was in the back with Sebastian. I was slowly nibbling on a cherry macaron as we pulled up to Daniels's home. It was an A-frame cabin located near the base of a mountain, with huge redwoods and pines soaring into the sky like giants. Their dark green leaves fell in slow lazy patterns, covering the floor in a multitude of colors and pine. It even smelled like Daniels: woodsy, outdoorsy, with a hint of fresh air.

The house was perfect for privacy, but I could see how uneasy Daniels may have felt with no one to hear anything in the middle of the woods. I felt the pull of the protective wards before we even stopped the car.

As we stepped out, I said to the guys, "There is a protection spell around the house. We will need to break it before we enter." I walked up the steps to the large wooden door with a coven's symbol carved into it. Seared into the doors by a witch's fire was an infinity cross with a rose sitting in the center with sharp thorns. The eternal glow from the fire burned bright. I always loved our symbol of the coven; it was beautiful and dangerous.

I smiled sadly. Of course, this home was Daniels's. It wasn't as big as the estate, but it was big enough. He could have a few people from our coven for meetings or even a family to stay. It was a dark chestnut color with a black roof and ironwork to create the windows and trim around the door.

"Since Daniels is dead, we should be able to break it quickly. Go on, Princess, show us what you got," Bash said in a low voice. He placed his hand on my back, guiding me to the door.

I blew out a breath and put my hand on the door, feeling the warmth of the wood from the eternal flame.

Then I closed my eyes, opening myself up to the magic as I felt a sizzle go up my spine. As my magic mixed with Daniels's, I whispered the words he taught me, "Ouvres-vous et dévoilez-vous." I felt the drop of Daniels's magic go, and I knew I had broken the wards down. I turned and looked at Bash with a cocky smile on my lips. "Easy-peasy."

Bash chuckled. "Here. I don't feel comfortable opening the door, Princess, and I have a feeling Daniels would have only wanted you to do it." He placed a gold skeleton key in my hand. I put it in the lock, and it turned with a click.

I pushed the door open, and the smell of cigars, pine, and whiskey hit me. It was so familiar to me that my eyes filled with unshed tears. I took a deep breath as I stepped through the door, the spell dissipating as soon as I entered. I swallowed hard as I held my tears back. I didn't need to cry, I needed to find a clue that could lead us to Daniels's killer. The small living room had a leather couch with soft blankets resting over the edge and two wooden club chairs in a soft rustic brown with burnt orange pillows. An iron table sat in the center with a hand-carved wooden top.

I knew Daniels took great care to make this home his. I ran my hands along the entry table that he'd built himself. I had seen him work on it in the yard at the estate a few times. It made me miss him, but I found it comforting in every aspect, too. The wood felt as solid and strong as he was. And, just like the rest of us, it held imperfections in its beauty.

I shook myself out of my thoughts and turned to Bash. "Let's check upstairs. I know he has an office up there." I walked to the circular black iron staircase that led to a small library with a dark green desk covered in papers.

I didn't need to see if the boys followed me; I felt them. It wasn't a power, per se, but, being a siren, I had more of an awareness of someone's personality. Bash was deep, dark, and serious, but had a lightness to him. Tristian was energy and brightness, like the first day of summer, full of excitement and joy. Aden was like your favorite sweater that you wear on a rainy day: calming, understanding, and comfortable.

Aden came next to me and smiled. "This place is amazing, Lex. Look!" He pointed to the collage of photos on

the wall. I stepped closer and noticed every photo had me, Coco, or Jason in them. A few showed my parents when they were young. In one photo, Daniels had an arm around my dad's shoulder, and my mom was clasping Daniels's arm and smiling into the camera.

"I have never seen these." I smiled sadly, running my fingers over the glass.

Bash brushed my shoulder. "He loved you, Lexi. Your entire family was his, wasn't it?"

I nodded, holding tears back. "He was always there at the house. He and my dad were like brothers, similar to you three." I sniffled. "Okay, let's focus. I already broke my promise not to cry." I wiped my cheek, finding it wet from an escaped tear.

Bash placed a hand on my shoulder, giving a light squeeze. "Lexi, it's okay to grieve for him."

I turned to him. "We need to focus on finding out who killed him first. Once we do that, I will be able to grieve for him. I don't want his death to be in vain."

He just nodded solemnly. "Then that's what we do, Princess." He walked over to a desk to look through papers. Tristian was working through the filing cabinet, and Aden was looking through the computer.

"Aden... did you already hack into his computer?" I said, giving him a confused look.

Aden simply shrugged. "Wasn't too hard to figure out his password; it was your birthday and your parents' names." He continued to click and type before pulling out a small adaptor and plugging it in. I walked over to see what he found. He looked up at me, smirking. "I am pulling all the

data and virtually uploading it to my computer. Then I will wipe the computer clean so no one else can get anything off it. I don't want this falling into the hands of humans or for The Wishmaker to find it."

"Don't you think The Wishmaker would have looked through this after he killed him?" I asked.

"Not likely," Bash said from the small loveseat. He lifted a few papers toward me while continuing to look through a stack of paperwork. "Nothing looks like it was moved. Most likely, The Wishmaker killed him in haste. I think it was unplanned. He must have found something here that made it necessary. He was in a hurry, which made him sloppy, so we will find something."

I pushed my tongue to my cheek. "Bash, it is scary that you know that from just looking around."

He shrugged. "It's one of my many talents." His eyes gleamed wickedly as he stared at me. I ignored him and headed over to the bookshelf, examining the many books he had, all organized from fiction works like Faulkner to Sylvia Plath, even a modern vampire book sat on the shelf. I picked it up and tossed it at Tristian. "Need a bit of light reading?"

Tristian looked at the book and rolled his eyes. "Really? Damn humans," he muttered.

I laughed at my joke. "Aww, come on! They have some things right. You do drink blood."

Tristian looked up at me with a deadpan stare. "Lil' Star, do I need to demonstrate what they have correct and what they have wrong? Would you like me to eat garlic, stick my hand in holy water, or bite you to see if you turn?"

I held up my hands in surrender. "It's just a joke. Don't

get your panties in a wad."

I heard Aden chuckle, and Bash couldn't hide his smile. "Trist gets a bit irritated about the whole human-vampire thing. Don't get him started or we'll be listening to it for the rest of the week."

I pushed my lips together, trying not to laugh. "Okay, sorry I brought it up."

I moved back to the bookshelf, running my fingers over the countless aged spines. The leather binding guided me, and then I noticed his collection of botanist books, some going back to the early 1700s. That was when I noticed a dark green leather-bound book with intricate lines in gold and a lock that looked like it was made of thorns. I sank to the floor and slowly rested it on my knees, careful not to cut myself.

"The Lost Magic of Botany," I read aloud in a whisper. It felt warm, almost like I just dipped my hand in a bath. A small humming went through my hands, and the gold lines began to move to create a rose. "Uhh, guys!" They were there in a vamp-speed second as the book began to glow. I looked up at them. "I'm not sure how to open it." Bash took my hand and placed it on the rose, pressing it to the thorns "What are you... OUCH!" The lock clicked open, and I glowered up at Bash. "Why is it always blood with you lot?"

"Blood is a life source, Princess. It is the most precious thing you have. Blood holds power."

The lock crumbled to the ground, and I was able to open the book. Tristian sat down next to me with a first aid kit he must have found, taking my hand and slowly cleaning the blood away and wrapping it up.

I gave him a small smile. "Thanks."

His hand was warm next to mine, and he held it as I opened the cover. The front page had our coven's symbol on it. It was hand-drawn with tiny details that were added over a period of time, judging by the fading in some inks and the different types of ink that were used. When we had more time, I would study it more. I carefully turned the pages, not wanting to rip them. Each page had handwritten spells and drawings—spells from how to make your garden have a fruitful spring to love spells and hexes.

I gasped as I recognized the handwriting, "Holy shit, this is my father's grimoire! I thought this was lost for years, but I remember him showing it to me when I was little."

The guys looked over my shoulder in surprise. "You mean the original Silver Pearl Coven grimoire?" Bash asked, getting a better look at the book in my lap.

"Exactly." I was getting more excited looking at each page when I noticed Daniels's handwriting on the bottom of one of the pages. It was his initials and a simple line of symbols. I didn't know what they meant; they didn't make sense. They almost looked like hieroglyphs. I turned to the back of the book and saw a small bump in the leather. "Wait... Bash, look at this... Aden, can you shine your flashlights closer to the binding of the book?" Aden instantly turned his flashlight from his camera on, and Bash moved closer. "It looks like it's a concealment spell, but it was poorly done. You can see the raised pocket."

Bash ran his fingers over the spot where a small bump was protruding. "It was either done by someone who isn't a witch, or the person was in a rush." I looked up at him. "Possibly the

latter, Princess." My shoulders slumped in disappointment.

I sighed, "How are we going to open it? I don't even know how to undo it."

Bash stood up and offered me his hand. I took it as he pulled me to my feet. Aden and Tristian followed.

"You don't, but it just so happens that I do." Aden and Bash followed Tristian to the desk where he had been sitting with smirks on their faces.

"What am I missing?" I demanded, looking at the guys.

Tristian grinned wolfishly. "Ahh, Lil' Star, I am good at many different things, but breaking concealment spells are my specialty. Blame my pops. He used to conceal the booze from us kids, and I happened to be able to break every single one of his spells," he said with a laugh. Everyone knew that Tristian's father was a powerful witch, and the fact that Tristian could break most of his spells meant he had significant power of his own.

"Sure you aren't a witch, Trist?"

He laughed. "Nah, I'm vamp through and through, but spells are just basic physics and math."

I rolled my eyes. "Tristian, spells are anything but basic."

He smiled at me. "May I?" He reached for the book, which I carefully handed over to him. He took it and sat in the desk chair, spreading the tome out beneath him. He placed his hand gently on the cover, whispering a few words I couldn't make out. A breeze lifted around the book, and a slight sheen of sweat appeared on his brow as he whispered more words forcefully.

All of a sudden, the wind stopped, and he looked up at us with a cocky smile. "Easy-peasy." I returned the gesture

as he turned the book towards me. "Ladies first," he said as he sat back, wiping his brow. I smoothed the page out gently and lifted the slit, pulling out a card that read The Oddity.

Aden looked at the card "Why do I know this name?"

Sebastian growled, "Because we know who owns the bar. That's Trinity Coven's bar, owned by Grayson."

My breath left me for a second. "Shit," I whispered. I walked to the corner window and looked over the forest. "What were you doing, Daniels?" I looked to the ceiling and noticed a cord that was covered by a piece of paneling that went straight into the bookcase. "What the hell?" I went over to the bookcase and followed it down to a set of books about mold and fungus. I tried to pull it, but it was stuck. I yanked harder, and the entire bookcase popped open. Bash was at my back in an instant, and I fell against him, laughing. "Did I just find a secret room?" I grinned. "I always wanted to find a secret room!"

Bash smirked wickedly with excitement. "Yeah, Princess? Well, congrats! It does seem like you did." I started to go in, but Bash grabbed my waist. "For fuck's sake, Princess, let me go first. I don't need you getting impaled. Aden, watch her. When we get in, do not touch a fucking thing. We don't know what's in here yet."

We all walked into a small brick circular room with shelves filled with different glass bottles and a variety of liquids in all different colors. Plants like belladonna, nightshade, witches' hazel, and even mudroot were scattered around the room.

A small lap table sat with different beakers, cucurbits,

microscopes, and instruments like crucibles, flasks, and alembics—even a laptop sat on the edge of the table. A small fireplace was placed in the corner as well.

"Well, this is simply medieval," muttered Tristian.

I rolled my eyes at him. "It's an alchemy workshop, asshat." I looked over Daniels's writings and noticed the words "pixie dust" written in multiple sections of formulas he had been working on, and my heart dropped. "Bash, what does pixie dust do to you?" I asked in a whisper, knowing he could hear.

Bash walked behind me looking over my shoulder, reading the formula. "Pixie dust puts you in a state of intense ecstasy; I hear it's like being the happiest you've ever been but multiplied by ten. What makes it so dangerous is that when you come down from the high, you turn into your worst self. You are angry with everything and everyone and then you sink into a depression so bad that you will not just end up horrifically killing yourself, but you will kill anyone else with you. People have lost their entire family because of this drug. It doesn't just affect one person. It can wipe out an entire coven if we let it."

I felt the tears roll down my cheeks. "I think I found out who created it..." I looked up at Bash.

He shook his head in disbelief. "We don't know that, Lexi." He cupped my face, wiping the tears from my cheeks. "We need more answers, and that half-dragon asshole owes me a few favors. We start with Grayson and then figure out what the fuck is going on." Bash stepped away from us, pulling out his phone and angrily typing a message, which I assumed was to Trinity Coven's leader.

Tristian wrapped his arms around me and rested his chin on my head. He whispered in my ear, "This could mean a million things, Lil' Star; we are pretty close to Grayson's territory, so we will get our answers soon." He kissed my head and walked over to Bash, speaking to him in hushed tones.

Aden pulled me to his side as we headed to the door. "You knew Daniels better than anyone, Lexi. You knew his heart. Do you think that he would do this?"

I shook my head. "No, not without a really good reason. I can't see him creating this."

Aden bent down and kissed my cheeks, then my lips. "Then don't lose faith, Lex. We will find out what Grayson knows first."

I sighed, "Okay, let's go see what secrets he's hiding."

As we all headed back down to the lower level, I ran through the many reasons he would have the formula to such a powerful drug. As I approached the exit, I turned around to look at Daniels's life one more time.

"Goodbye, Daniels," I whispered.

One last tear took my grief into the new stage of acceptance as I closed the door on a chapter of my life I would never get back.

Chapter Seventeen

The car ride to the outskirts of town was quiet. Trinity Coven's territory was located in the valley, the mountains separating them from Providence Village. It was isolated from the city, just like the coven itself. "I'm feeling The Hills Have Eyes vibes," I muttered.

Tristian pulled my hand to his lips and smirked. "Don't worry, Lil' Star, I will protect you from the big, bad dragon." His fangs slid out tauntingly.

I rolled my eyes at him. "Put those things away before you hurt yourself."

The sun slowly sank into the horizon, its orange, pink, and purple disappearing into the abyss of darkness. We turned off the road onto a dirt path that was surrounded by great redwood trees and giant Douglas firs. We were so close to the trees that we could touch them if we put our hands out the window. It was like walking into a long-lost fairy isle; lush green encased us, and we could see a small river become a peaceful waterfall flowing like a blanket of diamonds. Wildlife was everywhere: Birds flew back and forth, and a rabbit family gathered at the base of the trees. It was as magical as the night sky mixed with daylight. I even thought I saw a pair of amber eyes staring back through the thickest brush.

The road began to widen out and soon, we reached a huge, curved gate that had a scene of dragons flying through the air with wolves and hippogriffs running through the woods. Peering closely at the gate, I also saw fairies flying around flowers, gnomes by the huge trees, and even a cyclops peeking out from a tree trunk. "That's beautiful," I said in awe.

Bash huffed, "Grayson is a carpenter, and it was one of the first things he did when he won the leadership of the coven."

"Won? I thought he was voted in?" I asked curiously.

"No, Trinity was run by Grayson's uncle, Hugo. He was a cruel leader and punished men for even small misdemeanors. He hated women and despised children. It's the reason they don't have a lot of families in the coven. Grayson has been working for the past eight years to get more and more fae to come join them, but Hugo had such a bad reputation. People are still nervous around them."

I looked out the window and caught sight of the yellow eyes again. A wolf the size of a small horse appeared out of

the brush near me, and I let out a yelp.

Aden smirked from the driver's seat. "The better to hear you with, my dear."

I glared over him, which made Aden grin from ear to ear. The wolf was a dark grey with streaks of white running along with its fur. It was beautiful and stoic. Then the air shifted and felt thicker as the wolf howled to the night, and a ripple went through its body as a man emerged, very naked, in front of us.

"Grayson," Bash growled.

"Wait, I thought he was a dragon. That was a wolf," I stated.

Tristian laughed. "Oh, yeah, a lot of people don't know that Grayson is a half, just like you, Lil' Star."

I shrugged. "I am just half siren and half witch, and not very good at it."

Bash huffed. "Princess, you have more power in you than you know. You just need training."

I raised my brow at Bash. "Was that a compliment, Sebastian Ryder?"

He chuckled. "Don't get used to it, Princess."

I stared at the very naked man in front of us. Grayson was about six foot four and lean, with wide shoulders, tan skin, dark hair, and a five o'clock shadow. What made him truly beautiful were his grey eyes, which were so light they almost looked white and hypnotic. I tried not to look below his waist, but his V cut dipped so low that I couldn't help but notice, even on a chilly night, that the man had a lot to offer.

"Careful, Princess, you are drooling over the mutt," murmured Aden with a sneer. Grayson had on a seemingly permanent smirk as he strutted to the driver's side window. Aden rolled his window down. "Holsten, you smell like a wet dog."

Grayson smiled and leaned his head into the car before licking up the side of Aden's face and laughing when Aden tried to punch him. He dipped away, howling to the sky. "Welcome, Assholes and Ms. Rose." He bowed his head to me. "Welcome to Trinity Coven. I believe we have a lot to discuss tonight, so if you could kindly make your way inside, we can begin a tour and then go to the meeting." He looked back at Bash. "Your father is already here."

The large gate slowly opened, and we made our way to the house. It was surrounded by huge oak trees with lanterns hanging down from the branches with small lights flickering in and out. I looked closer and noticed it wasn't lights, it was a group of pixies flying around, dancing throughout the branches of the trees.

A willow tree was situated at the edge of a pond, with small wooden houses sitting around the base. A gnome popped its head out and glared at our light as it swept over the rippling water. Sitting back from the grove of trees was what looked like a cottage on steroids. Hell, it was closer to the size of a castle. It was at least four stories tall with dark brick adorning the exterior and a steep roof shooting to the night sky. Trails of smoke came from the four chimneys and colorful ivy climbed the sides, spilling over the balcony and brushing the forest floor below. Many fae of all shapes and sizes laughed, danced, and drank around a large fire pit.

Aden pulled up into the circle driveway where several cars sat. "Goddamn it," growled Bash.

"What's wrong?" I asked in concern.

"Nothing, but Grayson is right. Father is here with his little lemming, Franklin," he sneered.

"That kid gives me the fucking creeps. He's always staring at Ella, and I even caught him once watching from behind a bush while Lexi was swimming at your house years ago," Tristian snarled.

Aden full-on looked like he might gut the poor kid as he caressed his gun in his lap. "If he even looks your way, Lex, I will put a bullet in his head."

"I promise I can take care of myself, guys. A kick to the balls and a grinding stomp in combat boots does wonders on any man, whether they be six foot six or five foot two." I crossed my arms, smirking at them.

All three guys covered themselves, and Tristian looked at me in horror. "You are a monster, Lil' Star! Why, why would you?"

I laughed so loud, a few people on the porch turned their heads to the car. "Well, mess with a siren, and she'll destroy you." I hopped out of the car and walked to the porch, where a group of fae stood.

Aden and Bash quickly caught up with me, and Bash mumbled, "Don't leave our side, Princess. You don't know what kind of monsters are out tonight."

I grinned up at him, batting my eyelashes. "You forget, Bash. I am a monster myself."

Bash stared down at me, his eyes looking like he wanted to say more, but he merely shook his head.

In the doorway, now fully dressed, stood Grayson in dark jeans, a brown jean jacket, and a black Henley underneath. "Grayson is packing." Aden said quietly to Bash.

"How can you tell?" I whispered as we stepped up to the group.

Grayson smiled as he leaned into my space and stage-whispered in my ear, "It's the way I stand, and I assume Vamp Boy saw the heel of my gun." He smiled wolfishly, which made sense, given his breed.

I had only met one half-fae before, and she was half-witch, half-gorgon. I think Mom thought we would be besties, but I couldn't stand her vanity. Then she tried to turn me to stone; she was surprised when this little siren beat the shit out of her pretty face. But with Grayson, I was curious. I tilted my head, trying to get a read on him.

He stared down at me with his steel eyes. "Lexi Rose, why, you are as beautiful as your mother was. I only knew her when I was a pup, but my mom and dad were friendly with her. I do believe they even joked about us being betrothed one day." His voice carried a small southern accent that made him seem like a gentleman, but I saw right through that.

"Sorry to inform you, Holsten, but you couldn't handle me even on your best day." I patted his cheek and walked past him to sit on a porch swing.

Grayson barked out a loud laugh and clapped Bash on the back. "Bash, you have your work cut out, bro! That seductress is going to be a handful."

Bash smirked, and his eyes raked over me in appreciation. "You have no idea, Holsten, but let us get the tour and introductions going so we can get to the meeting. Let's not let the old man wait too long."

Aden had followed me over and held his hand out to help me up. I brushed it away and walked back to the group. "Let's go. Where to first? This place is so big; how are we going to get to everything?" I looked up to the top window, where a

small candle sat.

Grayson puffed his chest out. "Big enough to hold a small village, but I am only going to introduce you to the heads of each group, and they are in the great room behind us. I'll give you the basics and maybe one day when it's not midnight, I can show you more of the Trinity Coven."

He swept his arm out, directing us into the great room of the cabin. About a dozen or so men and women stood around drinking a plethora of drinks, from basic beer to fancy bubbling cocktails.

What was most impressive were the fae themselves. A man by the fire looked over and transformed into a cyclops. He stared at me with interest before returning to the stunning blonde with big blue eyes in front of him. She was wearing a sheer white dress, but what was most stunning were her beautiful green, purple, and yellow fairy wings.

The other girl next to her was so pale her skin was a light shade of blue. She had two horns curling out from her head adored with green leaves. The middle of her forehead had an intricate tattoo that swirled out with a delicate flower in the middle. She had a brush of freckles across her face, and her eyes were solid white. She was horrifically beautiful.

Four people sat at a table playing cards: a very drunk leprechaun with a green hat, a gnome with spiky hair, a sparkly girl with a horn sticking out of her head, and a huge dude with bat wings tucked into his back. He looked as mean as a snake. His head snapped up to me, and he bared his fangs in a hiss.

Grayson jumped up onto the stone coffee table and let out a huge whistle. Everyone stopped what they were do-

ing and looked at him. "Trinity leaders, how are we doing tonight?"

Every creature besides us four let out a huge cry: "Vivre une vie d'amour c'est mourir heureux!"

I repeated in English to the guys, "To live a life of love is to die a happy person."

Bash raised a questioning eyebrow at me.

"Hey, my French is not too shabby, Vamp Boy." I grinned. "Now, let's go meet some fae."

I headed over next to Grayson, and he held a hand out to me. I took it, and he pulled me up to the table. I smiled up at Grayson, thinking maybe I could actually lead a coven... with the help of friendly allies, or who I hoped would be allies. Each fae gave me a token of themselves, which was a tradition amongst the leaders of our coven when a new leader was anointed. A werewolf gave me a moonstone, the unicorns presented a jade scroll to me, and Grayson gave me a small necklace that held dragon fire in the center of it.

After a few hours of chatting and getting to know Trinity Coven, I was exhausted and wanted to get some sleep. I looked around the room, noticing everyone had either gone to bed or were completely drunk. Some were passed out on the couches or curled up in a corner of the room. A six foot five werewolf had his long tongue hanging out of his mouth, making whiny sounds. I placed the throw blanket over him, and he cuddled around it. I laughed silently at him and turned to the boys, who were gathered around an island drinking a beer and talking shit to each other. Bash was even laughing with Grayson. I walked up and grabbed Aden's beer, taking a sip.

"You know you should laugh more, Bash. It suits you." Tristian and Aden smirked at him, and Grayson clapped him on the shoulder.

"I like her. She's got spunk," he slightly slurred. "And you need coffee, and so do I."

I yawned loudly. "Where is it?" He pointed behind him to the most magnificent espresso maker I had ever seen. My eyes widened as a smile spread across my face. "Come to Momma!" I walked over to it and started pressing the espresso down and fiddling with the buttons. Grayson came behind me to show me how to use it. His body felt warm behind mine. I pressed my lips together.

"Thanks," I murmured as I produced a cup for him and one for me. I turned to hand it to him only to see all three guys glaring at me. "What?" I pouted, trying to make myself look as innocent as possible.

Aden growled, "MINE!" He walked up to Grayson with a dangerous-looking knife pulled from God knows where, holding it to Grayson's throat. "Too. Fucking. Close. To. Our. Woman." He enunciated each word. Tristian and Bash did nothing but stand with their arms crossed, glaring at Grayson.

I set my coffee down and placed my hand on his bicep—holy shit it was large—Damnit, focus, Lexi. "Aden..." He glanced down at me and then growled at Grayson's exposed fangs.

Grayson looked smug and drunk, not caring about the danger of three vamps who looked like they were ready to tear him into pieces. He hiccupped and smirked. "My bad, man. Didn't know you owned the seductress. Is it like a three-for-one deal or what?"

All of a sudden, I was yanked back to a hard chest, and Grayson was thrown across the room. Tristian wrapped his arms around me, caging my back to his front.

Bash strode toward Grayson, throwing a punch into his face before he could even get up. Grayson sobered up fast and finally got a few blows back at Bash. They rolled on the ground, cursing each other and hitting each other's stomachs.

Bash managed to slam Grayson to the ground, holding his throat and snarling into his face, "Do not talk about her that way."

Grayson started turning blue, and I was worried Bash wouldn't stop. "Bash!" I yelled, about to step in, but Tristian's hands tightened. "Let him, Lexi. Let him finish this. You know this is the way we do things."

I ground my teeth, knowing it was fae on fae and to interrupt it was more shameful than not to, but I still didn't like them fighting over my feelings. I could handle myself. "Fine." Grayson got a clean hit into Bash's temple, throwing Bash off of him as he gasped for air.

They both stood ready to charge at each other when I noticed Morgan walking in, looking bored. The young, skinny man from Ella's party stood next to him in a dark navy suit. He looked maybe twenty-one with light blond hair and small round eyes behind dark frame glasses. This had to be Franklin Morgan's assistant. He appeared shocked by the two huge men throwing punches at each other. Morgan turned his head and murmured something to Franklin. A smirk formed around the kid's mouth as he closed his eyes and muttered a spell.

A burst of wind picked up both men and began pulling them apart. Black smoke slithered up from Franklin's hands, wrapping itself around Bash's and Grayson's throats, cutting off their air supply. Grayson gasped for air. Bash's lips curled in rage as he glared at his father's face, beginning to turn red, his eyes bulging.

That was when I realized this wasn't the first time he had been spelled before by his father, and that made me furious. As a witch, the number one rule was to never use magic to cause harm unless it was a life-or-death situation. The fact that Morgan used magic as a disciplinary method made my blood boil, and something snapped within me.

"STOP IT!" I felt my power rise to the surface. Scales broke out over my skin, and I raised my hand to Franklin. "VOLER!" Franklin went flying through the air and hit the far wall, hard. Bash and Grayson fell to the ground, and no one made a sound.

The silence was deafening.

I whispered to Tristian, "Check on Grayson." He quickly went to him to check his pulse and gave me a nod that he was okay. I ran to Bash, pulling his head into my lap. I glared at Morgan. "You should be ashamed of yourself. You know better," I hissed at him. Morgan tilted his head as he looked at me with interest.

Aden walked over to Franklin and checked to see if he was alive. "Damn, the fucker is like a cockroach." He grabbed a bottle of water from a table, dumping it onto his head.

Franklin yelped awake and looked at me with fear in his

eyes that quickly changed to a menacing glower. I returned the gesture. "I know you now, Franklin, and I will ruin you if you touch him again." I turned back to Bash, who still hadn't opened his eyes, but I felt his heartbeat underneath my hand. I ran my fingers down his cheek and pushed my power into him, luring him out with my voice. "Sebastian, come back to me," I said softly. It was only meant for him. His eyes slowly opened, and he looked at me with worry.

His hand cupped my cheek. "I'm okay, Princess." But his voice sounded otherwise, scratchy and rough. I nodded, letting him see the anger in my eyes that I felt for his father.

He sat up looking at his father, daring him to challenge him again. Morgan straightened his cuffs and looked at his son. "Now, if we are done, we have a meeting, gentleman," stated Morgan. "Let's get on with it. I have been waiting for hours for you to finish this little gathering." He sounded disgusted with the party.

I glanced over at Grayson, whose eyes were glowing in concern for what just happened.

Then his expression changed, and a nonchalant smile spread across his face. Standing, he dusted off his pants. "This way, Mr. Ryder," he said in his southern twang. He gestured to a wooden door in the corner.

Bash stood up and pulled me with him. I kept my hand in his; his warmth was something I craved, as I was definitely more scared of Morgan Ryder now... and concerned that maybe we just met The Wishmaker himself.

Chapter Eighteen

"Come on, Princess, it will be okay." Bash placed my hand in the crook of his arm. It wasn't something he would normally do, but I had a feeling he was doing it to placate his father. We walked towards the door, which led down a set of stairs to what looked like a very expensive wine cellar.

I noticed the walls were damp and rough. It looked familiar enough. I had seen these rocks growing up here near the woods. "Is this part of the mountain?" I asked Grayson.

"It's the best way to keep wine at the perfect temperature." He gestured to a long oak table. "Leaders, please sit. My second is on his way down."

In the middle of the table were the most incredible-looking wine glasses. They had a silver branch of leaves and flowers wrapping around the stem of the glass up to the clear crystal globe that sparkled in the dim light.

Under the glasses, embedded into the wood, was a carving of all three covens: Pearl, Blood Moon, and Trinity, all meeting in the middle. I took a seat next to Bash, staring at the carving and admiring the intricate workmanship.

I looked over at Grayson. "You did that, didn't you?"

A blush crept onto his cheeks. "I did." He gave me a small smile.

I felt Aden's hand on my shoulder as he stood behind me. Tristian began to pour wine into each of our glasses. The large man from earlier who fell asleep on the couch came down the stairs. He stood behind Grayson silently with his arms crossed over his chest.

"My second in command, Hudson James."

I nodded a greeting to him.

"Shall we start?" Morgan sounded annoyed at the pleasantries. We all agreed as he raised his glass. "To the covens; to honor, to protect, unto death!"

I raised my glass as we repeated the mantra. Then I took a sip of the red wine, and the tangy-sweet liquid slid over my tongue. No one said anything until Morgan finished his sip. He carefully smelled the wine and swirled the glass in a lazy, circular motion. He was so pretentious. Not that I expected anything less from him. I struggled not to roll my eyes.

As Morgan placed his glass down, he looked down at his phone and sighed. "Daniels's death is a tragic loss to us all. The Silver Pearl Coven lost a leader of great potential, and,

of course, we lost a friend, a mentor, and a hell of a witch. Sebastian, where are you with the investigation?"

Bash looked at his father with a face void of emotion. "We went to his home today to see if we could find any clues."

Morgan looked slightly impressed. "What did you find?"

I wasn't sure how much Bash would tell him, but I hoped he would keep a lot of our findings to himself until we knew more from Grayson. I wanted to hold everything close to the chest. "Not much, a bunch of scribbles talking nonsense. From what I gathered, it seemed like Daniels was caught by surprise. We did find a lab that had a possible formula breakdown of pixie dust. I am not sure if he was trying to distribute it or what, but I assume that is what got him killed."

I reached for Bash's hand under the table, squeezing his fingers. He kept his face neutral but wrapped his fingers through mine, his thumb making slow circles around my wrist. I paid close attention to Morgan's emotions and how he reacted to Bash's news. If he was The Wishmaker, we were in trouble because Morgan's emotions were on lockdown. I couldn't get anything from him.

Morgan nodded at Bash. "Very well, and any more notes to our dear Ms. Rose?"

I spoke up, "Yes, we received one this morning. I am not sure what this sicko wants from me, but I am going to enjoy putting his head on a spike." I smiled sweetly.

Morgan's right eye twitched as if he was going to laugh, but he held it in. "So, the pixie dust is the root of this. It seems to be a bigger issue for all of us than we realized. I want each of you to spread the news to your covens. If you catch any of them using, you will be sending them to me, and I will take care of them—full rehab and rehabilitation. Franklin has started a program for fae who are addicted to pixie dust."

Franklin puffed his chest and smirked. "Of course, there will be fines and punishments for using. We do need this drug problem to be kept under control."

Everyone agreed; the rest of the meeting was approving new businesses; Tristian's whiskey bar The Gold Rush was given the final green light, and his speakeasy Belladonna's new secret project was approved. I looked at Tristian, smirking. I would figure out what this secret project was once this whole mess was over. After a few bottles of wine, everyone besides Morgan were a bit looser-lipped. Grayson cracked a joke that even had Franklin laughing.

Finally, Morgan stood up and shook Grayson's hand, then Bash's, and finally mine. "I will say bonne nuit to you all. Franklin let us make haste. Oh, and Grayson? Sebastian?"

Bash and Grayson both looked up at the same time.

"If you ever fight over la douce petite chatte again, I will make sure that young Franklin here doesn't just send les ténèbres as a warning. I will make sure he uses les ténèbres to take your damn soul." He turned and walked out with Franklin at his heels.

I rolled my eyes at his back. "He knows I can speak French, doesn't he?" I glanced over to the guys, and they seemed ashen. Bash looked like he was about to bust a blood vessel. I shifted my gaze to Grayson, who didn't appear much better. "What is 'the darkness'?"

Bash raised both eyebrows "You are a witch, and you don't know about The Darkness?"

I poured another glass of wine because politics made my head hurt. "Don't practice, remember?" I pointed to myself while taking a deep swig of wine.

Grayson smirked at me. "Les ténèbres, or 'The Darkness', is deep black magic. It is pretty much taking parts of yourself and trading it into a dark abyss in exchange for power. The problem is that it destroys your soul and mind, and the magic doesn't last forever, so you have to continue giving yourself to les ténèbres. The black smoke you saw tonight is les ténèbres's fae form. They crave souls to take into the other enfer."

Just as humans had heaven and hell, we had enfers. We had the Light Paradise for when we moved on from this world; then we had the Night Enfer which was for the wicked, sadistic, and amoral fae. Then there was the Other Enfer. The à mi-chemin was an in-between place where souls roamed, lost—not quite alive, not quite dead, just nothing. Basically, the Other Enfer was purgatory.

I was glad I swallowed my wine because if not, I would have spit it all over Bash.

Grayson spoke up, "It's more than that. Les ténèbres controls the à mi-chemin, and to keep the à mi-chemin alive, it needs souls. Eventually, the witch will succumb to the à mi-chemin, and their soul will remain there to roam."

"Moving on to the next thing," said Bash, pulling out the card and slamming it in front of Grayson. "Can you take a gander as to where I found this?"

Grayson lifted an eyebrow, crossing his arms. "I am

guessing it's not from a pixie named Trixie."

I stood and walked over to Grayson. Hudson straightened up and crossed his arms in case he needed to protect his leader. I pointed to the card. "Why would Daniels have this, Grayson? In a secret room that had the chemical compound for pixie dust?"

Grayson sighed and looked up at me with sympathy in his eyes. "If I tell you this, you swear it stays in the room?"

He took my hand in his, and a warm, tingling sensation went through me. When any fae made a promise, we were bound to it until our death.

I nodded. "Deal."

Grayson ran his hands over his face. "What do you know about pixie dust, Lexi?" I repeated what Bash told me, and he nodded. "You know the basics, but what you don't know is that you just don't inhale it like most think. You have to mix it and drink it. You... you have to mix it with mermaid tears to get the high."

My mouth dropped open. "WHAT?! Mermaid tears are sacred. Even using one can cause the mermaid pain physically and mentally and they are never the same again." I gasped in horror. "It's like taking the moon from a wolf or denying blood to a vampire."

Hudson shuttered at the thought. "Or a siren's song, a dragon's wings to fly, or sphinx a... Yeah, it's bad, darling."

He gazed at me with those light eyes, and I saw the pain he held in them. "I lost someone whom I loved to pixie dust. Daniels and I were working on finding an antidote. That was what you saw was his lab. I would procure pixie dust from an anonymous source and then hand it over

to Daniels to analyze so we could find a way to cure the addiction and get rid of this shit, and dammit, he was close." He slammed his hand down, making me jump, and Aden moved closer to me.

Tristian's hand rested on the butt of his gun, and Bash closed in like he would tackle Grayson if he went too far out of control. I shook my head slightly, knowing it wasn't anger; it was grief over the loss of someone he loved.

"Someone found out, and that's what got him killed. Lexi, I think I got him killed." He paced and ran his hands through his hair. "But that's not the biggest issue. Mermaids are now going missing and showing up dead a few weeks later. I know of two mermaids who have already died from pixie dust. More will go missing if we don't stop whoever is doing this. This is going to hit all of our covens soon."

The reality of pixie dust hit me. Kidnapping and killing mermaids, for what? Tears? Two mermaids were dead and more would go missing if we didn't stop this now. Grayson and Hudson were trying to handle it, and so was Daniels, in his own way. Before I had a chance to open my mouth, Grayson held up a hand.

"Look, I'm sorry you didn't know about any of this, but you made it clear as rain you didn't want to be part of any of the covens. I told Daniels you had the right to know, but he was so damn protective of you."

I rubbed my temples in frustration. He was right; I wanted nothing to do with the coven until Daniels's death. "I understand, but do not ever keep something like this from me again, Grayson. You should have told at least the covens' leaders." He nodded, opening his mouth. I held up my hand to stop him. "I am not done. Let me finish, please," I said, this time softer, trying not to sound harsh. "I know what I said to Daniels years ago, and the truth of the matter is, I wasn't ready to come into a leadership role for the covens, but I am here now, ready to take my throne. I cannot do this alone. We all need to work together to find the antidote and whoever The Wishmaker is. We will see an end to this, I promise you."

Grayson's eyes held a look of determination in them. "Well then, seductress, let us begin."

CHAPTER NINETEEN

Bash rose to his feet and held out his hand. "We will help, too, but not tonight. It is almost three in the morning. We need to get back."

Grayson bowed his head and kissed my hand. "We will meet again soon, Ms. Rose."

Bash glared at him, and Tristian whispered, "Motherfucker!" under his breath. Aden guided me through the living room where fae were still passed out.

The cold night air hit my face as we walked under an inky black sky that had tiny diamonds twinkling and winking at me. I leaned my head back, looking at the shimmering night. "Beautiful," I sighed as Aden wrapped his fingers around mine.

"Yeah..." he murmured. I grinned at him, but he wasn't looking at the sky; no, his gaze was on me.

I tightened my grip on his hand. "I want to keep these small moments with you, Aden. Sometimes they are the only thing that gets me through the day."

He gave me a half-smile. "Always."

I looked back and saw my guys walking towards me with Hudson and Grayson stopping at the door. I waved goodbye to them and yelled, "We'll talk soon!" He nodded and gave a small wave as he and Hudson headed back into the cabin.

Tristian came up beside Bash. "Well, I think I can say more shit has officially hit the fan."

Bash scoffed. "Yeah, I think our problem just grew exponentially, and I don't trust that fucking dragon/wolf."

I rolled my eyes at him as I climbed in the car. "No one does, genius."

Bash climbed in the backseat, hanging up his cell and sliding next to me. He sighed with relief and exhaustion. "Let's get back home. We will fix it tomorrow." He looked wrecked.

I threaded my fingers through his and rested my head on his shoulder. "Let's fix it tomorrow," I repeated, smiling faintly.

Bash smirked at me. "Thanks, Princess."

I snuggled closer to him as his arm went around me. I needed him right now. The anger I had felt before was beginning to dissolve. Over the last few days, he had been there for me in every possible way I needed. I wondered if he could give me just thirty more minutes... "Can we get burgers at least before heading back?"

Aden laughed. "And milkshakes?"

Bash rubbed his face in exhaustion. "Sure." He tilted his head back and closed his eyes as Tristian started to sing "Milkshake" by Kelis.

I giggled and closed my eyes as the night finally sunk into me and I felt how exhausted I was. "I'm just going to rest my eyes for a second." I didn't hear what anyone said as I drifted off to sleep.

In my dreams, I stood in an old factory. The atmosphere was sterile and cold. I watched tiny bottles being filled by men and women in dark glasses and masks. The glittery substance sparkled in the pale moonlight. A figure in a dark hood took one of the bottles, examined the substance, then walked over to an empty space where cages hung from the ceiling. The figure looked up and raised his hand as a cage was lowered.

A girl was curled in on herself. She was completely naked, shivering and whispering, "No, please, no! Please... you can't." The figure cast a spell and les ténèbres snaked out, catching her arms and legs, sitting her up.

The black smoke caught the back of her head, holding her still as the hooded figure spoke in a soft, gravelly voice that was neither male nor female. "Thank you. You will make our world safe again. You are the cure."

A single tear ran down her cheek. As the figure caught it with the bottle, the substance sizzled and turned a bright shimmery green. The figure turned to look right through me. "It is done."

I jolted awake with a gasp.

I was curled up around Bash. I nuzzled my head into his chest, wanting to sleep more. His soft breathing let me know he was asleep too. I opened one eye and saw Aden looking back at me. His eyes were narrowed in concern, his gaze hard on me and Bash. "You okay?" he asked.

I nodded to him. "Bad dream." I gently pulled away from Bash, then stretched and yawned.

"We got food," announced Tristian, holding up a greasy bag of deliciousness. The smell of freshly cooked fries drifted in, and my stomach let out the loudest rumble. Tristian chuckled. "Aden is finding a spot up on the hill so we can get out to eat and let Bash sleep."

Even asleep, Bash looked concerned; a slight frown rested on his lips. I looked out the window and noticed we were far up the mountain with nothing but the night sky over our heads. Shiny stars winked at me from above and tiny dots below set a glow across the city.

Aden pulled off the side of the road. We bumped along as he made his way into a huge opening. He parked, and both he and Tristian got out, pulling open the trunk. Tristian grabbed a big blanket as Aden opened my door. I looked at him with a question in my eyes, and he held his finger to his mouth, shushing me so I didn't wake up Bash. I took his hand, and his warm fingers intertwined with mine. Tristian laid out a blanket and as we settled split the burgers and fries between us.

I teased. "Are you guys wooing me?"

Aden smirked as he wrapped his arm around me. "Nah, this is normal for us... When you cause as much death and

chaos as we do, sometimes this is the only place you can find peace."

I knew Morgan had been using them as enforcers for years, and they had killed before, but I never thought of how much that weighed on them. I sat between them as a frown formed on my face.

"Hey, Lil' Star. It's okay. We knew what we were getting into a long time ago, and in the end, it keeps all of the covens safe. You have to have some sort of rule, or it would turn into the apocalypse." Tristian's smile didn't quite reach his eyes as he said his words to me, so I reached out and squeezed his hand.

"Just don't lose yourself to it, Tristian."

He shook his head and laughed. "Damn, Lil' Star, I think I just fell hard for you."

I laughed as I sipped my lemonade and opened my burger, taking a huge bite and humming with delight as the mixture of meat and heavenly cheesy goodness exploded in my mouth. Aden and Tristian were still as statues, looking at me with hunger in their eyes. Tristian licked his lips, and Aden looked at me like I was his prey.

"What?" I asked innocently. "I like burgers. Are you surprised?"

Tristian laughed. "No, Lil' Star, I'm not, but if you make that noise again, I will show you how much I enjoyed it." I looked down and saw him adjusting his pants. I blushed and grabbed a few fries, popping them in my mouth.

"No, I need food. Don't get any ideas until I get fed." I glared at each of them.

"Who are you saying that to, Lex?" Aden asked as he bit

into his burger, I noticed it was a veggie burger. Some things never change. Aden had been a vegetarian since he was ten. He watched a documentary on the cruelty of animals, and he could never eat meat again. Of course, humans and other fae were a different story. He said blood didn't count. To each their own, I guess. I personally loved a good burger.

I swallowed my bite and took a long sip from my cup, waving my hand at them in dismissal. "I don't know. To both of you, I guess…" I continued to snack on my fries as I looked at the tiny lights of the city below. "Do you think they have any idea how much danger is around them all the time?"

Tristian scooted closer so our shoulders touched, and Aden leaned back, crossing his arms behind his head and looking up at the sky. "No, Lex, I don't think humans do. They see us as the stories they have heard of for hundreds of years. To most of them, we are similar to celebrities. Most humans don't see the danger in us." He smirked with his fangs out.

"It's hard to take you seriously with a big glob of ketchup on your face." I laughed as he wiped his chin clean, glaring at me. I finished my drink and laid back into the crook of his arm. We all sat in silence as we gazed peacefully at the stars. Tristian pointed out all the constellations he knew, from Cetus to Vela, and explained what they meant.

After a while, I heard Tristian's breathing slow and sat up, finding him asleep with an arm over his eyes.

"He's out, isn't he?" Aden glanced at me, and I nodded. He stood, pulling me to my feet. "Can I show you something?"

I looked at him and then to the woods behind me. "You gonna take me into the woods and kill me?" I joked.

"You are always safe with me, Lex."

I felt my heart begin to beat faster as he held out his hand for me to take. I clasped his hand as he led me across the road to a clearing where a group of trees shot to the night sky like giants. We walked into the forest where green leaves fell to the ground and moss grew in a bright green along the tree trunks. The rustling of leaves stopped as whatever was walking around fell silent. The deeper we walked into the woods, the quieter the world became. The overwhelming smell of fresh flowers hit my nose, and the air around me became crisp and cold.

I crossed my arms over myself as the cold seeped deeper into me. The shadows of the brush and ferns became larger and sharper. Every little sound of a cracking twig or a whispering of the wind made me jump. Being a siren, the further I was away from the water, the more anxiety I felt. So, when I reached for Aden's hand, his warmth made me feel safe.

"Aden?" I asked in a shaky voice. "Are we almost there?"

He wrapped his arm around me, pulling me close to him. "Yep, it's right around the corner." We turned as he pointed to a small pond in the distance. It was surrounded by an array of birch trees, pine, and hemlock. Large boulders sat by the pond, creating the perfect spot to sit or to slide into the glowing water below that glittered underneath the moonlight. It looked otherworldly. Three small waterfalls fell into the pond, creating dazzling ripples. Warm steam billowed up, surrounding the edges of the water.

"It's a hot spring that the water witches created over a hundred years ago. Humans can't find this, and anyone who isn't fae will become lost. This is just for us, Lexi. It's something we have as our own that no one can take away," he whispered in my ear.

I smiled as I climbed up to the boulder sitting at the edge of the pond. I took my shoes off and sank my feet into the warm water. Aden pulled his shirt and pants off so fast I let out a laugh.

"What the hell are you doing?"

He smirked. "Not just me. Both of us are getting in."

I laughed as he jumped into the pond. "Damn vampire, I swear if you start to sparkle..." He splashed me as I pulled my top off and worked on peeling the leather pants down. "Hey!" I put my hands on my hips. "Listen, vamp boy, I will drown you if you aren't careful."

I was down to my black lacy underwear and bra. I waded into the pond. As a siren, I had control over my magic. I could transform if I wanted to, but I knew tonight was not about flexing my magic. It was about something more. The warm water soothed my muscles, and I sank underneath. Aden swam over to me.

"Aden?"

He gripped my waist. "Hmm?" His head resting against mine.

"You're naked." He lifted me by my ass, pulling me closer. I wrapped my legs around his waist as he wrapped his arms around me.

"That I am," he sighed. "Lexi, I was so angry earlier today with Grayson. If Bash didn't beat the shit out of him, I was going to. You are ours." He growled and pushed his hardness into me to let me know how much he wanted me.

I pulled back and shook my head at him. "Aden, you three can't just claim me like a trophy. I am not a prize to be won."

Aden looked at me. "But aren't you? I don't mean to be misogynistic or a dick, but Lexi, you are one of the most powerful faes that we know of. The fact you don't see that is astonishing. The need for us to protect what is ours overcomes us. That is what makes the three of us so drawn to you. It's not just from your power, but it's as if we are connected by something greater. Like we are meant to be together."

I shook my head. "I am not the same girl you knew. I am not some weak girl who needs three knights in shining armor to rescue her."

I pushed away from him, heading to where our clothes were. I felt Aden wrap his arms around me, pulling me back to him, my back to his chest. "I think I am realizing that now, Lex, and I can't apologize enough. We fucked up, baby, but I still want you as much as I did back when we were kids. Even more now. A part of that is the power you hold, but the other part is because I love this new person you have become." His fingers glided across my arms as he laid a gentle kiss on my neck. "The question is, Lexi, do you trust the devil within me?"

CHAPTER TWENTY

His words sunk their way into my heart. The sweetness behind them had me turning into his arms, wrapping my arms around his neck. Could I trust and forgive all three of them? That was the million-dollar question. At this moment in time, I wanted to. I didn't think I had wanted anything more in my life, but I knew I would always have a tinge of caution towards each of the Devils.

Instead of focusing on the hate and revenge that lived in my heart, I decided to embrace the need I had for Aden. "It's not that simple, Aden, but for now I will do what I've wanted to do since Ella's engagement."

I pressed my lips to his, and a growl escaped as he claimed my mouth with his tongue. He stroked and teased my lips with his nipping. Our kiss became more intense, as if every moment, every thought we had towards each other finally imploded. His fingers ran up to my sides and over my stomach as I panted and pushed myself into him.

I pulled back and reached between us, running my fingers over the silky tip of his dick. I felt the cold steel of a piercing running through the end of him. "You have a Prince Albert," I gasped.

He let a masculine chuckle out, "Reverse Prince Albert, baby." He pushed himself more into my hand, and I let a breathless moan out. "Lexi," he breathed out.

He moved his fingers to the top of my underwear, pushing them to the side, caressing me slowly with purpose. I moaned as we moved back onto the boulder. Each stroke led me to panting his name as he began to play with my clit. I leaned my head back as he lifted me out of the water, laying me back on the smooth rock. His fingers working magic as Aden fucked me with his hand. "Fucccckk, Adennn...." I was so close that I opened my eyes. I saw Tristian in the shadows.

I swallowed my scream, my eyes never leaving Tristian's. I opened my mouth to say something, but at that moment Aden lifted my hips. He slowly peeled off my underwear and with a flick of a wrist threw my bra behind us. Aden reached for my breast, teasing my nipples as he trailed kisses down my stomach. "Aden," I whispered his name.

"Yes, Lexi?" He kissed right above my hip, moving his way to my inner thigh.

"Stop teasing me," I begged. My moans became louder as he began to lick me slowly, teasing my clit with his tongue.

He teased me with his fingers, drawing slow circles around my inner thighs, never stopping his tongue from bringing me to the point of explosion. "Aden, don't stop."

His masculine chuckle tickled. "Never, baby. Never." He pushed his finger inside me, making me buck into his hands.

My fingers gripped his hair as he continued to lick me. I turned my head to Tristian, and he was stroking himself, enjoying the show. Our eyes locked in the moment. I felt my body begin to rise in heat and tighten around Aden's fingers. I exploded into a million pieces as I came hard, screaming Aden's name to the stars. I watched as Tristian spilled himself into his hand.

Aden grinned. "Baby, if you come like that every time..." He kissed his way up my body to my lips. "You are unbelievable, baby. You know that, right?" I let a breathy laugh out and looked back, only to meet Tristian eyes.

"Enjoying the show, brother?" Aden asked.

"It's not over yet," replied Tristian, losing his clothes and coming up behind me. "Show him what he's been missing, Lil' Star."

I moved to the soft moss that lay on the boulder. Aden walked out of the pond, laying down next to me. His cock was hard and ready through his boxers, and I moaned, biting my lips as I sat up, leaning over Aden. I let my finger trace down his chest over the shining nipple rings, down to the demon tattoos that swirled across his stomach.

I leaned down, taking his nipple in my mouth and tugging at it lightly. He let out a low growl. "Want me to show you why most fae crave sirens?"

Aden breathed an airy, "Yes."

Tristian ran his fingers through my hair, down my back, slowly teasing me. His rough fingers made me break out into tiny shivers. I felt him move and spread my knees apart and slowly caress down my ass. He leaned back and spread me as he sank two fingers into my slick self.

"Fucccck," I breathed as I pulled Aden out from his boxers and took the head of Aden into my mouth, slowly sucking on the tip and circling my tongue around him. I teased his piercing and stroked him until he was panting my name.

"Fuck. You are a damn good little siren, aren't you, baby?"

I took as much of Aden as I could, moving up and down, cupping his balls in my hand and using my tongue to tease the tip of him. A hand was placed on my head, and I heard Tristian whisper, "Will you let him fuck your face, Lil' Star?"

I nodded and Aden moaned, "I'm not gonna last much longer," as I took him all the way down to the back of my throat hard and fast. Tristan pushed my head down until the only thing I could do was swallow him whole, trying not to gag on him.

"Good. Now it's my turn to taste her," said Tristian as he lifted my ass higher. He licked me from front to back, pushing two fingers into me as his thumb teased my clit. I moaned and continued to suck and tease Aden; as his movements became faster, and so did Tristian's. He moved back to tease my other hole. I gasped as he began teasing around it and pushing his tongue into my tightness as he fucked my pussy with his fingers.

He moved his tongue back to my clit and pushed a finger into my ass. "This will be mine one day, Lil' Star." He continued to pump his fingers inside me, I felt so full.

I felt myself tighten around Tristian's tongue and fingers as Aden spilled himself down my throat. Once I came down from my high, I laid curled next to Aden, catching my breath, and Tristian fell on my lap. "That was amazing, Lil' Star," he said dreamily.

I smiled, running my fingers through his blond hair. The night air was silent as we bathed in bliss. I slowly stroked Tristian's hair as Aden's fingers moved up and down my back.

I heard what sounded like a bird screeching in the wind. "Does anyone hear a honking? Like a goose?" I asked.

Aden and I suddenly sat up quickly, pushing Tristian out of my lap.

"BASH!"

We all quickly dressed, the vampires faster than me, and we raced to the car. Aden and Tristian laughed the whole way. "Don't say a fucking word, asshats!" I hissed back at them when I ran right into a solid wall. I looked up into Bash's deep green eyes.

"Two words, Princess: Vampire. Hearing."

I gaped at Bash in shock, gulping in a deep breath. I should have been ashamed, or guilty, but I wasn't. The way Aden and Tristian opened up to me and shared their deepest secrets with me was more meaningful to me than Bash realized. For the last ten years, I've felt so alone moving through the day-to-day without really having a purpose. Tristian and Aden both saw more to me than just some heir to the coven's throne.

I bit my lip and placed a hand on his chest, leaning in close to him, my eyes boring into his. I licked my bottom lip and smirked. My power flowed through my veins as I opened up the gate, letting my siren song pour out. "Did you want to join us?"

He gripped my arm and pushed me away gently. "Get in the car, Princess."

I turned away and sauntered over to the door, opening it up and looking back at him. "You know, Bash, if you wanted to join, you could have just asked."

He folded his arms as a smile played on his mouth. "Oh yeah, Princess?" His eyes turned completely dark. "What would you do if I did? Would you take us one at a time? Or use all of those sweet little holes on each of us?"

I felt his compulsion trickle along my arm, and I had a sudden vision of Bash underneath me, pounding away as Aden took my ass and Tristian my mouth. I moaned at the vision and used my own gifts to break away. "Fuck you, Sebastian." I got in the car, slamming the door. He may think he won this time, but he was sorely mistaken because this princess wasn't going to play fair anymore. If Bash wanted me, he needed to earn me. I needed him to prove to me he wasn't the same guy who used and humiliated me.

When all three of them returned to the car, Bash pushed his way into the passenger seat. He was fuming. I could swear I saw his fangs biting into his lip. Tristian sat next to me, his hand covering his mouth as a chuckle came out in a hushed whisper. I elbowed him a few times when Bash would look back and glare at him. Aden drove, focused on the road ahead of us as we made our way back to my home.

I would catch him glancing back through the rearview mirror at me, a slight smile across his lips. I rolled my eyes, shaking my head at him. I felt the tension growing with

each one of them the longer we were in the car together. Every time Tristian laughed, Bash would growl, and Aden's hands would tighten at the wheel, his teeth grinding together. Bash caught Aden looking at me and snapped at him.

"EYES. ON. THE. FUCKING. ROAD. ASSHOLE."

I could see that Aden was growing increasingly tense with each minute that ticked on. I frowned at the back of Bash's head. His attitude was beyond extreme if he was this upset about what had happened between the three of us.

I sighed and leaned forwards whispering, "Bash, look...."

He held up a hand and shook his head. "No, Lexi, just don't," he whispered with a hint of sadness sinking into the last of his words.

"Okay, when you are ready, find me." I sat back, giving him the space he asked for. He had to know that I couldn't belong to just one person when all of them meant more to me than they would know. I told him I wouldn't ever pick between the three of them, and I meant it.

As Aden pulled up to my front gates, the lights swept over the road, and my stomach dropped as a large red box with a white bow sat in front of the gate.

"What... the... hell...?"

All eyes snapped to the box and a string of curses left each of their mouths. Aden slammed the brakes and put the car in reverse, driving back down the road, leaving a trail of dirt in his wake.

Bash had his phone up to his ear in an instant. "Ethan, I need to drop Lexi off with you. No, Aden will stay with her. A box was dropped off at the front of the gates and we don't know what the hell is in it." He continued to talk to Ethan as Aden drove so fast, I gripped the handle of the door.

Tristian was typing with the speed of a mongoose on his phone. "Morgan knows, Grayson is aware, and I contacted our explosive expert. He'll be there in fifteen," he said without looking up from his phone.

Suddenly, the reality of what might be in box crept in, and I became scared and aware of what it might be in the box: a bomb.

"Wait!" Every eye in the car snapped to me. "Turn back!"

Bash shook his head "We don't know what's in the box, Lexi. We have to keep you safe first and foremost. You will stay with Ethan and Ella while we work in shifts until we secure your home." Bash was in his boss mode. His voice was calm but held a source of power to it as if his demand could not be denied. If it was a bomb, the only thing that made me scared was a little white fluff that meant more to me than most people.

"DYNA! NO, BASH, GO BACK!" Before I knew what I was doing, I pushed to the front of the car trying to pull the wheel. The fear of losing my little floofy murder paws had my blood running cold.

"Lexi STOP! We can't..." Aden pushed me back, but I held onto his arm as the car jerked to the side.

"Fuck!" Tristian said, grabbing me from my waist back into his lap, his arms in an iron grip to keep me from moving. "She'll be okay, Lil' Star, don't worry. Bash and I will bring her to Ella's, okay?" He spoke in a soft tone to calm me down. I turned to look at his eyes. The fear must have shown, and he took my chin and locked his eyes with me.

"She will be okay, I swear, Lexi."

I nodded, wrapping my arms around myself as he tugged me closer to him, holding me and running his hands up and down my back.

We made it to Ella's and Ethan's condo in ten minutes when it normally took twenty. I didn't want to think about how many laws Aden broke to get us here. The only thing I was focused on was my cat. I prayed she would be okay.

We pulled into the underground garage. Aden parked in an emergency zone and got out with his gun drawn as he walked to Tristian's side to open the door for me. He took hold of my hand as I got out of the car. Bash circled the vehicle and was standing next to me, gun pulled out, ready to use. Tristian flanked us, scanning the garage for anything that was out of the ordinary. Aden pushed me slightly toward the elevator, placing me in the middle, Bash in front, and himself and Tristian to each side of me. Bash quickly punched in the code to the penthouse. We all stood in silence as the elevator crept to the top of the building.

When the doors swished open, I saw two very large men standing next to Ella's door. "I didn't think Ella would have guards, too," I murmured.

"Father didn't want anything to happen to Ella or Ethan, so he assigned all of your family and friends guards," Bash said in a tone that was too neutral to be the truth.

Squinting my eyes at him, I poked his arm. "Your father or you, Bash?" I knew his father didn't care about my family. Ella, yes, he cared for her, but Coco and Jason? He couldn't care less about them.

We walked to the door as Bash knocked. "I might have

suggested it to him the first time we found out about Daniels. Then maybe I had Tristian set up everything," he said with a shrug.

My heart tugged at the act. "You've always made sure I was safe, haven't you?"

He glanced down at me, and I saw a smile form on his lips "Maybe I have kept close eyes on you for a while to make sure you never get hurt again." He looked straight ahead, his eyes focused and a glint of chaos playing behind them. This wasn't Bash, this was Sebastian Ryder. This was who people feared: the bringer of death and destruction.

But he was my protector. He had been my protector for years without me even knowing.

I took his arm, pulling him down to me, lifting on my tiptoes. I laid a gentle kiss on his cheek. "Thank you for keeping me and my family safe."

Bash was controlling, demanding, and more possessive than a leprechaun with gold, but he would always protect our families. He looked down at me, opening his mouth to say something when the door suddenly swung open. Ella and Ethan, who both normally were well put together, appeared to be in disarray. Ella's hair was pulled into a messy bun with her robe tightly wrapped around her, and Ethan's looked as if he was woken out of sleep, his hair shooting in different directions. Ella shoved Bash to the side, grabbing my hand and pulling me into a worried hug I didn't know I needed.

Chapter Twenty-One

I wrapped my arms around her. The comfort of her sweet perfume tickled my nose, a mix of sweet jasmine and citrus that encased me. I finally let all of the tension leave me. Just knowing she was here made my anxiety lessen. I gave her a small smile, pulling back to look at her. "I'm okay, Ella."

Her eyes glistened with unshed tears. She nodded, pulling away and looking over the state of my dress. "Well, you look like shit. Let's get you a shower, comfy pajamas, a bottle of wine, and watch stupid movies until dawn. Maybe you'll pass out?"

I nudged her. "Hey, I looked hot earlier. Ask them!" Humor was my new defense mechanism, apparently.

I waved to the Three Devils standing behind me as I walked to Ella's bathroom.

When I passed Ethan, he stopped me with a hand on my shoulder and smiled down at me gently. "I'm glad you're okay, Lexi."

I grinned at him. He was perfect for Ella in every way. "Thanks, Ethan."

He grinned and whispered in my ear, "Wanna tell me why you smell like my little brother and a blond vampire I know?"

My eyes widened, and I shook my head, saying I didn't want to talk about it.

He smirked. "Hey, not my business, right?"

I patted his shoulder. "I promise to fill you in on it later, but don't tell Ella, not yet."

He grimaced at me. "I don't like keeping things from her, Lexi, so I will give you time. But you should tell her soon. She will be hurt if you don't."

I nodded and went straight back to Ella's all-white bathroom that looked like it came straight out of a magazine. It had a huge walk-in shower, which looked nice, but I dreamily looked over at the new deep jacuzzi bathtub. Oh, yes, that's what I needed. I turned the handles and started to fill it up with warm water and then added a fancy bubble bath to try to help me relax and possibly sleep.

I looked out the small window and noticed the dark sky was getting lighter, knowing that the sun would rise soon. "I'll be quick," I said as I undressed, leaving my damp clothes in the corner.

I stepped into the tub. A small moan escaped my lips

as the warm water lapped over my sore body. I sank into the tub, letting a breath of air out to try and relax. I set my phone to soft music and closed my eyes, trying not to worry about my poor cat and what the hell was in that box. I sank under the water, letting the warmth soak into my skin. The oils from the bath soothed my aching muscles. I leaned my head back and let the music take over my body, beginning to relax a little more the longer I stayed in the tub.

A small knock came from outside, and I opened one eye before the door opened. Bash walked in, taking in the scene of me naked in a bathtub with the tops of my breasts peeking out. I pulled more bubbles around me, trying to cover myself. "Sebastian, this better be good if you are going to interrupt me trying to relax."

He frowned slightly sitting on the edge. "Tristian and I are heading out, but Aden is staying with you. I promise I will bring Dyna back to you."

Worry must have been etched on my face. "Okay."

"I'll be back shortly. I will debrief you once we return."

I opened my eyes, looking up at him. I saw the conflict in his eyes and gripped his hand. "Bash, Thank you."

He nodded and bent down, kissing my lips lightly, taking me by surprise. He murmured against my mouth, "I'm still angry at you, Princess, but we can get into that later. Right now, I am going to go rescue your cat and figure out who the fuck is behind this. Then..." He trailed kisses from my mouth to my ear. "Then I am going to show you how angry I am, and you won't be able to walk the next day when I'm done." His hand slipped into the water, brushing between my thighs. I snapped my legs closed, trapping his hand before he could do anything.

I swallowed hard, calmed my breath, and tried not to lose my grip on his hand. "Just bring me back my cat, and then we can 'fight' later." He chuckled darkly, pulling his hand out and trailing it up over my stomach in between the valley of my breasts and up to my neck, where he wrapped his hand around my throat, squeezing it lightly, bending my head back to look at him. He was so close that our lips were almost touching.

"Using the wrong 'F' word, Princess. Trust me: You'll be in Heaven and Hell at the same time when I'm through with you." He stood and walked out the door, closing it behind him. I groaned, sinking lower into the tub.

That vampire was going to be the death of me.

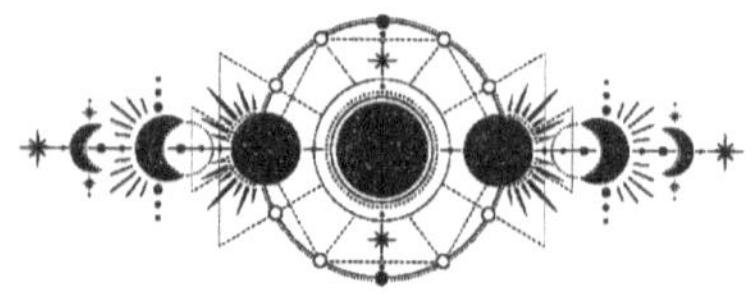

After a longer-than-normal bath, I found a pair of black silk pajamas waiting for me. I made it to the living room, where I found Aden in a pair of Ethan's sleep pants, shirtless, his tattoos and nipple rings shining in dim light. A pair of reading glasses sat upon his face, which made all parts of me shiver in excitement.

I walked over, smiling. I wrapped my arms around him as I looked at the papers spread out. "Any news?"

Aden pulled me onto his lap. "Yeah, it wasn't a bomb,

thankfully, but Bash is still bringing Dyna over and thinks we should leave her here with Ella. She is probably safest here."

I sighed. I didn't want her away from me, but I knew Bash was right. Dyna loved Ella and vice versa, so I knew she would be fine. "I don't love the idea, but I agree." I laid my head on his shoulder.

He looked surprised. "I thought I would have to fight you on that one."

I shrugged. "It makes sense. Where are Ella and Ethan?"

"They both fell asleep while waiting on you. I told them to go to bed and I would watch you." He pulled me close and kissed my head.

"Oh, I wanted to talk to her." I pouted.

"You can talk to me, baby." He slowly ran his fingers up and down my spine.

"It was about personal things that sometimes you just need girlfriends for. It's okay; I will talk to her tomorrow." I kissed his cheek. "I like the glasses, but do you really need them? Aren't vamps supposed to have, like, excellent vision or some bull like that?"

Aden huffed out a laugh. "No, baby, we aren't these indestructible creatures. Yeah, we're hard to kill, but my eyes have always sucked, especially when I am on the computer with the blue light and all that. But it's hella cute that you think that." He kissed the tip of my nose as he held me with one arm, reading over the notes and reports. I slid off his lap and sat next to him, looking over the notes as well, trying to find anything that could lead us to who was stalking me.

Soon, minutes turned into hours, and we had full pages of notes to go over with Bash and Tristian. Aden had a theory that maybe demons were behind it. I thought it could have been a group of humans who were known to hate the fae, but honestly, we had no clue who or what was behind this.

I yawned, stretching and bending back with my arms over my head. My shirt rode up over my stomach, and I let out a soft moan. I opened my eyes and Aden was staring, licking his lips. He reached his hand out and ran the tips of his fingers across my rib cage, sending shivers throughout me.

"No." I pointed at him. "No, focus." I pointed to the paper.

He saluted me with two fingers. "Yes, boss." With that, he went back to reading.

Aden had a map of the city out, with different areas highlighted in colors that matched notes on the side of the map. "Can you explain what we are looking at?" I asked as I stood and started the coffeemaker again, fixing two cups for us.

"This is a timeline from the morning of the engagement party to when Rengard tried to arrest Bash." I filled our cups with the magical goodness that was coffee as he continued to explain the map. "This is what we found in Daniels's lab and his paperwork. I am trying to figure out what he was doing wrong that the antidotes failed. Which ones were not working, and which ones were. The chemicals make sense, and I know he was close. He was really fucking close to solving it."

I handed his coffee over to him as I took a drink from mine. "You think someone found out that he had an antidote or was close to one?"

Aden nodded. "I think that is exactly what he was doing, and I think they killed him so it wouldn't ruin the business."

I took another sip of coffee, thinking through everything.

"Damn it, Daniels, what are we missing?" I whispered to myself. I looked over at Aden. "If Daniels had found out how to make an antidote, he would have hidden it. He would have protected it with everything he had."

Aden's expression turned intrigued. "But where?" He stood and started to pace back and forth. "Okay, we have to think like Daniels. Where was the one place Daniels would have held close to him? Obviously, he couldn't tell you, Coco, or Jason. He wouldn't want someone to hurt you to obtain this information. He knew it was dangerous."

I looked out the window. "He wouldn't want us hurt, but he would want us to find it should anything happen. There has to be a clue here."

Then it hit me.

The book that was hiding the grimoire! It was about botany and planting. Of course, I knew the one place Daniels spent most of his time. No one knew about it besides my family. It was the one place he told me never to go to until I was ready to take over the coven. "Holy shit, I know where the formula is."

Aden looked over to me. "Where?"

"Daniels had to have known that someone could come after him if they found out what he was working on, right?"

"Yeah, he would have."

"And so, he would have hidden it somewhere that no one would have thought of looking for it?" I saw the answer click in his head as he realized where it was hidden. "The conservatory is for basic spells, and upstairs is surrounded by poisonous plants. Our very own security for anyone who doesn't know how to handle them."

He shook his head with a smile. "Brilliant man."

I laughed. "The apothecary table is full of the rarest plants around the world. What if he has hidden the antidote in the table?"

Aden's eyes sparkled with excitement, and a grin spread across his face. "Well, aren't you a little Nancy Drew? Baby, I think you might be onto something."

The front door opened as Tristian and Bash walked in, looking grim. Bash was carrying a bright pink carrier and a duffle over his shoulder.

"Your damn cat clawed the shit out of us when we tried to get her in the damn carrier," he grumbled, sitting her down on the couch next to me. "I almost lost an eye because of that fluff of a demon with murder paws!"

I rolled my eyes. "You have to trick her with treats. Every cat owner knows that." He huffed and stomped out of the room. I laughed. "You'd think a big bad vampire who is nicknamed 'The Devil' could handle a little fluff ball." I opened the carrier, and Dyna came out, slowly looking around and then up at me with a question in her eyes. "We gotta stay here for a little bit." I kissed her furry head and wrapped her into my arms, kissing her and petting her soft white fur. Her purrs started immediately. "I missed you too, baby fluff," I cooed.

Tristian cleared his throat, eyeing Dyna from a safe distance. I saw that his arms were, in fact, scratched up. "We have good news and bad news; what do you want first?" He sat in an armchair near a fireplace far away from me and the cat.

Bash walked back in with low-slung black joggers and

his chest bare, looking like sin itself. Bash sat on a loveseat, spreading out and looking at the papers dispersed about the coffee table. They both looked exhausted, and I knew I did as well. I was ready for this night to be done.

"Just tell me the bad, then the good. Then you two need to shower and we all need sleep." Bash pulled a linen envelope from his back pocket and handed it over to me, not saying anything.

The envelope was black again with the same red seal. I shuddered, knowing it was from The Wishmaker. I took the heavy envelope and opened it, pulling out a thick piece of paper addressed to me. A small UBC drive fell out onto my lap. Aden snatched it up and was pushing it into his laptop before I said anything.

A grainy film showed up. I couldn't place it until I noticed the trees, the rocks, the pond, and Aden kissing me. "Son of a bitch." Aden whispered.

"That's not...."

"It is, Princess," Bash grumbled, glaring at Tristian and Aden. Tristian smirked as his eyes stayed on the screen, watching Aden place me on the rock and spread my legs, catching Tristian behind us with his cock out, running his hands up and down his shaft. My eyes widened when I saw myself come the first time from Aden's tongue, then when Tristian walked over, I knew I had seen enough. I turned it off with a click.

"Okay, okay, we know what happened, so please continue...." I waved my hand for them to move along. I felt violated. I knew my Devils would deliver his head to me when we found out who he was.

"Well, it was only us three, Lil' Star, but now Bashy-boy here knows exactly what happened." Tristian chuckled, smirking at Bash. "If you got off your high horse maybe it could have been you, frere."

Bash growled at him. "Let's see how you feel after I destroy that pretty face, Trist." His fists clenched, making his knuckles turn white.

"Okay, no fighting! Let's continue. Sebastian, what else did you find?"

Bash took a deep breath. "You should read the letter." He shook his head, his expression darkening. "We also found one of our guard's heads in the box." He ran his hands uneasily through his hair. "Lexi, the guy had a family and was just doing his job. Now we have two murders, and we don't know how many more will happen." He looked lost, like he wasn't quite sure how we would be able to protect our covens.

"Four. We have four murders now, Bash. The guard, Daniels, and my parents." I walked over to him, taking his hand in mine and pulling him slowly onto the loveseat with me. I laid my head onto his shoulder.

"We will find out who is behind this and when we do, we will make them pay for their crimes." He nodded to me, lacing his fingers through mine. He brought our hands to his mouth and kissed the back of mine, a gesture he used to do when we were younger.

I suddenly felt the pain of his betrayal all over again. I pulled my hand away from him, and hurt reached his eyes.

I noticed the dark circles on his pale skin. "Bash, when was the last time you slept?"

He looked up, confused, and shook his head. "I dunno, a day or two ago... The days are kinda blended now."

I pushed my pain aside for the moment. I could go back to hating him tomorrow. "I'm going to help you sleep, okay?" He nodded, and I felt my compulsion sweep over my skin onto his. I pushed it into him as I felt it fall away from my own body. My vision blurred for a second, almost like a silent release. I opened my eyes to see his shoulders relax and his arms becoming heavy at his sides.

He tried to fight it off because he was Bash and also one of the strongest vampires in his coven; he didn't let magic overcome him easily. With as little energy as he had and without blood for days, it wasn't hard to break through his blockade of emotions. He had so many emotions that surfaced at that moment. I could read them like a book. Excitement for the fight, sorrow for those we lost, anger for not knowing who did it, and loneliness sat at the heart of it all. He had happiness too, that I was close to him again.

I took all of those emotions and pushed him into a deep sleep. He immediately went into a tranquil state, slumping back onto the couch, his eyes closing. I pushed peaceful dreams into his mind as he shifted to lay on his back. I curled up onto him, my head on his chest. Let him dream of peaceful days and wild nights. This man needed his heart to be filled with more than the coldness, darkness, and heaviness he carried for so long. I was more than happy to give him a bit of peace.

When his breaths were deep and steady, I moved off of him, looking at Aden and Tristian. They both seemed like they were about to pass out, too. I smirked. "Did I leak my power onto you two as well?" At this, they softly chuckled.

"Yeah, Lil' Star, you did." Tristian stood, wobbling a little to get his balance, turning to me. "Morgan gave us a day off tomorrow, so when we wake, we will head back to the house. But for now, I am getting a shower in. As much as I love the scent of you on me, Lil' Star, I have to get all this blood off me."

I scrunched up my nose with disgust. "No offense, but please shower, both of you. I will just sit with Bash."

Both nodded, and Aden stood with a stretch, kissing my head before he headed to the door "Goodnight, baby; dream of me."

I rolled my eyes and smirked. "Asshat, go." I curled up next to Bash as his soft snores echoed through the room. The letter sat on the table, taunting me with its flourished lettering shining up at me. The dread of reading it created a knot in my stomach. "Screw it," I whispered, and opened it up. The first thing I saw was my sick nickname in dark red ink.

My Beautiful Rose,

Do you like my gift?

You disobeyed me, but I am a forgiving soul. It's not their fault you let your guard down.

I know you need to be reminded: You are mine, forever.

I saw you with two of those demons. My love, do you not feel them feasting on your soul? They will burn you to ash. They tried before, and they will do it again.

You keep forgetting who you are. You keep forgetting what they've done to you. You keep forgetting everything I've done for you.

So, I will keep reminding you with more gifts. I will keep reminding you of my love, my protection, and my strength. I will lay your enemies to waste, even if you still don't see them for what they are.

It is not yet time for us to meet, so I will say this once, Lexi Rose: Stop digging into places you have no business going. Trust me to take care of you. Trust me to make all your dreams, all your wishes, come true. Remember this, and I won't need to send you so many reminders.

I will never hurt you. But I will take you in hand if I must.

Even if that means taking someone you love away from you until you learn.

Ella, Ethan, Coco, or Jason...?

I wonder who it will be?

Until next time, my Lovely Rose. I will keep a watchful eye over you.

XX
Wishmaker

He had eyes on me everywhere. He knew what we were doing even before we did. We needed to figure out how.

But first, we needed to figure out what his agenda was. Why my family? What did we have that he needed?

I am not sure how long I stared at the letter; it could have been two minutes, it could have been two hours. I pinched the spot in between my eyes to think of anything else as the sun rays slowly spilled through the room. My muscles were sore; I felt so fatigued from everything.

I made my way to my bedroom to find both guys passed out. I climbed onto the middle of the bed, snuggling up against Tristian's chest. He smelled of soap and pine. I felt an arm wrap around me as Aden, my dark knight, curled against me. He nuzzled my neck, letting out a deep sigh.

I knew I felt safe with the three sleeping Devils in my midst.

Chapter Twenty-Two

When I awoke, alone, I knew it was late because the sun was high in the sky, shining through my window.

Voices carried in from the next room. "Ella, you need to listen to what Bash is saying. He is trying to protect you, Love." Ethan's pleading voice held a shaky panic to it.

I snuck out of the room to stand in the hallway and saw Ella and Ethan in the kitchen with Bash. The siblings faced off, both with arms crossed and a look of determination on their faces.

"No, Ethan! Look, Bash, I appreciate the protection, but you already have two guards here and one following me all the time. I do not want to be a prisoner in my own home!

I need to be able to go to work. I have not one but three charity events I have to organize and throw for the orphanage. I also have the fae events for the covens, the ritual for the Blood Moon Coven, that you hired me to do, and a wedding to plan!" Ella shrieked at him.

Ella loved her job; she had the energy for it, and no one else could keep up with her. She was always working for a cause, not only for the humans but for the covens as well. She organized almost all of our social events, so to just get ripped away from everything she loved was going to destroy her.

I knew the magnitude of the destruction if Bash put her under house arrest, but at the same time, I understood where Bash was coming from. The Wishmaker said he would come after my friends and family if I didn't stop our investigation. Of course, we weren't going to stop. We needed to play this carefully, though, and I needed to make sure our friends and families stayed safe.

I walked back into my room, grabbed a robe, wrapped it around myself, and headed into the kitchen to pour a cup of coffee. All eyes were on me as I took a sip and smiled sadly at Ella. "Ella..."

She looked at me, her baby blue eyes on the verge of tears. I couldn't keep this from her. She needed to know the truth. I looked over at Bash, who was staring down at the counter, his brows furrowed.

"Did you tell her everything, Bash?" I asked.

His eyes snapped to me, and his anger radiated off of him in hot waves. "I told her enough," he seethed.

I held up a hand, not wanting to fight with him. "She's

not a child anymore, Bash, or did you forget she is the same age as me?" He continued to glare at me. "Tell. Her. Everything," I said sternly.

Ella looked between us, confused. Then her eyes landed on her older brother, and the look she gave me scared me. "Sebastian Ryder, if you do not tell me this instant what the hell is going on, I will rip your nipples off and feed them to the birds."

I snorted into my coffee to cover up my laugh. It was a weird threat, but that's Ella; she didn't really threaten people.

Bash glared at me. "Fine," he hissed. "Let's go to Coco's to get food and coffee and I will tell you then." He stomped out of the kitchen and headed to the guest rooms to change.

Ella looked at me with tears pooling in her eyes. "It's bad, isn't it?"

I set my coffee down and rushed over to her. I hugged her close and whispered, "It isn't great, but just know that if I didn't have you, I wouldn't have made it; your friendship through the years has changed things for the better. Blood isn't always family; sometimes you forge your own. And Ella, you are my family. Never forget that, okay?" My own eyes mirrored her tears.

She nodded, finally understanding the severity of our problem. "Okay, I promise. I love you, Lex."

I smiled, wiping away a tear. "And I love you, Ell."

Bash came out in jeans and a black shirt, his hair slicked back with a pair of sunglasses on his head. "Ready?"

She silently headed to the door with Sebastian at her back; he looked back at me, and I gave him a little wave and mouthed, "Good luck." He gave me a small smile and followed her out onto the porch. I knew he had heard our conversation. I could only hope he understood that this was the right thing to do.

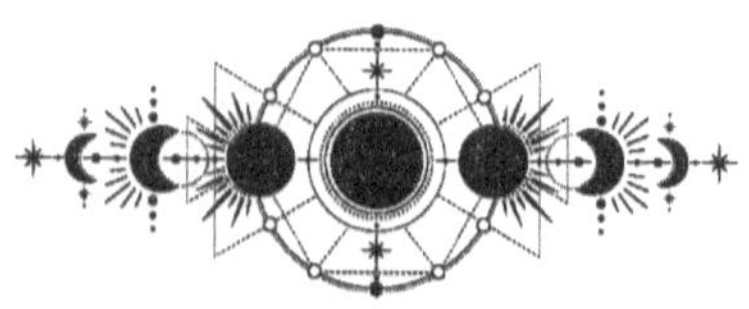

Bash must have been telling Ella everything from the past decade because Tristian got a late afternoon text from him to head back to my house and to wait for him there. I borrowed a pair of flip-flops, leggings, and a sweatshirt from Ella that said, "Live like there is no midnight." I was heading to the living room when I heard Ethan and Aden talking on the sofa.

I froze when I heard Ethan ask: "Petit frere, tell me what's going on with you two?"

Aden shrugged. "Lex and I have always had a connection beyond what words can say; she's like the light in my darkness, frere. I forgot how much joy she brought into my life, not just as a friend. She makes all of this seem okay. She makes me stronger."

Ethan clapped Aden's shoulder "You got it bad. I know that feeling well. Ella is my sun, moon, and stars. I would kill for her, and I will do everything I can to make her happy until the day I die. That fire I see in your eyes is the same I have in mine." He paused for a moment. "I gotta say this, dude: I love you, but if you hurt Lexi again, I will castrate

you. That girl has been through enough. Do not destroy her again. It took years, and I mean years, for Ella to get her to be more like herself."

Aden's face looked down at the floor, hurt and guilt flashing over his face. "I know what I did, and I swear it won't be me breaking hearts this time."

I walked into the light and cleared my throat. They looked over at me, eyes wide. "Hey, Aden, are you ready?"

Aden didn't say anything for a minute, like he didn't know how to handle me being there.

Tristian came into the room, whistling as he smirked at us. "Sooooo… what are you guys talking about?"

I rolled my eyes at him. "Let's head home, Mr. Nosy Pants." I picked up the white ball of fluff. "Come on, Dyna, time to go back home." I placed her in her carrier, giving her a few treats, which earned me a sweet little, "Meow."

Tristian glared at Dyna. "So that's how you play it, huh?" Her big blue eyes looked up at him as she turned and swished her tail and curled up in a small ball in her carrier.

I smiled at Tristian. "Told ya so," I sang as I walked to the door, putting an extra sway into my hips. "Don't feel bad, Tristian, we have a bond that can't be broken by some flirty blond sparkly vamp," I teased him.

He threw his head to the sky and laughed. "I do fucking sparkle, Lil' Star."

Aden interrupted us before we started on each other. "Let's go, you two." He shook his head as he gathered up all the files we went through last night.

I gave Ethan a huge hug and whispered, "Thank you for everything."

He grinned. "Don't break his heart, Lexi. I don't think he would survive it again."

I looked into his eyes and gave him the only truth I had. "I'll try not to." I let go of him and walked to Aden, taking his arm in mine. "Lead the way, devil of mine."

He smirked, shaking his head at me. Leading us to the elevator, he called back at Ethan, "Love you, dumbass!"

Ethan shook his head, but a smile shadowed his face. "Don't be idiots!" he called back as we stepped into the elevator. Before the doors closed, Tristian flipped him off.

The ride down to the garage was quiet. All of us were tired, and the anticipation of what lay ahead of us felt like a heavy cloud over our hearts. I closed my eyes and leaned against the elevator wall, letting a breath out I didn't even know I was holding in. The doors opened to the garage, and we headed to the large black SUV that sat between Ella and Ethan's cars. I slid into the back with both boys in the front; they were on full guard duty now. While they scanned and checked everything, I thought I could use a distraction. I opened my phone to text Coco.

Lexi: Hey! Can we have brunch or dinner soon? I'm missing my favorite aunt, and I desperately need your famous chocolate cheesecake.

Coco: *I am your only aunt, little lady, but yes, let's make this happen. How about next week? Are you going to have your "bodyguards" with you, too?*

Lexi: I don't think the Devil himself will let me out of his sight. I will probably have one if not all with me.

Coco: *Bash is here at the shop now with Ella, so I guess*

you're with Trist and Aden? Anyhoo, I'll talk to Jason. We can figure out a day, maybe invite Ethan and Ella, too!

Lexi: I was with both of them last night. Yes! Let's invite Ella and Ethan, too.

Coco: *You didn't stay at the beach house last night?*

Lexi: No. We had an incident.

Coco: *Everything okay?*

Lexi: The boys kept me safe. Just needed to stay away from the house.

Coco: *You didn't answer my question. When you are ready, you can fill me in. Just be safe.*

Lexi: I will, soon, I promise. Love you, Coco. Stay safe.

Coco: *Always. Love you, too.*

It killed me not to fill her in on the events that had occurred over the last few days, but I needed time to process, and I would tell her in my own time. It was reassuring to know that Coco never judged me for anything. That she knew what was in my heart and trusted my decisions.

I looked out the window and closed my eyes, just wanting to rest them for a minute. The next thing I knew, I was being pulled into the arms of one of my men. I opened my eyes to see Tristian carrying me, and I snuggled closer to him. "Go back to sleep, Lexi. We can wake you later."

I nodded and let my eyes close again, hearing mummers from both of them. I felt Tristian lay me onto the bed and I curled on my side as someone took my shoes off.

"Okay, you little monster. She needs you, so go cuddle,

you fluffy demon."

Then a small fluff curled up against my arms with a soft purr. I slept hard and dreamlessly.

I cracked open my eyes to see the sun setting. The orange and pink sky sank into the night. I stretched and looked for Dyna; she had abandoned me sometime during the evening for something better. I felt gross and desperately wanted to get the grit and grime off of me. I walked into the bathroom and started the shower, letting the steam fill the bathroom.

I stepped in and allowed the hot water to hit my back, moaning softly. "Now this, this is heaven," I murmured to myself, leaning back to let more of the water wash over me.

After I washed, scrubbed, and shampooed myself until I shined, I dried and curled my long brown hair, put a small bit of makeup on, grabbed my softest jeans and a soft white cropped sweater, and headed barefoot out into the kitchen and living room. There were pizza boxes, beer bottles, and chips out on the counter, but no one was in the kitchen or the living room. I saw a flicker of fire from outside and heard one of the Devils laughing. All three of them were sitting around the fire pit.

Bash was back, and the guys were lounging with beers hanging from their hands, laughing and cracking jokes with each other. Aden had a joint hanging out of his mouth as he told an elaborate story, his hands waving about. Bash was smiling so big, I didn't think I had ever seen him that happy. The thought of it made me sad. He didn't smile enough, and I wanted to change that.

Tristian was laughing so hard tears rolled down his

face and he clutched his side. I slowly opened the door, sneaking out, hoping no one would notice me. With their hearing, I was sure one of them would notice me, but I slipped outside undetected into the shadows. I was curious to see how they acted when it was just them, when they didn't have the pressures of the covens hanging over them. I also didn't want to interrupt. This was their moment, and I could see it didn't happen often.

Bash began to pour a glass of Chimera whiskey. Normally, it would just make a person very intoxicated, but this particular Chimera whiskey was stolen from a high lord by Daniels one night at a coven meeting. Later on, he handed it over to me to keep in a safe spot, which just happened to be my bar. This whiskey was so pure that not only would a guy get drunk, but he'd also get the bravery of a lion, the anger of a dragon, and the stubbornness of a goat. Bash passed out the three glasses and they all raised them to the sky and drank it back in one go.

Tristian leaned his head back on the chair and turned to Bash and said, "You know, we are supposed to be figuring out what to do with the Lil' Star." He hiccupped.

They were drunk as sailors. I threw my hand over my mouth to keep a laugh from escaping.

I looked at Aden, finding his shoulders were relaxed, a small smile spread over his face, focusing on the glass of whiskey he was sipping with glassy eyes. All three of them had similar expressions. I let a small giggle out. Luckily, they couldn't see or hear me as I settled onto a chair near the patio doors. I sat Indian style and watched each of them with mild entertainment.

Bash looked over to Tristian and ran a hand over his face "Yeah...hiccup...I guess...hiccup...we should... You ever notice how Princess's eyes sparkle when she sees us?" he slurred. Aden and Tristian perked up, moving their chairs closer to him. "Do you think she'll hate us forever?"

Aden gazed out over the ocean. His eyes held a pensive look.

Tristian shook his head. "I don't think she hates us, frere. I think she wants to, feels like she needs to, but I don't think she can hate us anymore."

They were all silent for a heartbeat, and I found myself frozen in my spot. Did what Tristian just state hold any truth behind it? Aden and I seemed to have this newfound relationship, and I knew we both felt it was more than just random hook-ups with each other. The question was, how did I feel about him now? Aden made me feel less alone, that was one thing I knew for sure. He knew me better than myself.

I sighed internally and looked at Tristian. He made me laugh. Yeah, he was a flirt, but there was so much more to him than that. When Tristian kissed me, it felt like being wrapped up in the sun, and Bash? Well, Bash was my knight, my Devil, he protected me at all costs, and my heart was slowly opening up to him, but I feared he would ruin it all over again.

I knew I needed to really think about how I felt about each of my Devils.

I started to stand up and head back inside when Bash quickly stood up and whipped his shirt off. "I'm a god damn eagle!" He ran towards the pool and jumped in with a loud splash. The water came over the edge as Bash's head popped up through the surface. Tristian looked at Aden, and they

both grinned at each other, whipping off their shirts as well.

Tristian yelled after Bash, "An eagle, man? You're more of a peacock who fucking struts around saying 'oOoOO oOoOO! I'm a peacock! Look at my fucking feathers! Look how I struuut!' You don't share your toys, dude, and an eagle would share!" He ran and cannon-balled into the pool right next to Bash.

Aden moved to the diving board and sat on the edge, looking down at them and swaying slightly. "He's more like…" He trailed off, and then with a perfect imitation of Bash, he finished, "You want a feather? Nope, those are my fucking feathers!" He half-smiled down at Bash.

Tristian swam up to his side, gripping Aden's ankle and arm as Bash took the other side, pulling Aden into the pool with them.

Bash floated on his back and drunkenly stated, "Fuck you! I'd give you a feather, frere! I can share the feathers, but only with you two assholes because you know what she needs. She needs us, and that includes you two assholes." He flipped back over and swam to the edge, pulling himself out. "She's ours, she's yours, but she's minnnneee too, MINE!" he screamed to the night sky. "You hear me, Wishmaker! You can't take her!" he cursed the sky as he stumbled to the nearest lounger and fell face down, passed out.

Bash was so close to me that if Aden or Tristian walked over, they would see me for sure. Aden was staring at Tristian with so many questions in his eyes "Did that mother-fuckin' asshole just say what I think he said?"

Tristian smirked. "Yep, he just gave us free rein of Lil' Star." His fangs slid out of his mouth, glistening in the moonlight, which sent shivers up my spine.

I had to wonder what it would be like for those teeth to sink into my neck. Tristian pulled himself out of the pool and started to walk to Bash. I knew he would for sure see me; drunk or not, they were still vampires.

I decided that instead of getting caught spying on them, I would just make my presence known. I stood from my seat and walked to Bash, sitting next to him and running my fingers through his wet hair. His soft snores told me he was asleep.

Tristian stood frozen, looking from the shadows I came from to where I sat.

I watched Aden run into his back. "What the fuck, man, why did you just stop?!" Aden looked over Tristian's shoulder to see me. Both of them had a look of desire etched on their faces. Aden walked up to me, fangs out, and sank to his knees. "How much of that did you hear, Lexi?" he whispered.

"Everything," I choked out.

Tristian stood behind me, moving my hair from my neck, his fangs lightly scraping right beneath my ear. "Everything, Lil' Star?"

I moaned, pushing my throat to his fangs, not even meaning to. The feel of them against my skin stirred something carnal in me. I dropped my wall and let my magic flow through me. It washed over me quickly, my eyes turning hazy as they focused on Tristian's emotions. Lust was there, but worry, confusion, and a small bit of loneliness trickled over him. I gazed into Aden's eyes; he was full of want, happiness, and fear.

"Have you ever been bitten by one of us?" Aden's voice

was deep and predatory.

Tristian's teeth pushed more into my neck, not breaking skin but just enough to send a shiver of fear down my spine.

"No," I said breathlessly.

Tristian pulled back and wrapped his arms around me, his chin resting on my shoulder. "Hmmm, seems like Lil' Star would like each of us to fulfill that fantasy," he growled.

I bit my bottom lip to cover up a moan from escaping me. I tasted the small droplets of blood as they filled my mouth.

Aden's eyes had a spark of desire in them as he leaned in to steal a kiss; he sucked my bottom lip into his. I let out a groan as he completely overwhelmed me with his mouth and his feather-light touch up my arms set every part of me on fire. As he expertly teased my lips, sucking the droplets of blood from me, I pulled him closer, wrapping my fingers around his strong arms, my nails biting into his biceps. Tristian moved a hand across my stomach. His cold touch gave me instant chills. He lifted my shirt, cupping my breast and tugging my nipple free from my bra.

I lifted my hips trying to get closer to Tristian, but the feeling of Bash's heavy body against me had me pausing. I forgot he was next to us as I got completely lost in the two of them. I pushed back and Bash mumbled sleepily, "I am so sorry we hurt you, Princess. I will not let anyone ever hurt you again, not until I take my last breath on this goddamn earth. I am yours and you are ours. You belong to us." I covered my mouth as I looked down at my sleeping Devil bringing me back to reality.

I pulled away from Aden and brushed my hand over Bash's hair. "We need to stop and get this peacock to bed."

That seemed to break whatever haze we had been in. They both blinked hard and began to move so I could stand as they pulled Bash under their shoulders and walked to the door. I rushed forward to open the door for them as they led Bash to my room. Then I went back outside to the fire pit and gathered all the glasses and empty bottles of alcohol.

I walked back inside with my hands full as Aden and Tristian came out to the living room. "You guys are pigs. Go clean up the rest of your mess. Then you need to get some rest," I jokingly said to them, trying to break the tension in the room. They chuckled and silently headed outside to gather the rest of the trash.

Once they were gone, I snuck back to my room and watched Bash's deep breaths move up and down. I shook myself as I pulled on leggings and a large shirt and curled up next to him, my back to his front. He automatically wrapped his arm around me and pulled me closer to him. His deep breath brought me comfort. Tristian and Aden walked in and looked at us, both frowning.

I spoke before they could. "I don't want to be alone tonight. Will you sleep in here with us?"

Tristian and Aden looked at each other in silent conversation. Aden spoke first. "One of us will need to stay up. I will take the first watch." He walked over and kissed my cheek. "Sweet dreams, Baby."

Tristian changed into grey sweatpants and climbed in beside me. "Aden, wake me up when you're ready to switch," he said with a yawn. Aden waved him off, and I felt sleep take both of us over as Tristian turned to face me, his hand on mine. "Good night, my Lil' Star," he said as his eyes fluttered shut.

Chapter Twenty-Three

The sun was shining, streaming in through the green glass today. I sat in the conservatory re-potting a plant while my cauldron was bubbling green smoke. "You know it's going to turn bad if you don't watch it," said a gruff voice from behind me.

I spun on my heels in surprise to face Daniels. "How... how...?" I gasped. A million questions ran through my mind, but none came out.

Daniels let a full-belly laugh out and smiled. "Hey, kid."

I looked around the conservatory—it seemed to move, to change at every glance. The table I worked on was now a café table with tea and sandwiches. The waterfall in the corner had moved, and in its place was a huge cage.

"This is a dream, isn't it?" I stared back at Daniels, feeling the heartache of him really being gone.

Daniels placed his hand on my shoulder and gave me a sad smile. "Ahh, you know what they say about dreams?"

I rolled my eyes at him and scoffed. "What? 'A dream is a wish your heart makes'?"

Daniels took my hand, pulling me along the conservatory up to the stairs. "Come on, kid, this way." I looked at his face, desperately trying to memorize him. He even smelled like the woodsy fresh scent that I remember so clearly. "Here we are," he said a little cheerily, standing in front of the apothecary table. "The answers you seek lay within here." He placed his hand on the table. "But the sacrifice is not a small one to make. You must find the strength within yourself to defeat The Wishmaker, Lexi."

I stared at the apothecary table and saw a pattern I had never noticed before. There were multiple carvings and lines that, to me, were always in a random order, but looking closely, I saw that they weren't random. Now, they melted together, forming a symbol somehow. A symbol I couldn't make out clearly because of the changing movements throughout the conservatory. I knew I would need to come here when I was awake and sit at the table and figure out what it was and what the hell it meant.

I truly knew that if I could solve this puzzle, we would be closer to defeating The Wishmaker. It was a small step, but it could give us the advantage we needed.

"Thank you," I said, looking back at Daniels. He seemed paler, thinner, and more fragile than just a second before. I took his hand as tears swam in my eyes and a lump formed at the back of my throat.

The words I wanted to say wouldn't come out. How could I live without him? I wanted to scream, "Please don't go! Please stay. Don't leave me alone. Just stay with me!" That was selfish, though, and I knew in my gut I couldn't be selfish anymore. Not with this, not with him. He was so selfless most of my life; he deserved to be at peace for once. He was my one force that kept me strong and, as much as I have tried to stay that way, seeing him now broke my heart into a million pieces.

So, I said the one thing I have wanted to say since I found out he died. "I miss you, Daniels."

He smiled with a warmth that I knew was only for me. "Ahh, kid, I miss you, too, but just know if you ever need me, I will be right here." He tapped his chest. The tears that I begged not to come did so anyway, and I felt them roll down my cheek.

"Forever, always."

I turned to the stairs, and we walked down them slowly to the table that was now back where my cauldron sat. The once green smoke was now black, and a pungent smell was filling the room. "I told you it would ruin," said Daniels from behind me.

I turned around and let out a laugh, but the person who stood behind me wasn't Daniels.

The Wishmaker held up a small bottle of sparkling liquid.

"Pixie dust," I whispered. He snarled hideously at me from beneath his hood and threw the bottle at my feet. Blackness spilled out from it, wrapping its way around my feet.

"Les ténèbres," I gasped.

It was already up to my arms, pinning them together, clasping my hands in a vice. I began to pull at the smoke but the more I fought, the more it weighed me down. My legs were now completely intertwined within the shadows, and I struggled to stand.

Panic set in.

The Wishmaker was giving me over to les ténèbres.

Daniels's voice drifted into my mind. "When the darkest of nights seem to be more than one can take, look to the light. The sun will always guide your way to the heavens."

I grunted and yelled to the empty room. "Daniels! Not the time for your riddles, old man! Give me more! How do we get rid of them?!" The darkness engulfed me, clasping around my throat, cutting off my scream for help.

A distant voice... someone I knew was screaming. "Lexi! Wake up! Dammit! Get me water, now!"

A splash of cold liquid covered me as les ténèbres disappeared. I opened my eyes to see all three of my Devils standing above me with frowns of concern etched on each of their faces.

Bash's eyes were wild as he held his phone in his hand. I could hear someone yelling on the other end. "Damn it," he cursed, returning to the phone. "Anderson, no, no, she's fine. I am not sure. A nightmare, it seemed like? I dunno. Yeah, yeah, I will. Listen, I gotta go. Yes, we will be there soon. Let me make sure she is okay. Yes, I will bring her. Yes, I know! We are coming, but let me make sure my siren is okay first," he growled.

He hung up, turned to me, and walked over. I was shaking so badly that I couldn't stop. Aden's hands were at my

back to help calm me, and Tristian had a towel in his hand as he sat at my feet, rubbing my legs to warm me back up.

"Wha... what was that?" I asked in an unsteady voice.

Bash took my ice-cold hands in his warm ones. "At first, we thought it was a nightmare, but we couldn't get you out of it. You wouldn't wake up."

I glanced down at my clothes, which were now plastered to me. "Water?" I raised a brow.

Aden spoke up. "Ocean water, to be exact. We tried everything, calling your name, shaking you, even jumping on the bed, but nothing worked. Tristian figured it out. Water is your fae half's element of power. We figured we would give it a shot. He ran and got a cup of tap water, and you reacted but never woke up. It was then that Tristian went to the beach to get the ocean water that jolted you awake."

I looked at Tristian, who looked a bit guilty about dumping a bucket of water on me. "Thank you, Tristian, I think you saved my life." His face went cold and serious, a look I'd never seen him wear before. I realized something at that moment. The happy-go-lucky, funny Tristian also was a cold-blooded killer.

"I will find who is doing this to you, Lil' Star, I swear it." He stood, putting his fist over his heart as he bowed to me. Aden and Bash stood next to him repeating, "I swear it," in unison, their fists over their hearts, bowing to me, mirroring Tristian.

In our world, this kind of promise was huge. It meant they wouldn't stop searching for The Wishmaker until he was dead or they were.

I stood and said, "Je suis honoré de t'avoir a mes côtés." I

bowed my head to them, lowering myself, making a promise to them, as well. We all stood looking at each other, holding onto the moment and the promises that we just made. I turned to Bash, changing the subject "Anderson wants to meet?"

Bash sighed, running his hand through his hair. "Yeah, we need to head out soon to his office." I looked at my soaked pajamas covered in ocean water. "I will go get ready." Heading to the bathroom, I stripped down, showering quickly. I wrapped a towel around me and jumped when I saw Aden leaning against the door.

"WOW, privacy please!" I tried to shoo him out.

"Sorry, baby. Bash doesn't want you alone. Plus, it's not like I haven't seen it all," he said with a shrug.

I crossed my arms and glared. "Be a fucking gentleman and turn around!"

Aden gave a masculine laugh. "Okay, but it's not like I wasn't between your sweet thighs a few days ago." He licked his lips as he was remembering us doing all of the dark deeds we had done. Finally, he spun around. "Better?" He eyed me through the mirror. I balled up my towel, throwing it at the back of his head.

"It's respectful, asshat!"

I walked into my closet and changed into lacey matching black underwear and bra, a navy plaid pencil skirt, and a black top that showed a bit of cleavage but wasn't too revealing. I paired it with strappy black sandals that had sharp silver heels that doubled as a weapon. A girl couldn't be too careful. I did my hair in a high ponytail and painted my lips in my favorite fucking fabulous lipstick.

I walked out and looked at Aden, who hadn't changed yet. As soon as he saw me, he smiled. "Welcome back, Lex. You kinda looked like a drowned rat earlier." He pulled out his phone, checking a message.

"Haha." I rolled my eyes. "Go change. We gotta go."

I headed to the living room to find Bash in a navy suit with a grey vest, a white button-up shirt, a navy tie, and a white pocket square. Tristian was dressed in black pants and a khaki jacket with a white shirt. His top buttons were undone, showing off his chest and his tattoos. I poured us coffee as we waited for Aden. He came quickly, pulling a black trench on with skinny black pants and a cream turtleneck. Once again, they all looked like they walked straight out of an ad.

I stood there sipping my coffee and admiring the view of my Devils who I knew would walk through the fiery pits of hell for me. Bash walked up to me. "You have a bit of drool, Princess." He ran his thumb along the edge of my mouth.

I pursed my lips. "Well, I can't say I'm gonna complain about the suit." I plucked at the button of his sleeve. "You all clean up nicely, but you know that. Too pretty for your own good." I shook my head. "Let's go, boys, we have lots to do and little time to do it."

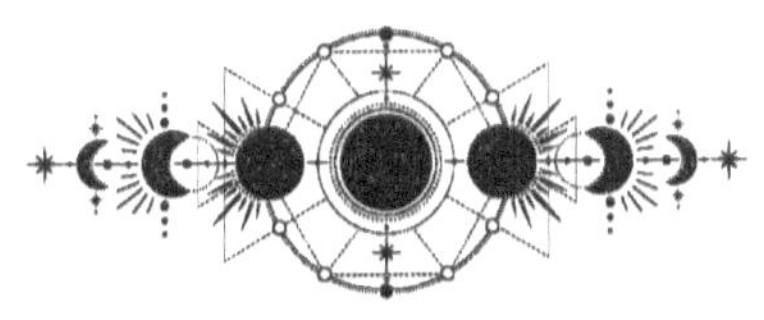

As we pulled into the city, the fog rolled in, covering the ground with a thick blanket of cloudy mist as we approached a dark, ominous, soaring building that had Anderson & Ryder Associates etched in gold on the side. I stood with my head back, staring at the tall building and sighed.

"Ready?" Bash said beside me.

I nodded. "Yeah, let's just hope this goes well."

Tristan and Aden flanked us.

"Don't worry, Lil' Star. If you get in trouble, we'll get you out."

I smiled. "Or you'll get us all killed."

Aden wrapped an arm around Tristian and Bash's shoulders. "You know what J. M. Barrie said: 'To die will be an awfully big adventure'."

We all walked into the posh lobby, the boys surrounding me as we approached the security desk. Bash nodded in greeting to the older security guard, who promptly dropped the book he was reading. "Mr. Ryder, your father didn't mention you coming in today."

Looking at his phone and then up to the security guard, he said, "Hey Steve, he wouldn't know. I am not here to see him. Can you let Mr. Anderson know we're here?"

The man smiled as if he loved the idea of keeping something from Morgan Ryder. He picked up the phone from his desk, holding it to his ear. "Hey, Gina, tell Mr. Anderson Sebastian Ryder is here for him...right...yes...sending them up now." He reached around, pulled out four visitor badges for us and led us through the lobby to an elevator located farther away from the ones in the front. "This will take you right to him."

Bash nodded. "Thank you, Steve. Tell Eliza and the kiddos I said 'hi'."

He gave Bash a smile. "Thank you, sir." He bowed his head slightly to him before returning to his desk.

The elevator ride was quick. We came to the top of the 100-floor building. "Before we go in, just remember one thing, Lexi: Always be aware and take what he offers with a grain of salt. Anderson seems to be on our side, but at this point, we can't trust anyone."

I knew this and leaned my head to the side. "Don't worry, Bash. I can play the politics game."

A shadow of a smile flickered across his lips.

The doors opened to a long cement desk and exposed brick walls. It was modern with a twist of traditional elements placed throughout the lobby. A twenty-ish-old girl sat behind the large desk with big brown eyes and wild, dark curls, dressed in a red cape dress that fell to her knees. She looked up as we approached. Her eyes hit Bash and lust appeared as she looked him over; a pang of jealousy hit me, and I instantly knew I didn't like her.

She stood, walking over to us. "Hello, Sebastian." She kissed both of his cheeks, greeting him in a sweet voice with a slight French accent.

He smiled sweetly at her, and the jealousy hit harder. "Hello, Camille, how is your grandmother?"

She bit her lip, grinning up at him. "Great! She said to come by the restaurant soon so she can show you her newest dish. Maybe we could even eat together?" She batted her eyelashes at him hopefully.

Okay, I officially disliked her. I glared at her and walked

up to Bash, wrapping my arm through his and leaning my head on his arm. "Hi! I'm Lexi Rose. I believe Mr. Anderson is waiting for us. I know he is such a busy man. I am sure he would love to know we are here and wouldn't want to be left waiting," I said sweetly, with a smile that held more venom in it than she probably realized. I pictured about twenty different ways I could cause her pain.

Camille looked a bit shocked. She walked over to the phone, picked it up, and in a flustered voice said, "Mr. Anderson? Sebastian Ryder and associates are here... Yes, she is with him... Okay, thank you. He said to head into his office." She led us to an empty office that overlooked the entirety of downtown. "Do you need anything? Water or coffee? I could order lunch?"

Tristian smiled gently at her. "No, thank you. We are fine." He dismissed her quickly.

I unwrapped myself from Bash's arms and walked to the window, crossing my arms and looking down at the city below. Aden walked up beside me, pulling me against his side. "Looking a bit green, Lex," he chuckled. I huffed, but kept my mouth shut, grinding my teeth. "You know he doesn't want anyone but you, right?" he whispered.

I arched an eyebrow at him and was about to say a snarky comment when Bash walked up to me and pulled me from Aden's arms, kissing my lips softly.

I deepened the kiss, tugging him down to me and growling into his mouth, "Miiiiiiiiine."

He moved back slightly, his lips quirked up. "Damn straight, Princess."

I pulled him closer as his tongue found mine. I pulled

away quickly, remembering where we were, leaving my red lipstick stained on his mouth. "Better use that pocket square, Bash, before Anderson gets here." I walked over to a mirror, fixing my lipstick, glad it didn't smudge too much.

Bash laughed and cleaned up his mouth. "Oh, we aren't even close to being done, Princess. You owe me, and I will make you pay tenfold." I huffed and warmed from his statement. Sebastian Ryder and I had unfinished business we needed to tend to one day, and that day seemed as if it would come quickly.

Just as I finished the final touches, Anderson walked in with a few folders in his hand. "Lexi, Bash, Aden, Tristian, nice to see you all. Please sit." He gestured to the small sitting area that had a couch and two chairs. Camille came in with a teapot and cups for us all. She set it down, bowing her head to Anderson as he thanked her. She left quickly. We all took our seats, and Anderson poured tea for each of us. We didn't touch our cups until Anderson took a sip of his.

He smirked. "Smart, but nothing is poisoned here. Bash, I swear to you, we want the same thing." Bash nodded and lifted his drink to his lips. The cup looked so tiny in his hand. I covered my mouth, trying not to laugh.

Anderson noticed and arched a brow at me. I shook my head to tell him not to say a word. He cleared his throat and continued by picking up a folder. "Let's not waste anymore of your time, Ms. Rose, and get straight to the point. I was working with Grayson and Daniels in hopes of finding the antidote to pixie dust."

We jolted, and our eyes narrowed in on him.

He held up a hand, telling us he needed to finish first.

"I am building a facility as we speak where we can produce the antidote in a safe environmental lab, research the drug, and hopefully find a cure. But, since Daniels's death, it seems like we might have to stop construction." He turned towards me with a somber face. "It has come to my attention that you, Ms. Rose, might have the answer we've been looking for."

The tension suddenly became thick, and I felt Bash move closer to me, pressing his thigh against mine as if he was ready to pick me up and run. I knew I needed to stand my ground and let Anderson know he didn't scare me, even if he was ruthless.

I picked up my teacup, taking a swig of floral liquid. "I don't know how much help I will be. Yes, I have access to Daniels's home, his ingredients, and I am assuming you know about his secret lab, but I am not nearly as talented in potions as Daniels." I gave a small shrug, deciding that telling the truth was better than lying about it. I hoped it would help in the long run, and it wasn't like I was giving too much away. Anderson was perceptive and rich. He could have found all of this out easily enough.

Anderson smiled wolfishly at me. "Ahh, but, my dear, that is exactly my point. I do need you. My researchers will help you find the antidote. With Daniels's notes, your smarts and natural talent, I know we can develop this antidote and hopefully cure millions of fae. This isn't just a Providence Village problem, Lexi. It spans beyond us, and I need to know who is behind it and destroy them and their business," he growled. "My question is, will you help me do that?"

I looked into his eyes to see if he would give anything away. I wanted to know the reason behind it all. I flexed my magic, and it slowly casted an invisible rope around his emotions. Why was Anderson so damn desperate to find out about pixie dust? One would only hope it was for the good of all fae, because hell, that drug destroyed many lives, and not just fae. It could kill a human as well, and from what we'd heard, it already had.

"I can't sense anything from you, so what is the reasoning behind this? Why are you so desperate to rid the world of a drug?"

He smirked. "You want to know if I have an agenda behind it all?"

I took another sip of my tea, raising my eyebrows. "Maybe just call it curiosity."

He laughed. "Curiosity can kill you sometimes, Ms. Rose, but if you want to know, a dear friend of mine was lost to pixie dust. And let's just say it hit harder than I thought."

I saw the pain in his eyes, and he let his wall slip enough for me to feel his emotions spill from him. It was like a sucker punch to my stomach; his grief was so strong it came in waves, and he was drowning in it. Then he put his wall back up as quickly as he let them down. I felt my hands shaking slightly, and I set my cup down. I slid my gaze to Sebastian, and he gave a slight nod as if he felt it himself.

I looked back at him with sadness in my voice. "Yes, we will. We will help find out who is doing this, and we will help find a way to cure everyone who has been affected by this soul-sucking drug."

He smiled, though it didn't reach his eyes. "Thank you, Lexi."

I returned the gesture. "You are welcome, Mr. Anderson."

He loosened his tie. "Please call me Kane. Mr. Anderson was my father, who was a total prick."

I laughed. "Okay, Kane it is."

Aden flipped through the file. "What is this, information on pixie dust?"

Morgan's smile fell into a frown. "Sadly, no. This file is from the FBI regarding the four mermaids that have gone missing within the past forty-eight hours."

I put my teacup down in shock as anger filled me. "No news outlets have reported this!"

Morgan shook his head. "No, we are trying to keep it on the down-low because we don't want The Wishmaker to kill any of these girls. One of them is only seventeen."

I glanced over at our group and saw each of my Devils fuming. "Why the hell are we just learning about this, Kane?" I hissed. The anger must have shown in my eyes because Morgan took my hand.

"Lexi, you have been dealing with a lot personally, with Daniels's death, the death threats, and a possible stalker. Look, truth be told, I also wasn't sure if you were trustworthy enough to help with this; obviously I was wrong."

I was about to lay into him when he said the next words that shook me to my core.

"They are from your coven. I was hoping you could do a bit of investigating."

I yanked my hand back as if he had burned me. "From... my... coven?"

I looked around the room at each of my Devils. Tristian stared at the floor with a look of shame. Aden glared at Bash, and Bash remained calm as he looked into my eyes.

"I didn't know about it until this morning," he explained. "My father didn't think it was important for me to know anymore, and with what happened this morning, I felt it would be better to talk to Anderson about it here."

He had to be joking. I stared at him as if he had grown three heads and was dancing in a pink tutu. "You didn't think at all, Sebastian," I muttered, turning back to Anderson. "We will look into this right away."

"Thank you, Lexi."

I nodded got up to walk to the door. "But Kane, if anything ever comes to you about my coven again and you do not let me know ASAP, then I swear you will find yourself in a watery grave."

Kane cleared his throat as he took my threat to heart, holding up his hands innocently. "Understood, Ms. Rose."

I flipped through the file, glancing at the pictures of four girls. Cordelia Higgins was a twenty-two-year-old girl with long dark red hair and bright blue eyes. Chelle Sanderson, twenty-eight, with curly blonde hair and bright green eyes. Viviane Lu, the seventeen-year-old, looked young even for her age, with delicate pearl skin and long black hair. The last girl, Nyx Lu, twenty-five, Viviane's sister, had the same long black hair but her eyes were light blue, almost white.

I knew her.

I touched Aden's arm. "Fuck. Aden, it's Nyx."

Aden moved closer and put an arm around me, peering at the photo. "Shit. How the hell was Nyx caught up in this shit?"

Bash and Tristian moved closer to see for themselves. "God damnit," Bash said under his breath. Tristian's face

was grim in disbelief.

I looked up at Anderson, finding him watching us with curiosity. "She went to school with us. She was a friend."

My throat felt tight as I held back the tears. Bash wrapped an arm around me as Anderson spoke softly. "Lexi, look at me. You have a stalker who is psychotic and who is kidnapping young women to make a drug that is making him a lot of money. It's sick and disgusting. When we find him, and we will, he won't be able to hurt anyone again, and you, my dear, will be the one to ensure his demise."

I stared at Anderson. I was hurt, sad, and angry, but mostly, I was determined. Determined to find out who The Wishmaker was. I would destroy him and his world, making him wish he never messed with any of our covens.

Chapter Twenty-Four

We said our goodbyes to Anderson and made our way down to our car. Then we took the highway through the mountains and popped out on the other side of a tunnel where palm trees lined the roads and white sandy beaches stretched alongside them. Beachgoers sunned themselves, and children played in the exquisite lagoon-blue ocean. Bash pulled up to a parking lot that was always full of cars, even on a weekday afternoon.

I stepped out, watching the hypnotizing waves lap against the shore. Falling under the spell of the ocean, I was dying to strip down to nothing and swim for hours...but we had other matters to discuss and mermaids to find first before I could let myself go.

Sighing, I looked back at my Devils standing behind me. "Okay, let's do this." I turned to The Oddity, taking in the elegant building that sat at the edge of the ocean.

It wasn't a typical beach bar. Yeah, it had palm trees and sand, but it was like walking into a dreamland. The front doors were arched by two palm trees with dark green fronds that opened to let us pass through. Large white, sheer tents raised high above, allowing the sun's rays to leave a soft warm glow on our skin. A few fae sat around on white couches. The tables were mother-of-pearl with white shell chairs encircling them. There were lavish green plants everywhere. I walked closer to the wall and saw thin, snakelike vines climbing the pillars of the tents with small white flowers opening and closing so slowly you wouldn't have noticed if you didn't look close enough.

We entered a room with a huge, turquoise sea glass bar standing in the middle. The same white fabrics draped across the ceiling allowed natural sunshine to shimmer through the windows, keeping the bar light and airy. Verdant green glass lights hung from the top of the ceiling with a fire witch's internal glow powering them and illuminating the glass dome.

One side of the bar held a set of tables with high rattan barstools and a plant of sea witch that sat in small vases, making the whole room smell like saltwater and fresh air. The bar had magical swings surrounding it; they were never uncomfortable to sit in and always held guests in place until they were ready to leave.

I slid into a swing and waited for the bartender to come over as I scanned the drink menu. "I don't know what to

order." I looked behind at the guys. "What do you suggest? A Lost Boy?" It was a rum drink with peaches.

Aden smiled. "I like Hold My Juju because it is made with two different rums and pineapple juice."

Tristian snatched the menu. "Ohh, look at Color of the Winds! It's 'a milky sweet drink with many colors swirled together'."

"The Cheshire Cat is refreshing, Princess," Bash added over my shoulder.

I glanced at the description: vodka berry mixture with fizzy water. It sounded delicious and lord only knew I needed a drink after the week we'd had.

A few minutes later, a bartender noticed me and walked over to our group. He had a nervous look about him, but that could have been because of the three deadly vampires that stood at my back. He was very handsome, with dark green hair, bright blue eyes, and a close-cut beard and a mustache that came down his chiseled jawline. He was shirtless, and you could see a tattoo of two guns attached to his hips as they dipped down into his pants.

A smile formed on his mouth as he licked his bottom lip in a nervous tick. "Well, hello beautiful, what can I get you?"

I smiled sweetly, hoping that we could play nice. His smile widened at me, and his eyes raked over me; this man knew he looked good. I could feel that he was a siren as he pushed a bit of his power toward me, but I held up my own inner shield.

I smirked and let my eyes turn their hazy purple. "Hi, can you do me a favor? Can you tell me if you know any of these girls, and then you can get me a Cheshire Cat?"

Bash took the photos out, laying them on the bar for him to see. The bartender swallowed hard, looking up at Bash, Tristian, and Aden. He visibly shuddered at the three of them. I turned around to see what they did, but they simply stood shoulder to shoulder with their arms crossed, wearing smug smiles. My brows arched as I turned back and looked at him.

"Umm yeah, I have seen these three, but not this one," he said, pointing to Viviane. "Makes sense, she's underage."

I ran my fingers over the top of his hand, pushing my siren gifts past his shield and into him to help him relax more. He was shaking so bad I knew he wouldn't tell us anything. He sighed, and his shoulders slumped slightly as I saw my power send him calming energy.

He looked back at the guys, licking his lips. "I...I know I saw Nyx a few days ago. She was hanging out by the lagoon, surfing." He nodded his head to Bash. "Do they need to stand behind you the whole time?" he asked in a small voice.

I turned around and glared at my Three Devils. "Why don't you go down to the lagoon and ask if anyone talked to or saw the girls?"

Bash glared back, grinding his teeth. "One of us needs to stay with you."

I mentally rolled my eyes. "Fine..." I said with a sickeningly sweet smile. "Tristian can stay."

Bash's fist clenched as I batted my eyelashes at him. "Why Tristian?" he barked out.

I turned in my seat and pulled him closer as I hissed, "Because, unlike you, he won't fucking scare every fae in the

bar. Now, go talk to the others and try not to kill anyone." I patted his cheek and turned back, not waiting for him to say anything. I found myself looking at a tall, colorful glass waiting for me. "You're fast!" I grinned. "Thank you." I raised my glass to him as I took a sip, rum coating my throat. "Sorry, but what is your name?"

The bartender returned my smile. "Liam."

I stuck my hand out. "Nice to meet you, Liam. I'm Lexi."

He took it and kissed it. "I know who you are, Lexi Rose."

I heard Tristian grunt a bit from behind me. I glanced over my shoulder and glared at him. "Forgive my friend here; he's not usually the grumpy one."

I turned back to Liam, smiling. "We are desperately trying to find them to get them back to their families. Could you please take another look at these photos? The coven and I would be grateful for your help." I gave him a sad smile.

He nodded and took the time to go over each of the photos. "Cordelia is the ringleader. She's a party girl, always in here, but I haven't seen her in about a week. She had been coming in with some young dude. She wasn't acting like herself lately, though."

My expression fell as a frown formed. "What do you mean?"

He ran a hand over his face. "Listen, Cordelia came in about a week ago, and...she was pale; her skin wasn't as luminous as it normally is. Her eyes were so dilated they were pinpoints. I knew she was hooked on something. My best guess was pixie dust with the way she was talking about flying and reaching the stars. Chelle is her roommate; she worked over at one of the high-end bars in the city—Smuggler's Club, I think. I only know because she tried to get me to apply for another bartender's spot there. She didn't come in a lot, but on occasion she would stop by the bar. I saw her about two weeks ago with Cordelia. They were fighting outside. Not sure what it was about, though. Nyx is always here, but she surfs most days and usually pops in for a post-drink with her boyfriend and his crew."

Now that piqued my interest. "Boyfriend? Where is he?"

Liam pointed to the beach. "Surfing. I saw him heading out before I started my shift."

I sipped my drink. "Okay, thanks. Liam, if you hear anything, can you call me? You would not only be helping me but our coven, as well."

He smiled at me and nodded. "Yes, ma'am. I will call if I hear anything."

Before I could give him my number, Tristian was writing a number on a business card and handing it to him. "Use this number, Liam. It's a direct line to me. The three of us are always around Lexi, right Lil' Star?" He said smugly.

I rolled my eyes. "Yeah, it seems I can't lose you," I replied sarcastically.

"That's not what you said the other night when I was making you come over and over again on my fingers."

I almost spit my drink out, swallowing the last sip down and glaring at Tristian as a blush formed across my cheeks.

I turned to Liam, forcing a neutral expression. "Thank you, Liam, truly."

I stood, and we walked out of the bar to where Liam had told us Nyx's boyfriend would be. We headed down to the

beach to meet Bash and Aden. Bash was standing with his arms crossed, eyes narrowed at the ocean, and Aden had his hands in his pockets, fuming at Bash. As we approached, I saw a group of four guys on surfboards out in the middle of the ocean flipping Bash off.

I rolled my eyes. "So, I am guessing the whole talking to people isn't working out too well for you. Bash, did you even try to say hello, or did you simply demand answers from them?"

He huffed, not saying a word. Aden smirked down at me. "He threatened to cut out their eyes if they didn't talk to him. One threw up earth magic, and they ran off with their boards. They were in the water before we could chase them down. Someone didn't want to get his shoes wet."

"Damn it, Sebastian." I turned from them, throwing my head back in exasperation. "I will get them back here, give me a second. You three stay." I took my heels off since I was sinking in the sand and walked to the edge of the water.

"How?" Aden called out.

I grinned at him. "Like this, pretty boy."

I walked to the break and bent down to the cool, salty water, letting my fingers run through the ocean. I let the power of the sea call to me, and I felt it flow through my veins. I opened my mouth and began to softly sing a soft, haunting melody to draw them in.

All four men sitting on their boards turned to me and almost immediately began to paddle back to shore. I sang louder as more and more people surrounded us. A few tried to reach out, but I saw Bash push them back. Eventually, my Three Devils moved to my back, creating a border between me and the people on the shore. I closed my eyes, letting my abilities take over. I felt the call of the ocean. Before I could stop myself, I walked into the briny water. When I opened my eyes, the water was hitting my knees and soaking my skirt. I looked to the four men ahead of me. They were wrestling with each other before coming to a complete stop before me.

"I got to her first!" said the blond-haired surfer kid. A red-headed kid, who looked only around twenty, was caught in an arm lock and grunted to be released. A black-haired skinny guy was bent at the waist as if he got tackled, a giant grin on his face.

A British accent came from a tall six foot five guy with the most beautiful deep rich brown skin I had ever seen. Tattooed sleeves reached all the way up to his neck. "No way, mate, she looked at me first," he said as he approached me with a twinkle in his eyes. He was the leader, and I knew this was the one I needed to talk to. His eyes were a copper brown, and he had a wickedly handsome smile that would make any girl melt.

"Hi, I'm Lexi." I held out my hand.

"I know. Name's Oliver Wright, Ms. Rose. What can me and my crew do for ya today? Are ya ready to ditch the vamps and hang with the sirens?"

I frowned a bit. "I thought you were mermaids, men? Is it mermaid or merman?"

They all laughed. "Ma'am you may call us whatever you want, but I am not a mermaid, I am just like you. I am half mermaid and half siren, Damon is a full mermaid, Gage is a warlock, and Andre is an incubus. I gotta say, Luv, your

call is strong. I couldn't even resist it myself. It was like the ocean was calling me home," he said dreamily. I heard Bash huff behind me and caught his eyes rolling as he muttered something under his breath.

"I'll try it on you next time, Big Boy." I yelled at Bash. "I'll even make sure to drown your ass in the bottom of the ocean once you are fully enthralled." I raised a brow in a challenge. He stood silent, glaring at me. Tristian looked like he was about to start laughing. I chuckled as I turned back to the group of four. "Don't mind the Three Devils behind me; they seem to think they can lay claim to anyone because they look like that."

Damon looked at the three of them with interest.

"I am looking for a girl named Nyx or any of these girls?" I showed them their pictures, and all of them shifted uncomfortably.

"What do you want with Nyx?" said Andre in a deep French accent.

"She's a friend." I tilted my head, looking at him.

"Nah darling, you aren't Nyx's friend. I would have met you. I've known Nyx my entire life," retorted Damon.

I whipped my head to him. "If you know her, then you know she's missing."

They all shifted uncomfortably, exchanging uneasy looks. "Yeah, we know she's missing, Luv. We've been looking for her everywhere. But my question is, why are the leaders of our covens just now giving a shit about a few missing mermaids?"

Oliver looked behind me, asking Bash the question, but before he got an answer, I walked right up to him and grabbed his face between my fingers. "Don't look at him because he won't help you. You look at me, your leader, and answer my damn questions." I pushed my enthrallment into him to persuade him to answer me. His eyes became unfocused as he went into a dreamy state.

"Nyx and I fought three days ago. She kept talking about how we had to help Cordelia. She was big into the dust and I guess had gone off the rails. I figured it was just Cordy being a royal bitch as always, but then later that night she was supposed to meet me at my house, but she never showed."

I released him, and he stumbled back into the guys as they caught him.

He growled, his eyes shifting to green slits as he shook off the enthrallment. Then he started to run at me. I was prepared for the hit when I felt myself being whipped out of the water and was suddenly behind Aden's back.

Bash held Oliver by the neck, walking to the shore. "I will end you, fish boy, if you lay a finger on what is mine," Bash snarled.

Tristian had the other three down on wet sand, casually holding a gun to Andre's head. The other two looked pissed as hell.

Bash growled at him, "Now you listen to me, you little dick, a member of your coven goes missing and you didn't inform any of the leaders or bring any knowledge forward? Makes you look pretty fucking guilty, asshole. So, you wanna try this approach again with your leader?" Oliver grunted as Bash continued, "Now, be nice before I rip your heart out of your chest."

Oliver finally looked scared and spluttered out. "I didn't

know! Nyx and I are on and off all the time. I thought I'd go down for what she did, but I've been looking for her every night. Viv is like a little sister to me. I wouldn't let anything bad happen to her."

I paced around him. "Look, we just want them safe, so what are you not telling us?"

The redhead, Gage, spoke up. "I'm dating Chelle; she was with Nyx, and so was Viviane. She has a crush on Damon. We were supposed to go to a party and since Cordy's the party girl, she knew of a secret party that night, but none of us even knew the name of the club or where the party was held. All we knew was that someone would text you an address, a password, and time to show up. We all met at the girls' apartment when we were supposed to, but they never showed up. We broke into the apartment, and it was empty, but it looked like they had been there that night. That's all we know. We haven't seen them since." He dropped his head, distraught, running his fingers through his hair.

Oliver started to turn blue from the hand around his throat, and I spoke up. "Bash, let him go. Tristian, give them a card. They told us everything."

Tristian flicked four cards at each one of them and holstered his gun, walking to me as Bash dropped Oliver from his grasp.

"If you hear from any of them, call me. I want them safe. And I'm sorry I haven't been the leader you want, Oliver, but I'm learning. I'm trying to do my best." I turned and walked to the car, wanting to get the hell out of here and back to the house.

"Wait!" Andre ran to us. "Chelle told me that Cordelia

kept having a guy in a suit over. They would go to his room and would be in there for hours. She never said anything sexual happened, but Cordy always came out high as a kite. If you can find that guy, you'll find the girls."

I nodded. "Thank you, Andre."

He gave a small smile and turned and walked away.

"I need a minute." I slumped my shoulders, slipping my shoes back on. A pair of arms wrapped around me, pulling me close and kissing my head.

"Of course, Princess, we will be right here."

I numbly shook my head and walked back into The Oddity, heading to the back where the bathroom sign hung. I entered and splashed water on my face, looking at myself in the mirror; my eyes swirled purple as the stress and the pain overwhelmed me. I wanted to scream, I was so frustrated with everything. Not finding these missing girls would be my coven's ruin. It would ruin everything Daniels had worked to build.

The coven would think I wasn't able to handle our major issues. It made me seem weak or even worse—that Daniels didn't want to protect our coven.

Shit! What was the real reason to kidnap them besides their tears? Why not from another coven? Could it have been a coincidence?

I closed my eyes, trying to get rid of the emotions stirring inside me. I felt the weight of them on me as if they would crush me. I needed to get myself back under control. I dried my face off and walked out the door, back to my Devils to figure out what our next steps would be.

Chapter Twenty-Five

"M s. Rose," a gruff voice said behind me. I turned, and a hand came over my mouth, muffling my scream. My body was lifted into the air by two very hairy arms. As I was being dragged through the back exit, I saw Bash's head lift and the green of his eyes fade to blood red. Tristian growled, and Aden ran towards me. I screamed and threw my head back into the kidnapper's face, hearing a loud crack and a grunt from the male voice who held me. I kicked my heel back into someone's legs.

"Fucking hell! You stupid slut! I am going to enjoy making you scream," a deep, rough voice yelled in my year. I felt spit fly into my face as I continued to fight with all my might. I bit his hand until I tasted blood.

He yanked his hand away from me, and I knew I had an

opportunity I couldn't waste. I pulled all of my power to the surface and let the loudest scream out I could manage. The windows all began to shatter all around us, raining glass down onto the crowd. Little pieces hit my skin and sliced small cuts across my face and hands.

That's when I heard gunshots.

"Lexi! We're coming!" Aden yelled, giving me the motivation to fight back as the kidnapper's hands faltered to keep hold of me. He slipped enough that I was able to pick up an almost empty bottle of vodka, break it down over the bar, and shove it into the guy's throat. He grasped his throat as I shoved harder, but his blood covered my hand, making the bottle slippery, and it fell to the ground.

He let go, and I hit the ground, scrambling to get myself up to run toward the exit. The bar was empty besides a few people cowering under tables. I almost made it to the door before I was jerked back by my ponytail. I let out a yelp as thick hands grabbed ahold of my neck and around my waist.

"You fuck twat! I will enjoy killing you," he roared. I screamed again. As he snarled, his spit hit my face and ran down it, mixing with blood and sweat. "I think I am going to take my time with you, maybe have you take my cock a few times before I play with your insides. Tell me, have you ever been fucked by a troll? I'll destroy your sweet little siren pussy. I bet you'll bleed pretty."

I should have been scared, but the threat just fueled my rage.

I threw my elbow as hard as I could into his stomach,

stomped on his foot, and twisted around so my knee met his junk. Only a glimpse of pain hit his face.

This was not going to be my end.

I screamed again, sending more glass flying and bottles breaking. He threw me into the wall, my head hitting hard. I heard more than felt the sickening crack before I blacked out.

When I came to, he had moved us to the back room and barricaded us in an office, piling a desk and a filing cabinet against the door. He punched the door's window out and started shooting at my Devils. I tried to get hold of his arm to pull him back, but my body was weak and my energy completely drained. Then he turned to me, threw me into an office chair, and pulled out a set of handcuffs.

I kicked as hard as I could in his shin and fought to search for any weapon I could use. I found a sharp pencil and slammed it into his hand. He shrieked, pulling the pencil out before punching my side, knocking the air out of me. He wrapped a hand around my waist and yanked me up, then took my hands and clasped them around a low-hanging pipe. I had to stand on my tiptoes; my head hung low as a trickle of blood dripped down my neck from a cut in my head.

I kept going in and out, trying my hardest to stay awake, but my head was foggy, and I kept seeing double. I could hear the guys shooting and trying to get in. I was not sure what happened, but something made them stop.

The troll turned to me, looking me up and down. He smiled with an evil glint in his eye. "I think I will take some-thing now, my pretty little siren."

He moved behind me, ripping my shirt and grabbing a knife to slice up my skirt. I whimpered as I tried to move and fight him.

"Shh, little siren, it will only hurt a lot," he chuckled as he unzipped his pants, taking his dick out. "I think I'll fuck that perfect little ass first."

I wrenched and screamed as much as I could, trying everything I could to stop him. I thought this was it. This is how I die. At least I would see my parents again and maybe Daniels. I felt the fight start to fade from me physically, but mentally, I still had hope, because if I didn't have hope, then I didn't have a chance.

He was behind me tugging my underwear down when the door burst open, sending the filing cabinet flying across the small room. The door began to splinter away, and a piece flew off, slicing the troll's face.

The troll yelped and quickly wiped away the blood from his face. He growled at me, "I'm going to destroy you." The look in his eyes told me nothing would stop him from taking what he wanted. I prepared myself for what was about to happen and only prayed I would be dead soon after.

I still fought with jerks and movements, kicking and screaming. I wouldn't make it easy for him. The troll sliced my stomach, and I screamed as the blood spilled down. "If you move again, I will slice you from top to bottom and still enjoy you while you bleed out, while you pray for me to kill you," he snarled. I sagged in my cuffs turning my head to the door in hopes to see a glimpse of my Devils one last time before I left this earth. The troll pushed his knee in between me and I took in a shaky gasp, not letting the whimper escape my lips; I didn't want to give him that satisfaction.

A loud crash hit the door, and pieces of wood shattered

away, creating a hole. Bash stepped through as the troll snarled at him. A gasp of relief escaped my mouth as he took in the scene: me hanging off the pipe with a bloody cut across my stomach in nothing but my underwear halfway down my thighs and my shirt ripped to shreds. I saw the fire rise into his eyes; his fangs fully extended past his bottom lip. His eyes turned even darker red. He let out a feral scream as he lunged for the troll, tearing him away from me as he ripped into the troll's throat almost to the point of decapitation. Inky red blood flowed down Bash's mouth onto his white shirt. Bash pulled the troll close and began to drink deeply, letting most of his blood fall to the floor until he didn't move anymore.

Bash looked up, the rage still in his eyes as he let the troll fall dead to the floor. I sagged in relief, knowing I was safe because my Devils came for me. Darkness began to swim into my eyes, and I faded in and out, hearing voices yelling orders to someone. I felt someone lift me as someone else carefully cut the handcuffs off from the pipe.

A whisper caressed through my mind. "Lil' Star, stay with me, baby. Open your eyes. Please, baby, please."

I slowly opened my eyes to see Tristian carrying me. I was wrapped in Bash's navy suit jacket and turned to look at Bash, who held my hand.

"Lexi, you have to stay awake, okay?"

I blinked and gave a small nod.

Tristian walked us out of the bar and over to the car, where Aden had someone tied up with his gun pointed at him. "This asshole isn't talking... Fuck, is she okay?" Worry filled Aden's eyes.

Bash sneered, "She needs to be healed. She got hit pretty hard and has a gnarly cut across her stomach. I fucking killed the bastard. He is nothing more than skin and bones now."

I struggled to keep my eyes open. "He...threw me back... wall...boom...big ouchy," I said, trying to make a joke.

Tristian sat with me gently cradled on his lap. "Just close your eyes, Lil' Star. It will be better soon." He murmured a healing spell. A warm tingling sensation washed through my body as the cut on my stomach stitched itself back together. "Damn it, I'm out of energy. Aden, give me yours."

Aden didn't hesitate. He handed Bash his gun and walked over to grip Tristian's hand. Both of their energies mixed and finished healing me from the rest of my cuts and the head wound.

I felt my own energy return. I was still light-headed as I tried to sit up. Thankfully, Tristian held onto me. "Lil' Star, just wait..." He frowned.

"I can stand," I said, shakily climbing to my feet. I patted the jacket, making sure I covered all the important parts of myself, then walked slowly over to Bash. His eyes held a worried look into them as he stared at me. "I'm okay, Sebastian, thanks to my Devils."

His eyes changed from worried to what could only be described as psychopathic. He turned back to Aden, who had the guy tied up. He was a skinny man with oily dark hair, scarred skin, and yellow eyes. He looked high as a kite. With teeth bared, he snarled, "Tu n'échapperas plus à la mort, les Wishmaker auront leur récompense."

I turned to Bash. "Please tell me we can kill this motherfucker now." A menacing smile formed around my lips. I

peered down at the man beneath me, letting my full siren show so he could see my true self: my violet eyes, my thin fangs elongated, and my pearlescent skin. "You tell the Wishmaker that if he wants me dead to come and kill me himself."

The guy was visibly shivering, like he just realized he was amongst bigger monsters than himself. I smiled cruelly, tilting my head to the side, and let my full compulsion hit him. "You are going to tell us everything we want to know. Then you are going to get two bullets to the chest and one to the head, which is me being merciful, you pathetic piece of shit."

He glared at me with hate in his eyes. "A la vraie révolution, aux souhaits que nous devons faire et aux sacrifices que nous acceptons." He snapped his mouth closed, and it began to foam.

"No!" yelled Aden as he reached for him. The guy began to convulse as his life left his eyes. Blood seeped from his mouth, nose, and eyes. I held a hand to my mouth in a silent gasp; he was dead before Aden got to him.

"Damn it!" Bash cursed, kicking the sand around us. Before any of us could do anything else, we heard sirens in the distance and a large grey SUV pulled up next to us.

The door swung open as Agent Rengard stepped out and removed his sunglasses. He took in the scene of a very dead man at Aden's feet, Bash fuming, and me only in a jacket looking as if I'd just survived a hurricane.

"Mr. Ryder, Ms. Rose. Why am I not surprised to see you two here?" He looked at the four of us, frowning. "Ms. Rose, are you okay?"

I hated that question. "I was almost your next victim,

Mr. Rengard."

He looked shocked for a second, then covered it up, walking to me.

"Tell me everything."

I sighed and told him everything from the troll who tried to kidnap and rape me to the dead guy at our feet who took his own life. Agent Rengard took notes and by the end, he was so mad he couldn't shield it from me anymore.

"Ms. Rose, we didn't think The Wishmaker would attack you like this. I will send in my report and give you a police escort to ensure your safety. I am sorry for all the trouble."

I folded my arms and moved next to Bash. "Your apologies are a bit too late, Mr. Rengard. If these men hadn't saved me, then you would have been reporting another murder to your superiors."

Rengard bent down to examine the body and nodded. "And what about him?"

Bash stepped forward. "Aden captured him and tied him up. When we tried to question him... It seems he had a deadly nightshade capsule. He took his own life."

Aden took out a phone and handed it to him. "I found this on him, Agent."

Agent Rengard pulled out a bag and took the phone with a gloved hand. "I will run it for prints and have our forensics team look through it."

Bash took my arm gently. "Now, I am taking Lexi home; she needs rest." Aden led me over to the passenger side of the car, opening my door as I slid in. I played the part of the helpless girl because I knew it would save us from being questioned for hours on end, and we didn't need the FBI

involved anymore.

Truth be told, I wasn't sure we could trust them.

Rengard and Bash exchanged a few words outside the car. "Suspect", "murder", and "coven assholes" were some of the colorful phrases he used. I couldn't hear everything, but by the look on Rengard's face, I could tell Bash was scolding him and his agency. When they were finished, Rengard nodded briskly to Bash and walked to my side of the car. He knocked on the window, and I reluctantly rolled it down.

"Yes...?"

Rengard looked me over carefully. I had no cuts or bruises, thanks to Tristian and Aden, but he knew I was telling the truth. "My sister is a therapist. If you need to talk to someone about today, feel free to get in touch with her. PTSD is real, Ms. Rose, and again, I can't say sorry enough. It was never my intention for you to be wrapped up in all of this." He handed me a card. I nodded my thanks, took the card, and rolled my window up as my Devils piled in.

Bash took my hand and kissed it. "Let's get home, Princess."

Chapter Twenty-Six

We headed down to the cliffs, the ocean waves big and dark as clouds covered the sun. I closed my eyes, thinking how lucky I was. I'd come close to death, and I had beat it, but I knew that without these three men I would have never seen another day. I would have never seen Ella, Coco, or Jason again, and that made my heart ache. I couldn't imagine never speaking to them again or having a funny meme sent to me about sparkly vampires.

I jumped as I realized our biggest mistake. "Damn it, that phone was our only clue!"

All three started to smile and Aden chuckled. "Lex, you think I didn't upload the phone already? Or that I gave

Rengard everything I found?" He shook his head as he handed me a card that had the words "Mort Noire" scrolled across it. It was an exclusive speakeasy where the darkest dealings tended to happen. I turned the card over, and engraved on the back were two words.

"Hemlock Falls?"

Aden smirked. "I'm pretty sure this is the club that the girls were supposed to meet at."

I grinned, pulled him into my arms, and kissed his cheek. "Aden Charmante, you beautiful vampire thief."

"Also, I texted Ella and told her what went down when I saw the state you were in. So, she couriered a package for you." He handed me a white shopping bag, and I pulled out a white summer dress with large black buttons going from the bottom to the top, and brown slip-on sandals.

"Thank you." I pulled off Bash's jacket and quickly threw the dress over me as my Devils avoided looking at me.

"Hey, you know, just doing what I do best," Aden called from the front.

I slipped on the shoes as Tristian huffed out from the driver's side, "We helped."

I gave him a small smile "Yes, you did, and I am grateful for my Devils who dove into hell to pull me out." I squeezed Bash's hand.

"Your Devils, Princess?" Bash asked with a raised eyebrow.

"What?" I tilted my head to the side with a smile "You call me your Princess." I bit my lip. "What else would I call you three?"

He leaned in close to my lips. "You have no idea how much I like that, Princess."

Driving back to the house was quick. I think the stress of the days finally hit us; we were so quiet in the car. We pulled up to the gate as one of our guards waved Aden down to stop. He was carrying a black velvet box under his arm, and he had his gun out. Aden rolled his window down, his hand on his gun. Tristian pulled his out as well. No one wanted to take any more chances.

"Boss," the guard said in a low voice.

"Marcel, what's going on?" He lifted the box to Aden.

"Got this today. Don't worry, we checked it out already. Ain't nothing in there but umm... I don't know if Boss Man is gonna be happy about it." He lightly laughed as he handed the box over.

I moved forward to the front and leaned between Aden and Tristian to see what was in the package. Aden placed the crushed velvet box on his lap. The top had gold swirly letters with all of our names painted on the lid; a huge gold satin ribbon held the box closed.

"Open it." I smiled.

Rolling his eyes at me, Aden pulled the ribbon, and it fell open, revealing a black invitation and a gold lace masquerade ball mask. "We are cordially invited to attend a masquerade ball Saturday at midnight at the home of Morgan Ryder and family. A mask must be worn the entire evening."

Tristian whistled. "Damn, we've been summoned, frere."

Bash just growled from his seat.

I took Bash's hand. "It will be okay, Bash. Plus, you might even get to stab someone."

He smirked at me. "True, Princess, I always do feel better when I can get a bit stabby."

I hit his arm, laughing playfully as a smile played at his lips. "Was that a joke, Sebastian?"

Maddox looked at us like I was off my rocker for teasing Bash. He quickly recovered, gave a two-finger salute, and walked back to his position by the gate.

Right as we were pulling in, I heard "LEXI ROSE!" I turned around and saw my seventy-nine-year-old neighbor Mrs. Wilson running in a full multi-colored kaftan and heels towards us.

I rolled my window down. "Hey Mrs. Wilson!" I waved. "What can I do for you?"

She smiled brightly as Aden rolled down his window, and she pulled her sunglasses down to get a good look at him and Tristan.

"Well, hello, darlings, I have a tiny favor to ask of you three strapping gentlemen. See, I have this piece of art I just got in my backyard that needs to be moved to its proper place, and, since I'm not as young as I once was, I thought I might be able to borrow your boys to help?" She waggled her eyebrows up and down.

I let out a small chuckle. "Of course they will, Mrs. Wilson. Right, guys?" All three looked at me with irritation and turned around. "They'd love to. Just let us park the car."

Aden grumbled under his voice and pulled into a spot. I climbed out and walked over to her as she pulled me into a tight hug and kissed both of my cheeks.

"Think they will do it shirtless?" She stage-whispered. "Wouldn't that be nice?"

I grinned. "Maybe I can convince them to."

She wrapped her arm in her mine and walked back to

her home as my Devils followed, leading us to her large backyard. "Ahh here it is, gorgeous." It was a huge purple oval shape that looked like a giant eggplant. "They call it 'Sliding into DM's' and here is the best part." She picked up a remote and pressed a button as water sprayed from the top. "It's a fountain!" she exclaimed.

I covered my mouth and laughed. "Mrs. Wilson, do you know what that is?"

Aden joined me and chuckled. "That is one big auber-gine."

I smirked, leaning in close to his ear. "I've seen bigger," I whispered, biting the inside of my cheek, trying not to laugh harder than I already was.

Bash walked up and stared at the giant eggplant as if it offended him. "You can't be serious?"

Tristian was already being pulled next to Mrs. Wilson as she had her hand wrapped around his bicep. "No darling, you don't want to get dirt on this nice shirt. Just pop it here and I will make sure nothing happens to it."

I walked over, unable to hide my smile. "She's right, you know, I think all of your shirts might get ruined if you don't take them off." I batted my eyelashes at him.

Tristian turned his eyes to me with a look of mischief about them. "Oh, yeah, Lil' Star? Like this?" He slowly popped open a few buttons on his shirt until his tattooed stomach with that lickable V was revealed. He ran his fingers along the sides of his shirt until he pulled it off in one fluid motion, throwing it in my direction. I caught it with one hand.

Mrs. Wilson cleared her throat "My darling Lexi, bring

an old lady her afternoon tea. it's sitting right over there. I should supervise this. She motioned to the outdoor bar where a martini glass sat empty next to a pitcher of clear liquid.

"Of course, Mrs. Wilson."

She chuckled as I tossed Tristian's shirt into a chair near her and walked over to Aden "It's really a shame you guys can't help Tristian. I think he might be my favorite now," I teased.

"Oh yeah, baby? We will see."

Aden walked backward toward Mrs. Wilson and Tristian, whipping his shirt off and tossing it my way. "Hold that for me, Lex. Just try not to get it too wet."

Shaking my head, I looked at Bash with a coy smile. "Two outta three. You gonna play too, Bash?"

He grinned mischievously at me. "Oh, Princess, you are royally fucked." He began to unbutton his shirt and left it open as he helped them move the dick statue. I grabbed a few glasses and sat next to Mrs. Wilson as she yelled at the boys to shift the sculpture.

I poured the martinis out and took a sip as the cool taste of gin hit my tongue. "You know this isn't tea, right, Mrs. Wilson?"

"Of course, dear, but if you don't live your life to the fullest every day, my love, it's not worth living."

I looked at all three of them as a bit of sweat started to drip down their chests, and I imagined what it would be like if I could feel them underneath me. Oh, to be utterly worshiped by all of my Devils. I looked over at Mrs. Wilson, who was staring at me with an amused expression. I took a sip of the gin. "What?" I asked innocently.

"Which one?" She smiled, all-knowing.

I choked and let out a hard cough. "Umm... I am not sure what you mean... They are just my friends. I've known them most of my life."

Mrs. Wilson looked at me with annoyance. "No, darling, that's not just friend energy. Blondie over there looked like he was going to make a meal out of you later, and dark and broody looks at you like the stars shine just for you, and do not get me started on Sebastian Ryder. He looks like he is going to chain you up and say 'MINE'!"

Little did she know that she was hitting close to home.

"It's complicated." I didn't know what more I could say than that because damnit, it was so fucking complicated. I took another drink and smiled wickedly. "Turn on the fountain when they get it set up," I whispered to Mrs. Wilson.

She gave a small laugh. "You are truly evil, darling. I love it."

As soon as the guys placed the artwork down, Mrs. Wilson picked up the remote with a wicked grin and pressed the button. Water exploded everywhere, and a string of curses exploded from each of them.

"Lil' Star! I am gonna turn that ass red when I get ahold of you!"

Mrs. Wilson smirked. "Lexi, dear, he reminds me of my late husband, God rest his soul. Tell me, does he fuck as good as mine did?"

This time my martini slipped out of my hand and spilled all over Mrs. Wilson's table. "Mrs. Wilson!" I gasped.

She waved me off. "My dear, you really should start to run. Those devils are heading our way, and it looks like they are going to make that promise of turning you red."

I looked up and saw three very angry vampires heading my way with vengeance in their eyes. Big babies. "Damn, I gotta go, Mrs. Wilson! See ya later!" I waved goodbye, grabbed my shoes in one hand, and took off running as fast as I could.

I made it to the gate when I heard them gaining on me. I looked back and saw Aden was running full speed—so close to vamp speed that it was a bit scary. I crossed the street, leaping through the side gate and running as hard and fast as I could. I was almost to the door when Bash sped the rest of the way, stopped in front of me, and I crashed into his arms.

"So close, Princess. Don't you know vampires always catch their prey?" he growled, spinning me around to see Aden and Tristian coming up the steps.

"Someone has been a bad, bad girl," Tristian tutted, taking my chin in his hand.

Aden came up next to him, running his fingers down my throat. "So pretty, baby. Think her blood tastes as sweet as her pussy?" He ran his tongue over his fangs and licked his bottom lip. I should have been terrified. Most girls would be, but I knew they wouldn't hurt me. I grinned seductively at them.

"Do your worst, boys," I purred in a sultry voice.

Bash growled behind me, pulling me closer to his chest as his hands splayed across my stomach. "Such a good little siren. Is that what you want, Princess? Do you want us to spill your blood while you have all three of us on our knees begging for you?" His hand moved up to tighten around my throat, and a moan escaped me.

Tristian let out a low chuckle. "Bash, I think that is exactly what she wants," he said, sinking his fingers into my hair and pulling my head to the side, exposing my neck to Aden. "Hmm, Lex, you want my lips here?" He kissed my throat right under my ear, and I let another moan out, whispering his name. "Tell me. Yes or no, baby, my will is waning."

The air around us grew thick with tension as they waited for me to decide if I wanted them all. The truth of it was I always had wanted them. "Yes" was on the tip of my tongue when Bash's phone rang, breaking the spell.

Bash whipped out his phone and let me go so fast that I fell right into Aden and Tristian. "This had better be good." He stiffened, looking like he was going to punch a wall. He quickly hit the speakerphone. "You are on speaker."

Kane Anderson's smooth, deep voice came through. "Good evening, all. Agent Rengard has just informed me that he thinks The Blood Coven is behind the pixie dust and murders. An eyewitness has come forward accusing you of selling and distributing the drug in Mort Noire. The evidence is stacking up against you right now, son, so heed this warning: If you don't start thinking with your brain instead of the appendage between your legs, you are going to spend your best years in jail, or worse. Get your shit together and find those mermaids."

The call ended as quickly as it began.

I turned to Bash, but he was walking to the end of the porch. He let out a thundering roar to the sky. I glanced back at Tristian and Aden with pleading eyes, and they looked defeated. Aden ran a hand over his face, and Tris-

tian glared at the ground with pinched eyes like he was trying to solve it all.

"Guys…" I whispered, placing my hand on Aden's hand and then reaching out for Tristian's. "He needs us." I led them to him, to the vampire everyone was terrified of. I dropped Aden and Tristian's hands as I ran my hands up Bash's back, wrapping myself around him. Tristian and Aden looked at each other for a moment before they nodded and each gripped Bash's shoulder to show their support for their friend and brother.

"Come here, Princess," he whispered. I moved to his front and wrapped my arms around him again, resting my head on his chest.

"We will find them, Bash. I won't let them take you away. I know you didn't do this, but we need to figure out who did so we can end them." I buried my head into his chest, inhaling his scent so he wouldn't see the unshed tears and the fear in my eyes.

He nodded.

"We are doing half of the FBI's job now. We will find them, and we will get our pound of flesh, frere," Aden said angrily.

Tristian looked over to Bash. "'Til the end, frere. Je suis le démon qui vit dans ton Coeur ta douleur prendra vie!" A silent word exchanged between the three of them, and then Bash and Aden lifted their heads to the sky and yelled:

"Votre Douleur prendra vie!"

It was like the heavens knew what promises they made. The clouds became dark and grey as droplets started to fall around us. I smiled at them. I knew their bond would never fail. They were more than just brothers; they were

intertwined into each other's souls.

They stood surrounding me, each of my Devils at my side. I leaned back into Sebastian and looked up at his handsome face. "Wanna go order pizza, watch awful movies, and drink cheap beer?"

He looked down at me and smiled. "Princess, you are a true wonder." He tugged me with him inside as the others followed. Tristian made the call for pizza, and Aden went to the fridge to get the beer. It wouldn't solve all of our problems right now, but we could hide and forget them for a moment.

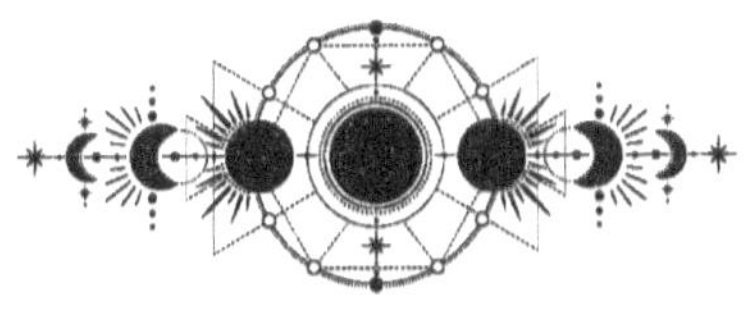

Once the pizza was delivered, we all gathered in the kitchen in our comfiest clothes. We all were quiet as we sat around the coffee table eating pizza and drinking cheap beer.

"We need to get a reservation to investigate Mort Noir for possible suspects," Tristian said to the room.

"How will you get us in? And when?" I asked.

"After the ball, Princess. I have a feeling that Morgan has an agenda to get us to come, so we need to tread lightly."

We all agreed unanimously that we would go after the ball.

The guys discussed logistics about security. I went

through my phone, texting back and forth with Ella, telling her what happened at The Oddity today and how Bash was now Suspect Number One in the investigation. I soon finished my pizza and walked over to the couch, turning on the TV to find a movie to watch. Tristian jumped over the couch and sat next to me as Aden plopped down on my other side. I pulled my knees up underneath me and watched Bash walk over, his shoulders slightly slumped and tension riddling throughout his body. I nudged Aden, and when he looked at me, I lifted my head in silence towards Bash. Aden then elbowed Tristian, who was almost asleep. He lifted his head to look at us, a knowing grin on his face.

Tristian yawned loudly, making Bash turn his head and raise his brow. "I'm tired. I think I'll head for a shower and bed," Tristian announced.

Bash lifted a hand in goodbye, and Aden stood.

"I'm gonna do a preliminary check before I head off to bed. Night Lex, Bash." He leaned down and kissed my cheek and whispered, "You might be the only one who can make him better, Lexi. He needs you now more than ever."

I gave him a small smile as he walked away.

I looked everywhere but at Bash. I felt his eyes on me, and I turned to see him staring at me intently. "What, do I have pizza sauce on my face?" I joked.

He smirked. "No, it's just... It's amazing to me how beautiful you truly are, Lexi. I don't just mean your face, but your heart. You truly care about all of it, don't you?"

I tilted my head, giving him a small smile. "I do, but you do too, Bash. You would do anything to protect your family, your coven. You may play the Devil, but you aren't truly

evil, Sebastian."

I stood, walking over to where he sat in the armchair as if he was on a throne; he was fully spread out, his hands resting on his thighs. I slid between his legs as he gave me a questioning look. I lowered myself to his eye level; he watched me like a snake watching a mouse. Still as a stone, almost to the point where I didn't know if he was breathing.

So, I did the only thing I was dying to do all night. I ran my fingers through his dark hair and pulled myself into his lap. He moved so I could straddle him.

I whispered, "I know in my heart you didn't kill Daniels and that you have nothing to do with pixie dust or the missing mermaids. I know this because I have seen how you protect me. I see the anger in your eyes when we think we've gotten everything, but then it's thrown back in our face. I see your fierceness for wanting to end the mayhem and have peace within our covens. I see it all because I see who you are, Bash, not what the world knows or wants. I've wanted you all this time, I was just too heartbroken to admit it." I closed our distance and slowly kissed his cheek, moving to the other side and laying light kisses across his face. I brushed my lips over his and murmured, "Am I right, Sebastian? Or is it all a lie?"

Bash's eyes tightened as he leaned closer, resting his forehead against mine. "You've owned my heart, Lexi, then and now. The truth is, I never fully recovered from you. I played the dutiful son and leader, but my days bled together. They didn't have hope, laughter, or joy; not until you came back into it."

I shivered and moved closer, kissing his lips slowly, de-

vouring each minute. His hands ran up my back along my spine, making me whimper as our kisses became frantic. I pulled at his shirt, wanting to feel more of his skin; he played with the top of my shorts while he trailed kisses to my neck.

"How quiet can you be, Princess?"

I bit my lip with a lustful moan. "Quiet, I swear."

He gave a husky laugh. "Doubtful," he said as he sank his finger into my shorts, rubbing right on top of my clit.

"Fucccccckkk...." I moaned into his neck, raising to meet his fingers as they moved my panties to the side. He sank two fingers into me. "Ohh! Bash!" His fingers moved to their own melody, playing me as I became slick to his touch. I arched into him as he continued to work me faster. I heard a door open but ignored it. Bash began to play with my nipple, pulling my shirt down to take it in his mouth. I moaned as I fucked his hand and moved my fingers to his plaid pajama bottoms, running it over his hard length.

"Jesus, Bash, I'm about to cum...."

He purred into my nipple, sending electric shockwaves throughout my whole body.

My fingernails bit into his shoulders as his fingers stayed the course. "Oh god, don't stop, Bash."

He happily obliged, and his lips soon found my neck. I felt his fangs scrape my skin, and I shuddered. He bit down but didn't break skin, just enough to send goosebumps across my body. He started moving faster and circling my clit with his thumb. I exploded as a full-body tremor ran through my spine.

He wasn't finished yet; he kept fucking me with his hand.

"There's my princess," he breathed. "Come again, baby, you know you want to." I continued to lift myself on Bash's hand and bit into his neck so hard I tasted his blood as I chased the next orgasm that hit me even harder.

I cursed Bash's name and moaned so loudly I knew that the whole house heard me. I sank into his lap, and he moved me so my legs were hanging over his; my eyes fluttered closed, but I made out two silhouettes in the shadows, and I smiled as I felt sleep finally catch up with me and drifted off to dreamland. The last thing I heard was hushed talking and a chuckle from Bash's chest.

Chapter Twenty-Seven

The next morning, I woke with a stretch, feeling a heavy arm wrapped around me, pulling me closer to him. I smiled. A hand started to trail down my stomach, and soft lips kissed my neck.

"Morning, Princess," Bash said as he pulled me back to his morning wood.

A small moan escaped me. "Bash..." I turned around to face him, finding his green eyes flashing with desire. I kissed his lips softly as his hand smoothed up my leg.

"Spread your legs, Princess. I need you." He gripped my shorts, pulling them off in one motion.

Who was I to say no to him?

I kissed him deeper, widening my legs for him. I giggled

as he moved above me, kissing my neck, lifting my shirt in one motion and tossing it behind me. He made his way down to the tops of my breasts, playing with my nipples, taking one in his mouth while he played with the other.

"Please, Bash, I need you," I echoed him.

He pushed his pants off, and I felt him hard and ready as he rubbed outside of me. I moaned as our kisses deepened, becoming feverish. It was like I never stopped craving this man. I ran my hands up his back, arching into him.

His phone started to ring, and I groaned into his mouth.

"I'll ignore it." He picked it up looking to see who it was. "Damn it, it's Ella. She never calls me this early."

I sank back on my elbows. "Answer it; then we can continue." I reached out to kiss his neck. He ran his hands down my front, holding the phone to his ear as he answered in a rough voice.

"Ella, what's up?" He sat back on his knees, looking down at me with a fire in his eyes, his fingers tracing circles on my stomach down my body. I arched into his hand, enjoying his touch, suppressing a moan. "No, I haven't seen her all morning."

He spread my legs slowly, licking his lips as his fingers teased my inner thigh. I pushed my face into a pillow to let out a whimper. Bash stilled and I lifted my head in question.

"Don't snap, Ella, I get you to want to talk to Lexi."

I sat up in a bolt, holding out my hand for the phone, but Bash pushed his thumb right on my clit and started rubbing me in slow lazy circles. I dropped back onto the bed and arched into his hand.

"Fuck, Bash," I breathed.

"You want me to get her now? She might be asleep still, but let me see." He slid two fingers inside me and began pumping them in and out of me. I cursed his name silently as he worked his hand right where I needed him. "I am only doing what Dad wants. You can see her whenever you want, little sister."

I was so close, and Bash knew it. He started to move faster. I rolled my hips over his hand as he continued to fuck me with his fingers, his palm grinding against my clit.

"Fuck, fuck, fuck, yes, Bash, don't stop!"

He grinned that mischievous grin, about to bring me to the brink, then stopped suddenly, his fingers still inside of me. I saw his eyes full of concern and slight fear. "You are on your way up to the gate? Now?"

What?! Okay, no. Ella could not see me naked in bed with her brother. I removed his hand from me with a small yelp and leaped out of the bed, making a beeline to my bathroom, where I started the shower. "Tell her I am in the shower!" I hissed from the door. I pulled Bash's clothes from the floor and shoved them in his arms. "Clothes. Dress. Out! Now!" I started pushing him to the door.

He seemed to calm down and now wore a cocky smirk, the bastard.

"You're enjoying this too much, Ryder." I glared at him.

He took his clothes and stole a quick kiss from me. "Yeah. I'll meet you, but I hear her shower going. Want me to get her?"

I glared at him, and he shooed me with his hands and pointed to the shower. I threw a middle finger in the air at him and jumped under the hot water to wash in a hurry. Like I could scrub any evidence that I had been with Bash away.

Sighing, I thought more about how I put a front up for those who I loved the most, and how around the Devils I could be my complete self. Yes, Lexi, Daniels, Coco, and Jason brought me joy, laughter, and happiness, but I think they always handled me with care as If I would break. In reality, I was already in so many shattered pieces that I couldn't be broken anymore.

Broken. Yeah. That was the perfect way to describe me.

I lived in my grief, I thrived in it for years, and I realized that I needed Bash, Aden, and Tristian, even though it came with some big baggage. I mean, who had three boyfriends? It was a big leap for me, who'd never even had a long-term boyfriend. Not to mention all of the feelings and egos I had to deal with. I think I knew deep down in my heart and soul that it had always been them. That's why I never had anyone serious; it was always supposed to be us four.

Sebastian was my first love, and like the ocean, always steady and there. Aden was my shore: soft, comfortable, relaxing. Tristian was the sun, always warm and there to bring a smile to my face even on the darkest days. I wanted to keep us quiet a while longer before we were bombarded with questions, and shouldn't I be able to?

I really hated lying to Ella, though. I would tell her soon, but I was scared of her reaction. Would she understand? Would she be mad, angry at me, at us? I banged my head lightly against the shower wall, letting the hot water run down me, when I heard the crack of a door opening and Tristian's sandy blond head popped in.

"Hey, Lil' Star, Bash sent me in here to see if you were okay."

I looked up, and his smile fell as he saw the worry that

was on my face. He walked into the shower fully clothed, wrapping himself around me. "Hey... what is it?"

I groaned into him. "I don't like lying to Ella about,"—I waved my hands between us—"all of this."

"Yeah... and what is all of this?" he asked, trying not to laugh.

I huffed in irritation. "Can we not talk about this all wet and naked?"

He bit his lip as he stepped back, admiring my body as the water fell. "You are the only one who's naked, babe." Which was true, but his white shirt was completely see-through now.

"You know what I mean."

Tristan threw his hands up in the air with a grin. "Okay, Lil' Star, whatever you say. I'm going to change." He stepped out of the shower. "But just so you know, Lexi, this is new to us, too. We never have shared women, not like this. You make our puzzle fit like you were made for us." He wrapped a towel around me, pulling me close to him and kissing my head. "I think when Ella sees that, she will be happy for you. But if you aren't ready, you aren't ready, and we will stand by your decision until you are ready for everyone to know you are ours." He moved to the door and stepped out before popping his head back in. "But, baby, just know if anyone else tries to join in with you, we will rip out their throats and bathe in their blood, because you belong to us." He said this with a sparkle in his eyes and a smile on his face, like he hoped that it would happen.

I dried off and dressed in soft cream jeans and a grey sweater, braiding my hair to the side. I threw on some mascara and lip gloss just to polish up.

Ella was on the couch with Dyna in her arms. I swear, animals loved this girl. I have seen her come home with a random dog, cat, and once even a few rabbits. I walked to the chair that Bash had me in last night, and a blush hit my cheeks.

Ella smiled at me. "I missed Dyna," she said, petting the cat's fluffy white fur. "Have those big old stupid vamp boys been mean to my sweet baby?" Her eyes suddenly creased with concern. "Hey, Lex, your face is flushed. Are you okay?"

I shook myself from the memory playing in my head.

"She's fine," a deep voice rang out. "Just a bit of sun from yesterday's beach day we had." I looked at Bash with a what the fuck face. He sat next to me in a chair that he pulled over, his legs brushing mine, a smirk playing on his lips. He leaned forward with his elbows on his knees and whispered, "Do you think she knows that I had my fingers in your sweet little pussy just half an hour ago?"

I glared at him. "Fuck off, Bash," I muttered.

Ella rolled her eyes. "Good to know you two still despise each other."

I beamed at Ella. "Well, once an asshat, always an asshat."

Aden and Tristian came into the room and sat down. "Hey, Ella, did Lexi tell you about us the other night?" quipped Aden.

"No...?" Ella gave me a confused look.

I stared icily at Aden.

"Yeah! She kicked all of our asses in cards the other night. I mean, I think she won at least a few hundred off each of us!"

Ella let a snicker out. "Go, girl!"

I smiled and immediately changed the subject. "So, I am assuming you are invited to the masquerade?"

She nodded. "Yep, Daddy Dearest calls and I come a-running." She rolled her eyes. "But hey, I have the coolest costumes for me and Ethan. It's like a devil/angel costume. It might be fun if you come, too!" She batted her eyes at Bash.

"She's her coven's leader, Ella. Of course she's coming," he grumbled.

I grinned. "Can't say no to a pretty dress and a mask!"

Ella laughed. "Yes! We can drink and dance 'til morning!"

I hopped in my chair at a chance to have a normal night of fun. That dream was nice, wasn't it?

Bash smiled broadly between me and Ella. "Yeah, and I'll be escorting you".

"And me." Tristian gave me a smug smile.

"Me too," Aden said in a low purr.

Ella frowned at us. "Lex, can we go take a walk on the beach... alone?" She turned and glared at Bash.

"NO!" snapped all three guys. Aden pushed his hands into his hair and looked at Ella "She can't go without someone with her, Ella, she could be—"

Ella sat up straighter. "Killed?" she said sarcastically. "Yes, I understand this, Aden Charmante. Lexi told me all about yesterday. But you three butt-faced cretins forget I am also just as dangerous." Her eyes shifted from her gorgeous umber brown eye to a dangerous canary yellow. She held her hand as her nails elongated to sharp needle-like claws. "I promise to deliver any attacker's heart to you on a silver platter." She blew out a breath, her eyes changing back.

All three of them stood solid, unmoving, and I sighed

with a slight pout to my lips.

"Look, I am asking for thirty minutes, max, just so we can talk." She turned to Bash, who narrowed his eyes and then gave us a short nod.

"Go, but we will watch from the backyard, and if I see anyone come near you, I will personally deliver their death by flaying them alive slowly."

Ella smirked. "Graphic, big brother. Come on, Lex, let's go before they change their minds."

I jumped up, and we both walked quickly to the backyard, feeling relieved to get a bit of privacy with her. We soon made it to the trail that led to the beach. I found my favorite spot and sat down, looking out at the horizon. Ella sat next to me, her knee bumping into mine.

"It's weird how they watch you like that... always has been." Ella and I turned at the same time to look back at the house, seeing three shadows standing at the window watching us. "Okay, spill it," she blurted out.

I looked up, trying to hide the shock on my face. "They are just being protective, Ella. Your father pretty much said that if anything happened to me, it would be their fangs." I played with the sand at my feet, letting it fall between my fingers.

Ella gave me a look that said I was full of it. "I call bullshit because the way they look at you tells me differently, mon amie."

I frowned at her words. I needed it to be just us for a little bit longer. Fuck! I just wanted to spend a bit more time in our little bubble. So, I made the decision that would make me hate myself later: I had to lie to Ella.

"Ella, seriously. Nothing is going on between us." I swallowed the words down as my stomach twisted in knots from the lie. Ella wrapped her arm around my shoulders, pulling me closer.

"I'm sorry, I just thought... I dunno, Lex. You've been happier these last few days. Happier than I have ever seen you in the past ten years, even with all of the crazy shit that has been going on around you. You just seem like you aren't carrying a dark, ominous cloud anymore." She grasped my hand to make me look at her. Ella's eyes brimmed with tears. I finally realized that she had noticed how sad I was all these years, which broke my heart; my grief and sadness were not hers to bear. "And if they are doing that, then that's great. But if not, then I am proud of you for finally being able to heal from all the pain you had to endure. It's like you're your old self again."

I laid my head on her shoulder and sighed. "That's the thing, Ella... I don't think I will ever be the same again. My soul is darker, and my heart has cracks in it. I learned to shine the light through those cracks, but I have been permanently changed. My parents' death wasn't just theirs; it was mine in its own way.

I wiped my eyes and smiled sadly at her.

"Hey. It's okay, the new Lexi isn't so bad. She can even cook now, thanks to Bash."

Ella let out a small laugh. "He had to cook for us because none of the chefs we hired were ever up to Dad's 'standards'." She mimed air quotes.

I chuckled because that was a very typical Morgan response. "Bash is a damn good cook. It's been a nice change, but I miss the Thai place. Think we could convince him to get takeout?"

Ella stood and pulled me up with both hands. "Ohhhhh, Lexi, one thing I know is how to make Bash do what I want. I have been doing it for years."

I laughed. "Okay, good! Let's head back before Bash's vein pulsates even more."

Ella giggled. "Oh my gawd, the vein! I forgot about that!"

We came through the back gate laughing and saw all three of my Devils sitting around the fire pit. Bash's back was to me and Ella. Aden and Tristian turned to face us. Aden was covering his face as he convulsed with laughter, and Tristian had his head thrown back, cackling openly at the sky.

I giggled. "Oops, I forgot... vampire hearing."

As Bash turned towards me and Ella, he was glaring at us so hard I could understand why people called him a devil, but there on his forehead was the very angry and red vein pulsating. I bite my lip, trying not to laugh, mouthing "sorry" to Bash, but he only glared harder as Ella burst into a fit of giggles.

"The vein!" she stage-whispered.

I winked at Bash. "If you get us Thai tonight, I'll stop the laughing."

Bash's dark glare turned into a look of amusement. "Deal, Princess."

A smile formed around my lips, and I began to softly sing "Ocean Eyes" by Billie Eilish. My compulsion fell over everyone around me, and then suddenly I saw everyone find a seat around the fire pit. Aden's whole body relaxed

in one fluid motion as he stared into the flames, Ella smiled and closed her eyes, swaying back and forth in her seat, and Tristian had his head back on the seat with his eyes closed, softly humming along. When I looked at Bash, he was staring at me with a look of amazement and a small amount of fear.

"I think the big, bad vampire finally realized how dangerous the little siren can be," I said with a husky laugh as I sat on his lap playing with his hair.

"No, Princess, I always knew how dangerous you were because when I was a kid, a little girl with bright blue eyes walked up to me one day and ripped my heart from my chest." He kissed my neck, and I relaxed in the comfort of my Devil.

He was mine. They were all mine, and I knew I wouldn't let anyone take them away from me. I had already had so much taken away from me, but my Devils, no.

They would stay with me forever.

Chapter Twenty-Eight

Saturday night came in faster than I had anticipated. Ella and I spent more time together, helping pick out clothes, shoes, and masks for all of us.

I was wrapping a towel tightly around me when Ella came barreling in. "Okay, I gotta go get ready, but I have everything ready for you. Hair and makeup will be here in an hour, so go get ready."

She pushed me into the bedroom, where a gorgeous black dress was laid out for me. After four hours of hair and makeup, at least Aden and Tristian kept checking on me and would sit and talk to me until they needed to get ready. I hadn't seen Bash at all this afternoon. Tristian said something about meetings with his father.

I was glad to finally get dressed as I pulled the dark-as-night, floor-length dress over me, letting it drop down my body and adjusting the high slit on the side. Its tulle was soft and silky with handmade black lace flowers placed around the bodice and feathers over my chest that reached the top of my shoulders. A small black diamond crown sat upon my head to complete my look. I slid my feet into satin, blood-red stilettos with delicate leaves climbing up the back of the heel. Then I touched up my dark red lipstick and stood back to see the entirety of the completed outfit.

I was someone I didn't recognize anymore.

The door clicked open, and Bash came in, fiddling with his cuff sleeve on his classic-cut tux. I turned to him and smiled. "Need help?" I asked, and he grunted, still looking down, and I reached for his hand to fix his cufflinks. He looked up and took me in, his grin turning wicked.

"You truly look like a villain now, Princess." He ran his fingers down my neck. "A true leader."

I shook my head. "It's just a dress and makeup, Bash."

He shook his head. "No, Lexi, this is not like when I saw you at Ella's engagement party. You were unsure about yourself and had an air of sadness about you even before Daniels's death, but now? That girl isn't there anymore. This woman is strong, which terrifies me a bit, but I loved how it has made you feel and how it makes me feel around you."

He placed the lightest kiss on my cheek.

"Ready to go see if we can get any more clues about who killed Daniels?"

I nodded. "Fuck yes, let's go cause chaos."

We walked together, laughing lightly at each other, as Tristian and Aden waited for us. Aden was in a dark red shirt that matched my lipstick with a solid black paisley jacket, and Tristian was in an all-black suit with silver thread sparkling through it, creating a filigree pattern throughout the coat. They were my three perfect mistakes. Tristian and Aden both stood still as I approached; I felt a blush creeping up my neck.

"Hey, Lil' Star." Tristian held his hand to me. "Ready to go cause trouble?"

I rolled my eyes. "Can we promise to enjoy the night a little bit, too? And if we find anything, we tell each other?"

Aden wrapped his arms around my shoulder. "Just fun." He winked at me, and a grin spread across his lips.

"What's so funny?" I asked, curious.

Bash huffed. "Nothing. Aden just won our bet." He handed Aden a few hundred dollars and walked to the door.

My face went from being embraced to pissed in an instant. "A fucking bet?" I spat at Bash. "After everything, you three... made another bet."

Tristian ran a hand through his hair. "It's not that kind of bet, Lil' Star."

I glared at him, pointing my finger at his chest. "NOT. THAT. KIND. OF. BET? You've got to be kidding me right now. Let's get this out here right now: Never fucking bet on me again because you will all lose." I stormed through the living room and out the door, wanting to scream at them after everything we'd been through. I started angrily texting Ella about what an idiot her older brother and his friends were.

I pulled the door open and tried to climb into the car's back seat, but with the dress and the shoes, it was more difficult than I thought. "Shit!" I hissed as I slipped for the third time, trying to get in.

A hand steadied my back. "Here." Aden held me as I lifted my dress and helped me slide into the car.

Once I was sitting comfortably, I glared at him. "You are a dick."

He tried to hide his smile. "I know, and I am so sorry. You are right. It was a stupid bet that we shouldn't have made; the bet was only to see if you looked like a goddamn goddess. We all knew you would, Lex. You just keep surprising us." He stepped up and slid next to me. "Please don't be mad." He kissed my cheek and held my hand.

I changed the subject. "You're not driving tonight?"

He shook his head. "No, Tristian is; I get to sit back with you and be your escort, if you'll have me."

I pursed my lips. "Only if you find me that cotton candy drink with the sparkles that Morgan loves to have at parties."

Aden beamed at me and held out his hand. "Deal, baby."

I couldn't help but smile back. "Deal." I clasped his hand.

Tristian climbed in the front, and Bash slid on the other side as we headed towards the city lights. "Why aren't you in the front passenger side?" I looked at Bash, who was staring at the window somberly.

"You will have two of us in your arms tonight, Princess, to ensure we show how powerful the covens are."

I smirked. "So, this isn't just about sending a big 'screw you' to Morgan and his little minion."

"Well... yeah, it's that, too." He chuckled and took my

hand into his, kissing the back. "I'm sorry, Princess, we won't ever do that again," he murmured into my hand, and I let my heart soften for Sebastian Ryder once more.

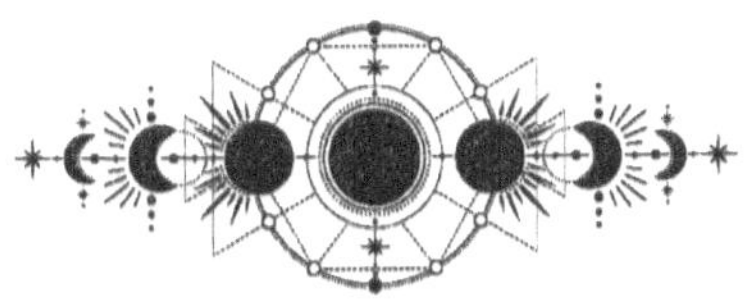

The Ryder Estate was straight out of a horror movie: Ivy crept up the iron gates, a small cemetery sat to the side, rolling down into foggy emerald hills, and a black steeple shot to the sky with a bell tower to the side. It was dark and gloomy and looked haunted.

"God, I hate this place," I groaned to Aden as he squeezed my hand in reinsurance.

"Seriously, why does this place always give me the creeps?" added Tristian from the front.

"Home sweet home," Bash said with a dreadful moan. We pulled up to the valet, and they approached to take the keys. Bash handed all of us our masks. "Here, everyone, put the mask on now."

I took the delicate mask from his hands. It matched my dress with dainty diamonds that swirled throughout the show. It wrapped around my face perfectly. I turned to Bash and smirked as he and the others wore identical masks. A golden mask sat upon his face with horns coming to a point that looked deadly, and two fangs were at the cutout of his mouth, so his beautiful full lips were on display.

"My Devils," I whispered, knowing they heard me.

Bash gazed into my eyes, looking like he wanted to say more, but he merely nodded. "Before we go in here, place this at your thigh just in case." It was a small, sharp blade with a holster that matched my dress.

I smirked. "Thanks; a girl could use some help."

He smiled. "As you wish." He raised my skirt, and I lifted my foot as he slid the blade up my leg, leaving goosebumps behind his fingers. He placed the blade at my thigh, tightening it so it wouldn't slip. As he pulled away, he eyed me like he was about to steal me away from everyone. "Shall we?" He gave me a small smile, knowing what he was doing to me. He held his hand to me to help me out of the car.

I took a deep breath and let it out in a puff. "Yep, let's rock this bitch."

They all laughed as we all stepped out and walked up to the door, the men flanking me on all sides. I reached for the door knocker, but it swung open, and Franklin stood there with a slimy expression as he licked his lips under his wooden Dryad mask.

"Lexi, you look lovely this evening." He held his hand to me, but I walked past him.

"Good evening," I deadpanned as I made my way into the grand room.

A large, winding staircase came sweeping down with gaudy black chandeliers and oil paintings of Morgan looking down at us. I felt Franklin's fear and hatred whip out as my Three Devils entered behind me. Franklin recovered quickly, throwing up a shield to keep me out, and he straightened his jacket.

"This way." He swept his arm towards a ballroom that sat off to the right of the grand room. Franklin stopped before two substantial oak doors and cleared his throat. "Just a few rules first."

Aden crossed his arms, glaring at Franklin. Tristian huffed a laugh, and Bash looked like he wanted to rip his head off.

"One, all masks are to be worn at all times, and two, no powers are to be used tonight. Lastly, we will have a surprise at the end of the night, and all three coven leaders must join in support of Mr. Ryder."

I rolled my eyes, irritated at him.

"Fine," Bash growled. "What kind of surprise?"

Franklin dared to smile. "You'll see," he said in a sing-song voice.

He pushed open two vast doors, and the entire room had been transformed into a dark fairytale; the space was encompassed in darkness with black raised pillars draped in black fabric that puddled at the floor. The only light came from glimmering chandeliers that hung low with forest greenery wrapping around them. Black candles floated like tiny stars in the sky, creating a twinkle that was cast throughout the room. In the middle was the dance floor. "Young and Beautiful" by Lana Del Rey played. A group of men and women were dancing in an abundance of colorful gowns and suits.

A man stood in the back. His grey suit was crisp, his hair pushed back, and he had a dark silver wolf's mask placed over his face. He stared at me with thirst in his eyes. I didn't need to guess who it was. Grayson signaled me with a nod to meet him over on the side, and I turned to Bash.

"Grayson."

He nodded, grabbing us champagne from a passing tray. He handed me one, and I took a sip of the bubbly as we headed over to meet Grayson, losing him in the crowd. I hoped we could find him again. We wove our way to a few pillars on one side, surrounded by only candlelight. A hand came out and clasped my wrist.

"Hello, seductress," Grayson said in his deep voice. "You look positively delectable." He gave me a wolfish grin.

"You clean up nice, too, farm boy." I grinned back.

He had the nerve to look shocked, clutching his hand to his chest. "She cuts deep! But seriously, sweetheart, you look good enough to eat."

I rolled my eyes, "You remember what happens to the wolf in most fairy tales, right?" I leaned closer to his ear and whispered, "You get turned into a pretty little area rug."

He shuddered at the thought. "I think being skinned alive by you wouldn't be too bad; tell me you would at least be scantily clad." He waggled his brows.

I let out a giggle. "You are relentless, aren't you?" I shook my head.

"Damn straight." He smiled and then turned his eyes to Bash. "Sebastian, good to see ya!" He held out his hand, and Bash looked down at it like it was diseased.

"Holsten, what can we do for you?" I wasn't sure why Bash acted like a world-class snob to Grayson, especially since he was helping us out.

"Ah, well, I was going to ask if Lexi would like to dance with me." He turned to me, holding out his hand.

I placed my hand in his and laughed. "Sure! Bash, be a dear and hold my drink." I passed my champagne flute over to him as I waved him off.

Grayson beamed and pulled me into the middle of the dance floor as "Lover" by Taylor Swift started softly playing. He guided me closer as he held my waist.

"You know he's going to be furious with you, right?" I tried to cover my laugh with my hand, but Grayson twirled me out to pull me into a dramatic dip.

"Nah, Bash and I have always had a bit of a competitive streak with each other."

I rested my hand on his shoulder as we began to move about the floor. Grayson Holsten was not only a great dancer, but I wanted to know more about our mysterious half-dragon, half-wolf leader. "Grayson, would you answer a personal question?"

He looked down at me with interest. "It depends on the question."

I took a deep breath and went for it. "What made you work with Daniels? Besides the obvious. Is there more to your reasoning than just wanting to get a drug off the street?"

His dark grey eyes looked down at me, and I could see the pain behind them. I knew that look because I had seen it in my own eyes for years. I moved closer to his ear and whispered so softly that I wasn't sure he heard me, "You lost someone to pixie dust, didn't you?" He gave me a pained smile as the song finished, and he took my hands and kissed each one.

"Follow me to the balcony, and I will tell you my story, seductress." I nodded, and we headed to the glass doors that would take us outside.

I glanced back at Aden and held up a finger to give me a minute; he raised his glass in acknowledgment as we stepped out into the night air. It was early enough that no one was out on the balcony yet. I walked to the railing to gaze up at the sky, admiring the full moon shining down on us and tiny stars twinkling as if they knew a secret. But I knew those bastards were heartless.

"It's wonderful, isn't it?" I turned to him as he approached. His eyes never left mine.

"Truly beautiful, indeed." He moved my hair behind my ear. That one touch sent shivers down my back, and I stared into his eyes.

I always felt a pull to him, as if we were supposed to be in each other's lives, a friendship that would last for years to come. There was something about Grayson Holsten that was like feeling warm inside, even on the coldest day. "Grayson, I...."

He leaned into me, but just as I thought he might kiss me, he moved to turn me slowly around to look down at the rolling hills below. He spoke in a soft voice filled with so much sorrow that I felt my heart crack. "My little sister was an addict; some boyfriend of hers got her started on it, but as much as you want to blame one person for introducing her to drugs, you can't, because in the end, addiction is a disease. For a long time, I blamed the whole world. I wanted to tear it apart and curse the skies to bring her back to me." He bit at the last words.

I felt his anger, his sorrow, and his pain. It tasted harsh and bitter. I let my power take the pain away slowly, and he

breathed in a sigh of relief.

I let the pain live on my tongue, feeling as if it would choke me down as he continued speaking to the night air.

"I found her drugged out. I tried so hard to get her better. I would hold her on the hardest days when she had no will to go on. I gave pieces of myself so she could be strong, and she was... she was damn strong for a long time. Then one day, she broke."

I saw a single tear fall from his eye and caught it on my finger as he continued entering a nightmarish memory.

"I found her on the northside in a cove that looked out onto the ocean. I want to think the last thing she saw was the sunset, and hopefully, she had one last beautiful moment before she was gone from this cruel world."

I turned to look at Grayson, letting him see the tears in my eyes so that he knew I felt the rough pain he was going through, and he didn't have to feel it alone anymore.

"Daniels found you, didn't he?"

He looked down and kissed the tears that had fallen from my cheeks. "I don't deserve tears, Lexi. I am not a good man. Daniels knew my sister. She was an air witch, so they worked together often. Daniels found me drinking myself to death one night at The Ironmoth after a few of the Trinity Coven called him."

I gave him a sad smile, tracing his hands. "Daniels would wake up in the middle of the night just to help someone out. He would yell and be a grumpy bastard about it." I laughed as I wiped more tears away. "But he would still help out anyone who needed it."

He grunted in response. "That old man kicked my ass,

then dumped me into the lake and told me that everyone bleeds, everyone has pain and loss, but it is what you decide to do with that pain that proves who you are. So, I could either face the fucking music and become the leader my coven needed, or I could end up just like my father and uncle." He ran a hand over his face. "I made the decision that night to be the man I wanted to be and to be the brother I knew my sister wanted. So, I became strong. I took back my coven." He looked down at me now with a fire raging in his eyes. "And made some shady deals with the other covens to be the middle ground for all of us." He hesitated for a second, looking at me, taking in my dress, my face, and finally landing on my eyes. "Daniels made a promise to me that night that we would find out who was bringing in pixie dust, and we swore to take them down. Can you keep that same promise, Lexi?" He gazed into my eyes, and I made my vow to the Trinity Covens leader.

"I swear we will find out who did this, Grayson; we will both get our revenge. I plan on making The Wishmaker's death as painful as possible and, finally, free us of him for good."

His eyes widened with my promises, and he leaned his head to mine. "Lexi Rose, you are the sun, the moon, and the stars. The Wishmaker shouldn't be scared of Bash or me. He should fear you and the wrath of a siren. I hope you bathe in his blood, seductress."

Chapter Twenty-Nine

I leaned closer, our lips just a breath away from touching. A deep chuckle came from the shadows. We both pulled apart and saw Morgan Ryder standing in the corner.

"Well, I guess my son does have some competition. Do we have two powerful fae vying for a piece of our siren's heart?" He turned to Grayson, tilting his head to the side. "Don't you know what happens when a siren song takes over, little wolf?" Morgan moved closer to us, and Grayson moved me behind his back to protect me.

"I'd rather drown in her than live in emptiness, Ryder," he growled.

"Remember the rules, Holsten. I could kill you here and

no one would know," Morgan said with a bite.

Morgan never lost his temper, but when he saw me with Grayson, something escaped under that cool and calm façade he always had. I moved from Grayson's back. "Nothing is going on between us, Mr. Ryder. Grayson and I just have similar stories; he was helping me with my grief over my parents and Daniels. We are just allies."

Morgan's expression softened when he looked at me. "My dear Lexi, I guess I am being a bit protective of you. I think of you as if you are my own daughter." He held out his hand. "May I have a word with you, Lexi?"

Grayson held onto my arm, not wanting me to leave.

"It's okay, just find Bash and let him know I am with his father." I eyed him as he still grasped my arm, unmoving. I patted his hand. "Grayson, I'll be okay." Grayson looked into my eyes before he nodded in agreement, and he made his way inside to the rest of the party.

Morgan motioned for me to join him at a table in a shadowy corner. "Please, sit."

I moved and sat on the chair. The cold of the metal bit into my skin and caused goosebumps to appear.

"You wanted to talk?" I asked him as he sat down.

"Yes, I just wanted to see how you were doing."

I was a bit taken aback, raising my eyebrows. "I'm okay. Ella has been there for me, so..."

He smirked. "Yes, Ella does have her mother's kind heart, but what about Sebastian? How is he treating you?"

I blushed slightly because Bash, even though he was a controlling asshat at times, had been treating me like he worshipped me. Not just with my feelings; the multiple

orgasms helped as well.

"It's no secret you hate him, Lexi. After your parents' deaths, I saw the switch with you. A crush on a boy, then pure hatred towards my son. It is the reason why I kept him away from you as much as I could."

I bit the side of my cheek before I spit out, "It's fine. We are learning how to get along."

He nodded. "Good." His phone buzzed. "Ah, I must go." Standing, he walked to the balcony doors. "How's the investigation going?" he asked me, looking up from his phone. He was cloaked in darkness. I saw only his silhouette against the moon's light.

"We have a clue. Once we know more, we will let you know."

He raised a brow, which made him look so much like Bash. "Good. My son better find something soon, or else he will have even bigger problems." Morgan walked back into the party, plastering a fake smile as a few fae came up to him.

"Fucking wanker," I muttered, heading back inside while also being careful to sidestep his fake political act.

I stepped up to the bar and ordered a bright green smoking cocktail called Medusa's Stare. I took a sip as the spicy flavor slid over my tongue. Bash and Aden walked my way, appearing even more brooding than normal.

"Hey, what's with the faces?" I asked. They exchanged looks but said nothing. I poked Bash in the chest. "Spill it, Sebastian."

He sighed. "I saw that my father talked to you."

I nodded. "He did." I moved closer and lowered my voice. "It was nothing, just a few threats if we didn't find out who was kidnapping and murdering fae." I smiled sarcastically, trying

to break the tension. "You know, a normal Saturday night."
I glared at Morgan across the room as he raised a glass to toast us. I raised mine with a mocking smile. "He is a royal dicktwat," I muttered.

Bash chuckled. "He prefers the title, 'King Dicktwat'."

Aden glared at Bash. "How the hell are you making jokes right now?"

"I'm not. And now I am being summoned by the king himself." He rolled his eyes and placed a quick kiss on my cheek. "If I am not back in thirty minutes, call in the guard."

I laughed. "I've got you covered." I turned back to Aden, downing my whole drink in one gulp. "Let's get drunk." I ordered two more drinks and handed one over to him. "Have you seen Ella or Ethan?"

Aden took a sip of the drink and then spit it back out. "Gross." He threw a hand to the bartender, who slid him a dragon whiskey instead.

"Better?" I asked.

He nodded. "Ella just got here. She and Ethan are dancing," he said, pointing to the dance floor where my best friend and her fiancé danced to "Good as Hell" by Lizzo. She had a huge smile on her face, and Ethan was laughing as he kissed her.

I glanced over at Aden. I saw the pain that sat behind his eyes; I saw how much he wanted that for himself. I grabbed his hand and interlaced our fingers, changing the subject. "So, you gonna tell me why you came over to me like a bat outta hell?"

He took a long swig from his whiskey, looking over the rim of the glass at me. "Some sleazeball was speaking about

you in an uncouth manner."

I wrinkled my nose. "And what did said 'uncouth slea- zeball' say?"

He looked surprised that I even asked but gulped the rest of the whiskey down before ordering another. "He said that you would be the perfect little girl to tie up and bleed while he had his way with you, while he watched your soul break." Aden glared over the crowd at Franklin the Coward, who stood next to Morgan.

I rolled my eyes. "Of course that little weasel said those things." Franklin looked up over at us, and I could see his disturbed smile as he waggled his eyebrows at me.

"Fucking bastard is dead," Aden spat out, slamming his glass of whiskey down. Ice, brown liquid, and glass shat- tered around us. I saw his fangs snap out and his eyes turn dark red; a vampire on the verge of a massacre.

My hand pushed at his chest, and Tristian was there in an instant. He moved close to his face, whispering, "Get it together, Aden."

Aden glowered at Tristian. "You don't know what—"

Tristian cut him off. "I caught the last bit. Look, Bash is keeping Morgan and Franklin occupied. You need to chill the fuck out, man. If you break the rule, you are dead. Morgan will make an example out of you, frere." Tristian looked down at me, pleading with his eyes for me to help his friend.

I took hold of Aden's arm since we were getting a bit of an audience. Many fae were whispering around us. "Aden, let's go upstairs to the library." I pulled on his arm.

He and Tristian followed me out of the ballroom to the

grand staircase. We climbed the stairs silently. I made my way through the halls of the home I knew so well. Even after not being here for years, these halls still held so many memories, both happy and sad. I made it to the two large French doors and pushed them open where the three-story library sat in a circle with a single circular staircase to the top. The moonlight lit the dark ebony room with larger-than-life bookcases filled with all kinds of books, mostly first editions, some rare, some from new authors. I knew there were a few romance novels snuck in by Ella.

I made my way to the big armchairs. Tristian followed me over to the fireplace next to them, flipping a switch to make the fire come alive, filling the room with a warm glow. I went to the bar and poured out three shots of whatever amber liquid was sitting inside and handed it out to each of us.

"A votre santé."

I raised my glass as they did the same. I poured the drink down my throat, feeling the sting all the way down. Tristian threw his back as Aden followed. Then he placed his glass down and looked at the fire.

"Aden..."

He looked up at me. The anger was still there, but it softened when he saw the worry on my face. I took off my mask and placed it on the small table near me.

I cupped his cheek. "He won't touch me. You are going to make sure of it. Bash and Tristian won't let me ever be alone with that worm."

Aden moved so quickly that I jumped, but he caught my arms before I could fall. "I swear on the moon and stars that he will never lay a finger on you. He will die by

my hands first, and never know the feeling of you." His eyes were still full of rage, but he had lust in there as well. I pushed for the latter.

"Then show me how much he will regret not knowing," I whispered, running my fingers over his mask and then to his mouth. Tristian moved beside me, his fingers trailing up my arms. He reached the straps of my dress and pulled them down.

"Both of us will show you, Lil' Star." He kissed along my neck, the cold of his mask hitting my skin. I leaned my neck back, looking to the second floor and seeing we weren't alone. A shadow in the stacks of books stepped forward. A scream bubbled up to my lips as the figure came closer, but then I realized I knew that shadow.

"Bash," I breathed. He held a finger to his mouth.

I nodded as Aden reached to unzip my dress, sliding it off my body. Tristian's hands moved, cupping my breasts, taking my nipples in between his fingers and twisting softly, causing small moans to escape. Aden knelt at my feet and looked up at me through the gold devil mask, a smile forming around his lips. He wrapped his hands around my ankles, taking my shoes off while kissing me, spreading my legs wider as the sharp fangs on the mask threatened to cut me.

I gasped at the sensation. "Aden," I whispered, "I need you now."

He growled into my thigh, and I felt myself getting wetter. Tristian brought my neck back farther and kissed me hard, exploring my mouth with his tongue. He twisted my nipple in one hand while his other skimmed down

my stomach, slowly circling until he reached my panties, playing with the top of them.

"Show us, Lil' Star. Show us how much you want us." He pushed a finger straight down to my clit just as Aden kissed me through my panties. I moaned so loudly it echoed off the walls.

"Tristian...more...."

Tristian lazily stroked my clit. "So fucking wet, so ready."

I whimpered, and my eyes snapped open to see Bash standing there, his hands clenched on the railing with a very obvious erection.

I wanted all three of them. I opened my mouth for Bash to join us when Aden ripped my panties in two, pulling them off of me, hooking one of my legs over his shoulder as he dragged his tongue over my center. I let out a breathy moan as the cold of the mask brushed the inside of my thighs. His hot tongue tasting me, he drank me in as his hands gripped my legs hard, lifting me to his mouth. I moaned his name as Tristian began to circle my clit faster with his fingers. I could not get enough of them; their touches pulled me into a euphoric high.

Aden ran his tongue slowly up and down, devouring me. "God, baby, you taste like a summer day." He pushed two fingers into me, and I arched my back.

"Fuck, Aden," I groaned as I pulled from Tristian with a gasp.

I looked back up to Bash. I ran my hands over my breasts, biting my lip, giving in to the desire of all three of my Devils watching me, knowing what they wanted to do to me. Bash moved closer to the railing, staring down at us with desire

dancing in his eyes. I thought I would explode. He wasn't hiding from us, but instead content in watching Aden and Tristian ruin me.

I was so turned on I found myself panting to them, "More... I need more..."

Tristian pulled his hands away from my clit and from my neck as he sucked hard on the pulse. "Greedy Lil' Star. Stay standing; don't lose your balance, baby," he murmured as he removed his mask and moved to my spine, kissing a path down to my ass.

Aden threw his mask off beside him as well and he continued to flick his tongue over my clit. I grasped Aden's hair, almost falling over. Tristian made it to the top of my ass and grasped both cheeks, squeezing, biting, and marking each one, sending a shiver of pain and pleasure straight to my core. He spanked me hard as he slipped a hand between my legs and sank two fingers into me.

"Trist," I whimpered as he licked and kissed me.

"Oh, fuck..." I looked up to see Bash biting his lip, his hand running over the front of his pants. I nodded as he licked his lips. He pulled himself out slowly and began stroking his hard cock. I moaned at the sight of him pleasuring himself to us.

Tristian and Aden started to synchronize with each other, fucking me with their tongues and hands. Aden licked my clit in small circles, and then he added a single finger to me with Tristian's two. He lifted his head as three fingers moved in and out of me.

"Baby, you're so tight and close... Come all over us." Aden spoke into my clit, humming, making me arch my back.

I was so close to the brink when Tristian suddenly spread my ass and began to lick me from the front to the back. He played with my smallest hole, licking and running his fingers over me as Aden attacked my clit, stroking me with his tongue, pumping three fingers into me as I began to tighten and tingle all over. I continued to grind on him, and Tristian pushed one finger into my backside. It felt like an uncomfortable pressure at first, but then I felt nothing but pleasurable fullness.

I snapped my eyes open to Bash. He was pumping himself up and down, and I could tell he was close, too. He mouthed to me, "Come. Now."

And as if on command, I felt myself fall over and over again. I cried out Aden and Tristian's names as I watched Bash spill himself into his hand. I bent over, holding Aden's shoulders so I didn't fall.

Tristian sat back with a giant smile on his face. "Now that's a sound I could hear over and over again."

I laughed, pushing back from Aden, finally able to stand on wobbly legs.

I heard the door open and jumped as Ella and Ethan walked in with a drink in her hand. "Lexi, I knew you'd be in…"

Chapter Thirty

She stopped with her mouth hanging open as she took in the scene: me completely naked with Aden and Tristian on their knees looking completely and utterly fucked. Her drink dropped to the ground, spilling everywhere, and I opened my mouth to explain but Aden and Tristian jumped to cover me up. I saw Ethan right behind her with his eyebrows raised in surprise. I glanced at Bash, but he was nowhere to be found.

I quickly pulled on my dress, leaving it unzipped. "Ella, let me explain..."

She looked up at me with a world of hurt in her eyes "No. You lied to me... TO ME!"

My mouth opened to try to explain, but no words came out.

"You have nothing to say now! You hate them! You've hated them for years! 'I hate Bash, despise Aden, and Tristian is barely tolerable' is what you told me a week ago, Lexi! Now you are just, what, fucking two of them!?! Why would you... Lex, why lie to me about this?" I saw tears fall from her eyes. Mine were there, too.

"I didn't want to lie to you, Ella... I just... I didn't know how to tell you."

She looked like I had just hit her. "You are such a fucking hypocrite! At least it wasn't my brother," she hissed.

I reddened. "Ella, please, let's just talk. I swear I'll tell you everything," I begged.

"Enough!" Bash's booming voice came from behind her.

She jumped and turned to him in shock, whispering, "You knew?"

Bash stared at me and didn't even give Ella a glance. "Leave now, Ella."

She looked between me and Bash. "Bash..." Then I saw the realization hit her. "My brother too... how long?... HOW LONG!?!" Her eyes changed color with her fury.

I flinched back as her words lashed me like a whip. I had no air in my lungs to answer her. My eyes pleaded with her as tears pooled in them.

Ella turned from me to Bash and shook her head. "We are done, Lexi, because if you can't trust me, your best friend, with this... we are done."

Ethan pulled her hand into his, glaring at his brother. "Not cool, little brother... all of you... not cool." Ethan looked so hurt and disappointed as he gently tugged Ella under his arm and pushed them to the exit.

Hot, salty tears slid down my cheeks. "Please, Ella, let me explain. I swear, I will tell you everything."

Ethan held up his hand to me. "No, Lexi, not now, not after this." He led Ella out the door and shook his head at us as he exited the library.

I turned my back from all three of them as I robotically gathered up my shoes, zipped my dress back up, and tried to tame my hair down. I slid back into my shoes and placed the mask back on my head. All three of them were dressed, staring at me.

"Let's get back to the party," I said with a hollow voice.

Ella was more than a friend; she was as close as a sister to me. I should have been able to tell her everything. To lose her would be just as much of a loss as Daniels, and I wasn't sure if I would survive it.

The guys didn't say anything, instead merely nodded, their heads hanging low as we headed to the door to go back to the ballroom. Tristian reached for the door as it opened again. I hoped it was Ella coming back.

"Ella, I am..." It wasn't Ella, it was Cassandra, standing there in an overly short purple dress with a long flowy cape attached to her shoulders that made it look like she had wings. She was slightly swaying in her tall heels.

"Oh, look, it's the Silver Pearl Coven's precious siren," she hissed at me. "Tell me, what makes you so special?" She lifted one of my curls and let it drop like it was poison.

I was so done with this girl. I snapped at her, "I don't have time for you, Cassandra, and you should go drink water since you look like you need it." All of a sudden, I felt drained emotionally over the entirety of the night. I tried to move past her, but she put her arm in my way and moved right into my space, towering over me in her heels.

"Bashy was mine, then you had to come back into his life, and now he doesn't want anything to do with me," she shrieked, crying. "He won't even return my calls." She pouted. "But that's okay... maybe I'll just ruin his new little pet, a little trick for our Blood Coven princes." Her eyes turned a fiery orange as her hand shifted to long fingers with sharp nails flicked out.

A hand shot out in a blur and wrapped around her throat in an instant as Bash raised her off her feet. "If you touch her, I will rip your spine out and feast on your blood as you take your last breath. Do you understand me?" His eyes were blood-red, letting his true devil shine through. the devil who loved violence, the kill, and rejoiced in the fear of others. I knew why his people feared him, but now I was able to see the way he protected them as well, and it was seriously a turn-on.

"That's so hot," I breathed.

Bash turned his head to me. "Hot, Princess?"

I bit my lip. "Insanely."

Tristian came up behind me. "I think he's going for scary, Lil' Star."

Cassandra clawed at his hands, gasping for air. As his grip tightened around her throat, she began to turn blue from the lack of air.

Bash turned back to Cassandra. "I... CAN'T... HEAR... YOU!" he snarled.

Cassandra's eyes widened, knowing he would kill her in an instant. "I swear I won't touch her," she whimpered. Bash

released her in an instant, and Cassandra fell to the floor.

"Leave, now. If I see you again tonight, I will have your head."

She scrambled as she stood, clutching her chest. Tears fell down her face as she ran down the hallway towards the other wing of the house.

Bash turned to me, cupping my face. "Princess, you okay? We lost you for a few minutes."

I looked up into his green eyes and willed myself not to break. "No, take me home, please."

As my lip trembled, Bash, Tristian, and Aden came to me, pulling me lightly against all three of them.

"It's okay, Lex, she just needs time." Aden kissed my head.

Tristian led us down the stairs. When we reached the bottom, Grayson and Morgan walked towards us. "Sebastian, I need a word, son." He pointed to a side door, demanding he come with them.

Grayson looked grim as he walked beside him. When he saw my face, his frown deepened, and he looked to Bash, who shook his head as if saying he would tell him later.

Bash turned to face me and the guys. "Take her home, Tristian."

Tristian nodded in agreement. I walked over to Bash as he started to leave. I knew I needed to say something.

"Bash, wait!" I brought my hand to his face. "Thank you." I laid the lightest kiss on his cheek.

He smirked. "I'd go to hell to and back to bring the fire back to your eyes, Princess. Now, go home, cuddle with the boys, and eat as much junk food as you want. We can only solve one problem at a time."

I gave him a small smile as I returned to Aden and took his arm, which he held out to me.

"Home?" he said.

"Yeah, let's go home." I laid my head on his shoulder.

We had just reached the grand entry when a piercing scream rang out through the entire house. We all stood still for a second before a crowd of people came rushing at us through the ballroom. A huge blur flew into the room. It was as large as a bear with dark pointy ears and razor-sharp teeth.

"It's a Quaggoth!" Tristian yelled. "Don't let it bite you! It's poisonous!"

Aden jumped into action, magic shimmering around him as he murmured words I couldn't understand. He yanked two swords from his back, looking like a god of war. Tristian pulled a gun from his back.

"Lexi! Get the knife out, now!" Aden shouted.

I pulled the knife from its sheath just as a girl who was mid-transformation into an imp lunged at me, sending me to the ground. The air was knocked out of me. My knife fell from my hands, skidding across the floor.

The girl's face began to elongate, and her claws sank into my arms. Fangs dripped in black blood and green venom as she tried to snap at me. Her pupils shrank to black pinpoints as she lowered her head to bite me, trying to fill me with her venom. Those razor-sharp claws slashed down my arms and I felt the blood welt. I was pinned down, but I began hitting her sides as hard as I could, hearing cracks, but she kept coming. I put my knee in between our bodies to avoid her snapping teeth. Then I looked for my blade

and saw it just out of reach. My fingertips barely touched the knife's hilt. I brought my legs together and rolled us as we both threw punches at each other.

I finally had the upper hand and scrambled for my knife. Once it was in my hands, I slammed it into her side, and it made a sickening popping sound. She howled from the pain and started to tear at my dress as I stabbed her over and over again until she stilled under my touch.

I stood up, painted in her blood, and looked around. Most of the guests had made it outside, but at least thirty of us were battling each other. I scanned my eyes to search for Tristian, Bash, or Aden. There was so much action going on that it was hard to find them. A creature who was shadowed in dark smoke with white hair approached me. I recognized this was a dark elf. They called themselves Drow. He wore magical armor, and his deep voice rang out.

"Daughter of the Rose, if you come with me now, no harm will come to anyone. My master wants but a word."

I scoffed. "The Wishmaker?" At this, he nodded. "Tell him I'd rather die than speak to him."

The Drow bowed. "And so be it." He raised a small axe, and it flew in my direction.

I jumped aside as it barely missed my head. I glared at him, lowering all of my shields and concentrating on him. He caught my eyes and dropped his weapons, walking slowly over to me.

"Bow."

He sank to his knees, his head bowed. "How...?" He asked as he tried to fight my call.

"No one can escape a siren's song, not even the Drow."

I glared down at him as my eyes bore into him. I could easily kill him; I killed the girl simply enough. But for some reason, my gut was saying not to kill this Drow.

He raised his head as the shadows swept back from him, revealing a handsome face with a scar that ran from his brow over his eye to the top of his lip. The scar didn't take away from his beauty; rather, it actually seemed to enhance it. His skin was so pale that it held a purple tone that shimmered in the light. His eyes were the palest blue; they looked white. His dark hair was pulled back in an intricate braid, and his white shirt fell open to show his wide chest with intricate tattoos flowing down his stomach. I saw each of the covens' symbols over his heart.

"You came to kill me?" I asked him.

"No, my mission was to take you to the Wishmaker." He sneered at me. "If you must kill me, do it fast, but know this: We don't want this war. We are forced by the Wishmaker. My people are enslaved by him."

I lifted my blade to his throat, the deadly blade just inches away from the main artery. I lowered my knife to his chest and bent closer to him so he could meet my siren's gaze. He didn't shudder or move away from me as I hissed, "Go... Take your people before they all die... This is your only chance. If I see you again, I will let my Devils kill you." I backed away, my knife still ready to attack, but he simply stood.

"We are in your debt. If you ever want to visit, I will not turn you away, beautiful siren." He let out a high-pitched whistle that echoed throughout the room. Many elves of all shapes and sizes stood as a dark smoke appeared and

they all vanished.

I scanned the room and in a small alcove saw a troll attacking a young girl, holding her down with his huge green arm wrapped around her, and the images of my own attack came back. Fury rolled through me, and I stalked up behind them. I slashed my knife across his throat, slicing deep as blood sprayed around us. Then I pulled the girl out as fast as I could as the troll held his neck, trying but failing to roar.

"Run!" I said to the wide-eyed young girl. "RUN!"

The troll came at me with a force I was prepared for. I spun and sliced my knife across his stomach and around to his back. He roared in pain as he turned to me, arms out, and I slammed my knife as hard as I could into his heart. His eyes widened for a second before he fell back onto the stairs. I yanked my blade out, wiping green blood on my dress, then climbed the stairs in search of my Devils. I spotted all three on the floor in the middle of their own fights, looking like demons straight from hell.

Aden was battling two harpies; he had flecks of blood across his shirt and a nasty cut on his arm. I searched for Tristian, who had one mean-looking troll in a headlock. A druid was coming up behind him with a gun out, ready to pull the trigger. Knowing I couldn't make it to him in time, I could only pray my aim was true. I took my knife by the hilt and remembered everything Daniels and Jason taught me.

Throw through the target; aim with strength and power.

I took a deep breath as the world slowed down and I aimed at the druid's chest. I threw the blade through the air, hitting him in his shoulder, not the chest, but it caused him to jerk enough to drop the gun to the ground. Tristian turned and saw me on the stairs.

I smirked. "You owe me!"

He grinned at me as he blindly shot the druid in the head. "I'm coming for you, Lil' Star!"

I shook my head, looking for Ella and Ethan, hoping they made it out. That's when I saw Franklin sneaking out the back way with them, with Morgan not far behind. Of course, Morgan wouldn't take part in the fight; he was such a weasel. More and more fae were fighting. I knew this would end badly. I hurried over to Tristian as he shot a dragon shifter in the chest, emptying his clip.

"We need to stop this, Tristian!" I yelled as he reloaded his gun. He looked at me in surprise, his eyes raking over me, probably looking for injuries. "I'm fine," I said as I deflected an attack from a small fairy, throwing him from my side to the group who were fighting below.

Tristian smirked. "Lil' Star... sing."

I looked at him like he was crazy. "What?"

He threw a punch at a gargoyle's face, knocking the thing out. I found Bash in the crowd in a fight with four guys surrounding him. He was like the Devil himself, throwing blows at people like they were ragdolls. The problem was that it was four against one and more were coming at him.

Tristian shook me. "Sing, Lexi! Sing! I got Bash." He took off in a run towards Bash as Aden's hand grabbed mine.

"Let's go, baby. Put these bastards to sleep."

That's when I saw a huge grey wolf bound in and rip a man's arm off, growling next to Bash, joining him in the fight. "Grayson!"

He must have heard me because he let out a howl before he began to run at a group of pixies. Aden's curse broke me from watching Bash and Grayson fight, and I saw him being held down by three centaurs at the bottom of the stairs. I kicked a small troll over as I made my way up to the second level. I dropped every shield I had in place for my abilities and allowed my power to flow through me. My eyes hazed over, and my skin turned pearly white. I felt my teeth sharpen and rip through my gums and my hands turn into claws.

I took a deep breath and began to sing. As soon as I finished the first verse, the whole fight slowed. Most of the lesser fae were already standing as still as statues. By the second verse, everyone was under a trance. Weapons dropped, and a few fairies curled up and fell asleep.

I looked to my Devils; their eyes told me they were okay, but even they were still. This was what most sirens feared: total control of fae, knowing we could kill so many with just the sound of our voice. I walked to Tristian, touching his hand to follow me to the top and brushing his arm with my fingers.

"Tristian, help Aden." I nodded to him on the ground. Tristian's eyes widened as he bent and helped Aden up.

Grayson was at the top of the stairs, and I saw him fighting the trance. I passed him, running my hand over his shoulders and he shook himself. "Thanks," he said dreamily. Bash slowly made his way to us.

"Now what?" I asked in fear, wrapping my hand in Bash's.

"Now we wait because one... two... three."

A powerful knock came on the giant wooden doors as

the police announced themselves. They came in, followed by Agent Rengard. He looked around the room, seeing more than thirty fae in a siren trance. His eyes settled on me, and a glimpse of surprise passed over his face.

"Release them, Ms. Rose," he ordered as he walked to where I stood. I felt the exhaustion seep in, but I slowly dragged my thrall away from the room and let it fall away. I watched as everyone slowly came out of the spell; some were confused, some were angry, and some merely stayed asleep. Agent Rengard approached me with caution.

"Agent Rengard... I can..." I started to explain, but he held up a hand and shook his head.

"Don't worry. Just get the hell out of here, will ya? And take one of your boys. A girl outside stopped me, explaining how you saved her life. You saved many fae tonight, Lexi."

Tristian and Aden pulled me by my hand out of the estate. I saw more people from the party; so many were confused about the fight, a few fae were crying in each other's arms, and some cowered away from me in fright. I crossed my arms around my body, wishing for warmth again. I noticed one of my Devils missing and frantically searched for Bash.

Aden pulled me closer to him, an arm wrapping around my shoulder. Leaning into me, he spoke quietly. "He'll be okay, Lexi. We've got to get you out of here, though. It's not safe for you right now."

We walked to the valet, and Aden retrieved the keys. His brows were furrowed with worry as he ran to pull the car around. Tristian stood next to me, looking menacing, his eyes scanning the area for any potential danger. Aden

whipped the car around, and we all climbed in and made our way out of the estate. I gazed back at the looming castle that Morgan had created, hoping Bash would soon be home, safe with us. Tristian sat next to me with his hand intertwined with mine.

I peered out the window as the lights of the city flew past us. "Why didn't we get questioned by the police?" I looked at Aden in the front.

Aden's eyes flicked to me, then to Tristian. "Because, Lexi, you just showed everyone how powerful you are. Sirens can control a small group of five, maybe ten people. But you had easily thirty people fully enthralled. The rest of us threw up a shield, but even Grayson, who is stronger than most, was struggling. Most sirens would be drained by exuding that much power. It should have killed you, baby, but here you are."

I frowned. "If I can control thirty without being completely drained, what does that mean?"

"It means that you are the most powerful fae in all three covens. Possibly the most powerful fae in the past hundred years."

Chapter Thirty-One

When we arrived at the house, Dyna meowed at me, looking up with judgmental eyes as she took in the state of my clothes. The beautiful dress was now in complete disarray, covered in different types of blood, sweat, and generally in tatters.

"We all can't be perfectly fluffy all the time," I murmured as I filled her cat bowl with treats and food. Aden and Tristian walked in looking exhausted, throwing weapons on the counter.

Aden's arm had a massive gash down the front.

"Your arm!" I pointed to him, my mouth falling open in shock.

"'Tis but a scratch." He smiled, taking the first aid kit out and tossing it to Tristian. "Wrap it up. I know you can't heal us because we are all drained, so we do it old school."

Tristian smiled. "Old school?"

I ignored him. "I'm going to change and go to the ocean to recharge." I headed into my room, slowly peeling off the dress. I didn't have underwear on thanks to Aden. Great. I fought an entire room of fae without panties on. I pulled a navy bikini on and jumped into a pair of flowy pants and a white long-sleeve top that knotted at my stomach.

I walked back out into the living room where Aden was drinking from a whiskey bottle as Tristian was stitching him up.

"You two okay?"

Aden nodded, and Tristian grunted at me. "One of us should go with you," Aden said as he took another drink, staring at the bikini top peeking through the shirt.

"I'm good, and I need this. If you insist, once Tristian is done mending you, he can meet me down at the beach."

He nodded as I closed the door and made my way to the beach. I slid out of the pants and tossed my shirt aside as I walked to the edge. As soon as I placed my foot into the water, I felt the healing energy of the ocean wash over me. The next thing I knew, I was wading waist-deep in the waves. I dove forward as bubbles came around me. Opening my eyes and seeing the ocean floor, I swam forward and farther down, zipping around schools of fish and large underwater arches where more colorful fish hid. I went farther down to the bottom where a shipwreck lay in the deep sand. The ocean had claimed it as its own, covering it in barnacles and algae. Seeing how it deteriorated over time and became a

home to many other fish and sea creatures always had me in awe. Yes, the ocean was full of trash, and humans were slowly killing its ecosystem, but sometimes I had to find the beauty in the ugly.

I wasn't sure how long I was underwater, but when I surfaced, I saw Tristian sitting on the beach with a towel and a blanket waiting for me. I rose out of the water, letting it fall around me. I sat next to him on the blanket and wrapped the towel around my shoulders.

"Do you feel better?" he murmured. I couldn't miss the concern in his voice.

I nodded. "Yeah, I do, and look! All healed, so don't worry." I bumped his shoulder with mine as I showed him my arms. He traced where the cuts had been.

We sat in silence for a while, just watching the ocean.

Then he said, "Do you want to talk about Ella?"

I shook my head. "No, because if I talk about it now, I will break, and I can't be broken anymore." There was a crack in my voice, and I inwardly swore I would not cry. I held onto that promise with all my might.

"When you're ready, we're here for you, Lil' Star." He wrapped his arms around me as we stared the ocean. After a while, Tristian's phone buzzed, and he looked down. "Bash is back." When I didn't move, he held my hand. "Lexi?"

I shook my head again. "Can we stay for a few more minutes?"

I kept my eyes on the waves, not looking at him, because if I did that would be the end for me. I would drown in my tears again. He kissed my head and pulled me closer. "Of course."

We sat for a while longer, then walked back hand-in-hand. Aden was sitting on the couch with a computer on his lap, and Bash stood with a tense look on his face and his phone to his ear.

"You think we could have prevented a bunch of fae from attacking us?" He stiffened. "Yes, sir. Yes, we will. Goodnight, Father." He placed his phone down and looked over at me. "You went to the ocean."

I hopped up onto the island next to him. "I had to recharge."

He took my arms, examining each one. "I saw you get hurt. Are you healed completely now?"

I took his hands in mine. "Ocean magic." I smiled teasingly, looking at him as well, trying to see if he got hurt. I found a bruise forming under his eye and a few cuts, but other than that, Sebastian Ryder was completely fine.

"I didn't know the ocean could heal you that quickly."

I ran a hand over his arm. "Cuts, bruises, and small wounds, yeah, but anything major would be more complicated to heal."

Bash smirked and pushed my hair behind my ear. "You surprise me every day, Princess. Tonight was, well, let's just say Morgan isn't happy. But Grayson is scared shitless of you now, so that's the silver lining."

Shaking my head, I jumped down and went to get a bottle of water.

A knock came from the front door. Everyone was on their feet in a second, and Aden pulled a gun out from who knew where. I raised my brow. "Guys, chill. It's just the door." I moved to answer it, but Bash pressed me back.

"Lexi, let me."

I stepped backwards with my hands held up to let Bash open the door.

The blue-haired tatted Deke stood there with another black box, looking grim. "Boss, another one was just dropped off." He handed the package over to Bash.

"Did you catch who dropped it off?" Bash asked, taking it from him.

"No, it was found on a perimeter check out of range of the camera. The only way we found it was because of the audio."

I looked over Bash's shoulder. "Audio?"

Deke looked down at me shifting uncomfortably. "Yeah… umm… it was a song—haunting, almost sad, I felt like I needed to go toward it, like an invisible pull."

Bash's eyes flicked over to me, and he murmured, "A siren song."

I shuddered.

"Thanks, Deke, we will look into this," Bash said in a grim voice.

"Night, Boss." Deke turned and left us with the black box. Bash placed it on the island as we surrounded it.

He opened the package, revealing four smaller ones. I picked one up and opened it. A bright blue, braided piece of hair sat in the middle; underneath was a picture of Nyx in a cage. She looked helpless with barely any clothes on, curled up onto herself. I could make out bruises on her pale skin.

"Bash…" I gasped.

He looked over my shoulder and growled. "Open them all," he demanded.

Each box was the same: a colored braid of hair and

photos of each missing girl all in the same condition as Nyx. Dirty, weak, and beaten.

"We need to call Agent Rengard, let him know what we found," Aden said in a low voice. All of us shot a Look at him. We could see the distress on his face as he examined each photo.

I placed my hand on his. "We will catch him, Aden."

He looked away and walked towards the window. I wanted to go after him, but Bash took my arm.

"I got this one, Princess. Tristian, I found this on the balcony after the fight at the masquerade ball. Can you two look more into it?" He pulled out a small clear bag and handed it over to Tristian's waiting hands. Tristan took it and walked to the back room, out of sight.

Bash headed over to the patio with two glasses and a bottle of dragon whiskey in his hands. He poured the golden liquid into the glasses, handing one over to Aden. He swirled the contents around and brought the drink to his lips, taking a deep swig. The tension in his shoulders relaxed. His throat bobbed as he drained the glass. "Another," he grunted, and Bash refilled his glass again with no comment.

Tristian soon came back, his eyes pulled in a frown.

"Is he going to be okay?" I asked as Aden slumped down in his chair, staring at the night sky.

Tristian's frown softened as he came up behind me, wrapping his arms around me. "He will be, but do you know about Aden's history at all?"

I turned into his arms, looking up at his copper eyes. "No, he didn't talk much about his family life to me or Ella. We

assumed it was similar to Ethan's. He was just always there for us when we needed him. He was the funniest, sweetest, and kindest guy I ever met."

Tristian gave me a half-smile. "He is still all of those things." He kissed my temple as he continued. "But his story isn't mine to tell. I think you should ask him what it was like growing up in the Charmante household. It might make things clearer about everything that happened and why he made the decisions that he did, Lil' Star."

I sighed and rested my head on his chest, needing the comfort from the evening and my twisted and complicated life. "What did Bash find?"

Tristian sped away to the guest rooms and came back with a gray case. He pulled out the clear bag. "Looks like a card and a vial of pixie dust." He took a pair of tongs and pulled out the card and the vial before laying them out on a silver tray. "I'll dust for prints and run anything through the system. Can you take a look at the card?"

I threw a pair of disposable gloves on and picked up the card. It was solid gold with a phone number and an engraving of a black moth with a skull head. There was a simple name written under the engraving in tiny writing.

"The Mort Noire." I stood up and took the tray with the card over to Tristian. "I am not sure why anyone would ever want to be invited there?" I sat next to him on the couch, placing the tray down beside the computer.

"I've been invited," Aden said in a gruff voice.

Bash came in behind him, typing out something on his phone. "Well, it looks like you'll be getting us five invites to Mort Noire then, because I am pretty sure that is where

the Wishmaker is planning everything. It will be the one way to find our missing mermaids." He put his phone away, clasping Aden on the shoulder. "Relax, it won't be that bad."

We all groaned. "Come on, asshat, why would you say that?"

He looked around, confused. "Seriously, are you guys that superstitious?"

All three of us scowled at him.

We continued to work into the night to figure out how, when, and where we would get into Mort Noire. I ran through Daniels's paperwork again, trying to break down formulas and to find anything that would be of some kind of importance. It wasn't until I heard soft snores coming from Tristian that the rest of us decided we needed sleep.

I kissed the top of his head as we headed to bed. "Good night, my soleil."

Chapter Thirty-Two

The next day, I sat at the bar, sipping coffee looking over the files that Anderson gave us, trying to find some rhyme or reason for the missing mermaids. My phone started to buzz, and I saw that it was Coco calling.

A smile broke out across my face as I answered in a sing-song voice, "Hello, my favorite tata!"

A laugh came from the other end. "I am your only aunt, fille drole, and I miss you. So, I am officially inviting you over for brunch. Bring your knights; I am making a feast!"

I heard Jason in the background, mocking her. "Coco, Baby, you've cooked enough food for an army." A crack sounded from the other end of the phone. "OUCH! What the hell?"

I laughed "Did you just...?"

"Crack him with a towel? Yeah, I did. If he's not careful, I will bring out the wooden spoon!" she yelled.

Jason's voice came on from the other end of the phone, "Damn it, women! You know how I feel about the wooden spoon!"

I giggled at their banter. "Okay, okay! Give me thirty minutes to get the grumpy vamps up."

Coco laughed again. "Okay, see you soon, Luv."

I hung up and took the last sips of my coffee then grabbed a glass of water. I wandered over to the couch, where Tristian was sprawled out snoring softly. His face held no sign of tension; he looked young and carefree. It was truly angelic.

I tilted my head. "Too bad it's gonna suck to be woken up this way." I poured the ice-cold water over his chest.

He woke with a shout and leaped off the couch. "You are dead, Lil' Star!"

I shrieked, throwing the cup at him, and he caught it with ease. I ran into the darkened guest bedroom to jump in bed with Aden, who was passed out.

He grumbled something incoherent. I shook him, and he mumbled, "Then she had a shiny penny for me. It was nice, but I had to make the bastard swallow it."

I laughed, shaking him harder. "Aden, help! save me from the big bad vampire!"

He blinked his eyes open slowly and smiled up at me. "Good morning, baby."

Tristian bounded into the room. I dove under the covers "Lil' Star... come out, come out, wherever you are!" He took

the sheets and ripped them away from me, exposing me in my tiny shorts and tank. Aden was fully nude, sporting his morning hard-on. Tristian jumped back. "WOW, dude, I was not prepared!" He covered his eyes with his hand.

Aden smirked and leaned back, his arms behind his head. "Leave us for a bit, mon frere. You can come back when her screaming stops." He gave me a suggestive smirk.

I laughed. "I've got something better than that..."

Aden sat up and tucked my hair behind my ear. "Oh yeah? What's that, baby?" he said as he tried to kiss my neck.

I moved out of his way to stand, putting both of my hands on my hips. "Coco's fresh ground coffee, fresh pain au chocolat, and les croissants." Aden fell back and groaned into his pillow. "We leave in ten. Get dressed." I threw a pair of jeans at him and walked out as Tristian's laugh faded. I headed back into my bedroom where Bash had crashed last night but found the bed empty, besides Dyna, who was curled up in a ball in his spot.

I quickly changed into black leggings and a grey hoodie, throwing my hair in a braid. I walked back into the living room with my shoes in hand. "Hey, Aden, where is Bash?" I called out as Aden walked into the kitchen in a pair of low hanging grey sweats.

He poured a mug of coffee for me and then himself and shrugged. I admired him walking over, dragging my eyes up his body, dipping my eyes to the V that disappeared into the grey sweats. He smirked and held the coffee out for me to take. I held the warm mug in my hand as I bit my lip, watching Aden's muscles move over his arms as he took a sip from his mug.

"You're staring, Princess," Bash murmured into my ear.

I would have spilled the coffee all over me if it wasn't for Aden's vamp speed. He snatched the coffee from my hands as I spun around, seeing Bash in running shorts and nothing more. Sweat dripped down his chest to his toned stomach, making me want to run my fingers down his front.

I cleared my voice, turning back to Aden. "Well, you try living with you three." I took my mug from him and walked to the counter, hopping up and taking a sip, giving them a catty look. "Not my fault you're showing off your body."

Bash licked his lips, walking up to me and moving in between my legs. "You want us to cover up? Sounds a bit sexist, Princess." He reached for a water bottle that was left out, took a long swig, then poured it over his head, letting it splash onto us. I set my coffee down and ran my hands over his stomach lightly up to his chest.

He let a rumble out and I laughed. "You seemed a bit worked up, Bash. We should probably do something about it."

He stepped closer, letting me know just how worked up he was, and I bit my lip.

"Coco invited us for brunch."

He moved back, pressing his head to mine, sighing and moving back. "Fine, but we aren't done here, Princess." He brushed his hands up my thighs, making me shiver.

"Go shower!" I pushed him away lightly, and he walked towards the bathroom. I looked over to Aden who was sipping his coffee.

"Don't mind me, Lex, I'm enjoying the show."

I threw up a middle finger at him, and he laughed as Tristian came back into the living room in just a towel

"Oh, jeez! For fuck's sake. I will be outside when you're ready." As I walked to the porch, I heard three of them laughing. Damn those three insanely hot vamps and my vagina for not listening to me. She was being a bit slutty these days, but I couldn't complain. The orgasms were worth it.

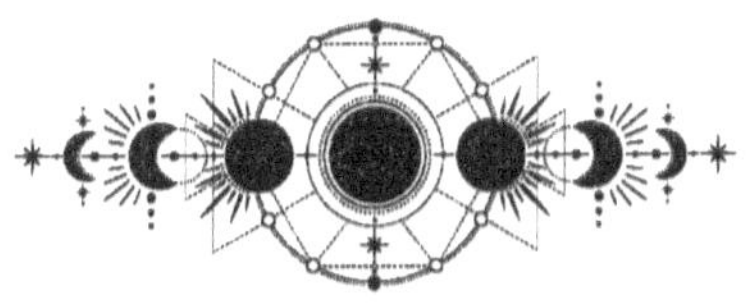

We pulled into my old family home in record time, thanks to Tristian driving like a bat out of hell. I bounded up the steps, walking straight into the main house. Everything was still the same and different at the same time. I eyed the staircase and was pushed back into a memory of that horrific night ten years ago. The early quiet of the house encased me, and I held my breath before I lost myself in the pain.

Coco's voice echoed from the kitchen, breaking me from the memory. "Jason, I swear if I catch you one more time trying to steal a croissant, I am going to beat you with a broom!"

I giggled and felt a hand wrap around my own. I looked up to see Bash staring down at me.

"We lost you for a second, Princess." A worried look passed through his eyes.

I gave him a sad smile. "It's always hard walking back into the house. It just makes me a bit sad."

He nodded and pressed a kiss to my head.

"Well, you don't have to do it alone anymore, Lil' Star," said Tristian, taking my other hand.

Aden hugged me from behind. "You have us now, Lex."

I looked at my three guards and realized they were right. We couldn't go back. A throat cleared from the side; Jason stood there with a huge smile on his face, and Coco stood behind him with a rolling pin in her hand.

"Jason, get out of my way before I get the wooden spoon out again."

Jason flinched and moved to the side, revealing my aunt, who wore a dark blue apron around her middle. Her red hair was pushed back in a headband.

"No, not the wooden spoon, my love," Jason teased as he kissed her cheek.

I laughed. "Is she still chasing you with the spoon?"

He grinned at me. "She never catches me. I'm too fast."

Coco glared at me and then at Jason. "I'll remember that for next time."

I let go of my Devils and walked to Coco, letting her take me into her arms and wrap herself around me.

"Hey, favorite niece."

I snorted. "I'm your only niece. Do I smell fresh coffee?"

Grinning, she dragged me into the kitchen, placing me in front of the island, which was filled with food, from a tray full of fresh fruits to Coco's famous French pastries and even the tiny almond cookies that tasted like something only angels could make. "Ta da!" A huge smile spread across her face. "It's all of your favorite food! Aden texted us last night telling us what happened at the Ryder Estate... I thought this might help."

I sat on the bar stool as Coco passed me a cup of coffee. "Chocolate does cure a lot of things, but this coffee will cure everything." She took a sip and hummed with delight. "Oh my god, it's so good! What's new about it?"

Coco grinned. "New blend grown here on the estate. It's Jason's new project. He's into coffee now." She gave a teasing eye roll. "The customers at the bakery are obsessed with it. We can't keep the bags on the shelf."

The guys walked in laughing as Coco poured each of them a cup of coffee. Aden kissed her cheek, and I saw a slight blush cross her face as Tristian offered her a flirty wink. Bash sat next to me with his hand on my knee, drawing circles slowly as he sipped his coffee. I eyed him, looking for any mischief in his eyes.

"I also just pulled some biscotti out." Coco brought a plate over to us.

I snatched an almond cookie and dipped it in my coffee. I moaned with delight as the chocolate and coffee mixed together, creating what I assumed heaven was like. "Holy crap, Aunt Coco. It's amazing."

Coco laughed. "I love you, too, Lexi."

Tristian sat next to me with his plate piled high. His hand brushed against mine. "It's almost as good as sex," he chuckled.

Coco chortled. "If I had a nickel for how many times I've heard that!"

She turned back around to focus on a sheet of cookies. Bash was talking to Jason about the latest basketball teams and who was a sure win. Aden sat talking to Coco, making her laugh.

I took in the moment of peace and serenity. We haven't

had much of it lately, and it was nice. Once everyone was finished, Coco shooed the guys out, and I helped wash the dishes as my aunt dried them. It used to be a ritual we would do when I was little. It was time we spent with each other to have our own private conversation without the ears of Jason and Daniels or even my parents listening in.

Coco appraised me. "You look different." I frowned, and she quickly added, "Not in a bad way, honey. You look... less sad, like you aren't as disappointed in the world. You look like you might even be happy." She kissed the side of my temple and whispered, "And if those three are behind that, do not give it up for anyone or anything."

I blushed and cleared my throat. "It's a bit complicated. Bash and I have history, Aden was like a brother to me, and Tristian, well, it's Tristian," I sighed. "Then there's Ella. She is so mad at me." I decided to tell Coco the truth because I knew she would be the one person who would never judge me. I just left out the explicit details of the library. "I lied to her about them. She's so mad. I don't know if I can fix it." I shook my head to hold back my tears.

Aunt Coco stopped and wrapped an arm around me. "Lexi, I love you with my whole heart, but you know what I am going to say. You need to be honest with her about everything."

I knew she was right. "I'm terrified she's going to hate me."

Coco shook her head. "She might be mad, and she might be disappointed, but she won't hate you. She loves you, and if you were honest with everyone,"—she gave me a pointed look—"you wouldn't be in this situation."

I sighed and nodded. "You know, I hate it when you're right. I will talk to her."

I tried not to think of the many possible outcomes that could happen between me and Ella, but I was glad Coco and I talked. I had to believe in our friendship.

Tristian, Jason, and Bash were drinking beer and playing a round of pool in the billiards room with the afternoon baseball game playing on the television. Coco curled up into a chair in the corner with her latest book, a My Fair Lady retelling.

I looked over to the group and walked over to them. "I'm going to head to the conservatory for a bit."

Bash was leaning against the wall and stood straight up, coming towards me. "Want me to join you?"

I shook my head. "No, I'm good."

He looked like he wanted to argue but merely gave me a quick nod.

When I walked into the humid dome, I could feel Daniels all around me, as if he never left. "Hey, old man."

I walked over to the tables and began to pull out different tools and grabbed the grimoire from its spot on the bookshelf. I looked over the notes I had made and reread the ones Daniels had marked up. I began to gather supplies, determined to make a potion for sleep to keep from people invading mine, and a healing potion to keep on hand at the house just in case we ever needed it. I made my way to the second level to gather a few key ingredients.

I paused at the apothecary table, remembering the dream I had from the other day. "The key to your wants and dreams lies within here," Daniels had said. I traced over the pattern, noticing it looked like the Silver Pearl Coven symbol.

"Hmmm."

I traced my fingers over the pattern until I felt a slight bump in the smooth surface. Using my magic, I pressed firmly, finding a small gold button encased into the wood.

The top of the apothecary table lifted. I slid the top back and inside sat an old scroll and a few vials of a potion sealed by wax with skull and crossbones labels on them as a warning. A silver knife sat on the side with ruby gems adorning the handle. I picked up the knife to examine it. I felt the power within it and immediately knew this wasn't just a normal blade.

"What did you find?"

I screamed in surprise at the voice and turned around with the knife in my hand.

"Whoa, Lex, I didn't mean to scare you! I called your name a few times." Aden looked at the blade in my hand, and I saw the color drain from his face. "Why do you have a pouvoir mort?"

I raised a brow. "Power of death?"

He held his hands up. "La mort a ceux qui la tiennent is the long version, but Lexi, that knife is dangerous. It drains the power of its victims. It's illegal for all fae to possess. So why do you have it?"

I frowned and placed the knife back inside the table and moved aside so Aden could see. "I found it here." I shrugged. "I didn't know what it was, but I can feel the power within it. It's dark magic, right?"

Aden nodded and picked up the scroll.

"It's in French," I said as he rolled it out. It was old, and I was worried it would crumble. A spell was written across the top in deep red flourishing letters.

"Lexi, do you know what this is…?"

I shook my head, looking over his shoulder at the old scroll.

"It's an answer to our problems." He continued to read through the scroll and grinned. "And this tells us what's in pixie dust. Look—a werewolf's fang, the blood of a vampire, crushed wings of a fairy, and a tear from a mermaid or siren. You combine all of this into a bottle under a blood moon and recite the spell four times. Je combine les quatre fées dans sacrifice dans les ténèbres, laisse ton pouvoir prendre une fois était perdu et maintenant est le mien. Four times while giving your own blood sacrifice to les ténèbres."

Aden cursed and looked up at me.

"Pixie dust isn't a new drug. It's old—thousands of years old. This tells us what it is and how to stop the fae from being able to use their magic."

I squinted at the spell in shock. "What? You mean to be like, what, a human?"

He nodded. "It seems like it. We need to get this to Bash so we can study it, see if we can figure out what the fuck this says. My French is good, but the old language is a bit rusty."

I ran to a storage closet, pulled out a box, and added some soft rags for padding. I took it back to the table as Aden and I carefully packed the box up. "The night you guys couldn't wake me up in my dream, Daniels was there. He said, 'When the darkest of nights seem to be more than one can take, look to the light. The sun will always guide your way to the heavens.'" I stood up and pointed to the scroll. "What if he wasn't talking about me, but talking about all fae?"

Aden gave me a small smile. "Maybe, or maybe it was just a dream."

I looked over the patterns below on the table. They were a bunch of lines etched into the wood in different directions. I examined them closer. "Aden, do the etchings look like they move?"

Aden bent closer, turning his phone light on and taking out a small blade. He pushed it in between the dark wooden layers and the small wooden line pushed down with a click. We looked at each other with eyebrows raised. "That answers your question, Lex."

I began to push other inlays down. Some didn't move while others did. I noticed that the more I heard pieces click into place, the more they began to form a pattern. I squinted my eyes because I had seen that pattern before.

It was inked on all of the Three Devils.

I jumped up. "Aden, take your shirt off!" I grabbed at his shirt, and he gave me the strangest look, like I was going crazy.

"Lexi, baby, I can't believe I am saying this, but umm… it's not really the time or place."

Confused, I looked at him. "What?" Then it dawned on me, and I punched him in the arm. "No! Not that, you asshat! Let me see your chest, where you have the tattoo of the covens."

His eyebrows reached his hairline, but he did as I said, revealing his chest, which was covered in tattoos. I sighed; it was a great chest.

Aden smiled. "Lex?" I looked up at his face as he chuckled. "You're staring."

I shook my head. "Sorry, just a bit distracted."

I ran my fingers over his left peck where the symbol of the Blood Moon Coven sat. Most covens used glyphs similar to the Egyptians; we used these for all kinds of spells, potions, and to hold elements of power. Each symbol was surrounded by a protective circle so whoever had it was guarded by their magic. Every fae had magic in them, and our symbols added extra protection.

I began to push on the etchings on the table to create the symbol and soon it was complete, but nothing happened. "Damn it."

Aden scrubbed his hands over his face, then pulled his shirt back on. "What are we missing?" he whispered to himself.

I closed my eyes, going back to my dream and thinking to myself. "Come on, remember, Lexi! You saw the table, why were those lines so similar to it?" My eyes snapped open "Wait, Aden, let's try this." I pushed on four lines, and they all went down easily. "That's the start of the Pearl Coven," I said excitedly.

He continued to push it down until it was complete. "It's a combo of all of the covens' symbols."

I began to push Trinity Coven's symbol down.

"Holy shit!" Aden laughed as I pressed the last line down. The bottom drawer popped open. An envelope with my name in Daniels's chicken scratch handwriting lay inside. I unfolded the letter from the envelope and began to read the message left for me.

My Dearest Lexi,

I fear if you are reading this, then my time has come to an end. Fear not, kid, it is what was meant to happen.

The truth is, I've thought of you as my own for a long time. I loved your father and mother as if they were my own blood. Lexi, you are the rightful leader of this coven. I have known this for years, but you never wanted anything to do with them, so I stepped up.

But it's time to accept your destiny. Look to the other covens to guide you. Grayson is a good ally—keep him close! That fucker comes in handy when times are dire. Sebastian is hot-headed, but I have seen the way he and his men look at you. They will protect you until their last breaths. Keep Morgan at a distance. I still don't know if he can be trusted.

Don't forget you have many friends between all three covens. Ella and Ethan will be powerful on their own, but they will always be there in your darkest times. Coco and Jason are loyal to a fault. Don't let them fall, kid.

Beware of the darkness, Lexi. Those who follow it may appear to be friendly, but they are waiting for you to fall.

Finally, lean on Kane Anderson. He has good intentions to help the covens succeed.

I love you, kid, and I am so damn sorry I had to leave you. I'll see you when I see you.

Love always,
Daniels

P.S. Whoever is making pixie dust is missing the main ingredient: a coven leader's blood. You have to protect all three of the leaders. If the Wishmaker gets any of your blood, our covens are doomed. I have been working with Anderson and Grayson to find the antidote. All we've found is a note about how the antidote lies in the place where the stars meet the sea, and the sun's rays fall onto the darkest moon. Whatever the hell that means.

Chapter Thirty-Three

I folded up his letter and held onto the scroll. I didn't
want to put it back. I wanted to run my fingers over it
and bathe in its ancient power. Aden placed his hand
on my shoulder, and I looked up at him. His eyes were
glowing red, and I knew mine had changed since the
haze had overcome me. The scroll was so strong. I now
understood why Daniels had it locked up.

"We have to put it back, Aden."

He nodded, not seeming to be able to speak. I gathered
all my strength and put the paper back into the envelope
and sealed it back into the apothecary table, locking it up
as tightly as we had found it.

I was breathing heavily when I turned to Aden. He came

at me fast, lifting me into his arms. I wrapped my legs around his waist as he kissed me hard. Our tongues mixed as if he were starving. I gasped and pulled him closer, trying to get to as much skin as I possibly could. He trailed kisses down me, and I felt his teeth scrape my neck.

"Yesss," I whispered as I grinded down into him. I pulled at his shirt and threw it over the rail. It floated to the ground below us. He moved us to the edge of a wooden table, dropping me and laying me back on the rough surface. "Aden what are we..." I asked breathlessly.

I felt the magic from the scroll move through us. The light buzz that danced across my skin was even more exaggerated with every one of Aden's kisses.

"Lexi. You. Feel. Like. Heaven. And. Hell," he growled out.

His fingers found the top of my tights, and he yanked them and my underwear down in one go. He pressed my ankles together, sinking two fingers in me. I arched my back into his hand and threw my shirt off to join his down below. His other hand found my breast, pinching my nipples, teasing them between light and rough touches. His head leaned down over my breast as he pulled my bra down, exposing my hard, peaked nipples.

He sucked and teased each one until he had me whispering his name over and over again. "Aden..."

He looked up at me and his eyes darkened at my statement. I nodded, letting him know I wanted all of him. He pulled back and removed his pants and stood before me with his perfect body. I watched as he hooked his fingers into his boxer briefs, which were already strained from his hard cock. He pulled them down impossibly slowly, letting me watch all of his muscles bunch and flex until he revealed a perfectly hard cock with a silver piercing right through the head.

He moved in between my legs, hard and ready to go. He gripped his cock and lined it up with my entrance, teasing me and running his head over my clit. Gasping, I arched up, grabbing his arms, as I already felt I would explode. He slowly pushed into my pussy, moving back a bit at a time, then moving slowly into me, making me whimper his name.

"Aden, make me yours."

He grunted and began to move his cock deeper, filling and stretching me. He teased my nipples with his tongue, taking each one into his mouth as he moved faster, thrusting so hard the whole table was shaking. "Fuck, baby, I've been wanting to do this forever."

I wrapped my legs around his waist as he pulled me up and went deeper. My screams echoed throughout the conservatory.

Kissing me hard, Aden began to fuck me fast and quick, his grip on my ass bruising me. He licked my neck, and I tilted my head to the side. "Do it, Aden."

He shook his head. "It's...not...about...that," he panted, but I could see it in his eyes.

"Aden, I want you to do it, I trust you," I begged, meeting him with every thrust. His grey eyes turned red, and his fangs descended down as he moved to my neck, kissing me softly, then snapping them into my skin.

The intensity of his fangs piercing my throat hurt for a second, and then I felt him suck. It was like he was drinking every part of my soul. The pleasure from his bite, his cock, and how I was meeting him thrust by thrust had me coming apart so hard that I was seeing stars. "Fuck...fuck...fuck."

His fingers moved to my clit once more and began to draw out my orgasm. He removed his fangs from my neck, healing my wounds with a swipe of his thumb.

He laid me back down on the table, circling my clit and fucking me slowly and deeply. I looked up at him, and he smirked as he kissed me. "Did you think I was done, baby?"

I groaned into his kiss. "Aden, please, oh god."

He licked his lips. "Hold onto me, Lex. I am going to enjoy this." He held one hand onto my hip, and he went totally savage on me. His fingers never left my clit as they continued to circle faster than before. He was fucking me so hard that plants were falling and empty potion bottles were breaking all around us.

I sat up, watching him fuck me, and held onto his hand. "Don't stop, Aden! Oh god, don't stop!" I felt him building up as he slammed into me deeply. I pulled him closer with my heels, taking everything he offered me. My climax came roaring back, and I was so tight it took one hard long thrust to push us both over the edge as we tumbled into total bliss.

Aden collapsed on me, and I relished the feeling of his weight on me. I ran my fingers through his hair down his back and up again.

He looked into my eyes. "Lexi Rose, you are the most beautiful woman I've ever known, and I will spend the next hundred years worshipping you." He kissed my neck and moved down to my breasts.

"Hmm, Aden, I think I like that idea." As I reached for him again, I thought we could go one more round. He was

already half-hard again. "Aden I...I think I'm..."

Aden's phone buzzed and I saw we missed five calls and about ten texts. "Shit... hey, Bash, what's up?" he answered breathlessly. He pulled out of me as I sat up and began to search for our clothes. "Oh yeah, we found something... NO! Don't come to us. I already put it in the car... Yeah, we will come to you... Awesome, I'm starving." He was staring at me, licking his lips.

I shook my head as I found my tights and bra. Now where the hell is my underwear?

"Okay, see you soon" Aden hung up the phone and smirked. "Missing these?" He was holding my top and panties teasingly.

"Don't even think about it," I hissed.

He tossed me my top and as I pulled it on, he said, "Oh no, baby." He held up my panties with two fingers. "These are mine for the night. I'll give them back when we get to the house."

I rolled my eyes at him. "Fine, but two can play at this game," I said to his back as he dressed quickly.

"And what does that mean?"

I gathered the envelope and walked to the door, tossing my hair back and grinning. "You'll see."

I headed to the house and took a quick look in the mirror. I looked like I had been thoroughly fucked. I tried to flatten my hair and remove any smudges from my eyes. I walked into the billiards room, sitting on the window seat, crossing my legs as I watched Bash sink the 8 ball and smirk.

"Game." He puffed his chest out confidently.

"What's your prize?" I asked, batting my eyelashes.

Bash looked at me with a slight glare. "Why, that would be you, Princess." He came up to me and captured my lips with his. I gasped at his boldness.

Coco giggled, and Jason cleared his throat. "Umm, dude I've known her since she was, like, five. Can you, like, not make out with her? She is like my baby sister."

He pulled back and gave me an amused look, turning back to Jason. "Apologies, Jason. I can't help myself around her."

I blushed, and Bash looked down at me, smirking as he pressed a feather-light kiss to my hair. He took a step back as Aden walked in looking smug as hell with his hands in his pockets. He walked over to Tristian, leaning close to him. Tristian suddenly looked as if someone slapped him.

"Dude, what the…" He took a deep breath and then snapped a look to me, his eyes turning red for a flash and a low growl escaping him. I tilted my head in surprise. Tristian never lashed out like that. I started to walk over to him to talk, but as soon as I did that, Coco hopped up.

"You guys want dinner? I can whip up something quick before you head out."

Aden stretched his shirt, raising it to show off his toned stomach, and yawned. "Food sounds great, Coco. Right, Lex? We worked up an appetite in the conservatory, didn't we?"

A blush ran up my neck to my face, and Bash glared hard, crossing his arms. I guess he figured it out, too. Damn, I needed to escape. I headed over to Coco. "Dinner sounds great. Let me help."

I passed Bash, who knelt down, whispering into my ear, "Princess, I can smell Aden on you, and I am guessing Tristian smells you on him. You are in so much trouble later, little

siren." I shivered as I raced to meet Coco in the kitchen.

She looked up as she placed her apron around her and gave me a knowing smile. "You look flushed, Lexi. You feeling okay?"

I nodded absently. "Yeah, I'm just a bit lightheaded. Bash can be overwhelming." I gathered pots and pans and found Coco looking at me like she thought I thought she was stupid.

"Sure, Lexi, but maybe it might not be just Bash. Tristian seemed a bit peeved about something that maybe involves Aden?" She started to gather the ingredients for lasagna.

"Maybe." I bit my lip, feeling the blush return.

She snickered. "And here I thought you weren't a true siren."

After eating way too much, we all piled back into the dark SUV and headed back to my home. It was too quiet in the car, and a heavy air settled around us in that small space. I walked in and turned on the lights, scooping Dyna up as Aden brought in the box, placing it on the kitchen counter. I sat back in a chair with Dyna curled up around me as Aden explained to Bash and Tristian what we found in the conservatory. I looked out the window to the ocean, reflecting on how my life had changed in the last few days. The hatred that ran through me for so many years seemed to have disappeared, and it was replaced with something else.

It wasn't love, but maybe caring for them, or infatuation? And maybe respect for these three men. I wasn't sure, but I knew one thing: I was falling hard for each of them. But there was a whisper in the back of my mind.

Which one would break my heart?

Or would they all shatter it again?

Chapter Thirty-Four

The guys worked all through the night looking over everything, documenting what they could find and going through every file we had on pixie dust. They discussed our next steps and strategies. Bash made a call to Anderson and Grayson to fill them in on our findings. The tension had grown throughout the day between each of them. Tristian's snapping at Aden and Bash's death glares had me rolling my eyes at the level of testosterone in the room.

I finally called it at 3 A.M. and when I woke up a few hours later, I knew I needed to spend some time away from my three moody vamps. I removed Bash's heavy arm and had to climb over Aden to make my way to the bathroom. I quietly gathered my bikini and a towel and made my way out the back patio and down to the ocean.

Once there, I threw the towel on the sand and stretched, letting the ocean's song wash over me. It flowed through my veins, making me dizzy. I walked through the cold sand, the waves lapping at my feet. It was calling to me, and I felt it deep within. I was in a trance-like state when I opened my eyes and found myself waist-deep in the salty water. I let the first wave hit me. The water stung my skin as I let the currents take me under. My arms hung loose around me, and the blurry ocean became clear as my eyes shifted. I kicked off the bottom of the sandy floor and moved over the coral reef and around the sea plants. A few fish swam next me as I explored. I picked up a few lost items: coins, a necklace, even a fork. By the time I came up from the ocean, I saw a tall shadow standing in the distance.

Bash stood next to my stuff with two mugs of coffee in his hand. I headed back to him, and he handed me my towel, wrapping it around me. "Thank you," I said, taking the cup from him. I shivered in the cold of the morning.

"I figured you all would be asleep for a while longer."

"Tristian and Aden are asleep, but I felt you wake, Princess. Plus, the bed is always lonely in the morning when you aren't there. And Tristian snores."

I smiled as I sipped the warm beverage. "Of course, you make coffee like a god."

Bash laughed. "Does that surprise you?" He threw his arm around my shoulder as we headed to the lounge chairs so we could watch the ocean waves. His forest-green eyes stared out as if a memory was playing out in front of

them "I had to take care of Ella and myself a lot growing up, including cooking because my father thought a cook was unnecessary. I guess he forgot about his kids. He was off on coven business most of the time and cheating on my stepmother with one of his many colleagues. Ella was just a kid. She had no one to look after her. Someone had to take care of her."

He looked down at his cup, sighing.

"Lexi... about Ella... when she was older, I still took care of her. I never wanted her to learn the truth about our father. I still hide certain things from her now. Things that if she found out, she would hate me for. The coven's activities are just the tip of the iceberg. Lexi, that night all those years ago was part of what my father wanted me to do. The coven told me to seduce you and to find out things about Pearl Moon Coven. When I realized you didn't know anything, Franklin suggested that if I could seduce you, it would put shame on your family's name." He looked over at me, taking my hand. "He said that I should destroy you for my father. At that time, I ached for my father's approval, so I did it, and I fucked it all up. I am so sorry, Princess. I am so damn sorry about it all, I am sorry for that night and how I treated you ever since."

He leaned closer to me, his elbows on his knees.

"I am not an honorable man, but damn it, I am willing to show Ella I might be able to be one, one day. I hope you are around to see it, too, because, I hope, one day, you will forgive me. I don't want to be just a mistake from your past. Lexi, I would carve my own heart out for Ella, but you? I would tear the world apart for you, because, baby you don't have just my heart, you have my soul. I will love you forever, until the last star burns out."

His words were barely a whisper, but I felt like he yelled them to the world. I turned to him, curling my knees under me. I gazed back into his green eyes.

"Sebastian Ryder, I think I forgave all three of you the day you swore your protection to me. I never hated you, even though I tried to. I told myself for years that I hated you with a fiery passion. I wanted to hate you, I needed to. I should have hated you. So, I shoved my true feelings down. I wanted you to only see me as your little sister's annoying friend, but you tore your way back in, and I can't pretend to hate you anymore. I am drawn to you. You are my tide; you push me to my limits, but you also pull me in. You care for me, protect me, and you make me feel safe, like I'm home."

I cupped his face and pulled his mouth to mine as I gave the lightest kisses, slowly pushing my tongue into his and wrapping my arms around his neck. He pulled me into his lap. We kissed like this for minutes or hours. Time was irrelevant for us in this moment. This was what it should have been all those years ago. This was how we should have fallen for each other on our own, organically. I hated Morgan for pushing us apart and Franklin for his lies and deceptions.

My thoughts of Ella and her anger pushed at my mind. I slowly pulled away, missing the taste of his mouth already. Bash looked confused as he tilted my chin up.

"What is it, Princess?"

I stared down into my coffee. "I should have told her, Bash." My voice cracked.

When my gaze lifted, I saw Bash frown. "I love Ella with all of my heart, but Lexi, this... us four... this is real and feels right. Not that I like the idea of you being with my best friends, my freres, but I understand it. We've been together for so long as the Devils. I think the magic of the covens wants us together for whatever reason. You are supposed to be a part of that." He leaned towards me, staring into my eyes.

I looked down as a blush reached my cheek. "I wanted it to just be us a little while longer. I didn't want her to know yet... I'll tell her... but just her and Ethan. I know they won't judge us, but the others? They don't need to know until... until we are sure we want to go public."

Bash smiled. "You're aware that Coco and Jason know, right?"

I nearly dropped my coffee cup in surprise, but thanks to Bash's super-speed, he just grabbed it and calmly handed it back to me. "Oh, my god, they knew about Aden and me, didn't they?" Mortified, I covered my face.

Bash burst out laughing. "Princess, we all knew. Even if I couldn't smell him on you or vice versa, his smile told us everything."

I threw a pillow at him. "Fucking bastards!" He deflected the pillow and grabbed my hands.

"Princess, Aden might have been the first out of us, but he won't be the last." He kissed my lips quickly as he pulled me up with him.

"I'll fix pancakes, come on." We walked inside, hand-in-hand. Aden and Tristian met us at the patio door with looks of dread on their faces. Bash dropped my hand and stiffened.

"What is it?"

Tristian shook his head and Aden looked at me with heart-

break in his eyes. "Agent Rengard called Bash. They found a body this morning."

Shock struck me in the center of my chest, and fear crept back in. "Who?" I barely whispered to Tristian.

He looked beaten. "It was Nyx, Lexi. I am so sorry."

I just nodded my head as I sat down on the closest chair.

The boys were talking around me, but I didn't hear their words. It was like everything was in slow motion. The next thing I knew, Bash was shaking me. My anger fumed inside of me as I planned on what I would do to The Wishmaker when I found him. I was thinking bamboo sticks in every orifice was a good start.

"Lexi!" Bash snapped at me.

I came back, standing and springing into action. "I'm her leader, so we need to claim her body... Where do we go to do that? The morgue, I guess... I need to call her family... What should I say? How do I get that information? Do I do that? Or is that, like, an assistant thing? Do I have an assistant? Oh, the coven should get together and do a ritual, I need to..."

Aden was suddenly in front of me in a heartbeat. "LEXI ROSE, STOP!" He shook me to snap me out of my spinning. When I looked into his grey eyes, that's when it hit.

I felt like the whole world was falling around me, like I was being smashed by an invisible force.

I looked down. I was holding onto Aden's arms, my nails digging into his skin so much that they broke through. That's when the first tear rolled down my cheek. "I can't breathe," I wheezed.

Aden pulled me closer, and I lost it. I screamed to the

sky and cursed the world. The boys moved me to the couch. "Breathe, baby, just breathe."

Bash was on his phone talking to someone in an urgent voice. Tristian walked over to us with a washcloth in his hand. He placed it on the back of my neck. His smooth voice rushed over me as he ran his hands down my back in small circles.

"Lexi, name five things in this room."

I didn't question him, just answered, "Chair, door, Aden, Bash, you."

He nodded and continued to rub my back in lazy circles. "Now, four things you can touch." He gestured for me to follow his instructions.

I touched the sofa's pillow, then the table. I reached out to Aden's shirt, then put my hand on Tristian's where he held the washcloth.

"Good, Lil' Star, good. Three things you hear."

I closed my eyes and listened. "Bash whispering, the birds outside, and Aden's breath."

He moved closer to me and pulled me to his lap. "Now, two things you can smell, baby."

I leaned my head onto his chest. "Your body wash and the jasmine plant from outside."

He smirked. "Okay, now one slow, deep breath."

I obeyed, inhaling and holding it, then letting it out slowly as the world that was spinning came into focus.

I blinked my eyes open and looked up at him.

"Better?"

I nodded. "A bit."

I sat up and glanced at Aden, whose eyes were on Bash

behind us. He looked like he was about to punch him when he spat, "You are fucking kidding me, right? Bash, you can't!" He shot to his feet, slamming into him. Tristian was in between them in an instant as Bash snarled at Aden.

"I fucking have to, brother. It's the only way you guys stay fucking safe!"

I whipped my head back and forth between the two of them. "Sebastian Ryder, explain everything now," I snapped at him. He turned to me, and his eyes were full of loss. "That was Agent Rengard. He was giving me a courtesy call. They found evidence that I was at the crime scene with Nyx."

I shook my head in disbelief. "No... Bash, you were here most of the night. We all saw you."

Bash's shoulders slumped. "They found evidence against me, and the police will be here in ten minutes to arrest me for the murder of Nyx and Daniels."

Panic flared through me. "We just have to explain! You can tell them where you went, Bash."

He shook his head. "I can't, baby. When you got up, I had just gotten in."

I was confused, and he continued, "I was missing while you were all asleep."

I shook my head, begging him. I didn't want to know, but I knew he would tell me. "Just tell me where you were then, Bash."

That's when I felt my heart shatter again just like it did ten years ago. I pleaded with him with my eyes, and he shook his head. I couldn't do this again with him, not after everything we'd been through, not after everything we just said to each other.

I asked the question I was dreading to ask. "Sebastian, where were you?"

His eyes softened, and he sat on a chair. He reached for my hand and tugged me to him. My stomach brushed his head as he leaned forward. "I had an anonymous tip about The Wishmaker. I was meeting a source in the alleyway behind The Oddity, but when I got there, the alley was empty, and I saw someone laying on the ground, a body.

"It was Nyx. I saw her, but she was alive. She was completely high on pixie dust. I tried to help her up and bring her back here. She fought me and transformed. She scratched my arms so much I was bleeding. She begged me to leave her, to let her die, but then there was a girl—no, it was a man who came out, and then I can't remember what happened." He banged his head against his hand. "The person said they would take her, and I just let them. I don't know why I was screaming inside not to, but I couldn't move. Something was wrong. I felt like a huge fog came over me. I can remember some things, but it's all out of place. Then before I knew it, I was back here crawling in bed with you. Then you woke up, and I just thought it was all a dream. I swear that's what happened, but they have my blood on Nyx, and it's not looking good."

Chapter Thirty-Five

I sat on his lap and ran my fingers over his cheek. "Sebastian Ryder, you will not give up like this. Let them take you, but know that we will get you out and you will come back to us." I kissed him softly.

He looked over my head at his brothers. Tristian and Aden joined us and put their hands on Bash's shoulder. We all stood quietly, just needing to be with each other. I wasn't sure what the future would hold for us, but I knew one thing: the harder I held onto my Devils, the more the world would try to tear them from me.

So, as I held onto Bash, I memorized every line of his face, inhaled his intoxicating smell of spicy and sweet, and listened to his steady breathing and the drum of his heart.

The sirens in the distance grew closer. All of our phones began to ping and as I pulled mine out to look down at a text message that had just come in from an unknown number, I heard three very angry vamps snarl and curse at the same time. Confused, I opened the text. It was a photo of the crime scene. Nyx's body was laid out naked with the Blood Coven's symbol carved into her skin. The scene was gruesome and gritty; her once beautiful face that had light in it was now a blank canvas, her eyes open, looking up at the sky in fright.

I noticed a dark figure standing in the shadows looking at the camera. Under the photo, the text said, "Your move, Little Rose. What will you do now that I took out one of your Devils? -The Wishmaker."

I growled as anger seeped into my body. I would find a way to keep Bash with us and figure out how all four of us could become what we always were supposed to be. I knew one thing for certain: I would avenge Nyx's death; I would destroy The Wishmaker. It was time to take back my crown and become the queen I needed to be. This siren had fangs, and she was about to show the world what happened when you tried to take one of her Devils away from her.

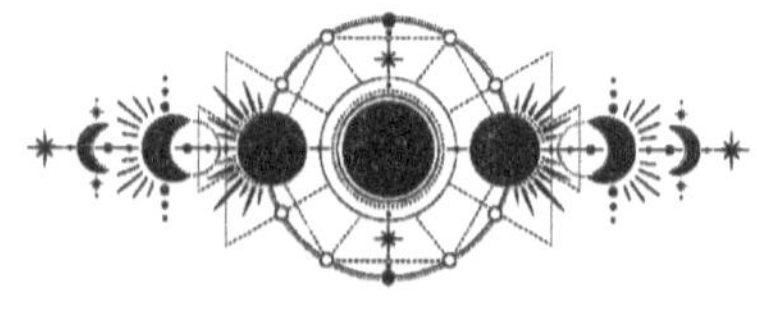

Franklin stood, looking out the high-rise building window, watching as the tiny dots scurried around. With a slimy smile and an air of delight, he raised a glass of champagne to his lips, smiling, "It is done."

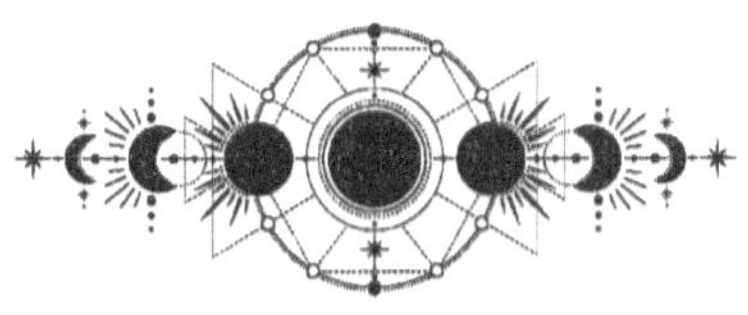

I moved slowly through the hospital room, my black robes swirling around me. My hood was covered so no one could see my face, not that they could even recognize me with all the charms I had put in place. I slammed open the door that read "Mortuary". The tiny goblin who ran the site jumped when I entered, about to yell at whomever had just interrupted his work. His eyes met mine, and he cowered as I slinked closer to him.

"Do you have it ready?"

He paled at the sound of my voice and nodded as he stood, his hands trembling. "This...this...wa...way, master."

He led me to a sterilized room where they performed autopsies. It was bright white, and the air smelled of disinfectant. Rows and rows of cabinets lined the walls. I assumed they had bodies in them, but the only one I cared for laid on a steel table covered in white cloth.

"This is the mermaid?"

The troll offered me one quick nod and tugged the blanket back. Her pale white skin and silky black hair was fanned out;

no life remained in her.

I frowned. "Terrible... such a waste. She was one of my favorites." I trailed my finger down her cheek. "And the blood?"

The troll acted as if I just hit him. "I collected the vampire's blood off of the body. Smart for him to be cut while under the spell. He never knew." He handed me a small vial with Sebastian Ryder's blood in it. "Yes, vampires heal quickly. By the time he was leaving, no trace would be left behind."

The troll covered the girl back up and stepped back. "Is there anything else my master would like me to do?"

I looked at the troll and saw my reflection behind him in the steel doors. My eyes were silver, my skin had paled, my grin revealed razor-sharp teeth. "No, thank you. We can continue with our plan." I let a nail-scraping laugh escape my lips.

With a flick of my hand, I was outside Morte Noire. "Now, I will finish what I started."

Author's Note

It's done! How did you like book one of The Covens?

First, Thank you! This was such an important story for me to share.

The struggle with grief affects not just a few of us, but all of us. I knew I wanted to create a story about how grief affects different people and how you can start your own healing process.

I lost my older brother several years ago. It made me realize that grief doesn't go away, but time can help you heal your pain. So, if you or anyone you know is struggling with grief, please reach out to betterhelp.com, or check out *www.griefshare.org* for many other resources to help you.

If your grief has brought you to an extreme place and you are thinking of ending your life, please, know you are not alone and reach out to **The National Suicide Prevention Lifeline, 988**. Grief looks different for everyone, but just know that there are people who understand the pain you are going through. I hope one day any of you that are dealing with such a loss can find peace.

I have wanted to tell this story for years and spent a lot of time trying to figure out how to intertwine my message with an interesting story and characters. So, how the heck did I come up with The Covens?

Well, one day I went to a destress tank (a saltwater tank where you float) and boom! The story flew out of me. I called my momma that day, and she said, "GO WRITE THAT DOWN!" so I finally just sat down and wrote it! It started very differently from where it ended, but that is the amazing thing about a story—it can change!

So, how do you like Lexi? She is a bit of a BAMF firecracker, which I love. We'd be total BFFs. Who's your favorite Devil? Bash is broody, sexy, and a big grumpy pants. Tristian has golden retriever energy with the hunger of a wolf, and Aden, well, Aden is the anti-prince charming with a shit ton of tats and a dark soul. Really, you can't go wrong with any one of them. AM I RIGHT? Or AM I RIGHT? Do you think we will see more of Grayson, Maman Brigitte, or even follow other covens around the world? Or possibly have a story about our Drow Prince in the next books?

Could they join the group? Nahhh, I don't think they would... or would they?

Oh, and UGH Franklin is kind of slimy and gross, right? I think I threw up a little writing him, to be perfectly honest. Lastly, can we all just say FUCK MORGAN because he is such a butt-faced miscreant? The Wishmaker?!? Who is she/he? (Could it be Morgan, Ella, or even Jason?)

Lastly, I have to thank a few people because, without them, this book would have never happened.

My team at Tala Editorial, Nikki, Tara, Ashley, Kristy, and Ben: thank you for making a dream come alive for me. Thank you for trusting my story would be something to make you laugh, cry, and maybe a little mad, too.

My hubby Tom: You keep me grounded. You believe in me so much and are my biggest fan even when I don't think I deserve it. You laugh at my horrible jokes, but more importantly, you love me for me.

My momma and daddy: You knew I would be an artist from a very young age. Maybe it was the singing (bad singing) or the fact I acted out every Disney movie ever made. You encouraged my love for the arts and for that I am ever so grateful for you both. I love you to the moon.

To my bestie group: Megs, McCalli, Hailley, Crystal, Brooke, Cissy, Katie, and so, so many more women who consistently not only make me feel so amazing but love me with full hearts. Thank you for the wine nights and dancing. It keeps me sane.

Jayde: You can't read this book yet (at least wait until you're eighteen), but I love you so much and your kind heart and smarty pants brain make me want to be better. I love you, honey, and your daddy. I know he is looking down at us now. He would be so proud of how you have grown, to see this amazing, beautiful girl standing before me.

And lastly...

To John: Bubba, I lost you too soon, and my heart breaks every night knowing I will never hear your voice again. Thank you for teaching me to be a better friend, to be a better daughter, aunt, and sister. I will love you to the end. One day, I hope to wrap my arms around you again. I love you so much, Bubba.

But seriously, can I just say thank you so freaking much for reading and coming to Providence Village with me?

I hope you all loved it as much as I did!

If you want to see more of Lexi and her Devils, follow me @CiciMyersauthor on Instagram, Facebook, and Tik-tok. Sign up for a newsletter at *CiciMyersAuthor.com*,; and lastly, join *The Covens* Oddity Reading Group. Let's see what trouble we can get up to!

Book 2: *Hemlock Falls* is in the works and will be out 2023. Here's a sneak peek to calm your aching hearts.

CiCi

Hemlock Falls

Your move next, my darling Rose. What will you do now that I took out one of your Devils?

The Wishmaker

I keep reading the line over and over again. "Your Move?" What is this, a damn chess match to him? I was too shocked to speak or even to form words on what the hell we were going to do. I couldn't see a future, how we were going to win from this.

I felt Bash's arms around my waist as he kept a firm grasp on me. I could hear the police sirens getting closer. Tristian and Aden were talking in a flurry around us, arguing about what to do. Aden's eyes were fully in a blaze of red, and

Tristian kept running his hands through his hair then gripping it. He sent out multiple texts.

"I told Ella, Ethan, Coco, and James… Do I send one to Morgan?" Tristian looked to Bash for an answer, but he just kept his arms around me and stared into the fire as if he had already accepted his fate.

"Bash…" I whispered.

"Yeah, Princess?"

I swallowed hard. "This is bad, isn't it?"

He sighed. "Yeah, baby, it is."

I looked down at his face. "I just got you back, I can't…"

His eyes snapped up to mine, and he shook his head. "Never. You aren't going to lose me, Princess."

I heard the car door slam shut and a shuffle of shoes making their way up the stairs. Aden was becoming even more irate, walking quickly back and forth with his fangs full on display as if he was waiting for a fight. Anger flowed through him and made him vibrate with the fury of a thousand demons.

"Aden?" His eyes snapped towards me, scanning my expression. Worry passed over his face.

I raised my chin and looked into his eyes. The red faded away, and his grey steel eyes showed his real emotion—he was scared. The sight of fear in his eyes pressed into my heart, and I saw the hope leave him. "I need you to quickly go and hide everything we have on The Wishmaker: all of the files, boxes we've received, and any photo evidence. We can't let the FBI get their hands on it," I ordered.

He jumped into action. Using his vampiric abilities, he sped through the house, grabbing folders and boxes.

I stared at the door with dread washing over me. "Bash...
I... I..."

Without warning, a bang came from the door. "Providence Village Police! Open the door!" Agent Rengard's smooth, deep voice came through the other side. Tristian made a move to answer the door, but he was stiff and let his anger roll off of him, so it hit you in the face like a hot, humid day.

"No! Tristian, let me." I looked down at Bash and kissed him one more time, because I didn't want it to be the last. "We will find a way, Bash."

He nodded as he let me go. I walked to the door, opening it to find Agent Rengard standing next to two large police officers.

"Agent Rengard," I coldly greeted him.

"Ms. Rose, we are here for Sebastian Ryder. We have a warrant to search the property for any possible murder weapons."

I scoffed. "You know he had nothing to do with this." I shook my head at him and the two police officers that stood behind him.

The first police officer looked young. He had a baby face with the lightest blond hair and big, bright blue eyes. He stared at me in awe, and I looked down and saw that I was still in my bikini.

I glared at him. "Officer...?"

He gave me a boyish smile. "Officer Watson."

I smiled sweetly as I let my venom drip. "If you could kindly not stare at my tits while you try to arrest a friend, I would appreciate it. I know it might be hard, but let's just keep our dick in our pants, shall we?"

Agent Rengard laughed and covered it with his hand. "Ms. Rose has a point, Officer Watson. Even if she is a siren, you should respect her regardless of how she's dressed." I raised an eyebrow as he handed me a piece of paper. "Here is the warrant for Sebastian's arrest." My eyes narrowed.

"Ma'am, are we going to have a problem?" One of the officers asked.

I looked at him. I could tell he was a giant of some type, not just because he was probably close to six-foot-seven and had a haziness of charisma around him, but what told me he was a giant were his tattoos. The tattooed cloud climbed up his arms with his tribe's symbol shining in bright gold ink. His thick beard made him look intimidating. His hair was buzzed short and bright blue, and his beady eyes looked almost black, they were so dark. The most frightening thing was his cold stare.

I crossed my arms, glaring at the officer, not willing to back down because I never backed down from dumbasses. I smirked as I looked at his tag. "Officer Hyde, I have two words for you—" but before I could call Officer Asshat all the words I could think of, I was lifted from behind and twisted around. I looked down, seeing tattooed hands that said "open book" written across their knuckles. I growled. "Tristian, put me down."

He sat me on the couch and pulled me close to him. "Easy, Lil' Star. You don't want Bash to have more problems, so shut your mouth, darling." He smiled at me, which may have looked flirty to everyone else, but his words held a bite to them, and I knew he was saving our asses from Agent Rengard.

I crossed my arms and glared at Agent Rengard as Aden

walked him into the room. The FBI agent looked around, his face suddenly flushed as he spat out, "Where is Sebastian Ryder?" I looked around for Bash, not seeing him in the room.

"Relax, Agent Rengard. I am right here," Bash said coolly as he walked from the hallway that led to my room.

Rengard straightened. "Sebastian Ryder, you are under arrest for the murder of Steven Daniels and Nyx Lu." Officer Hyde came up to Bash, throwing him against the counter and slapping a pair of handcuffs on him. Tristian and I shot up from the couch in an instant.

"He isn't resisting arrest; you don't have to manhandle him!" Tristian shouted.

Aden bared his teeth in fury. I was biting my tongue so hard I felt the blood fill my mouth.

"Tristian, get a fucking lawyer on the phone to meet us down at the station," Bash grunted out with a chuckle. Of course, not even a giant could bring down the great Sebastian Ryder.

They hauled Bash into a standing position as they led him to the front door. Opening the door, Agent Rengard looked back. "He'll need a few hours to be processed. If you get the lawyer to meet us there, he might be home tonight. But Lexi, the evidence is overwhelming against him at this point. I would expect the worse."

I took a deep breath. "Agent Rengard, you are all being played, and you know it. You just want to put a pretty bow around it to get the people off your backs, but that won't stop the drugs or the killings." I walked to him, still seething. "Good night, Rengard. Rot in hell." I slammed the door in his face and moved to the window where Aden and Tristian stood. "What's going on?"

Aden pulled me close, putting his arm around me and I watched out the window to see what they were looking at. The officers lead Bash out of the house, walking him down the steps to the waiting police cars that sat with all of their lights on. We saw that Agent Rengard had five police cars with him, and a news crew was set up along the fence with many of our neighbors gathered around, mouths agape. Newscasters and cameramen were running around trying to get the best footage. I shook my head.

"It's a goddamn circus," spat Aden.

"Come on, we aren't hiding from this. We will stand united," I said. They both looked a bit shocked.

We walked outside, and I wrapped my arms through Aden's and Tristian's. "Agent Rengard!"

He turned to me. "Yes, Ms. Rose?"

I let anger seep out towards him. "Your promises are small in comparison to what we did for you, and they mean nothing to me now. You will not destroy us. When I find out who The Wishmaker is, and I will find out, I will drag him into the depths of hell and set his soul on fire. We are the covens, and together, our power is strong. Do not mistake us for being weak."

Agent Regards' eyes widened in surprise for a second, but he recovered quickly, making his face as cool as stone. He finally saw the anger in my eyes.

"I truly hope you do, Ms. Rose, but, until then, Mr. Ryder comes with us. I'll see you at the station." The officers threw Bash in the back of a black SUV, and his head bounced off the window. He threw his head back, laughing like a damn maniac. Agent Rengard slid into the driver's seat, starting the car. I looked back at Bash, and he turned his head to me, his green eyes staring into my blue. A tear escaped and fell down my cheek. His eyes flash with pain, but he shook his head, telling me not to cry.

I swallowed deeply and nodded, giving myself the time to settle my emotions down. I wish I could just flip a switch and turn off all my emotions sometimes. Yes, my shield was solid, but I was feeling all the emotions from everyone here: anger, shame, guilt, despair, and hopelessness. The news crews called out to us to get a statement, and I memorized each of their faces.

"Lexi, let's go inside." Aden nudged me.

"Okay, let's go."

As I was turning to the door, I saw a streak of white-blonde hair in the crowd. Franklin was standing there with his arms crossed in a sharp suit with a smug look on his face. I glared at him and shot my power at him. My anger wrapped around him, and his eyes snapped to mine. He smirked and blew me a kiss, then moved back and slunk into the crowd.

"Was that..." Tristian started to ask me.

"Yeah, the slimy salamander himself, probably reporting back to Daddy Dearest." I walked in, locking the door, feeling a vulnerable feeling sink into me. Dyna trotted out, winding her tail around me and Tristian. Tristian finally gave in, picking her up and snuggling her fur.

"I think she wants you, Lexi." I looked down at Tristian's arms, and Dyna's big light blue eyes found mine. She gave me a cute meow with a stretch of a paw.

I smiled at her. "I know, I know, Dyna." I pulled her from Tristian's arms into mine, and she purred loudly. "What is our next move? You two have a plan, don't you?" I sat on the couch, looking around.

The house felt empty without Bash here. Aden moved to the kitchen, pulling out glasses and filling them with the dragon whiskey. He said, "First, we take a drink, then we make a plan."

I sighed, putting my head down into Dyna, kissing her head as she purred loudly.

Aden walked over to us, handing out the glasses. "Then we need to call Anderson. Cover our bases and such."

I nodded in agreement.

"The lawyer is on his way down to the police station, too." Tristian pulled his phone out, reading the text from the lawyer.

I sipped the dragon whiskey, trying to relax, but the longer I sat here doing nothing, the angrier I was becoming, because fuck The Wishmaker. Fuck him!

I groaned as the boys snapped their heads to me. "Lex, you okay?"

I took a huge gulp of my drink because I couldn't believe I didn't think of it first. "Morgan already knows about Bash, thanks to Franklin."

Both groaned and downed their drinks. Tristian's phone rang. "Speak of the devil and he shall appear," he muttered as he put the phone on speaker. "Mr. Ryder, we are here. You are on speaker."

Morgan's deep, smooth voice came through the phone. "I won't say this is a pleasant call for me to make in the middle of the day, Tristian. Would you like to explain why my eldest is being hauled away for murder?"

Tristian cleared his throat. "We just found out about this ourselves, Morgan. We got tipped off just thirty minutes before the police came to the door. We were waiting until we had a plan until we made our call to you." He looked up from the phone and gave us a half-smile for the white lie he was telling.

"I see, and the lawyer?" Morgan said, sounding indifferent to the fact that his son got arrested.

Aden cleared his throat. "He will meet Bash at the precinct."

Morgan cleared his throat. "Good, I will meet you there in forty-five. Ms. Rose, we have much to discuss. My last appointment just got here." The phone ended with a click.

I put down the rest of my glass and glared at the ceiling. "Fuck Morgan Ryder!" I screamed. I stood abruptly, sending Dyna scurrying off into my room. "I am not going to sit here like a goddamn soldier waiting for Morgan to tell us what to do."

Aden grimaced. "Lexi, we aren't Morgan's soldiers. We are the fucking generals. We say who does what, and we can end it just as quickly," he snapped as he stood in front of me with a speed unlike any I'd ever seen. I didn't jump, though. I wasn't backing down now.

I sneered, "Screw you, asshat. You are Morgan's sheep. You may get control of a few things, but Morgan is the puppetmaster, and you are just his puppets. You aren't Pinocchio; you won't actually become a real boy. Once a soldier, always a soldier."

Aden's face turned into a scowl, and he got up in my face, his fangs elongated. "Lexi Rose, if you think I am that same little boy you knew years ago, then think again. I take what I want, when I want, baby. That includes you." I heard the slap first before I noticed my palm sting with pain. I looked down and saw a line of blood ripped across my hand. I opened my mouth in shock, raising my head to see Aden's face jerked to the side, a trickle of blood rolling from his lip.

Tristian was in between us in an instant, pulling me to him as he walked us to the door, his anger leaking out of him. "Go for a walk, Lexi, get out of here." I shook my head, begging Tristian with my eyes. His gaze filled with pain as he pulled me close and hissed in my ear, "You are spewing your emotions everywhere."

I choke on a sob. "Oh, God, Aden... I am sorry" I put a hand to my mouth to cover up the whimper that threatened to escape. "Trist... I don't... I didn't..."

He shook me enough to get me out of my head, and his anger tasted bitter. "We both get it—you fucking love him, but it doesn't change a damn thing."

My mouth fell open. Tristian had never been angry with me or slashed me as much as he just did. The pain that sat in his eyes was something I realized I never wanted to see.

I turned and walked to the front door. "Fine," I whispered, shutting the door behind me. I headed to the gate as people were calling my name. I ignored them all and looked to the guards. Deke was pushing back a cameraman as he nodded to me, and Sonny gave me a sad smile. "You good, Ms. Rose?" he yelled. I waved him off as I headed to the back gate, where I saw one cop car sitting idling, watching me.

I walked over to the vehicle and tapped on the window. Officer Hyde looked up, annoyed, and rolled his window down. "What can I do for you, Ms. Rose?" His condescending voice carried over the noise around us.

"Officer Hyde, what are you doing here?" I eyed him suspiciously.

"I was told to watch the house and make sure no one left or came in." I raised both of my eyebrows.

"Are we all suspects?"

Officer Hyde smirked. "Now, you know I can't discuss that, but one of you is going down for murder. I can only hope it's Sebastian Ryder; that bastard deserves everything that's coming to him."

I rolled my eyes. "It's a vendetta then?" He said nothing as he sat still. "You should be wary of the green-eyed monster; it will destroy your soul."

He scoffed at me and huffed a laugh out.

"You aren't even half the man that Sebastian Ryder is." I walked away, heading down to the beach.

I heard a car door slam. "Ms. Rose, put your hands up now." I turned around and saw Officer Hyde's gun drawn. I put my hands in the air.

"You've got to be kidding me."

He smiled cruelly. "No, I am following orders, Mrs. Rose. You are under arrest for obstruction of justice." He came at me. "I can do this the hard way or the easy way, Mrs. Rose. I am begging you to make it hard, please," he snarled at me, his hatred for me clear in his eyes. I looked at his gun, then back at him, knowing he would have no problem shooting me.

Aden and Tristian bolted out the door, yelling my name. They turned to Officer Hyde in surprise. "What the hell?! Put your fucking gun down!"

Officer Hyde walked up to me and whispered, "I see their guns, Mrs. Rose. Now, I am sure they are a good shot, but they won't dare do that with you standing next to me. Listen closely, there something you should know about me: I am an excellent shot. I will put a bullet in each of their pretty heads." I looked back at Aden and Tristian and gave a small shake of my head not to interfere.

"It's done. I will go with you, Hyde," I growled. I held out my hands to him, and he slapped a pair of handcuffs on me.

"Good girl." He moved behind me as bile started to rise in my throat.

I looked at Aden, and he saw my anger. "We are right behind you!"

I took a deep breath as I walked to Officer Hyde's car. He pushed me in the back, smiling a crooked smile. "Don't get too comfortable, darlin'." With that, he slammed the door. He started to whistle, making his way around the car. As he drove me downtown, he looked back at me in his mirror. "Perfect Little Rose, all tied up. It is a beauty to see."

I shot my gaze to his eyes in the rearview mirror, tilting my head to the side. Only one person had ever called me that before—The Wishmaker.

"What did you call me?" I raised an eyebrow.

"Nothing," he muttered. As he drove, he would look

back at me a few times, trying to bait me, but I chose to ignore him and stare out the window. Hyde just gave away one important clue.

He had a connection to The Wishmaker.

I started to laugh. "Oh God, you are so screwed, dude. You fucked up. You know that, don't you?" I turned my gaze to him, watching my eyes turn purple in the rearview mirror. "We will come for you, so you might want to let your boss know that The Three Devils will be collecting soon." I laughed silently as I saw his eyes fill with fear over what he just revealed.

His eyes turned hard, the black orbs overtaking and filling the car with chilly air. He snarled at me "You think you're special?" He laughed. "I just want to know one thing. You grew up with everything, your life was set, and then you threw it all away for them? Rich boys with a pretty face? It's sad you think they won't break you into a million pieces again. You are either the most naive girl I have ever met, or your pussy must be made of fucking gold if you brought The Three Devils of Providence Village down to their knees."

I bit my tongue, denying him any gratitude. It wasn't about me choosing just one. We worked as a unit.

We were meant to all be together.

CiCi was born and raised in Texas but now resides in sunny California. When she is not writing *The Covens* series or her other works, you can find her spending time with her family, drinking wine with her girls, singing way too loud and off key in the car, or snuggling up with her cat, a cup of coffee, and a good book.

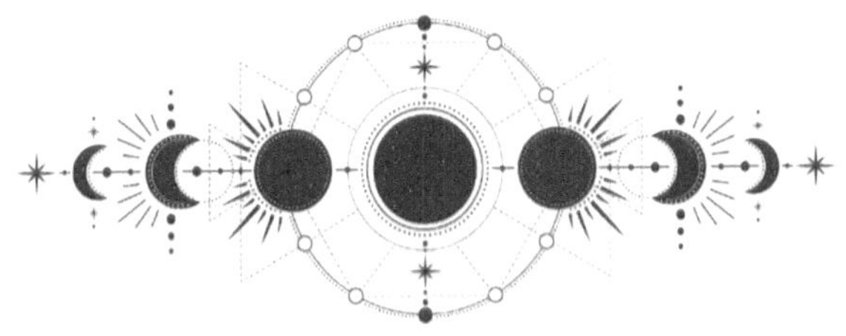

Want more of *The Covens* series?

Listen to the Official The Coven Series Playlist on Spotify!